MALL TIME

He sits among his weapons; and time tangles, time knots and skeins itself about his oily fingers.

Time is the enemy, time is the killer. There may be a body, he's fairly sure that there's a body in the kitchen – though he hasn't looked, not for a while now, not for a time – but still, it wasn't him that killed. That much is certain. It was time, that's all, it was only time. Everyone meets their death in time, and never mind who makes the introduction.

Time steals the life out of people, directly or indirectly, as it has stolen his; but it has other tricks too. As now, tripping him gaily by the heels when he's at his most vulnerable, most in need of balance.

Tripping him and setting him to fall back, far back: before this death, and all the way back to another . . .

**Also by the same author,
and available from Coronet:**

The Samaritan
The Refuge
The Garden

About the author

Chaz Brenchley was born in Oxford, but now makes his home in Newcastle. He has been a professional writer since he was eighteen, and is the widely acclaimed author of three previous novels for Coronet, *The Samaritan*, *The Refuge* and *The Garden*.

Mall Time

Chaz Brenchley

CORONET BOOKS
Hodder and Stoughton

British Library C.I.P.

Brenchley, Chaz
 Mall time.
 I. Title
 823[F]

 ISBN 0 340 574488

Printed and bound in Great Britain for Hodder and Stoughton Paperbacks, a division of Hodder and Stoughton Ltd., Mill Road, Dunton Green, Sevenoaks, Kent TN13 2YA (Editorial Office: 47 Bedford Square, London WC1 3DP) by Clays Ltd., St Ives plc.

For Philippa and Mike,
without whom something, perhaps,
but not this; someone, perhaps,
but not me.

Contents

Contents – continued

MALL TIME

WHERE THE ACTION IS

It's not the biggest in England, no, it's the biggest in Europe; and, of course, the best in the world. That goes without saying. It's bright, it's brash, it's modern, it's got everything you could possibly want; and you're welcome, you're very welcome to visit. Bring your credit cards.

It stands on a spit of land between two rivers, and it belongs very much to the area and its people. They built it and they own it, or one of them does (and never mind that he's an incomer, he's still an adopted son); and who said civic pride was dead? They love it.

Well, some of them love it. Others are more ambivalent, but you'd expect that. There have always been people ready and eager to poke a finger in the eye of progress. People who don't want change, and wouldn't recognise regeneration if it were sitting on their very doorstep. As this is.

Once it was an industrial wasteland, this spit of land. Then the recession came, and it was just a wasteland. But now – oh, now it's booming. Now they come from all over, to spend their time and their wages here. There are coaches from Scotland, parties of American tourists, day-trippers from Scandinavia. The people and the money, they just keep rolling in.

So what's the big attraction, you ask? Listen, I'll tell you. Hold onto your hats for a lightning tour of the busiest, the most exciting, the only place to be.

Shops, of course. Don't ask what's here, ask what isn't – and don't hold your breath for an answer, because it could be a long time coming. We've got all the major chains, all the minor chains and a whole lot more besides. I'll tell you, they're queueing up for spaces.

And restaurants. You can eat French, Italian, Greek, Turkish, Spanish, American, Spanish-American, Mexican, Chinese or Thai. Seafood or steak, vegetarian or vegan – if it's edible, it's here. You can have a quick hamburger before the movie, or a leisurely supper afterwards; a romantic dinner *à deux* or a mediaeval banquet for sixty guests.

Did I mention movies there? Ask me about movies. It's a multi-screen cinema, of course – and I'm talking twelve separate studios, maybe twenty different films a day. The seats are wide and comfortable, there's leg-room for the tallest man; and there's popcorn sweet or salty, hot dogs and chilli dogs, cold drinks on tap and a choice of thirty-two Italian ice-creams. Clean toilets, no smoking and a cry-room if the baby wants to yell. Envious? You should be, you've never seen anything like it in your life. But it's all sitting here, don't forget, only waiting for you to drop in. Open seven days a week, early till late.

And be sure to bring the kids, when you come. They'll love it. When they're tired of the toyshops and sick of sweets, just take them along to Dreamland. It's a funfair and a fantasy, it's got everything from the latest video games to a mini roller-coaster with maxi thrills. No tears, guaranteed; who could cry, in a world of candy floss and cartoons? You can even leave your youngsters in the care of a qualified childminder while you do your own thing; and it only adds to the giggle-factor when the childminder turns out to be Snow White or Rumpelstiltskin.

And I haven't told you the half of it yet. I haven't mentioned the Greek Temple, or the Tudor Village, or –

But enough for now. We're talking big, that's all you really need to know. This place was conceived – boldly and brilliantly conceived – on a massive scale; and it's growing all the time.

And where is it, what is it? It's the Meldon Centre, of course. It's right here, this is it; and believe me, this is where the action is . . .

THE BOOK OF HOURS

1

0400:

" . . . and that was 'Sweet As A Rotting Apple', the first single from a new band – or new to me, anyway, I gather they've been big in Glasgow for a couple of years now – called Good Man Feeling Bad. Where *do* they get these names from? And before you all start phoning in to tell me, let me just say that was a rhetorical question, okay – that's 'rhetorical', with an H, you can look it up later – because actually I do know where that one comes from, it's pinched from an old blues number, 'The Blues Ain't Nothing But A Good Man Feeling Bad'. Now *that* is my kind of music. Forget this modern rubbish, give me Muddy Waters and John Lee Hooker any day. Maybe I'll play some a little later, see if I can't convert a few of you ignorant hooligans out there. No, don't switch off – take your fingers off that dial, I can see you! – I was only foolin'. I love it all, really. And I love *you*, sexy listener. You're tuned to the louche, lubricious lady with the large libido, Dictionary Denise on Naughty Radio Nova, and Dirty Den loves ya, baby . . .

"Now don't panic, the music goes on in a minute, and I've got some supremely salacious stuff lined up for your lugholes tonight; but I just want to take a little time out to tell you what's going on at the Meldon Centre later today. I know you've heard it all already, but I'm going to throw it at you one more time, okay? So take your tongue out of your lover's ear, I want them to hear it too. Sit up and listen good.

"What it is, is a massive twenty-four hour splurge for charity. It's a telethon, of course; but forget the telly, because it's a radiothon too, and we're the people who count. Radio Nova's luscious new studio is right in the heart of the Meldon Centre – yes, folks, I'm sitting in it right now, with my beautiful boyfriend on one side and a teensy-weensy little vodka and tonic on the other – but we won't be in the studio much. Starting at midday today, the beat hits the street. All your favourite voices are going to be out and about, wearing their weird and wonderful bodies and talking to you the people. Getting interviews, getting dedications, and of course getting your money off you, because that's what it's all about.

"So just you be there, you hear me? It's a party, and I know you're all party people. What else is there to live for? So come along, bring lots of dosh, have a whale of a time and save a whale while you're doing it. The money's all going to environmental causes; Friends of the Earth get a share, so do Greenpeace and half a dozen others. How trendy do you want it?

"There's going to be plenty happening, all through the night, noon till noon; and like I told you, every one of our husky macho male jocks will be around, with live mikes and a bucket apiece. And if that's not enough to tempt you little boy-listeners out of your idle and selfish beds, then clock this: I'm going to be there too. Yes, me, Desirable Denise in person, exchanging kisses for cash. A pound a peck, it's going to cost you; and worth every penny of it, let me tell you. If you don't believe me, ask my fella.

"Talking of which, maybe you shouldn't expect to see me too early. That's not an excuse for you to be late, mind; there's plenty else to get up to, before you snatch a snog with me. And you'll be too tired afterwards – shagged out, as it were. But the thing is, like I said before, my man is right here with me now; and I don't get off the air till five, we won't be home much before six, and the way he's looking at me, the way he's – get *down*, boy! – well, never you mind exactly what he's doing, but I sort of get the impression we're not going straight to sleep when we get there. Bed, maybe, but sleep? I rather fancy not.

"So I may be just a tad late getting up today. Soon as I can, though, I'll be there. I promise. And you'll know me when you see me, I'll be the one with the shiny red eyes, the bonk-badges on my neck and a distinctly droopy microphone . . .

"But enough of my sex-life, I'm only making you jealous. Snuggle up, sweethearts, and let's get back to the tracks. Here's something seriously smoochy, just to get you all in the mood for later . . . "

"You don't half talk a lot of crap, Den."

"It's my job," she said, her fingers quickly double-checking that yes, the microphone was dead, no one was hearing this. With the headphones tugged off so that Simply Red was nothing but a tiny scratching in the air around them, she swivelled round to the turntables and lifted off the last single. Slipped it into its sleeve and reached for the light-pen as Matt said,

"What, crapping on about me?"

"Hang on."

She ran the pen back and forth across bar-codes on the sleeve and on a separate sheet, making a random guess at how long the record had played. The computer bleeped its satisfaction – machines were easy to fool, like the public – and she was free for a bit, at least, she could take time out to confront the messiness of real life. One quick gulp at the beaker of cold coffee on the console, and she turned her chair again to face Matt.

Tried a smile and wasted it, because he was sitting hunched over with his head low, watching the floor, nothing to see of him but black curls glossy with hair-wax and hands clenched tight into fists.

"It's not all crap, you know," she said instead of the smile, trying to make it soft and serious, but only sounding fatuously romantic even to herself.

"Isn't it?" He lifted his head now, too late; and his face was all stubble and shadow, and surrender. "You really think I'm going to take you home and screw you stupid tonight?"

"Oh, that's just image, it's for the punters. They don't believe it either, half the time; they just like to hear a girl talking dirty. It's not even you I'm talking about, really, just a mythical toy-boy." She lifted one headphone to her ear to check where the music had got to, and wondered why they always had to have these conversations at work, in three-minute segments. At home he would never talk at all. "But you are important to me, Matt. I mean, you do know that, don't you?"

"Important. Yeah, sure."

She sighed, caught as usual by the sheer futility of throwing words into the black hole of his self-disgust. Then, doing it anyway, futile or not: "Matt love, don't you think you ought to see a doctor?"

"What for? I'm okay."

"Like fuck you are. You're depressed, anyone can see that."

"Depressed. Right. So what, I need a doctor to tell me what I know already?"

"No, you need a doctor to help you get over it. You won't discuss things with me, or with your friends – Jesus, you never see them any more, unless I ask them round. Maybe a stranger would be more use to you, someone who can understand how your mind's working . . . "

"Ah. We're not talking 'doctor' here any more, are we? We're talking 'psychiatrist', right?"

"Doctor, psychiatrist, who cares? Just someone who can help, that's all. I'll come with you, if you want."

"Forget it. It's a job I need, not a handful of pills and a session on someone's couch."

"Yeah? And when was the last time you applied for a job? When was the last time you even *looked*?" She got only silence in response, and went on quickly, "I'm not blaming you, Matt. I know better than that. It's just got too big for you, that's all. But we both know it isn't only being out of work, not any more. You can't see anything straight these days. Really, if you just went and talked it over with a doctor – they're used to people with problems, they see them every day, it's not that special . . . "

"Forget it, I said."

That she wouldn't do, it wasn't in the job description; but she did the next best thing, and let the subject drop. For now. Instead she walked across the studio and kissed him; and never mind the slack unresponsiveness of his mouth, his utter separation. At least she'd tried, she'd set another marker by the wayside. That had to be worth something. Points for effort.

Then she glanced at the turntable and cursed, seeing the stylus tracking round the last, silent groove of the disc. She dived back to the console, her thumb stabbing the microphone to life; and,

"Whoops! Sorry about that, folks. You just caught me kissing the boyfriend, is all. Getting him fired up for later. Tell you what, let's have a couple of jingles and some ads, while I get myself straightened out here. I'm all in pieces at the moment, he does that to me . . . "

*   *   *

"Radio Nova – it burns all night . . . "

In the security complex, Alan Hudson leant back in his chair, folded his hands behind his head and twisted away from the bank of monitors to glance over at his partner.

"That Denise Anderson – you ever seen her?"

"Seen her? No. Why?"

"She's some sexy little bint, that's why. I looked in on Nova a couple of nights back while I was doing the rounds, and copped an eyeful through the studio window. Very tasty, she is. And she's got her hair done up in one of those Mohicans, you know, shaved clean up the sides and then this ridge standing up straight, all the way down to her neck? And would you believe it, she wears her headphones upside down, with the strap under her chin, so's it doesn't muck the hair up. Christ knows what it looks like in the morning – but I'll tell you one thing, I'd like to be there to find out . . . "

"Yeah, well. Not much chance of that, is there?" Peter Kerr leant forward suddenly, his eyes fixed on one of the monitors. "Saw something move, then. Sector D. Pan the camera left."

Hudson grunted, and turned back to the control board. After a moment the view on one monitor began to change, a small staff parking area sliding sideways, with buildings rising high behind. "What was it, then," Hudson asked, "one of them tramps?"

"No, too small. Hold it!" as a row of rubbish-skips appeared. "Yeah, there they are. It's those bloody strays again."

The picture showed a pack of half a dozen mongrels circling a skip, the largest of them leaping up to scrabble with its paws on the steel lip for a moment before falling back.

"Right." Kerr got to his feet and went to a canvas bag in the corner. "You log it. I'll fix them."

"Why bother? They're only dogs." Hudson had three dogs himself, and two of those had once been strays.

"It's part of the job, isn't it? And it looks good in the log. Shows we're alert."

"What are you going to do, then?" Kerr had something in his fist that Hudson couldn't identify, a bulky cylinder coloured army khaki.

"Scare the shit out of them. You watch."

Kerr grinned, and left the room; and for the practice, for

something to do or for sheer curiosity, Hudson did watch. He tracked his partner's progress from camera to camera, from the complex to the main buildings and through a narrow alleyway to the car park and the dogs.

Another switch turned on a microphone, so that he could hear Kerr's footsteps, loud as he passed near the camera but fading quickly as he walked on, out into the full glare of the security lights. He stood still then, and Hudson heard a distant barking from the dogs; watched as Kerr drew his arm back and tossed that cylinder in a high lob towards them.

It landed right in the middle of the scattering pack, and a second later there was a searing flash, a cloud of smoke, an explosion that made the control-room speakers boom and crackle.

Hudson swore, and flicked the microphone off with a thrusting finger; and was still swearing when the smoke cleared to show the car park empty and still, no sign of dog or man.

"What the hell was that?" he demanded when Kerr came in exultant, smelling of smoke.

"Thunderflash. Big bang, no damage. Scorched a bit of fur, that's all. Not even that, if they were quick. Worked, though, didn't it? Those buggers won't be back."

"I thought you'd chucked a bloody grenade at them. Jesus, you'd be out of here quicker than those poor damn dogs, if Johnnie Lee knew you were throwing those things around. I mean, for God's sake, what else you got in that bag of yours? Pistol, maybe, a sawn-off shotgun, what?"

"No, nothing. It was just those dogs, we've had them here before, and I figured a flash'd scare them off. So I've been bringing it in for a few nights, waiting for the chance."

"Where d'you get it from, anyway?"

"Oh, contacts. It's not hard to pick up stuff like that, if you know the right people. But keep it quiet, right?"

"You bet. Here." Hudson fished a loose-leaf file out from a shelf below the console, and passed it over to his partner. "God knows what you're going to say, but you can bloody well log it yourself."

0500:

and Julian sat rolling a cigarette around the bowl of an ashtray, watching the smoke rise. He had the radio on, turned down so low he could barely hear it; but that was just for company, he wasn't listening.

He lifted his head to see the sky brightening through the window, took a deep drag on his tab, almost made a decision to go, to leave now, silent and secret; and heard the door click open behind him, footsteps soft on the carpet.

He didn't turn round, even when hands closed warm and firm on his naked shoulders, even when a voice murmured, "Aren't you cold, like that?"

"No."

"Liar. You're shivering."

"Well, I didn't want to come back in, for my shirt. Might have woken you up, like, I didn't want to do that . . . "

"Shouldn't have left me, then, should you? That's what woke me up. Empty bed, cold sheets. No Julian."

He could find nothing to say to that, except, "I've got to get home, anyway."

"Have you?"

"Aye. I've never stopped out all night, there'll be questions from Mam . . . "

"And you don't want to give her any answers, right?"

"I can't. I just, I *can't* . . . "

Hard thumbs worked the stiff muscles of his back for a minute; then there was a sigh, and, "All right, you get some clothes on, if that's what you want. I'll make coffee."

Julian nodded, pushed himself slowly to his feet and picked his way through the party's debris, empty cans and overflowing ashtrays. But then a hand grabbed the waistband of his jeans, bringing him to a dead halt.

"Hey. Don't I even get a kiss good-morning?"

"Uh, yeah. Sure . . . "

So he turned and saw Richard looking like a monk, in a long white dressing-gown with the hood pushed back. Saw tired, concerned eyes that clashed significantly with the casual voice and the teasing smile; and then stopped looking, as Richard took a pace forward, looped one arm round his waist, slid the other hand up over his chest and round to the back of his neck, pulled his head down to meet him carefully, mouth to mouth.

*   *   *

Andrew Scott was asleep and dreaming when the music came, laying itself down like a movie soundtrack and seeming for a moment almost logical, almost a believable part of the action. Then he woke and rolled over, and only the music stayed with him, his radio-alarm turning itself on as instructed.

He squinted through the half-light to check the time, and grunted softly. Half past five and too early, far too early to be getting up on a Saturday, but that was also as instructed.

This was a big day, a day to impress the hell out of his boss if everything went smoothly; and he wanted to be at work by seven, sharp and ready for anything, just to make sure that it did.

So he sat up and rubbed his eyes one-handed, then headed naked for the shower, scooping his bathrobe off the back of a chair with a practised swing of his left arm. Wondering a second later how Dee would feel if she saw him do it. Knowing that however well-adjusted a person was, it was always the little things, the casual actions that could shake them . . .

Then he grinned, mocking himself. He should be so lucky. Chances were he'd never get Dee anywhere near his bedroom; and if he did, he wouldn't need to worry. If she could handle a night in bed, she wasn't likely to be much disturbed by the sight of him in the morning.

When he got to the bathroom it was automatic to check out his left hand, first thing. There was no problem, though. The hand hadn't been stolen overnight, it hadn't spasmed into an immovable fist or crawled away on its fingers to commit a foul horror-movie murder on Mrs Crawford downstairs. More realistically, there hadn't been a power cut overnight; according to the read-out the battery was fully charged, there were no malfunctions in the circuitry, the hand was only waiting for the rest of his body to get plugged in.

He touched the soft palm, and shivered a little as always at the warmth of it in the mornings. It was only the recharger doing its stuff, he knew that; but still, it felt alive. And it looked too damn real for comfort. He was willing to bet that for someone unaccustomed to prosthetics – someone like Dee – it was actually scarier that way than an obviously mechanical substitute would have been. With this one you could practically watch the nails grow while it was lying there on its bed of cotton-wool, all wired up and humming to itself . . .

Nails. That was a thought. He checked the nails on his right hand; and just as well he did, because they were going to need trimming again. It was one of the odd little things that people noticed, if the nails on one hand were longer than those on the other. And he was due to meet any number of strangers today, important strangers, so he'd best make sure they matched.

*   *   *

'Thank – thank you, nurse, it's very kind of you . . . "

Carol Easterman made one of those soft murmurs that sound to patients like *"not at all, you're very welcome"* but actually mean *"too bloody right it is, you irritating old man"*; and if the smile she forced onto her face looked more like the weary, meaningless grimace that lay behind it, what did it matter? Mr Quin wasn't going to notice, in the darkened ward.

She swathed the bed-pan in paper towels and began the long, long trek fifty yards down the corridor to the sluice, feeling every step of it in her suffering feet. She was carrying too much weight for this job, far too much. She'd stick with it now, though, she'd have to. What else was there for her? Answer, nothing. She'd been glad enough to get it, after so many months on the dole; and she'd always been stubborn, she had that going for her. When she took something on, she stuck with it.

But oh, why did that old fool always have to hold it all in until this end of the shift, when each separate step hurt so badly? Actually, she knew the answer to that one, too. He'd lie awake for hours, until he was sure that every other patient was asleep; then wait till she made her rounds, till she could be hailed in a whisper, too embarrassed to let anyone else know that he had bowels that functioned like their own.

Carol sighed, and twisted her head down to read the time from the fob-watch pinned to her uniform. A present from Audrey, that had been, joking congratulations: "Just to make sure you do the thing *properly*, darling. I bet half those young things don't use these any more, but dare to be different, that's what I say."

A quarter to six, near enough. Give or take. The wretched thing could lose five minutes in every hour, if it was in the mood; but that was the price you paid for Audrey's jokes. And if it was losing, at least that meant she'd get off sooner than she thought. Either way, she could be home in a couple of hours. Home and soaking her swollen feet in a bowl of cold water, with bed just minutes away and a long day's sleep ahead . . .

She'd heard some of the others on her shift – the young things – making plans to meet up at midday at the Meldon Centre, for some charity affair. They'd invited her to join them, of course, when they saw that she was listening; and bless them, they'd even argued a little when she refused, tried to persuade her. But privately, she couldn't imagine anything worse. Dragging herself out of bed too soon, making the long trail out by bus or train to spend hours more on her feet in a crush of youngsters, bored and exhausted and utterly out of place . . .

No, thank you. The future is famous for its uncertainty; but if anything was a cast-iron surety, it was that Carol Easterman was going nowhere near the Meldon Centre this weekend. Absolutely not. No way . . .

*   *   *

Peter Kerr sat in the control room doing a final check for the log, testing every camera in the Centre. The place was waking up now. He could see cars coming in, being passed through the security barriers; buses starting to arrive, bringing in store workers and cleaning staff; lorries queueing up at the delivery points, waiting to be unloaded.

It was in standing orders, to run a comprehensive check

like this at the end of every shift; but he was more scrupulous than the others, he knew that. It was just another proof that he should have got that last promotion to sergeant. And the fact that he hadn't was just another proof that he wasn't liked, by his bosses any more than his fellow guards.

He could hear the new shift now, getting into uniform in the changing-room down the corridor. Twice as many as usual, because of all the special events today and the huge crowds expected. And the worst of those crowds would still be here when Peter came back on duty at ten o'clock this evening – thousands of teenagers packing the malls, drinking more than they could handle, getting into fights, shoplifting and snatching purses . . .

The whole thing was a mistake, Peter was sure of that. A big mistake on the management's part, ever to have agreed to it. It was the publicity angle they were after, nationwide television and a fashionable cause; but it could backfire on them terribly, if it all turned to riots and looting and mass arrests.

Still, to set against that, there was always the possibility of Peter's finally making an impression on his bosses. He'd show the bastards what a balls-up they'd made, passing him over the way they did. He'd rub their bloody faces in it when they saw how he took control, mixed it with the troublemakers and stamped out any violence at the first sign, even before the police knew what was going on. There was only one good man on their whole bloody team, and they'd know it before tomorrow . . .

Hudson's laughter echoed suddenly up the corridor from the changing-room. Typical, that was. You wouldn't catch Peter changing out of uniform before the shift was over. He'd stay where he was supposed to be, run his checks and log them, then wait to be relieved like it said in standing orders. To the letter, that's how he liked to play it.

And at least he'd have the room to himself when he did go to change. He preferred it that way, the benches empty and the lockers shut, no press of other men's bodies against his. He liked his privacy, Peter did. He liked to be left alone, to dress in peace and leave in his own time, drive home to find his meal ready for him and his bed turned down and waiting . . .

0600:

"You coming to bed, then, or what?"

Thus Denise, standing in the living-room doorway, arms akimbo; while her lover sat slumped on the sofa, cigarette in one hand and beer in the other, eyes fixed on the vacuities of night-time television.

She fought to keep the edge out of her voice as she asked, but she might as well have saved the effort, because Matt didn't seem even to hear her. In any event he didn't reply with so much as a movement of his head, yes or no.

Denise leant over the back of the sofa to grab a handful of his thick curls and pull his head round; and spoke softer than her actions, softer than her words, even, as she said, "Hey, you. I'm talking to you. Are you planning to sit here all night?"

His eyes gazed at her across a gulf far wider than those few inches. "It's morning already."

"All morning, then."

"Why not? Nothing else to do."

"You could try sleeping. It's supposed to be good for you."

"I don't like waking up."

And it wasn't a pulling away from her, she couldn't accuse him of that; all he did was turn his head an inch or two, to move his eyes back to the television. But it was enough, because he suddenly wasn't there any more, not for her. She could feel the absence of him beneath her fingers, his skin only a wall turned against her, to close her out; and this was all familiar ground now, the fleeting contacts and the abrupt cutting off. She couldn't do any more tonight, he probably wouldn't say another word, however hard she pushed him.

She grimaced, touched her lips to his ear in a brief kiss — only a gesture, but that's how it was these days, she lived a life of unregarded gestures and kept them up more for her own sake than his – and went to bed alone.

* * *

The Coatman stirred, grunted and shrugged himself deeper into the warmth of his covers, his coats. He wanted nothing more than sleep, as much sleep as he could glean from these short summer nights. But the rumble of increasing traffic only yards away told him it was morning already, daylight too soon; the staccato click of a woman's high heels, hesitating only briefly as she passed and then hurrying on, warned him that he wouldn't be left alone much longer; and a dog's curious nose thrusting at his legs was enough to make him curse and lurch upwards on the bench.

He roared wordlessly at the stray, which flinched and scuttered away across the road, barely missing the bumper of a speeding lorry. Then the Coatman planted his feet slowly and solidly onto the pavement, first one and then the other. A convulsive cough shook his body; he hawked deep in his throat, and spat wet phlegm into the gutter. The bright sunlight made him squint and mutter, as he ran a hand over his long, matted beard. He gathered his coats carefully across his shoulders – the donkey jacket first, then the macintosh and the heavy overcoat, lastly the parka with the hood he could pull up over his greying, greasy hair – and reached for his tobacco-tin in one of the carrier bags under the bench. He fished with spatulate, yellowed fingers for the longest dog-end, put it between his lips and lit it with his last match; and coughed again, as he pushed himself up.

He stamped a few times against the pain and stiffness in his joints, and roared again – at the world this time, a world of dogs and dog-ends, hunger and hard beds. Then he picked up his bags and limped cautiously out of the bus shelter in which he'd passed the night. He sniffed at the breeze, and spat; and turned – muttering again, all but unconscious of his own voice running on – towards the industrial estate half a mile down the road. He'd find Ivy there, in the little camp she'd made herself, her ripped tarpaulin tent and oil-drum fire. And one thing was sure: where Ivy was, there would a bottle be, and never mind what was in it . . .

* * *

Andrew turned off the motorway onto the Meldon Centre feed-road, followed it in a wide loop around the main buildings and through the acres of colour-coded car parks, coming finally to the security complex, a series of interlinked one-storey structures which housed all the administrative offices.

He slowed down for the barrier and tutted in remonstrance when he saw it lifting even before he'd reached it.

He pulled up by the small brick gatehouse, trying to scowl ferociously at the guard inside.

"Norman! *Don't* lift the barrier before you check passes!"

Norman was quite unperturbed. "I know your car, Mr Scott."

"That's not the point. You couldn't be sure it was me driving it."

"Oh, aye. You're a terrible driver." Delivered deadpan, no concessions to the hierarchy.

"Thanks, mate. But watch out for Johnnie Lee, that's all. He'll bollock you, if he catches you at it."

"Don't you worry, Mr Scott. I know his car too. He gets the full treatment. By the time I'm through checking his face against his photo, even he's not sure he's himself."

Andrew grinned, waved an acknowledgement – *okay, I won't tell you how to do your job* – and drove on to his own personal parking-space. He still got a kick out of that. Maybe it was only one among a couple of dozen, he hadn't been singled out; but still, the reserved sign had his own name neatly lettered, his car's registration underneath, and a disabled symbol painted on just to make doubly certain no one pinched it.

He parked and locked the car, started towards the nearest door into the complex; saw one of the steel-plated surveillance cameras following him from the top of its long pole, and made a cheerfully rude gesture at it. Left-handed, of course. It had taken a while to master that, extending just the two fingers wasn't easy, but he had it down pat now.

Inside, he found that the guy he shared an office with was there before him.

"Well, if it isn't Captain Hook."

"'Morning, Dalek. Give us a twirl."

"Anything to oblige." Calum hooked his thumb over the joystick and his wheelchair span in a quick circle, without moving an inch from its place.

Andrew applauded, sat down at his desk and reached for the computer keyboard to log himself in. "I know about me, I'm sucking up to Teacher; but how come you're here this early?"

"My mother's on early shifts this week. By definition, so am I."

"You mean you've been coming in before seven all week?"

"That's right."

"Shit, why didn't you say?"

"There's nothing you can do about it, Andrew. It's just the nature of the beast."

"That's not true. I could pick you up on my way in, no trouble. I've taken you home before now, so why not?"

"You could pick me up, yes. But you couldn't get me out of bed, help me in the bathroom and give me breakfast first, could you? All that has to be done before Mother leaves. And I'd rather be here getting on with things than sitting around at home waiting for you."

Andrew nodded, accepting the point reluctantly. Calum's brittle-bone disease had left him with a normal head – and a highly superior intellect – on a tiny and massively deformed body, his twisted arms thin as sticks and dangerously fragile, his legs withered and useless. The hi-tech chair made him mobile, at least in a designed environment such as his bungalow home or here at the Meldon Centre; but he would always be dependent on others for domestic help.

It was a curious coincidence that the two of them had ended up sharing an office – Cripples' Corner they called it themselves, loudly and in public – but certainly nothing more than that, there'd been no intent behind it. Two jobs had been on offer in the Public Relations department; when the PR Director, Mrs Pargeter, had phoned to offer one of them to Andrew, she'd said, "Oh, by the way, you'll be working with a man who's physically disabled. Quite severely so. It's a bonus for us, to be honest; we'd have taken him in any case, he was an outstanding candidate, but it'll be good to have someone on the staff who really understands about wheelchair access and other facilities. Particularly on the PR staff. We're moving him straight onto the sub-committee that deals with such things, he's very keen. I can't see that there'll be any problems for you in sharing an office with him, but I thought I ought to forewarn you."

"No problem at all," Andrew had assured her, thinking, *here goes* . . . "As a matter of fact, I'm disabled myself."

A pause; then, "I'm sorry?"

"My left hand is artificial. I lost the original in an accident, when I was eleven."

"Oh. I see. I'm sorry . . . You didn't mention that, on the application form."

"No. The question asked if I was registered disabled; and I don't register. I manage very well without state assistance, and I don't want the label."

"Yes. I can understand that."

"I suppose I should have brought it up at the interview. I wasn't trying to deceive you, it's just a habit; if people don't notice, then generally I don't think they need to know. It shouldn't affect my work at all, except maybe making me a little slow on the computer, I have to more or less type one-handed . . . Um, sorry, but do I still get the job?"

She'd laughed then. "Yes, of course you do. Come along on Monday week, at ten. You can meet Calum, and I'll introduce you both around; and if you don't object, I'd like to take a look at that hand. I was a nurse once, many moons ago, and I can't believe that I didn't spot it . . . "

That was more than a year ago. In the months since, Andrew had watched Calum carving out his own niche in the department, never missing the chance to argue for a change of policy or design if the disabled could benefit; and although they were friends, although they worked very easily and effectively together, Andrew had felt himself being left behind. He lacked both Calum's ambition and his sheer force of personality – and of course he lacked the monumental advantage of a highly visible disability, which Calum made no bones about exploiting at every opportunity. *'If you've got it, flaunt it'* – that was the motto Calum had hanging on the wall above his desk. And he was constantly urging Andrew to exchange his discreet prosthetic for a large steel hook.

Still, there were hares and there were tortoises; and even if tortoises didn't always win races, at least they'd get there in the end. Andrew had the biggest job of his career on his hands – both hands – today, acting as liaison between the event organisers, the television people and the Centre's own administration. If he blew it . . .

But he wasn't going to blow it. No way. He turned back to his terminal and started punching keys, calling up his anticipated schedule on the VDU.

0700:

and as always Johnnie Lee had been up since five, despite not getting to bed till after one. "Eight hours' sleep, that is a luxury to me," he had been quoted as saying. "I have nothing against luxuries, you should not misunderstand me. You have only to look at my lifestyle. But sleep would not be my choice. I prefer to work."

And working he was, in the undeniably luxurious suite of offices below his penthouse at Burleigh Tower. He sat in a leather armchair by the picture-window overlooking the quayside, reading quickly through a pile of correspondence and dictating responses into a hand-held recorder.

"Burroughs – no, but politely. I do not want this door closed. The offer is good; but I think it will be improved. Carbondale – yes, provisionally. Ask Mr Adams to follow up on that. Mitchell & Mitchell no, and you may be as rude as you like . . . "

And so on, rapid staccato decisions that his secretary would convert into formal letters. He worked his way to the bottom of the stack, and flicked off the recorder. Good – there had been nothing there to waste his time, nothing he could safely have left to a subordinate to decide.

Johnnie walked through to the next room, where a girl was busy at one of the computer terminals. He dropped the pile of papers onto his secretary's desk, put the recorder on top and wandered across to peer over the girl's shoulder.

"What's this, Marie?"

"Just working on the spreadsheet, Mr Lee, updating profit forecasts on the basis of last month's figures. I'll do you a summary, as soon as I've finished. That's if the software'll stop arguing with me," she added, grinning. "It keeps trying to delete one of the columns. But I'll win in the end."

"Of course. I only hire winners." He nodded, remembered not to pat her on the shoulder – no patronising of employees, Linda had spoken to him about that – and said, "Where is the overnight status report, please?"

"I'm sorry, Mr Lee, it's not come through yet."

"Not?" He glanced at his watch. "It should be in before seven. This is seven fifteen."

"Do you want me to chase them up?"

"No. I will do it."

But even as he picked a phone up to dial, the terminal on another desk bleeped for attention, and a printer started chattering.

"I expect that's it now, Mr Lee."

"Yes. I hope so."

He went across and ran his eye over the fanfold pages worming out of the printer. That was it, yes: the summary he insisted on, everything noteworthy that had happened at the Centre in the past twelve hours.

There never was much in these overnight reports, of course. Teenagers causing a disturbance at the bus terminal, after the last film; that was a common occurrence, and the security people were well able to deal with it. One woman taken ill in the cinema, suspected heart attack, an ambulance called and two members of staff accompanying her to hospital; PR informed, and a press statement to be issued. Too late for the local morning paper, but it might appear in the evening editions. Journalists were always courteous to Johnnie Lee; their editors knew how much advertising space he took, and were careful to keep them so.

Little else on the report. A pack of stray dogs – 'dealt with', according to the security log. Peter Kerr, that came from. Dealt with how, Johnnie wondered; and decided to ask, next time he saw the man. Strays were always a potential hazard on site, with the inevitable accumulation of spoiled food and other rubbish. It could keep customers away, if the Centre got a reputation for dogs running wild. If Peter Kerr had an efficient method of driving them off, it was worth passing on to the other security men; and Johnnie knew enough about his employees to guess that Kerr wouldn't pass it on himself. He was a loner, that one.

The report ended with the change of shifts, noting the double staffing Johnnie had ordered. He nodded, scribbled his initials on the final sheet and dropped it onto Marie's desk for filing.

Then he left the suite, trotted upstairs to the penthouse and went into the master bedroom for a word with his wife.

She wasn't there, though. The bed was empty, and so when he looked was the dressing-room next door. He rapped on the bathroom door, got no answer, and pushed it open just to be sure. There was no sign of Linda, nor of the mess she usually left behind her in the mornings for the maid to tidy up. Probably she'd woken earlier than usual, and gone down to the basement gym for a work-out or a sauna. Johnnie shrugged, unconcerned; she'd be at the Centre when he needed her, he could count on that.

He checked his watch again, and took their private lift quickly down to the ground floor. His car was waiting outside, he could see it through the tall glass doors; but Johnnie allowed himself a minute just to stand in the foyer, gazing at the fine model ship that gleamed proudly white on a table in the middle of the marble floor.

The ship didn't exist yet, or not like this: not with Johnnie's logo emblazoned high on its funnels, not carrying Johnnie's name and reputation around the coasts of Europe. Somewhere, though, there was a ferry with worried owners, hauling too few cars and passengers from one port to another; and it wouldn't be long now before Johnnie found it. His agents were out looking already, dropping hints, murmuring about the Channel tunnel and the inevitable falling-off of trade on the sea routes. Mentioning no names, but talking about a customer they had, a man looking for a roll-on roll-off and willing to pay in any currency the owners chose. Someone would take the bait soon, that was inevitable. Johnnie would get his ship.

And then he would gut it, strip it right down to the shell and rebuild it to the vision in his mind, brighter even than the model on the table. It would be a shopping mall, and more: a floating hotel, a nightclub, a pleasure park, whatever the punters wanted. There was plenty of harbour space these days, with the decline in commercial shipping; he'd cruise it from port to port, dock for a week or a month at each and move on before the public got bored. He'd take it across the North Sea, across the Channel, perhaps even down to the Mediterranean. He'd run an advertising blitz at every port of call; men would come for the sports hall and the restaurants, women for the shopping, kids for the fun. They would all come, for the novelty. It would be a travelling Meldon Centre, the mall that comes to the public; and best of all, for Johnnie, it would still be a ship.

He nodded, smiled tightly, and decided to invite some people to dinner next week. He could show them the model, the detailed plans and the feasibility study, sell them on the concept and start talking money.

But that was next week. Today, this morning he pulled open one of the heavy glass doors and went running down the steps into bright sunshine, to where his chauffeur waited with the car.

*   *   *

Ivy sat singing on an upturned plastic beer crate, legs spread wide and bottle in hand, mistress of all she surveyed. This was her queendom, right enough, this little patch of waste ground; and she loved it here. She called it home, she called it hers, she counted every worn rubber tyre and every rusting engine and claimed them as her own. Not on a permanent basis, of course, that was understood. Sooner or later the bailiffs would come, as they always did; they'd have documents to prove that the land belonged to the council, other documents to show that the council had a use for it, that they wanted to build another factory or clear the ground for a car park. And then, once again, she'd have nothing. No documents for Ivy: no right of abode in the open air, no secured tenancy on a home without bricks or mortar or visible means of support.

So she'd move on, in the end. Drift around till she found another uncontested piece of nothing, somewhere in the urban wilderness, and staked her claim to it. Pitched her tarpaulin tent and hung her hat on the ridge-pole.

But that was for the future, that grey and greasy time she never looked at. For the moment here she was, and here she sat: drinking, singing, watching a shambling figure on the road draw closer step by step. A courtier he, coming to make his duty to the queen.

And, of course, deserving of a royal welcome. She struggled to her feet, and never mind the throbbing pains of all the corns and bunions that forced her wellingtons into such strange, distorted shapes; hobbled over to the oil-drum brazier, and prodded the fire into sullen life. Added a handful of twigs and branches she'd gleaned last night from the roadside, to make a blaze to greet him, and bent with a groan to pick up an old tin mug from the ground. Shook a beetle out, and watched it scuttle for shelter among the sparse grasses.

"Sorry, matey," she said, cackling. "I'm the bailiff, see? I'm the bailiff here."

She gave the mug a wipe-round with a corner of her skirt, said it again, "Oh yes, matey, old Ivy's the bailiff round here. Old Ivy makes the rules," and sloshed a dirty grey liquid from bottle to mug. Sniffed it, gave another little cackle, and held both aloft – high, high above her head like she was dancing, and she might have done that as well, might have tossed a caper or two if only her poor feet didn't hurt so much – as encouragement to hurry the Coatman along.

*　　　*　　　*

The baby's crying woke Charlie Campbell more quickly and more thoroughly than any alarm clock ever had. His eyes snapped open, he made a fast and accurate guess at the time – he was getting good at that, after three months of fatherhood – and waited. After a minute, when Sue still hadn't moved a solitary muscle, let alone leapt instantly out of bed like a devoted mother should, he slid an arm over to her side of the bed and prodded her lightly in the ribs.

"Your turn."

"Sod off," mumbled back at him through a mouthful of pillow.

"Oy." His fingers walked slowly up her spine, counting off the vertebrae. "We made a pact, remember? Turn and turn about. And I did it yesterday, so it's your turn."

"You've got to get up anyway. I haven't. No point both of us suffering."

And she hunched herself down further under the duvet, end of discussion.

"Bitch." He addressed it without heat to the top of her head, pulled on a pair of jeans and ambled out of the room, closing the door quietly behind him.

A couple of minutes later he shooed the cat off the

changing-mat in the kitchen and laid his son there instead.

"Here we go, then. Feels good to be back, doesn't it? Home is anywhere you get your nappy changed. And wasn't it kind of Erotica to keep it warm for you . . . ?"

The soft monologue ran on, while Charlie's hands dealt speedily with the baby's damp clothes and sodden nappy. The former went straight into the washing-machine, the latter into the bin; then a spot of cream on an incipient rash, and John Mark was left to kick and complain on his own for a minute.

Coming back with a fresh nappy and a clean babygro: "Bright yellow this morning, Master Campbell, how d'you like that? You'll match your breakfast. Lie there and play with it, while I fix a bottle for you. 'Tisn't breakfast-time yet, see, on account of your daddy's got to go dashing off to do some overtime, the poor bugger, and your mother is an idle hussy who doesn't love you. So you'll have to settle for a drink right now. Then I'll put you back to bed, and what I want you to do, I want you to sleep for one hour, then bawl your bloody head off, okay? You can give her a real hard time all morning, if you like . . . "

Under the influence of his father's familiar voice and the welcome attention, John Mark's screams had died slowly to quiet whimpers, and then to silence. Now he chuckled; and Charlie left the bottle warming in a pan of water, to go over and disentangle his fingers gently from the soft cotton of the babygro.

"Oh, you like that idea, do you, child of mine? Can't say I blame you, not at all. I've seen the way she treats you. She was even cutting your poor fingernails last night, wasn't she? Talk about over-reacting, it was just a tiny wee scratch you'd given her, and only on the cheek at that. It didn't even bleed much, did it? She'll not be disfigured for more than a month or two, and such a fuss she made! And so cruel too, with those nasty sharp scissors, hacking away bits of your beautiful body . . . "

He bent over to nuzzle the small hands sympathetically; and while he was there moved his lips to the baby's stomach and blew a loud raspberry, just to hear John Mark's shriek of laughter.

And was rewarded with a fine jet of urine, spraying all over his naked chest.

He straightened up, swearing; and heard another laugh

come from the doorway behind him, to blend with his son's.

He made a face at Sue over his shoulder and said, "We should have got a girl, I told you we should get a girl. They're not so accurate. Fetch me a towel, will you? When you've finished with the adolescent giggling?"

Instead she came to join him, wrapping one arm round his waist and using the sleeve of her bathrobe to rub him dry with the other.

"Thank you. Greater love hath no man than this. But listen, how is it that I make a martyr of myself, attending to our child's every need so that you can get a few more hours of sorely-needed beauty sleep, only to find that you spurn this selfless generosity and get up anyway? How is that? Were you spying, is that it, listening in on our man's-talk?"

"That's it," she agreed, through a yawn. "I hate missing out on your prattle. It's the only reason I haven't divorced you yet."

"Well, there had to be something."

"Yeah." She kissed him just below the collar-bone, and pushed him away. "Put the kettle on, I'll finish off sweetums."

"Aye, now that he's safely evacuated his bladder all over me. I know."

Half an hour later John Mark was getting his breakfast after all, spoonfuls of yellow goo administered by his mother while Charlie got himself dressed and ready.

"What are you two doing today, then?"

"Dunno. Nothing much. Maybe I'll take him into town, do some shopping. He likes it in town, can you imagine?"

"I know, I've seen him. Why don't you bring him out to the Meldon Centre? Bright lights, big shops; he'll go bananas. And if you're going to spend the money I'm sweating to earn, you might as well do it where I can watch you. I'll zoom the camera in on every penny."

She just snorted; Charlie grinned, and pushed his hand through her short bleached hair. "No, I mean it. Come on out, the pair of you."

"Charlie. It'll be hell out there. He'll get scared . . . "

"Not him – and you watch your tongue, woman. He's a Campbell, isn't he? All Campbell boys are born heroes, it's a matter of definition. Look at me, for example."

"Do I have to?"

"No. You turn your face away, I'll sidle quietly out of the door, you'll never know I'm gone . . . "

She turned her face up instead, and said, "Kiss."

So he kissed her and then the baby, smears of yellow goo notwithstanding; and left for work, pausing only to say, "By the way, your roots could use some attention. I mean, they really could . . . "

"Fuck off and die."

0800:

and brisk as ever, Linda Lee stood up and pulled the solitary sheet off the bed, leaving her lover – or her minder, her toy boy, call him what you will: her employee, at any rate – lying naked and exposed, languid but watchful, the sweat still glistening on his skin.

She wrapped the sheet around her, tied it securely above her breasts and went through to the bathroom. With her hair tucked under a cap she took a quick shower, a purely short-term expedient to cleanse the smell of him from her body and the possessive grip of him from her mind. She'd bathe properly later, up in the penthouse; but there was always this urgent compulsion to wash herself immediately after sex, to rid herself with soap and water of any other's claim on her person. It was more than dirty water she watched spiral away down the plughole, and more than clean skin she dried afterwards on one of Carl's towels.

Clad in the sheet again, she returned to the bedroom for her clothes; and found him still on the bed, flat on his back now with his legs spread and his hands tucked behind his head, making a brazen exhibition of his hard-built body.

Linda twitched a cool eyebrow at his smile, and said nothing. If he was expecting a compliment – and no doubt he was, young men were predictable as cattle – then he'd be disappointed. He ought to know that by now, he'd been on the payroll long enough.

She unhitched the sheet and let it fall, hiding nothing and displaying nothing, neither disturbed nor excited by the feel of his eyes on her. She dressed unconcernedly under his gaze, shorts and singlet, track suit, a sweat-band to hold the hair out of her eyes; sat on the edge of the mattress to lace her trainers, and felt it shift beneath her as he stirred and sat up.

His hands closed on her shoulders, probing for stiffness. There was none to find, she was confident of that; massage was another of his duties, along with regulating her exercise programme, and there at least he was an expert. In bed – well, he was competent, but there were the inevitable faults of his youth to overcome, as well as the benefits to enjoy. Swings and roundabouts, you couldn't escape them. She was still fighting a war with his ego, still seeking a way to set his macho self-confidence on one side for long enough to teach him a few of the subtler arts of giving a woman pleasure.

But not now. The massage was unnecessary, and – given that he must be aware of that, his fingers finding no knots, no tensions – the assumption that underlay it was unpleasant to her. Her body was not available to him, to be handled at will; that had to be impressed upon him somehow.

She endured his touch for a brief while, not to deflate him utterly; then she shrugged him away and stood up, with a crisp, "Thank you, Carl, that'll do. Now put your clothes on. I've a lot to do, and I'm short of time already, with all this nonsense going on at the Centre."

"What's the hurry?" he said, challenging. "Your old man'll be gone by now, I checked. Half seven, he wanted the car."

"That's not the point. I told you, I've got work to do."

"Yeah. Making more money for him, right?"

"Making more money for both of us." She scooped up his running-clothes from the floor and tossed them onto the bed beside him. "Hurry up, please."

But he still didn't move, he only looked at her and said, "You should leave him, that's what you should do."

"Leave Johnnie?" She laughed, crystal-clear and scornful. "What on earth for?" And when he didn't answer, "For you, you mean? Is that what you're getting at?"

"Yeah, why not?"

She drew a breath, to tell him exactly why not; and then

held it back as he went on, clumsy with words but supremely self-assured.

"I mean, he ain't giving you what you want, is he? You wouldn't be fooling around with me if he was. But I reckon you and me, Linda, we could really go places. And you don't need to worry about money. For fuck's sake, you've been married how long?"

"Fifteen years," she supplied neutrally.

"Yeah, right, fifteen years. You'd get half of everything, and that's one hell of a lot. And you'd be shot of him, and we could stop hiding it, stop sneaking around when he wasn't looking and be right up front. We could get married, and . . . "

"Carl." She arrested the flow with nothing but his name. "Carl, listen to me. I'm only going to say this once, so remember it. I don't stay with Johnnie because of his money; he's worth a lot more to me than that. I make all the money I need, in any case. You're quite right, he doesn't give me everything I want; but frankly, my dear, neither do you. I come to you for sex because I enjoy strong bodies and younger men, that's why I hired you; but that's all."

"What're you saying," Carl demanded with a deepening scowl on his face, in his voice, in every muscle of his body, "that I'm some sort of whore?"

"That's right," she said mercilessly. "And a fairly common sort of whore, I'm afraid. I've had a dozen like you over the years, and I expect I'll have a dozen more."

His fists clenched, and she thought that perhaps he might have struck her if he hadn't still been fairly ludicrously naked on the mattress, while she was standing and clothed some distance away. He did struggle clumsily to his feet, did come one furious pace towards her; but she stalled him by taking a step forward herself, and laying a hand coolly on his chest.

"Now, Carl, don't be foolish. And don't do anything that you might regret later, like walking out on me. It's a good job you've got yourself here. You're well paid, you get this flat for nothing, and the car – and, well, you get me too. Just look on me as another of the perks, if you like. You're a sweet boy, and I'm very glad to have you, in every sense of the word; just don't get ideas outside the job description, that's all I'm saying, because you'll only be disappointed. Now, I'm going up to the penthouse. You don't have to come with me yet. Take your time, have a shower, and come up when you're ready. Just so long as you're there before I want to leave for the Centre. Oh, and wear a suit. There'll be television, and I want you looking your best. A million dollars'-worth at least."

She patted him on the shoulder and left him standing, didn't look back.

*   *   *

Carol Easterman lay in her newly-acquired double bed – orthopaedic mattress for her poor back, which had been the excuse for it, and the wonderful width which was the real reason, she was just too big these days for a single – with two plump pillows under her head and her eyes closed, waiting for sleep.

Exhausted though she was, however, sleep wasn't cooperating. Half an hour it must be now since she came to bed, and she still felt wide awake. It might be her body, so shattered that it was turning fractious; or perhaps her mind was just too wound up to relax.

Then again, it might be nothing to do with her at all. Sometimes she saw sleep as a mischievous little creature with a life of its own, half Santa Claus and half Cupid: sliding down chimneys every night to send people into oblivion with the prick of a dart. Or not. Withholding it occasionally at random or for purely malicious reasons, in no danger ever of being called to account for its choices . . .

Vicious little beast, Carol thought, finding that she was tired enough this morning almost to believe that nonsense, certainly to prefer having someone other than herself to blame for her insomnia. She heaved her body over to the other side of the bed, where the pillows were cooler against her cheek, settled herself with a sigh and started to draw pictures of the creature in her mind.

He came to life quickly, bald head and pointed ears, as ugly as she could make him. Tattered leather tunic, dirt under her fingernails, bow and arrow in his hands – or no, this was the nineties after all, make that a hypodermic syringe. Give him a white coat, make him a doctor. All doctors were arbitrary, capricious, downright cruel on occasion . . .

So she did that, she made him a capering and malignant doctor; and he seemed suddenly so real that she half-thought perhaps she was slipping from imagination into dream, perhaps she was going to get some sleep after all, and *thank you doctor, just a little prick from that dripping needle if it's not too much to ask* –

– and a car horn blared suddenly in the street below her window, *shave and a hair-cut* and wake up Carol. Which she did, abruptly and thoroughly conscious again.

She opened her eyes to the dim light fighting its way in through the bedroom curtains, and cursed all inconsiderate drivers. Rolled over again, feeling the futility of it, bidding the good doctor farewell as he faded into unreality and left her as far as ever from sleeping.

Finally she sat up, heaped pillows behind her back for support, and reached for the remote-control unit on her bedside table. Nothing to do now but watch television for a while, try to numb her brain into obedience . . .

So she thumbed a button at random, the TV at the foot of the bed flickered into life, and Carol found herself watching a trailer for the Meldon Centre telethon.

" . . . As well as the main events there'll be buskers, jugglers, clowns to amuse the kids. Or there are plenty of activities you can join in with. If you're feeling brave, you can even abseil from the roof of the highest building in the Centre, under the watchful eyes of the Fusiliers. Remember, the fun starts at noon and goes on all day, all night and well into tomorrow. You can watch it all, on this channel; and the phone lines are open all weekend for you to call in your contributions. But better yet, why not come out here and be a part of it? I promise, it'll be a day to remember . . . "

*   *   *

Penny Polson was on her knees, hugging the toilet bowl and retching helplessly when she heard the door bang open behind her, footsteps on the lino.

"Whoops! Um, sorry . . . "

Nick's voice. Great. Terrific way for the new flatmate to catch her, head down in the loo chucking her cookies. Any of the others, she wouldn't have minded. Well, not so much . . .

"Are you okay?"

She rested her sweating forehead against the cold porcelain of the bowl, and tried a few deep breaths. Decided she could talk, and said, "Yeah, Nick, I'm fine. Never felt better."

"Sorry. Silly question, really, wasn't it? Um, I only wanted my shirt for work. I'll just take it, shall I, and let you, er, leave you alone . . . "

Penny took a chance, straightening slowly to sit back on her heels as Nick walked past her. Her stomach heaved, but settled again as she swallowed hard. She watched him slip a white shirt off its hanger above the bath, and toss it over his shoulder; then he turned round with a shy smile.

"Can I, you know, get you anything? Cup of tea, fruit juice, something like that? I could bring it up to your room . . . "

"No, ta. I'll come down in a bit. If I go back to bed I'll only want to throw up again. I always feel worse, lying down."

"Do this often, do you?" Another smile, and he was reaching past her to press the lever on the toilet cistern, flush her vomit away.

Often enough, yeah. But she didn't say it aloud, she only tugged at the hem of the baggy T-shirt she was wearing, where it was rucked up around her hips. Didn't know why she was bothering, chances were he'd got a nice view of her bum when he came in, and her cellulite thighs and all; but he was a nice guy, and he sounded embarrassed enough already. A quick flash of pubic hair as she stood up might just finish him off altogether.

"Well, I'll . . . " He broke off as she put one hand on the rim of the toilet and grabbed for the basin with the other, to pull herself up. His arms circled her waist from behind and lifted her carefully, held her till she was steady on her feet.

"Okay? Good. I'll see you downstairs, then. In a bit."

"Yeah. In a bit. Thanks, Nick . . . "

He shrugged, smiled, went out. Penny propped herself against the basin, leaning heavily on one arm, and filled the household tooth-mug with water to rinse the taste of bile from her mouth.

Ten minutes later, she was sitting in the kitchen with a pint glass of pineapple juice, sipping cautiously and watching Nick iron neat creases into his shirt.

"That must have been some party, last night."

"Yeah. Yeah, it was."

"Worth it, then?"

"What, worth the throwing up, you mean, and feeling like shit this morning? I dunno, are they ever?" But she thought back to the night before: to the playing and dancing and playing again, warm bodies and warm feelings, crowded rooms and noise, cans of cool lager flowing down her throat; and said, "Well, I guess, yeah. Worth it at the time, anyway. Richard's got a talent for making parties work. And he knows *everybody*, it's amazing. There were people there I haven't seen for years."

"That's nice. Are you going to be fit, though? For this afternoon?"

"I'll just have to be, won't I? With the television there, and everything. We'd be stupid to blow it."

A horn sounded in the street, and Nick looked at his watch. "Damn, that's my lift. I've got to go, Penny," pulling his shirt on, snatching up tie and jacket, already heading for the door. "I'll see you later, okay? And best of luck . . . "

"Thanks, Nick. Have a nice day."

When he was gone, Penny rubbed hard at the ache in her temples and turned to face Clarabelle, who was standing tall and silent in the corner of the room. Now there was a problem, if you like. How the hell was she going to practise, when standing up made her feel sick again and her head was throbbing already, to a rhythm of its own?

She looked at Clarabelle, Clarabelle looked at her; and at last she said, "Yeah, yeah, I know. I suffer, right?"

And supplied Clarabelle's response for her, flat and firm. "Right."

*　　　*　　　*

– and the first one died, just then. Died without much fuss, unnoticed by the neighbours: quietly at home, as you might say.

Though you wouldn't say that, not if you'd seen it happen. You might say a lot of other things, or you might say nothing at all; you might only stand and look, and shake your pitying head at the wonder and the horror of it all. Or else step queasily aside and bring up your breakfast, perhaps; or turn and run, stagger into the street outside and marvel that the road's still there, that cars still pass, that the sun still shines and the world still turns unheeding.

Might sigh, might even manage a thin smile as you say to yourself that life goes on, of course it does – until you remind yourself that for one person at least it does not. Later, you might enjoy the irony of your own clumsiness with words; but not now, no. Not with the smell of blood hanging in your nostrils, the stickiness of it on the soles of your feet. In the midst of death you are in life, maybe; but it's death's footprints you leave on the pavement, as you walk away.

0900:

and television had arrived, in the shape of two huge pantechnicons and a small fleet of cars. Had in fact arrived some time ago, and at least from Andrew's point of view seemed well on the way to taking over the entire Centre.

He stood with Bill Bruce the producer in the small car park that had been made over entirely to their use, and watched as technicians unloaded an apparently endless series of thick cables from one of the trucks. These were being locked into labelled sockets at the back of the other and then unreeled at a run, across the car park and out of sight.

"Jesus," Andrew murmured. "How many cameras have you lot brought with you, then?"

"There'll be half a dozen feeding live to the unit here. And then there's a couple of mobile units on top, small teams with a hand-held camera, recording to tape. They'll be on a roving commission inside – getting interviews, filming the buskers, that sort of thing. Vox pop. We'll patch their tapes into the broadcast during the lulls. That's something I was wanting to ask you about, in fact – is there anywhere on site that you'd rather they didn't go? Anything out of bounds? If there is, I'd like to know now, so I can warn them off in advance. Saves embarrassment all round. And one or two of the boys are liable to turn stroppy, if a guard tries to tell them there's something they're not allowed to film."

Andrew thought quickly. "Well, there's the security complex; but they wouldn't get in anyway, without a pass or a chaperon. I can't see any objection, though, if you want to take a camera in there. Just let me know, I'll arrange it. It'd be good PR for us, to show the public how careful we are. Other than that, I don't think there's a problem. I'd appreciate it if you could concentrate on the theme areas, though. I mean, I shouldn't say this, but one shopping mall looks much like any other, even ours. So if you could stick to the Greek temple and what we call the villages, the Latin-American arcade and the mediaeval square and so on . . . "

"Sure. We'd have done that anyway. As you say, they're more interesting visually. Now," Bruce gestured towards the nearest pantechnicon, "would you like a quick look round the OB unit? Before things turn hectic?"

"Love to. Thanks, Bill." But Andrew glanced around before mounting the steps; and what he saw checked him in his tracks. "Hang on a sec, though. There's Calum coming over."

Calum's wheelchair was slow over the tarmac, so Andrew walked out to meet him.

"Hi, did you want me?"

"You? No. What I *want*," the word spat out as Calum rolled past Andrew, the stately progress of the chair in marked contrast to the agitated man it carried, "is to be able to get from A to B with no greater hindrance than I usually have to confront. Which I cannot do at present."

"Why, what's the problem?"

"The problem," Calum glared up at Andrew, and then at Bill Bruce as he strolled over to join them, "is these bloody cables everywhere. What is the point of designing this place to be wheelchair-friendly, and promoting it as such – particularly for events like this – when you then go and lay trip-wires all over? Half a dozen three-inch cables would be enough of an obstacle-course for a woman with a pram to push; in a powered wheelchair it's impossible. And the way they're set out at the moment, they're totally cutting off my access to the main buildings."

"Oh, lord. You're right, Calum, I should have thought of that. I'm sorry . . . "

"*You* should have thought of it? Hell, *I* should have

thought of it! It's my job, isn't it?"

"Calm down, Dalek. There's time yet, we can fix it. We just need ramps, or something like."

"No problem," Bill said. "We've *got* ramps, they just haven't been unloaded yet. I'll get the lads onto that for you. At Two Rivers Television," he added smugly, "we think of *everything*."

Calum looked at Andrew, looked at Bill, looked back at Andrew; said, "I don't think I like your friend."

* * *

Rudy Bellamy sat on the pavement, fiddling half-heartedly with his motorbike while he watched the end of the street. It was far too early to be out here waiting, he knew that; she wouldn't show up for hours yet. She'd probably gone straight to bed the way he should've done, after he walked her home at dawn. *Lazy cow*, he thought with a private smile, picturing her in that silly Snoopy nightshirt he'd given her, snoring quietly beneath her posters with the photos of him tucked safely under the pillow, "where I can feel them in the dark," she'd said . . .

And then the smile stretched into a broad grin as he saw her turn the corner; and he was up on his feet in a moment and strolling down to meet her, wiping his oily fingers off on his T-shirt and trying to look seriously casual, as if his feet weren't itching to run all the way, his whole body wasn't burning just at the sight of her . . .

"Hi," he said, all the greeting he had breath to spare for; and reached a hand out for hers, needing the promise, the guarantees of touch.

She pulled back, wrinkling her nose at the state of him; then shrugged, still without talking, and stepped forward again. Her small body nestled against his, her lips nuzzled at his neck while he wrapped his arms around her and pressed his face into her hair.

"You smell all petrol," she said, after a while.

"Yeah, well, I had to be doing something, didn't I? Till you came?"

Liane giggled then, wriggled free and took his arm to tug him gently back down the street. "I cleaned the bathroom," she confessed. "Like it's never been cleaned in its life. Mam couldn't believe it, when she got up. But I had a bath afterwards," she added pointedly.

"Well, I'll have a bath too, if you don't mind hanging around."

"I'll survive."

"Want to come in and wash my back for me?"

"Rudy, all I want to do is go back to bed."

"Yeah, that's even better. Mine or yours?"

She hissed at him for silence and stared fretfully up at the house, wary of lip-readers. "I mean I'm knackered, that's all. I just want some sleep. Didn't get much last night, did I?" With a sly smile that made him ache for the dark again, for the secrecy of his bedroom and the door shut tight, the two of them shy with each other and nervous of the world, jerking alert at every sound outside . . .

"Tell you what, then. Why don't we go off down the coast somewhere? It's going to be dead warm again, we could find some quiet bit of beach, have a swim and a what-d'you-call-it, a siesta. Fish and chips for lunch, and a can of lager . . . "

"Rudy, we *can't*! We're going to the Meldon Centre, remember? We said we'd meet up with everyone there, there's all that stuff going on . . . "

"We could skip it," he murmured, slipping his fingers under the waistband of her jeans.

She shook her head hard, and slapped his hand away. "No. We've got to be there, we said. Anyway, I want to, it's going to be great."

"Thought you were knackered?"

"That won't stop me." She grinned up at him with another touch of sly, and stood on tiptoe to kiss his cheek. "We could go to the beach tomorrow, yeah?"

"It'll rain."

"Oh, you . . . "

She punched him under the ribs, and walked quickly through the gate into the Bellamys' front garden, stooping to pick Deena up from where she was playing on the lawn. "Hi, pet lamb. What are you doing?"

"Making a castle." Rudy's small sister gestured at the ramshackle pile she'd been constructing from upturned buckets and bits of wood.

"Oh, good. Can I play?"

"Rudy too."

"Rudy's going to have a bath, sweetheart, he's all smelly. So it's down to you and me. We'll make it a castle only for girls, shall we?"

So they did that; and were just agreeing on the disposition of the defences – Deena's vast collection of dolls – when Rudy reappeared, wearing a pair of white jeans and a towel around his neck.

"Quickest bath in history," Liane snorted, snatching the towel away and stretching up over his shoulders to rub at his dripping hair.

"Didn't want to leave you alone too long with the monster," Rudy said.

"We were getting on fine, mate. You just didn't want to be left out, that's all."

"Okay, yeah. I didn't want to be left out." He kissed her forehead, her nose and her lips; then said, "Mam's making coffee. You coming in?"

"I dunno." She glanced down to where Deena was standing watching, fascinated. "We're in the middle of a game."

Rudy sighed, reached down and swung his sister up onto his hip. "Want some juice, little 'un?"

"Yeh."

"Yes what?"

"*Please.*"

"Right, then. Let's go." With his other arm finding its way to where it most wanted to be, looped loosely round Liane's neck, the fingers hanging down to brush lightly, almost accidentally against her small breast.

Five minutes later, all of them settled comfortably in the kitchen and Rudy struggling to control his giggles as Liane's foot stroked its way up and down his calf, while she smiled at him all innocence across the table:

"So what are you two doing today, then?" The question came from his mother, sitting fat and comfortable at the far end.

"Going out the Meldon Centre, for this telethon thing."

"That's good. You can take Nadine, then, can't you?"

"What? Oh, no, Mam!"

"Yes, please. Your dad and me want the day to ourselves."

"Yeah, but – well, we can't take her, that's all. We're going on the bike. And we're meeting all our mates out there . . ."

"So she won't be any trouble, will she, if there's that many of you to keep an eye on her. I want you to take her, Rudy. I'll give you money for the bus, and something extra so you can take her to Dreamland and give her a few rides. She likes it in Dreamland, don't you, Nadine?"

Deena nodded, eyeing her brother warily. Rudy sighed, looked across at Liane and saw her shrug a surrender.

Said, "Okay, then. We'll take her."

*　　　*　　　*

"You get yourself closer to the fire there, old Coatman, old love. Always cold, aren't you? Yes. Always cold." And she tore a damp cardboard box into panels, dropped them into her home-made brazier and said it again. "Get up nearer the fire. And if that doesn't warm you, you could always try asking old Ivy." With a cackle, patting her heavy stomach. "*I'm* not cold, no. Ivy's never cold, they all know that. There's a furnace in Ivy's belly, they used to say that, a burning fiery furnace in her belly. And maybe I'd share it with you, old matey. Maybe I'd take you into my tent there and lay you down in my blankets, press my hot belly against your cold back and warm you through and through. Now that'd be a thing, wouldn't it, old love? If I'd do that for you? That'd be a story for the news."

The Coatman lifted his head slowly, to peer up at her from under the shadow of his hood: dark rheumy eyes buried deep in bony sockets, no flesh anywhere on his face, only ridges and hollows. And the hood and the beard and the long lank hair all something more to hide inside, like the coats he heaped around his bowed shoulders that never got him warm. Like the mutter mutter and the filth that he used as a weapon against the world, even against her; and the silence that wasn't really any different from the mutter mutter, that he was using now.

Looked at her, and turned his head away; for a minute saying nothing at all, and then only, "It's busy, that. That road."

"It is. Is it Saturday? Must be Saturday. Always busy on Saturdays. And it's time we were busy too, old love."

"Unh?"

"Follow the cars, we must. That's what we must do, follow the cars. Kiss the wife and the kiddies, and go to work. No point sitting here in the good sun getting hungry, when there's food just a short mile down the road, and people with money and all, and all."

He coughed, and spat. "Get turned off."

"Of course we'll get turned off. We always get turned off. But we might get some food first. Or some money, even, and then they won't turn us off. Treat us like kings and queens, they will, if we've got some money. King Coatman and Queen Ivy we'll be, till the money's spent. Up you get, old love, up, up, up. And if they turn us off too soon," slipping her arm under his to ease him onto his feet, slow and gentle, "well then, we'll just go back again, won't we? That's all."

She threw a pile of damp rags and sodden wood onto the fire, to keep it smouldering till they got back. Matches were precious and soon gone, especially with the Coatman around, with his dumpers and his rollies that were always going out, always needing another light.

And then she was ready, he was sour and muttering, ready as he'd ever be; and they set off. Down to the road and trudge trudge along the verge, single file with him five yards behind and both of them watching the ground under their feet, stooping for a dog-end or the glint of anything metal that might just possibly be a coin.

THE BOOK OF THE DEAD

I: Father to the Man

He sits among his weapons; and time tangles, time knots and skeins itself about his oily fingers.

Time is the enemy, time is the killer. There may be a body, he's fairly sure that there's a body in the kitchen – though he hasn't looked, not for a while now, not for a time – but still, it wasn't him that killed. That much is certain. It was time, that's all, it was only time. Everyone meets their death in time, and never mind who makes the introduction.

Time steals the life out of people, directly or indirectly, as it has stolen his; but it has other tricks too. As now, tripping him gaily by the heels when he's at his most vulnerable, most in need of balance.

Tripping him and setting him to fall back, far back: before this death, and all the way back to another . . .

He was a boy then, soldier's boy, son of a soldier and a soldier's wife; but the wife didn't live with the soldier, no. He didn't live with his dad.

"Women?" his dad said, sloshing gin straight, bottle to glass and glass to mouth; or like as not bottle to mouth without the glass between. Licking and sucking, shaping words indistinctly around the green neck of the bottle. "Don't talk to me about women. Bitches and cows. Not your mother, mind, not her. Fine woman, your mother. God, I loved that woman. Still do, come to that. Still would. Half a chance, that's all, give me half a chance."

A long guzzling drink, a slow belch after.

"She wouldn't have it, though. Wouldn't have me now. Ah, you can understand it. Can't you, son? You can understand. I'm no fit man for her these days, no man at all. And there's you to be thought of. She wouldn't want me on her hands, not with you there to see, to see the state of me. I'm lucky she lets you come at all. And I'm glad, son, I'm glad to see you here. Have I told you that? I'm glad you come, it's good of you, find the time to see your old man. Can't say that often enough, how glad I am to see you . . . "

So he said it again, and many times more. Every visit he said this, and cried a little over his bottle, easy tears to prove the truth of it.

"Bitches and cows," again, another time. "If you knew, if you'd seen what they'd done to your old dad . . . It's no wonder, it's no wonder your mother won't have me in the house."

And, "*You* love me, I know that. You don't say it, I know, you don't need to. Embarrasses you, doesn't it, me talking like this? But that's all right, a boy like you, sure to be embarrassed when your dad gets soppy.

"But you do, you do love me. That's important, to love your dad. Even if he's a mess, like I am.

"Your mother, too. She wouldn't say it, not now; but oh, she loved me well. Back when I was in the army, she did. When I was a proper soldier, when those photographs were took. And a love like that, it don't die, son. You can't kill it off, not however much time you take to try it.

"So there's you, and there's her; and that's it, there's no one else. No buddies left, no mates. But you're all I need, see? My wife, and my boy. That's enough. I don't have to be with you, I've got you right here, in my head, son, in my head. You live in my head, all the bloody time. Shouldn't swear in front of you, I know, but you've heard worse at school, of course you have. And you'll hear worse in the army, when you get there.

"You're all I ever wanted, you know that, lad? You're it, for me. You're the tops. It's all a proper soldier ever wants, when he gets to my age. A boy, a son to follow after. That's what I've got, what your mother's give me; and I'm so grateful, son, I'm so bloody grateful . . . "

And again, "Don't you listen to your mother, boy. Not on this. What does she know?

"She would say that, of course she would. She's a woman, isn't she? Of course she stands up for them. That's only right. But she's got them wrong, see, she doesn't see them straight. Well, she wouldn't, would she? Being one of them.

"Bitches and cows.

"No, you listen to your dad. This is a warning, see. Word to the wise, that's what this is. You've got a wise head on those shoulders, anyone can see that. So you listen to me. Don't have nothing to do with them, sunshine. Don't you do what your dad did. You can see where it got me, can't you? If it hadn't been for the women, I'd have been home with you now, you and your mum and me, one big happy family like we ought to be.

"But I got tempted easy, I was always a sucker for a big smile, big tits. Sorry, shouldn't say that, should I? But I was always a soft touch. And being in the army, being posted all over – well, it was easy, see? You'll find that, after you join up. You'll find out how easy it is.

"But don't you be tempted, son. Don't you follow your dad. Keep yourself clean. Keep away from the women, that's what I'm saying, see? See what I mean, do you? They're poison. They poisoned me, and I don't want to see that happen to you. I want to be proud of you, son. I am proud, and I want to stay that way. I don't want you talking to your kid the way I'm talking to you now.

"Better to be dead. And I mean that. I'd rather see you dead than all messed up like I am. And it's the women do that to you, they're the ones that did for me. You keep away from the women, son. Just keep right away, don't have nothing to do with them. It'll be hard, sure. Young men, they get tempted easy; and you'll have all your mates, you'll see them going off with girls, hear them boasting about it after. They'll laugh at you, maybe, for holding back. But don't you worry about that, don't you listen. Don't let them get to you. Remember your father, right? Make me proud. That's all, just make me proud . . . "

And would he be proud now, would his father be proud? Seeing the weapons set out so neatly on the bed, the guns oiled and ready, the primed grenades? Seeing further, perhaps, seeing more: seeing the woman's body on the kitchen floor, the necessity of that death and the inevitability of others to come, would his father still be proud?

He doesn't know, can't say. Certainly can't ask. His father's dead too, it was his father gave him his first taste of death, too early and too strong.

Like this, he found his father . . .

*

Coming to visit one Sunday afternoon – twelve he would
have been by then and long used to the routine of it, barely
able to remember a time when he had more than a sentimen-
tal Sunday father – he'd climbed the stairs, lifted his hand,
knocked politely on his father's door.

Got no answer, waited, knocked again. Knocked louder
against the good chance of his father being well into a bottle
already, maybe fallen asleep with waiting for him.

Still no answer.

He'd tried the door out of curiosity, too young yet to
worry; found it unlocked, and walked in to the familiar
smells of gin and stale tobacco, damp and sour clothing.

Saw his father lying sprawled and naked on the unmade
bed; hesitated, moved slowly forward step by uncertain step,
reached to touch a cold shoulder, to wake him up.

Saw how his father's mouth had fallen open, how it was
filled with a green and crusted vomit.

Scuttled back hurriedly, away from the stink and the
sudden understanding; but still looking, his eyes still
gripped, he saw something more now, something that stirred
his own stomach and brought a thin bile spewing out of his
mouth.

Saw his father's genitals half rotted, half eaten away by
corruption; and made sense at last, some sense of all the
warnings.

And now he cleans his weapons one final time, now he
handles smooth and silent metal and thinks only of glory, of
headlines in tomorrow's papers, something to make a father
proud. Not at all of the body in the kitchen.

He's his father's son, yes, and glad to be so; but not, not at
all the man his father was.

THE BOOK OF HOURS

II

1000:

and Johnnie Lee's electronic organiser sang a soft alarm at him, from his jacket pocket.

"Ah, yes. I regret you will have to excuse me now, Inspector . . . "

A security guard approached him, walkie-talkie in hand. "Mr Lee? Control called. That coach with the Japanese has just been passed through at Gate Three."

"Good." He double-checked the time on his watch. "Exactly on schedule. Just confirm, please, that my wife has arrived." The guard nodded, and spoke softly into his set as Johnnie turned back to the policeman. "I must leave you here, Inspector – unless you would care to walk with me to the hospitality suite? If there is anything further you wish to discuss?"

"I don't think that's necessary, sir. The operation seems well in hand."

"Yes, I think so. We have very little trouble here ordinarily, and I have doubled our own security for the twenty-four hour period. I doubt if your men will have much to do, beyond helping with crowd control and arresting shoplifters. You will liaise with my Chief of Security about such matters?"

"Yes, sir. That's all in hand, I've spoken with Mr Pritchard already. And we'll be as unobtrusive as we can, I promise you that. I'm not out to spoil anyone's day with heavy-handed policing. With any luck, my lads'll be going home thinking it was a waste of time them being here at all. But still, it's as well to be prepared."

"Yes. I was a boy scout myself in Hong Kong, and that was a lesson well learned. I'm glad to have you here, Inspector; but I share your hope, that your presence will prove to be unnecessary."

He nodded solemnly, turning away as Inspector Holborn

lifted a finger to his cap in a gesture that was halfway to a salute.

Johnnie was already moving towards the nearest lift when he glanced at the guard, looking for the confirmation he'd asked for about his wife. But the guard said, "Sir? Control reports that Mrs Lee hasn't arrived on site, sir."

"Are they sure?"

"Yes, sir. Positive."

Johnnie frowned and pushed a hand through his thick greying hair, aware of the Inspector's eyes still on him, registering this first hiccup in the smooth running of the day.

"Very well. Ask them to phone the Tower, and find out if she has been delayed. There may be a problem with the car. When she does arrive, she must be directed straight to me. I shall be in the hospitality suite with my guests for the next hour; after that they can use the walkie-talkie to locate us. Mrs Pargeter will be with me, and she carries one. Understood?"

"Yes, sir."

The lift took Johnnie down to the Plaza, a wide area of fountains and greenery, interspersed with tables and seating for two hundred. Around it stood a dozen fast-food outlets, serving everything from burgers to Danish smørrebrød. The place was filling up already, he was glad to see; he had a twenty-percent interest in each of these businesses. The main attractions of the day were all taking place outside the Centre, on the open land that surrounded it, but he was confident that few people would come this far without spending at least a little time – and a little money – in his arcades and restaurants. People got hungry, people needed groceries and clothes. *Two birds with one stone*, he thought, with a private smile. That was how he'd got from Kowloon to here, by always looking for a way to double his advantage. That was the secret of good business.

He walked quickly through the Plaza and came into what they called the Victorian Market. This was a single-storeyed section of the complex with a glass roof, a huge open space with six lanes of stalls, each having its own awning and its own produce to sell: a tourists'-eye recreation of its nineteenth-century namesake, complete with cobbles and flickering gas-lamps down the central aisle, and every employee in costume. Even the security guards here were dressed as peelers, and encouraged – for a small monthly bonus – to grow bushy moustaches and sideburns.

Another look at his watch, and Johnnie hurried through towards the far end, acknowledging the nods and smiles of the stall-holders with brief waves of the hand. Again he owned a percentage of many of these businesses – those he trusted to turn in good profits at the end of the year – as well as charging rent on the units. It was that doubled advantage in action once more, and very successfully so.

They were busy here, too, and due to get a lot busier before the day was out. As the rest of the Centre would; as he would himself. He frowned, dodging between clumps of customers shuffling from one stall to the next, and wondered where Linda could be. He had been counting on her to take over a lot of the peripheral socialising that was unavoidable on a day like this, the visiting VIPs who expected to see the Lee empire in the company of a Lee . . .

As well as the many public ways in and out of the Meldon Centre, there were any number of hidden access doors to the service areas that ran beside, above and underneath the malls. It was a maze, a warren of interlinked corridors and stairways where strangers could lose themselves in minutes; but Johnnie knew the whole system intimately. He used one of those secret doors now, pushing at a single tall panel in a wall of panels and stepping through as it swung open.

Beyond the panel was a long passage floored with concrete and walled with breeze blocks, no superfluous decoration here. He stood still for a moment, watching the camera that hung from the ceiling nearby; and nodded with satisfaction as it turned to direct its lens at him. Good: they were keeping alert, then, back in the control room. Opening any of these doors caused a light to flash on the main board, and it was in standing orders that every such signal should be followed up, to be sure that no unauthorised person had found their way into the service areas. If the men on duty at the monitors didn't recognise him, Johnnie knew that a call would go out immediately to the nearest security guard, to chase him down; but there was no danger of that. Everyone at the Centre knew Johnnie Lee.

He made his way down the passage and around the corner to another door, this one heavy and secure, marked 'Private' and kept locked.

Johnnie opened it with a master-key and walked through into a world of plush carpets and plastered walls, soft lighting and the smell of money.

His guests were a group of Japanese businessmen, all managing companies in the UK. He found them drinking coffee in the VIP lounge, and went straight in – with a nod to Judith Pargeter, and a slight shrug to her murmured query about his wife – to shake hands and mingle, as he had with a hundred similar groups before.

There was one fundamental difference this time, though; and prepared as he was, Johnnie still had to repress a slight shudder, a sense of unease and danger, as he made his way around the room. He'd dealt with Japanese before, of course, many times – that was inevitable in the shipping industry, where he'd built his fortune – but he'd done it through intermediaries as much as he could without giving offence. And there were so many here; he hadn't been shut in with so many since the bad times, the war years in Hong Kong.

Canapés had been laid out on a long table to one side, with bottles of champagne on ice. Johnnie closed his eyes briefly, remembering other rooms on the other side of the world: remembering himself as a boy, working in a commandeered hotel to bring home a little money and what food he could beg or steal. Too thin and always hungry, always scared, he'd spent many an evening serving food and drink to the officers of the occupying army.

It was those years as servant to a hated master – enduring the cuffs and blows when he was clumsy or insolent or in the way, the constant contempt of conqueror to conquered – that had seeded Johnnie with the burning desire that hadn't left him yet, the insatiable hunger for success. That was all it came down to, in the end: being too rich and too powerful for anyone to hit him or scorn him or shove him aside.

And he might almost be there now, was getting there for certain; but still he wanted Linda beside him now, he wanted not to confront his memories alone. And still she hadn't come, so he had to do it.

It didn't take much to draw the room's whole attention to himself. He had a percentage already, few people actually watching him but each of them aware of where he was, what he was doing. So just a cough and a movement of his hand,

and every eye was on him, every voice was stilled.

Power, he thought briefly. *Yes. This is what it's for*.

"Gentlemen," he said – no women in this group, the old order still ascendant – "I regret the interruption, but if I may have your attention, only for a minute . . . " Keeping his voice controlled and confident, no obsequiousness in it, no going back. *Remember who you are, who you have become. Not who you were.* "I want to welcome you all to the Meldon Centre, my honoured guests." One hand rising to the wall behind him, to where a map of the site hung behind glass; and now he was away and it was easy, he'd done this so often before.

"Here you see a plan of the whole Centre – or I should say the Centre so far. We have two hundred and twenty acres, with most of the development completed; we're still waiting for Stage Four, the section you see here with the dotted lines. That should be ready to open in the spring. No. It *will* be ready to open in the spring. There is no question. Every stage so far has been ahead of schedule, and I am certain we will achieve that again. It is very much in the contractors' interests to do so; the contracts are structured that way. There are generous bonuses for finishing the work early, and heavy penalties for being late. No-strike clauses also, and no unions. Every worker on site signs an agreement to that effect, and they are subject to immediate dismissal without compensation if they default.

"This is already the largest shopping and leisure complex outside the American continent; and I have options to buy another hundred acres adjoining, here to the east. These options are good for three years, and I will not hurry into a decision. As you may know, gentlemen, the Meldon Centre is not now my only, ah, iron in the fire. I have another project taking up a good deal of my time and attention at the moment." Smiles from his audience, to which Johnnie responded with a comfortable chuckle. "But the Centre will not be allowed to stagnate. It is a living and growing thing now, an organism; and growth is what counts in business today, as it always has. Expansion. Staying ahead of the opposition. One has to be better; and that means one has to be bigger, one has to offer more.

"What we have done so far has been very successful, but I am not content with that. We will continue to grow. I have the best team in the world working for me here, and actually they don't need me any more. The Meldon Centre has its momentum now, it has confidence; and that is all it needs to survive and to flourish. People ask me often what is my secret, what gives me the Midas touch; but it is no secret. Confidence is all. I had confidence when I began this project, and for a year or two everyone else fed themselves from that; but they all have confidence now. They know this horse is a winning ride. Johnnie Lee is redundant here, and proud to admit it. That is what frees me to move on."

One man started clapping, and they all joined in. Johnnie let it go on for a few seconds, then lifted his hands to quieten them.

"Please, don't applaud me. Judith, the champagne must be cold? Good. Gentlemen, will you join me in a glass of champagne, and drink a toast to the Meldon Centre's continued prosperity in a difficult world?"

They would, and they did; and Johnnie was taking a bottle around offering refills – finding nothing but comfort now in his memories, his slow transition from there to here, from skinny boy to magnate and millionaire, *too big to hit* – when the door opened, and his wife came in.

He went to fetch her a glass, and found her at his elbow as he filled it. She looked immaculate as ever, perfect for the occasion, simply but expensively dressed and not a hair out of place; his guests would get no hint of anything amiss. But he knew her well enough to see that she was flustered. He could read the tension in the corners of her mouth, feel it in the hand she laid lightly on his arm as she took the glass.

"Johnnie, I'm sorry. I was waiting for Carl, I'd asked him to drive me in, and he's always been reliable up to now. He didn't come up, though, and his phone didn't answer; so I had to go down to his flat first, to check. Lord knows what's happened to him, because he wasn't there, and his car's gone too, but . . ."

"Later," Johnnie said. "You understand?" And when she nodded, he turned her round with a hand on her shoulder, and said, "Gentlemen, permit me to introduce my wife, Linda. Wife and financial manager, I should say. She handles all my money for me. I work for a year to make an honest living, then she doubles everything in two minutes at a computer . . ."

*   *   *

Denise had dozed and drifted ever since she came to bed, seldom more than half awake but never properly, never deeply asleep. A muffled thud roused her instantly, breaking the slender threads that had bound her to uncomfortable dreams; she sat up, fully alert and anxious.

"Matt? You okay?"

No answer. She tossed back the duvet and hurried to the living-room door, gazed in and surprised herself with a sudden, unintended giggle. He was lying full-length where she'd left him, propped up on one elbow, blinking in sleepy confusion; and the heavy glass ashtray was upside-down on the floor, where his head had all too clearly knocked it off the arm of the sofa.

He turned slowly to look up at her, rubbing a hand down over his shadowed face.

"Den . . . ?"

"Yeah." She stepped lightly over the scattered cigarette-butts and slipped both arms round his chest, pulling him awkwardly into a sitting position. "Come on, lover, time for bed. If you're going to sleep, you might as well sleep with me."

Another heave and he was on his feet, standing precariously in the circle of her arms. She held him steady for a minute, until he found his own careful balance.

"Here we go, then. Nice and easy . . . "

It wasn't easy, in fact, supporting his twelve stones against her seven, step by step through to the bedroom; but she'd done this often enough before, when he was too drunk to control his legs properly. Not that he was drunk this morning. He'd been drinking, to be sure, she could smell the lager on him along with the cigarettes. But no, he wasn't drunk. Only sick and exhausted, his mind more than half divorced from his body and barely understanding where he was.

Denise eased him down onto the mattress and stripped him quickly, hindered more than helped by his own fumbling attempts at the intricate demands of belt and button. Then she pushed him flat, slid a pillow under his head and tugged the duvet up to cover them both.

That done, there was nothing left but to lie there and look at him, watch him slouching towards sleep again, say nothing and simply hope. Not for a miracle, or any instant remedy for all his ills; that level of faith was far beyond her now. She didn't even believe in love any more as a potential panacea – only as a bitter reality, greater than loneliness and more abrasive. But at least she could hope to find enough strength, enough will-power for another twenty-four hours of this. Not to give up on him today, that was what counted. Tomorrow was something else, but she could worry about that tomorrow.

*   *   *

With his camera sitting comfortably heavy on his shoulder, Charlie Campbell went looking for his sound man Guy, and found him talking to Bill Bruce.

"All fit, Charlie?" Bill asked.

"Aye, no problems here."

"Good. You two might as well get off, then. There's nothing much happening yet, but you can get the feel of the place at least, check out some locations. And you might find someone interesting to talk to. You shouldn't have any problem with the light in there, it's pretty bright; give us a shout, though, if you want extra. And bring me back some good material, will you?"

"Bill, man, have we ever let you down?"

"Just don't do it today, that's all I'm saying."

"Okay. Do we get a front man for the interviews, or have we got to do it all ourselves?"

"Do it yourselves, I've no one spare. Bring me something in every hour or so, if you can. I might need it in a hurry."

"Will do. All right, Guy?"

Guy nodded, and swung the microphone over his shoulder on its long boom. Charlie grinned, quite used to his partner's silence; theirs was a regular pairing, and he wondered sometimes if that was deliberate on Bill's part, setting the taciturn sound man against his own constant stream of patter. Deliberate or not, Charlie approved. It pleased his sense of balance, as he'd said to Guy more than once in the course of their one-sided conversations. "Yin and Yang, you see? Bacon and tomatoes. Haggis and neeps. Blue sky, green grass and a yellow sun turning red for setting. Me and you. It all hangs together, if you see it right."

Now they walked side by side through automatic doors, out of the warming sunshine into the cool air-conditioning of the Meldon Centre; and the first thing Charlie saw was two men coming towards him, one of them in a wheelchair, his body strangely deformed.

Charlie's first response was to put his eye to the viewfinder, and bring the lens to bear; his second to turn the camera sharply away, a moment ahead of Guy's warning nudge.

"No, you're right, Guy," he murmured. "Not quite the thing, really . . . "

But as they got closer, he saw that both men wore staff badges on the lapels of their suits; and the journalist in him couldn't resist stopping them, saying, "Charlie Campbell, Two Rivers. You two work here, do you?"

"For our sins, we do," from the man in the chair. "I'm Calum Rafferty, this is Andrew Scott. Can we help you gentlemen in any way?"

"Aye, you can. If you'd care to say a few words to the folks back home, that is." Charlie tapped the camera suggestively. "If you could just tell us something about what your jobs involve, and what you'll be doing today, that'll be fine. How you're involved in the special events, you know the sort of thing. And, uh, Mr Rafferty, if you wouldn't mind talking a bit about your own situation, whether you've run into any particular problems with the chair and so on . . . "

"No need to be shy, Mr Campbell. It's all part of the job. In fact it *is* the job, more or less. I'd be delighted."

"Terrific." Charlie looked around him quickly. "In that case, can we get a few shots of you making your way round the mall here, to start with? On your own, I think, that'll make the point to the viewers . . . "

And Bill's going to cream his pants, he added, strictly to himself, while his tongue ran on unheeded. *He'll get five minutes out of this, if he dubs on a commentary about big-hearted Johnnie Lee doing his best for the disadvantaged. Which he will, he won't need telling. Might even hold it back for a while if he's not pushed, try to get a word from the man himself. Oh boy, is he going to be chuffed with me. Mr Rafferty, I think I love you . . .*

1100:

Richard hadn't slept at all, after Julian left him. He'd gone back to bed for a while, and just lay there with his mind and body buzzing, change and possibilities dancing in front of his eyes. At half-past six he'd got up again and had a slow, sybaritic soak in the bath, scalding water up to his chin and Django on the stereo in the next room. After that there was a bacon sandwich for breakfast, a pot of coffee and *The Guardian* for an hour; and since then he'd been tidying the flat.

He'd filled four rubbish-bags with bottles, cans and other detritus, done the washing-up and run the hoover through from front door to back. Now his eyes moved over the instruments that hung from copper nails on the white wall – bodhran, zither, balalaika, mandolin, three guitars – and he lifted down his favourite of those last, the one he'd be using later at the gig.

By rights, he should do an hour's hard practice; they'd be playing a couple of new tunes this afternoon, and he was still a little uncertain with his solos. But, hell, he was no more under-rehearsed than the rest of the band, and none of them was interested in military precision. They'd cover for him if he fluffed; or else they'd just laugh, and let him dig his own way out of the hole. Either way, it wouldn't matter. Cock-ups were almost a part of the act, for Hot Ginger.

So he dropped onto the sofa, settled the guitar on his knee and picked out a few quiet chords, letting his fingers stray into a gentle, easy riff as he thought about Julian.

Richard was a man of quick enthusiasms, he knew that much about himself. Or you could give them a stronger name, and perhaps be closer to the mark. You could talk about lust, as some people did; or possession, or simply the fascination of what's new. Personally, Richard preferred to talk about love.

It wasn't always people. Music could have the same effect, the same crippling effect on his social life and his state of mind. If he started experimenting with a new instrument or a new style of playing – well, the mandolin had eaten a month of his time, the blues another. Only let something take a grip on his imagination and he was gone, for as long as it took to work itself out.

Something, or someone. To Richard every affair was like a first adolescent crush, he'd heard that said, and accepted it. A lover – and they were always lovers, Richard's partners, or at any rate always beloved – would possess him beyond his ability to resist, taking over mind and body and every detail of his life.

So with Julian. He'd known him, what, twelve hours now, or fourteen; and already priorities were shifting in his head, whatever he valued being shoved ruthlessly aside to make room for this one overmastering factor, this boy to claim first place in everything.

The phone's abrupt ringing was an unwelcome intrusion; Richard scowled at it, thought of leaving it, at last reached out a reluctant hand to hoist the receiver.

"Yeah, what?"

"Richard, it's Penny. I just wanted to check when you'd be here. We're supposed to get out there by twelve, aren't we?"

"Half-past. But – look, did I say I was going to take you?"

"Yes." Her voice went flat suddenly, as though she already knew what was coming. Richard winced, thinking that she probably did.

"Ah, shit. I don't think I can, Penny. I've promised Julian a lift out, with a friend of his; and you wouldn't all fit in the car, not with Clarabelle on top."

"No, obviously not. Can't they get a bus, or something?"

"I suppose – but, hell, Penny, I did promise." No doubt he'd promised her, too; but that didn't, couldn't count any longer. And no doubt she realised that, which was why she didn't throw it back at him. "And – oh, I don't know, I just don't want to give him an excuse to pull back. Not this soon. He was dead nervous about it all this morning, and I think I've got to keep myself visible, you know?"

"Uh-huh."

"You can take a taxi, can't you? We'll pay for it out of band money. Get one of those big estates, and you could pick the others up on your way. You've squashed three in before, even with all the instruments."

"Sometimes. Just depends if they have to fold the back seat down for Clarabelle. Okay, Richard," giving way as he'd known she would, as she had to, "I'll get a taxi."

"Good. Thanks, Pen. See you there, then. About half twelve, right?"

"Right. Don't be late."

"I'll try."

No promises now; he knew himself too well to make them. Penny grunted, and hung up. Richard sighed at this early evidence of trouble ahead, and took the easy way, the quick way of escaping from it. Moved his hand and his mind back from telephone to guitar and sought out the beginnings of a tune, something new. Something perhaps to be worth writing down — perhaps to be worth calling 'A Song For Julian'.

*   *   *

Rudy lifted Deena off the bus in the centre of town, and then couldn't resist dangling her threateningly over a concrete waste-bin on the pavement.

"Drop you in here, will I, little nuisance?"

"No!" With a gurgling laugh.

"No what?"

"No *please!*"

"Why not? Go on, give us a good reason."

His sister squirmed and wriggled so hard that he nearly did drop her, then yelled, "Mam'd be cross with you!"

"That's not a good reason."

"*I'd* be cross with you." That was Liane, reaching past him to take the little girl. He shrugged, grinned, and surrendered her.

"Okay. That's good enough."

"It better be." Liane settled Deena on her hip, then reached out her spare hand for his. "So where do we catch the bus out, then?"

"By the memorial — but I've got a better idea. Let's go down the station, get the train. Deena likes trains, don't you, pet?"

"Yeh . . . " Then, glancing uncertainly up at Liane, "I want to walk."

"Suits me. You're too big to carry, anyway."

So they walked down towards the station, past department stores, shoe shops and fashion houses. Rudy's eye wandered away from the girls (*my girls*, he thought, getting a curious kick out of the words, the responsibility they implied) to the bright windows; and he stopped suddenly, giving a little tug to Liane's hand to warn her.

"Hang on a sec. There's no hurry, nothing's going to start for an hour yet."

"It's not me that's hurrying," she said, with a glance down to where Deena was fidgeting impatiently at her side. "What are you looking at?"

"Them jackets."

Liane looked, and snorted. "Yeah, they're terrific. Have you seen the price on them? And you've got one, anyway."

"It wasn't me I was thinking of. You're always saying you want a leather jacket; and you should, for the bike. I've seen gravel scars on a girl, and I don't want to see them on you."

"Dream on. I couldn't afford that in a hundred years."

"It's your birthday next month, isn't it?"

Finally, she caught on. "Oh no, Rudy. No, don't you even think about it. That's far too much, it's stupid. Just wait, we'll find one second-hand somewhere . . . "

"Well, maybe. I just think you'd look dead pretty, in one of them big baggy ones . . . "

"Hey. I said no, didn't I? And I mean it, too." Frowning up at him, and that frown only adding to the glory of his day. He loved it when she got bossy. It meant more to him even than her smile, underlining just how far they'd gone together, that she had the right to make rules for him.

Not that he was going to give way this time. He wanted her to have a leather jacket; and more than that, he wanted to be the one who gave it to her. Okay, she'd make a fuss, she was sure to; but it wouldn't last. She'd be dead pleased inside, as long as he picked the right one.

So he said nothing at all, only turned and started walking again; and with Deena hauling imperiously on her other arm, Liane didn't get a chance to pursue it.

Their route took them through the central square, where girls in green uniforms were handing out leaflets and gas-filled balloons, decorated with the logos of the Meldon Centre and Two Rivers Television, one more promotion stunt for the telethon.

Rudy tossed a handful of change into one of the collection-buckets, and got a balloon in return.

"That's for me," Deena said firmly. Adding, "Aren't I *lucky?*" to Liane, just to be sure she got it.

"You sure are," Rudy said, crouching down to her level. "Now give us your hand, I'm just going to tie a loop in the string here and slip it round your wrist . . . "

"What for?"

"You'll let go of it, else; and then it'll go flying away into the sky, and you'll start screaming. I know you."

Deena took a firm hold of the string, and gazed anxiously up at the balloon, in case it showed any tendency to fly away of its own accord. Then her eye went further, higher; and she squealed, and pointed excitedly.

"Look! There's one, someone let go of that one, didn't they?"

Rudy looked, and laughed. "That's not a balloon, silly, that's an airship."

"It's like a balloon."

"Yeah, it is. Like a great big one. And it's got the same slogans on the side, too. I expect we'll see it again later, out at the Centre. Now come on, let's go and catch that train."

He lifted her up and sat her on his shoulders; and they went on their way with Liane walking beside him, her arm loosely through his as she talked about the bands that were due to be playing later – "after we've taken Deena home, we can come back again, can't we? On the bike?" – and his sister's small fists gripping his hair painfully tight as she twisted and strained her neck to watch the airship out of sight.

*   *   *

There were more cars on the road than the Coatman could remember ever seeing before – though to be fair he couldn't remember too much, and didn't want to. That was why he drank, why he drank anything that Ivy offered him without question, to kill off a few more brain cells every day and forget a little more. The past was for burying, along with the name he used to carry and the life that went with it, heavier than all his coats and more burdensome.

And to be honest, he couldn't see that well either, and didn't try. Kept his blurry eyes on his feet, watching for dumpers or coins, only his ears registering the steady noise of the traffic through the muffling of his parka hood. But some part of his mind was still alive to its implications, despite the numbing distance at which he kept the world. He knew what it meant all right, this constant stream of cars all headed in the same direction as Ivy, as himself: it meant extra crowds and extra opportunities, to be sure, but it also meant extra guards. Extra uniforms, and extra trouble.

So it was no surprise to be hailed almost as soon as they left the highway, as they followed the cars off the road and down towards the glitter and shadows of the Meldon Centre. To look up and see a policeman making his way across the grass towards them. No surprise, and only a moment to feel grateful that at least it was a policeman, not the Centre's own security; then he was with them, standing arms akimbo against the sun, saying, "What are you two after here, then, eh?"

"Who's that?" Ivy demanded, squinting between her fingers. "Is that you, is it, George, trying to scare poor old Ivy and her good friend the Coatman?"

"Aye, Ivy, it's George."

And he was defeated already, George was; the Coatman knew that, right enough. Names were a weapon in this world. Names and knowledge, that was all the power you needed; and Ivy had them both. She knew half the busies on the river. This youngster, now, he wouldn't stand a chance . . .

"Well, and good morning to you, Georgie, old love. And what are you doing all the way out here, all these miles from home? Taken your nice fast car away from you, have they, with the blue flashing light and the siren that won't let a body sleep at night? Set you down in the car park and left you, have they, Georgie? And what for, are you going to tell old Ivy that, then? So's you can keep the cars moving, is it, George," and her arms jerked in a semaphore mockery of a policeman directing traffic, "or is it something else, did they put you here just to stop us old ones from having a sit-down and a nice cup of tea down the shops there?"

"Never saw you drink tea yet, Ivy. Other stuff, aye, but not tea."

"Well, you just let us through like a good boy, and you can see it now. That's all we're after, see, just a cup of tea and a bit of a sit."

"Pull the other one, Ivy, it goes ting-a-ling." The policeman sighed, scratched the back of his neck, looked around
for help or inspiration and didn't find it; finally said, "Oh,
what the hell. You go on down, if you want to. You'll not get
far. Centre security'll turn you off as soon as they spot you,
you know that; but it's not my job. Just don't let me catch
you begging off people, that's all. Or pinching stuff."

"There's a good boy, Georgie." Ivy reached up to pat his
cheek, cackled, then walked boldly out into the road and
played traffic policeman again: thrusting up one hand to stop
the approaching cars, beckoning the shambling Coatman
over with the other.

*   *   *

Andrew stood on the dais erected below the Centre, and
looked around him. Away to his left he could just see the
huge marquee for the bands; ahead of him was a wide area
of grass running down towards the spit where the two rivers
met, cordoned off to stage the telethon's major events.
Crowds were already massing behind the barriers, eager for
the show to start.

Bill Bruce was standing by the dais, talking urgently to
Vernon Melville, anchorman from Two Rivers' local news
and magazine programme and the closest they came to a
national celebrity. Technicians hurried across the dais,
checking microphones and murmuring into walkie-talkies. A
photographer crouched on the grass in front, and seemed to
focus his lens directly on Andrew's face for a moment. More
likely it was his companion the man was interested in,
though; Andrew checked his watch, and turned to her with a
smile.

"Ten minutes to go."

"Yes." She looked up at him enquiringly. "Are you nervous?"

"Me?" He grinned. "No reason for me to be nervous, it's
not me that has to face the cameras. Or the questions afterwards, if the whole thing's a disaster. But – hell, yes, I'm
terrified. How about you?"

She smiled, and shook her head. "Not really. It's been too
well organised to fall flat, I'm sure of that. Johnnie Lee
wouldn't have put his name to it if there was any chance of
failing. Frankly, we wouldn't have got involved either, un-

less we were very confident. Green issues are very fashionable at the moment, but we could still lose all the support we've gained in the last couple of years if we were seen to be closely associated with a resounding flop. I'm sorry if that sounds cynical, but we've been the laughing stock of the political scene for too long, we're not about to risk having it happen again. As for the cameras – well, you get used to that pretty quickly, in my position."

"Yes, I suppose you would." *You'd have to.* Three months earlier, Gina Lambton had been the Green Party's candidate at a crucial parliamentary by-election. No one had expected her to win, of course, in a safe Conservative seat; but with green issues all the rage – and being female, attractive and still under thirty – she'd received a lot of media attention at the start, and substantially more when she started moving up rapidly in the polls. By voting day, she was running neck and neck with the Tory candidate; and after three recounts and with a margin of just twenty-four votes, she'd become Gina Lambton MP. As her party's first ever representative in parliament, she'd retained her position as media darling, and it had been a considerable coup for the telethon when she'd agreed to open the proceedings today.

Andrew saw a chunky figure making his way through the barrier, heading towards the dais. "Here comes Johnnie. Right on time."

"Well, of course. You wouldn't expect him to miss the chance of talking on nationwide television, would you?"

And in a day full of new experiences, Andrew added another first to his list – the first time a member of parliament had openly and unequivocally winked at him.

"No. That's right, I wouldn't. But – don't you object to sharing a platform with him? I mean, the guy's an out-and-out capitalist, I doubt if he gives a damn about the rainforests or the ozone layer or anything you stand for . . . "

"So do I; but no, I don't object. It's good for us, actually, it stops people writing us off as just another kind of socialist. And in any case, he'll talk for two minutes, then I'll talk for ten; it'll be what I say that sticks in the mind, if anything does."

"Right." Andrew grinned again with purely private pleasure, at the thought of his ultimate boss losing the limelight to a girl half his age.

Then a voice behind him called out, "Five minutes, everybody. Can we have the stage clear, please, except for whoever's meant to be there?"

"That means me off, I'm afraid," Andrew said. "Do you think you can cope with Johnnie on your own?"

"I'm confident of it."

Me too, he thought, looking at her. *You're not much older than me, but there sure ain't any flies on you, lady.* Aloud, he said, "Well, the best of luck, Ms Lambton. Here's hoping it's good for all of us."

He shook her hand and left her, jumping off the back of the dais just as Johnnie Lee vaulted on at the front. Vernon Melville was coming up the steps on the far side, while Bill Bruce ran off towards his lorries and his seat at the controls.

Overhead, the rented airship was heading purposefully their way, from north of the river. There was a camera up there too, slung below the gondola and sending its signals by radio direct to the OB unit. It could be that the Centre's best publicity shots would come from that bird's-eye view, showing the vast complex of buildings and the packed car parks, the milling crowds. *This is the place to be, folks. This is where it's at, where the action is . . .*

1200:

and Denise had been awake for half an hour or more, had finally accepted that that was it: that tired as she was, weary to the very bones of her, she wasn't going to sleep any more today.

She eased her shoulder out from under Matt's head and slid a pillow in to take its place, a Denise-substitute to stop him waking up. Then she shambled slowly through to the living-room, pushing her fingers through her tangled hair and stopping off for a quick pee on the way.

The way she felt, she was tempted to skip her wake-up routines, just this once. But habit took her over to the telly and flicked it on, laid her down on the floor and kicked her into the first of fifty slow press-ups while Vernon Melville's face filled the screen, his warm voice filled the room and her mind; and with her body working so hard there was no space left to worry or wonder about Matt or anything, anyone else . . .

" . . . The whole of the Meldon Centre has gone green for the day; for those of you watching in black and white, I should say that even this platform I'm standing on is decked out in green canvas. As you can see, there's a big crowd here already; and they haven't simply come to enjoy themselves. Here in the north, we care as much as anyone about the environment, and I think we're going to prove that in the space of the next twenty-four hours. But we do have a packed programme of entertainment, for those who are here and for you watching at home. The first band is tuning up already over in the music tent, that's, uh, Dick Friction and the Frotteurs – can I say that? Too late, I already have – and we'll be going over there in just a few minutes, to give you a taste – no, better make that a sample of their performance. Other bands coming up later, of course, including a couple of major coups, apparently, that I'll leave it to someone else to tell you about. If it's not Frank Sinatra, it's just noise to me.

"But meanwhile, there'll be plenty happening in the main arena here. We've got the police motor-cycle display team coming up shortly – and every bike, let me assure you, running on unleaded fuel. We've got Chinese acrobats, and martial arts demonstrations; we've got a team of tribal dancers from Indonesia, making their first appearance in this country – they're on a world tour to publicise the destruction of their rainforests, and believe me, they are like nothing you've ever seen before. Amazing stuff. Then of course there's the final of the GXO Oil International Challenge to find the world's strongest man; that starts at four o'clock. And plenty more after that, the list just goes on and on.

"But first, before we get this show on the road, I'd like to introduce Mr Johnnie Lee, otherwise known as Mr Meldon Centre. After he's had a word or two, it'll be my great pleasure to invite Gina Lambton, the youngest and prettiest MP in the Commons, to remind you of what all this palaver is in aid of, why we're all here. And after *that*, I promise you, no more speeches. We've got a few videos we're going to run for the audience at home, to underline how serious the environmental crisis is, how close to disaster we're treading; and there's a film-tent and information booths for the people here. And, of course, we're asking everyone to dig deep into their pockets today. Send us as much as you can spare, and maybe just a little bit more. It's your children's future we're talking about here. There'll be phone-numbers coming up shortly, for pledges and credit-card donations. But still, let's not forget that we're here to have fun, too; and I promise you, fun we are going to have.

"And now, ladies and gentlemen, let me introduce you to the man who's made this whole affair possible – Mr Johnnie Lee!"

Denise rolled onto her back, breathing hard, feeling the blood pump through her aching arms and shoulders. Enough, give them a rest; she tucked her hands behind her head and groaned at the thought of sit-ups to come as the round, Asiatic face of Johnnie Lee filled the screen, as he started the ball rolling with a donation of a hundred thousand pounds and a promise to match any larger gift pound for pound.

*　　　*　　　*

" . . . Thank you, ladies and gentlemen, thank you. Yes, indeed. If you'd like to look down towards the river now, there's going to be a demonstration of parascending, by the members of the Two Rivers Parascending Club. Who, I may say, number last year's British Champion among them, so you can expect a pretty impressive show. I'll just hand you over to this year's champion, Clive Darkin, for an expert commentary, as it's a sport which to be quite frank I know nothing about whatsoever . . . "

Neither, of course, did Ivy; but she wasn't even pretending an interest. She paid no more attention to the loudspeakers than she did to the drone of the speedboats down on the river or the bright-coloured kites rising behind them with their payloads of people. Ivy had come down here for the punters, the crowds: wanting cash in her pocket before she risked the gauntlet of Centre security to take the Coatman inside.

Inevitably there were security guards out here too, but their uniforms made them easy to spot, and the crush made them easy to avoid. Much easier here than in the malls; and touching the punters would be easier here as well, where they were looking for a good time and not thinking about spending money. Giving it away was something else, they were doing that all right: everywhere she looked she could see kids dressed up in stupid costumes and shaking gaudy yellow buckets, people laughing and joking as they fished in pockets or purses for coins or even notes to throw away.

"Maybe we should get ourselves a bucket, eh, old Coatman?" she muttered, though she knew he was too far behind her to hear through his thick hood. "Maybe we should just rattle a bucket at these good people, and take their kindness that way. Or maybe not. Maybe you're right, old dear, maybe they wouldn't believe us. Maybe we're not dressed up silly enough, maybe we look too ordinary, is that it?" With a cackle and a glance down at the torn nylon mac she was wearing, that wasn't long enough to cover the printed cotton dress with its huge purple flowers, hanging loose over the tops of her wellington boots. "Or maybe they just wouldn't give us one of their pretty buckets, mmm? That's right. No bucket for Ivy, she'll just have to ask the nice people for their money, like she always does. While the Coatman keeps himself good and back out of the way, so he doesn't scare the nice people while Ivy's asking ever so nicely for their nice money . . . "

And she glanced back to check on that, to see that the Coatman really was holding back far enough. No good as a beggar, him. Didn't have the charm. Except at night, maybe, when he could surprise the little students on their way home from the pub, maybe frighten the odd quid out of them. In daylight, they saw him coming and crossed the street.

But no one crossed the street for Ivy. Sometimes they just walked past with their eyes dead ahead, making like she didn't exist even when she was pawing her hands at their sleeves; but that was people for you, there were always some who wouldn't see what they didn't want to. And the others made up for it, the ones who looked at her and saw an old lady down on her luck. Or a nuisancey beggar-woman to be paid off quick and forgotten about, that was just as good. She didn't mind what labels, what names they gave her, so long as she got cash to go with them.

Once she'd checked on the Coatman and looked around for uniforms, for guards, she limped up to a woman who was counting coins in her hand, obviously getting ready for the next bucket that came past; put a tremble in her hands and a little whine in her voice, and said, "'Scuse me, old love, you couldn't spare just a little bit of that for a tired old girl, could you, to buy a cup of tea on a hot day . . . ?"

*   *   *

"So why've you come here today, then, girls?"

It wasn't easy, to operate the camera and do the interview at the same time; but he'd had to do it often enough before, when Two Rivers had proved too mean to send a front man along on a story. Charlie kept his eye on the viewfinder and the lens steady, five teenage girls neatly framed, sitting on a fake adobe wall in the Latin-American Village; and he could trust Guy to move the mike between them, to pick up both his question and the girls' answering giggles.

They should pay me extra for this, he thought cheerfully, knowing full well that they wouldn't. *It's not in the job description*. And seeing that he wasn't going to get any more response than those irritating giggles if he didn't shove a little, he picked out one of the girls and focused both the camera and the question on her.

"Janine?"

She was the tallest of them, possibly the oldest, and his instinct told him she was the leader; but still she glanced from side to side before she answered, needing her friends' encouragement or else just checking that she had their attention.

"We always do, don't we?"

"What, you mean you're here every Saturday?"

"Nah. Every *day*."

That was what Charlie had been looking for, the story he'd sensed when he saw them – *you know, I'm bloody good at this, they should definitely pay me extra* – but he kept his voice calm as he said, "Today's no different, then, with the telethon and everything?"

"Nah, it's nothing special. Bit more crowded, maybe, bit

more going on. But we'd have been here anyway."

"I see. So why is that?" He gave her a second to reply, then when she seemed to be floundering a little, turned to one of the other girls. "What do you come here for, Kelly? What's the attraction?"

The girl shrugged thin shoulders, said, "I dunno. It's somewhere to go, innit?"

Janine threw her a scornful look, and snatched back the initiative. "It's *exciting* here, see? Better than anywhere."

"Better than hanging around at home, or on the streets, you mean?"

"*Miles* better." To grunts and nods of agreement from her cohort. "There's always something new around here, if you know where to look. And we do, we know every inch of this place. I love all the lights, and the shops, and the smell of it – it's just the best place to be, you know? It's the tops."

"Right, I get it. You know, the Americans have a word for kids like you."

"Yeah?" She frowned at him, suspicion and interest mixed. "What's that, then?"

"Mall rats, they'd call you."

He waited to see how they took it, and of course to let the camera see; and saw more or less what he'd expected, the hesitations, uncertain glances, faces turning to Janine for a lead. She thought about it, and smiled; and that set the rest of them off, laughing and nudging each other, happy thoughts.

"Yeah, that's us," Janine said positively. "We're a rat-pack."

And you're Queen Rat, right?

Charlie finished with a close-up of Janine nodding and grinning, then stopped the camera and eased it off his shoulder.

"That'll do, I reckon, Guy. I'll just run this back to Bill and pick up a fresh tape. Do you want to come with, or would you rather stay here and guard the gear?"

Guy glanced at his watch, and said, "Lunch-break."

"Right you are. Let's hit the road." He hoisted the camera again, then glanced back over his shoulder and said, "Thanks, girls, that was great. I don't know if they'll use it or not, it's not up to me; but if you want to get yourselves to a telly, you might catch it going out sometime this afternoon."

More giggles and over-casual shrugs, clearly designed to

suggest that they had far more interesting things to do today, and so what if their faces were going to be on the box, *they* weren't impressed. Charlie just grinned, and laid a bet with himself that they'd spend the next couple of hours kicking their heels outside a TV shop somewhere in the centre, staring in at the windows just in case.

Heading back through the packed malls, watching his feet in the crush and keeping both arms tight around the camera, Charlie got his ankles rammed hard by a baby-buggy. Came to a dead stop, looked up with a glare – and swapped one swear-word for another, a stronger, as he saw his wife beaming at him above the handles of the buggy.

"It's all right, walk straight past us," Sue said with sweet reason. "*We* don't care, do we, John Mark? We're quite happy, being ignored . . . "

"Bitch," Charlie said equably. "That hurt." He crouched down and cooed at his son for a little, and was rewarded with a wide and toothless smile. Then, "We're just going for lunch. Want to come?"

Sue shook her head firmly. "I just want to do the shopping and get out of here."

"She's got a phobia," Charlie explained to Guy. "Doesn't like people. Not even her own son, she wouldn't be trying to starve him to death, else."

"I just fed him, you blitherer. That's why he's being so nice. Do me a favour, Guy, take this man away? He's blocking the path."

THE BOOK OF THE DEAD

II: Mother's Little Soldier

Television's on, in the living-room. Television tells him it isn't time yet. Soon, yes, but not yet. And time's important, he's got to get the timing right.

So he goes back to his bedroom and starts to pack, feeling every minute heavy on his hands and on his mind. Impatience tugs at him, but there's danger there. He mustn't let himself be rushed.

He makes his selection carefully, what he'll need and what can be left behind, what's superfluous. Grenades are stowed in a small rucksack, packed in tight among ammunition-clips, all he's got for the Kalashnikov. You can never have too much ammunition.

The rucksack and the rifle fit comfortably, discreetly into a kitbag. Once that's zipped up and waiting, ready to go, he turns his attention to what's left; and ever the neat one, ever responsive to his training, he puts his other weapons back into the steel cabinet, runs a chain through their trigger-guards and padlocks it, closes the cabinet and locks that too.

Then he hammers the floorboards back into place, where he's ripped them up to get at his secret, unlicensed armoury, what he's taking with him when he goes.

With the room straight and his preparations complete, he strips his clothes off and sets the shower running. He's got time; and if he's going to do this – and he is, no question: it's time again, his hour come round at last – then he wants to go into it clean.

That's what his father would have wanted, so it's what he wants, too.

His mother, though, what she would have wanted – now that's another question, that's something else entirely.

He steps under the jet of water, reaches for the soap and ponders on that, what his mother would have wanted. Rubs a thick lather across his chest, rubs a few years away inside his head, feels for an answer and finds one of sorts.

While he played with his guns in the bath, while she knelt beside the tub and shampooed his hair for him, a long time ago now:

"You're going to be a soldier, aren't you?" she said, as she had said so often before. A game that was, a ritual, he loved it; but this time he changed the rules on her.

"Like my dad," he said.

"No," she said, fiercely, her hands suddenly rough on his head, digging deep, driving her words hard into his soft skull. "*Better* than your dad. A man to make your mother proud, you're going to be. A man for the girls to look up to, a handsome lad in uniform. An officer, even. You'd like that, wouldn't you? I'd like that. My son, the officer . . . "

He shook his head, not in denial, just to break free of the relentless pressure of her fingers; squirted his water-pistol silently at his feet, tried to imagine being better than his dad. And couldn't.

Years later, when he found his father dead with a mouthful of nasty and a nastiness between his legs, when his mother came to fetch him from the boarding-house and found him cowering away from the landlady's kindness:

"Come on, then, son," she said softly, reaching to comb his wild hair straight with her fingers. "Let's go home."

"Don't touch me." And he jerked his head aside from her hand and said it again, with all the violence he had in him. "Don't *touch* me!"

Later again, when he was fifteen:

"I wish you'd get out more," she said, speaking loud above the noise from the television. "You'll ruin your eyes, staying in every evening watching telly, the way you do."

"I've got homework," he said grudgingly, not taking his gaze from the screen.

"Not doing it, though."

"I'll do it."

"Yes, but you don't, do you? It was dreadful, your last school report. You'll never make officer if you don't work."

"I'm not bothered."

"Well, you should be. Do you want to end up like your dad?"

Nothing. No response, only his stillness to answer her.

"That's what'll happen, if you don't look out. You'll be just another squaddie in the ranks, a nothing soldier like your father was."

At last he was stung into movement, lifting his head, looking at her bleakly. "My dad was okay."

"That's what you think. If you knew . . . "

But his eyes told her, reminded her forcibly that he did know; and she shifted her ground fast, came back to where she'd started.

"You ought to get out more. You ought to have friends, a lad your age, it's not normal to keep yourself so private. Don't you get on with any of the boys in the cadets?"

A shrug. "They're okay. They don't take it serious, though. And you should make your mind up, you should. D'you want me off out all the time, or do you want me working for my exams?"

"Both," she said, trying a smile, trying to lighten his mood and her own. "I want a son I can be proud of, officer class, with lots of friends. But most of all I just want you to be happy, and I'm not sure you are."

When he didn't answer that, she tried another tack again. "What about girls, then, any girls you fancy at that school of yours? I bet some of your classmates are driving their mothers wild by now, hanging around at discos, sneaking girls up to their bedrooms at night. Why not you, eh? When are you going to give me a few grey hairs from worry?"

He turned his head back to the television.

"Come on, talk to me," she said gaily. "That's it, isn't it? There's some girl been messing you about. You can tell me, son, I'm your mother . . . "

And she reached to twist a lock of his hair around her finger, as she used to do when he was a teasable little boy, seeming to forget that he was older now and setting rules, setting limits.

He jerked away, jumped to his feet in a fury, snarling. "Don't *touch* me!"

"Sorry," she said, cold now, pulling back fast to the distance he preferred, he insisted on. "I forgot, you're untouchable these days. What is it with you, for God's sake? What are you angling for, do you want to be some virgin bloody hero or what?"

And he nearly opened his mouth, then; nearly gave it to

her straight. *Yes,* he nearly said, *yes, that's what I want. I've seen my father, I know what the other way does, the way you're telling me to go; and no, I don't want to end up like my dad.*

And once more, after another passage of years: when he was home on leave, when he told her what he'd done.

"You volunteered," she repeated dully. "Christ, I can't believe this. I just can't believe *you*, you know that?"

He shrugged. "They're sending a lot of men from our regiment anyway. I just made sure I was on the list, that's all."

"Yes, but – Northern Ireland, for God's sake!"

"It's what I want."

"What, you want to get killed, do you? You want to get sniped at from across the street, or blown up in some stupid bloody booby-trap? God, I can see that so easily. You'd walk straight into it, you would."

"No," he said. "I'm a good soldier."

"Good soldiers don't volunteer," bitterly. "Not for anything. Didn't your father ever tell you that?"

Never you mind what my father told me. "I'm sick of pissing about," he said. "I want the real thing; I trained to be a soldier, not to piss about. I want to see some action, and that means Ireland, there's nothing happening anywhere else."

"Oh, yes," she said, her voice harsher suddenly, touched to life. "Now that, that I can believe. You want action, of course you do, a young man like you; but you're still looking in the wrong place, aren't you? All the other squaddies are out getting their rocks off, but not you. You still don't go for that, do you? Oh, no. You still want to be a hero." And letting her anger break through, just this once: "Ah, go on, then. Volunteer, be a bloody hero, what do I care? Get yourself blown to bits, it's your choice. Just remember this much, if you can: your father's not around any more to see you do it. And me, they may fire a stinking salute over your grave when they drop you in it, but one thing's for sure, I won't be clapping. You'll get no applause from me."

And he'd get no applause from her today, either, he knows that much.

It didn't stop him then, of course, and probably it

wouldn't have stopped him now; but it doesn't apply any more, in any case. His mother's dead as well, she's gone after his father. Down into corruption, leaving him this last chance at writing his own headlines.

So he showers and dries himself carefully, methodically, behind the ears and between the toes; then he dresses like a soldier one more time.

And finally time is his friend, his buddy, time says it's time to go.

The television only confirms it, showing him what he's been waiting for all morning, or all his life.

He walks out to his car, kitbag heavy on his shoulder; lays it gently on the passenger seat, stands just for a moment with his hand on the thick canvas, glorying in the power, the potential of what's beneath.

His power now, his potential. He belongs to this day, this hour; and the hour, the day belongs to him. Claimed and chosen, that's how he feels. And he exults in it.

He deserves it after everything that's happened, everything that's been done to him. It's a debt he's owed, with interest due; and today he's out to collect. He can't stand back, he can't be patient any longer. The body in the kitchen denies him that, forbids him his proper place in the eyes of the world, steals any chance of true recognition.

It's a dirty trick, but he's long familiar with life's tricks, they've been played on him too often. And if he can't be a hero – except to himself, of course, he knows his own worth – he'll be a soldier at least; and he'll by God go down fighting.

He closes the car door, smiling. Goes unhurriedly round to the driver's side, gets in and starts the engine.

Starts the war.

THE BOOK OF HOURS

III

1300:

and Penny leant against a wall of warm bricks in a staff parking area, sun on her face and Clarabelle in her arms, tuning up. Laura stood beside her, fiddle under her chin to give the note; while Adam sat on the tarmac rolling a cigarette, his guitar still in its case beside him and a bright yellow bucket conspicuously empty beside that.

While time ticked away, time they could and should have been using to take people's money off them in the malls; while Richard was God knew where, when he should have been here.

"I vote we give him another ten minutes," Penny said, "then go in and start anyway. He can come and find us, when he gets here. If he bothers to come at all."

Adam grunted neutrally; Laura played a couple of quick arpeggios, and lowered her fiddle with a frown. "What are we going to do about his solos?"

"Skip them, or busk them. Adam knows most of 'em anyway, and the punters won't notice. It's just bloody stupid, kicking around like this. And we've done it too often, I'm sick to death of waiting for Richard. Maybe he'll sharpen up a bit, if we show him that we really don't need him that much."

"Well, maybe . . . "

But just then the wide brown bonnet of an old Rover came nosing slowly round the corner. Laura huffed with relief, and waved her bow in welcome; Penny balanced her double bass carefully against the wall, folded her arms and waited coldly, a classic figure – as she well knew, almost a cliché, but at least it might get the message home – of impatience and irritation barely held in check.

And had to hold it in check a while longer, as Richard parked the car in the last remaining space, got out with two passengers, lifted his guitar from the boot and stood talking

for a few moments before coming over to join them; and
even then he had Julian still in tow, the other guy hanging
back by the car.

"Hi, gang. Sorry I'm late, we got held up. Any idea where
we're going to be playing, so's Jules can come and find us
later?"

"They want us in the Tudor Village," Laura said. "Wherever that is."

"They *wanted* us there half an hour ago," Penny added
pointedly. "They said to play a set there and then move on,
wherever the crowds were." With a glance at her watch,
which might be coming on a bit strong but hell, Richard
deserved it, keeping them waiting so long . . .

"Right." Richard turned back to Julian, and Penny saw
his hand move towards the kid's waist and then jerk back
again, wary of the other boy's seeing. "You okay, then,
sweets? There's no pressure, you don't have to come if you
don't want to. Just play it by ear."

"Aye." Julian nodded, looked round at the band and
sketched a wave, half greeting and half farewell, before he
went sloping back, hands in pockets and very casual, to join
his friend. Richard stood still, watching until they rounded
the corner out of sight; then he drew a breath, let it out
slowly and gathered up the band with his eyes. "You lot
ready, then?"

"Oh, yes," Penny said. "*We're* ready."

"Good. So let's do it, eh? Which way?"

*   *   *

Rudy had taken Deena up onto his shoulders again, to
prevent either or both of them panicking if she got separated
from him in the crush. He grabbed her swinging ankles
firmly and paused outside the doors to the Centre, grinning
across at Liane.

"Hang on tight, pet. I don't want to lose you either."

She nodded, and slipped her arm through his. "Okay.
Where are we going first?"

"Dreamland!" Deena shouted.

"Surprise. But what if Liane wants to go to the shops, or
down to the field to see what's happening, eh? What then?"

"No! Dreamland first!"

"I don't mind," Liane said. "Really."

"I dunno, love. We're supposed to be meeting the others, remember? Some of 'em must be here by now, they might be looking for us . . . "

"Yeah, but they're never going to find us anyway, are they? Not in this lot. We should've said somewhere to meet, but we didn't, so . . . "

"They'll never think to look in Dreamland, that's for sure."

Deena tugged at his hair, and spoke with a suspicious tremor in her voice. "I want to go to Dreamland. You *promised* . . . "

Rudy sighed, and gave up. "All right, then. But just for one hour, you hear me, you spoiled brat? And no sulking when your time's up, or I'm taking you straight home."

"I'm not spoiled."

"Of course you are. What's the point me having a kid sister if I don't spoil you? Just mind you duck as we go in, or you'll bang your head."

The automatic doors slid back at their approach; Deena squealed and ducked fast, hugging Rudy's head as they passed through, jerking her balloon after them just before the doors could close on the string.

They picked their way slowly through the crowds, stopping every time they found a busker or someone in costume, feeding small coins to Deena for her to throw wildly towards the yellow collecting-buckets. She'd miss, inevitably, and shriek with laughter as Liane went scuttling off to retrieve the pennies from under people's feet; then she'd have another go, Rudy holding her wrist carefully above the bucket's mouth, and shriek again as the coin clattered in.

And then they'd move on, Deena the only one talking and Rudy not even trying to listen in the hubbub. He thought instead, and watched the windows of the shops as they passed; and eventually, long before they reached Dreamland, he stopped and urged Liane into a quiet corner.

"Listen, pet, d'you think you could cope with Deena on your own, just for half an hour? Take her on some rides, she'll be fine . . . "

"Yeah, sure – but why, Rudy? What are you up to?"

"It's a secret. I'll be as quick as I can; and then I'll take over, if you want to nip round the shops or anything."

"I thought you said you didn't want to lose me?"

"I don't. And I won't. I'll find you easy enough, as long as you stay in Dreamland. I just thought of something, that's all; and it's something I've got to do by myself."

"Well, if Deena doesn't mind . . . "

When she was consulted, Deena's lower lip stuck out obstinately, and her grip tightened on Rudy's head; but she relented quickly enough, after Liane promised her a ride on the roller-coaster and candy floss afterwards.

Her brother swung her up off his shoulders and settled her onto Liane's, saying, "Are you sure you can manage her like that? She's pretty heavy."

"Of course I can manage."

"Yeah, right. Dead macho, you are," skipping back quickly to avoid Liane's sharp punch at his ribs. Then he stepped close again, to kiss her; stood on a nearby bench to gain height enough to kiss his giggling sister; said goodbye, and watched them all the way up a crowded escalator and out of sight before he turned back to the shops, and his big idea.

*   *   *

With his guests dispersed for the afternoon, each of them carrying the little golden voucher that would entitle them to a meal and drinks anywhere in the Centre at his expense – each of them, he hoped, ready to spend far more than they would save – and the telethon successfully in progress, Johnnie Lee was free to take his own lunch with his wife.

They had their favourite place to eat, a small French restaurant tucked away in the heart of the Centre. Johnnie hesitated briefly, at the prospect of forcing their way through the dense crowds in the malls; but Linda smiled and linked her arm with his. "Doesn't matter. Let's face the hurly-burly, and enjoy it. Taste the triumph, and count the cash . . . "

"Yes. You're right."

So they shuffled their way through the halls and the arcades, nothing but the cut of their clothes to distinguish them from the hoi polloi, nothing at all to say that they had a totally different relationship to the walls and roofs that surrounded them, the floors they walked on: that they owned what the others were only using. Today of all days they were simply two units in the mass, unrecognised and unremarked –

– except that Linda stopped dead without warning, bringing her husband to a halt beside her with a tug on his arm.

"What is it?"

She stared back at the milling crowds, the countless faces surging past them, and said, "No. I must have been mistaken. Only . . . "

"What?" Johnnie said again.

"I thought I saw Carl. Back there, watching me."

Johnnie followed the direction of her gaze, said, "I don't see him."

"No. Nor do I, now. It was just a glimpse, a man in a combat jacket; and he's got one, he wears it a lot when he's off-duty. That's what made me glance at his face, and I thought, I did think it was him."

"There are many men who wear combat jackets."

"Yes. Just someone with similar features, I expect. He's on my mind at the moment, that's all. If it had been him, he'd have come forward. Wouldn't he? We had a, something of a disagreement this morning, but nothing to make him behave so strangely, I'm sure of that . . . "

"No. Forget it, Linda. It was not Carl."

"No . . . "

*   *   *

They had money now, or Ivy did; and the Coatman was content to follow her lead, as always. She gave his world the focus it lacked when he was alone, she was all the brightness his dimming eyes could find; and if sometimes she gave him other things, drinks that twisted that focus strangely awry – well, moths got burned around candles, that was all very normal and natural.

So he followed her now, away from the field with its booming loudspeakers and its generous crowds, all the way up to the nearest doors into the Centre proper; and would have followed her inside without a thought, if a hand hadn't gripped his arm roughly to pull him back, if a voice hadn't said, "Oh, yeah? And where do you think you're going, like?"

He turned slowly, under the impetus of another tug on his arm, and looked blearily down into the face of a boy half his age. Short, overweight, his skin so badly marked with acne that at this distance even the Coatman could make out the scars, this young man derived his only authority from the clothes he wore; but they made up the uniform of Centre security, and that was more than enough.

"I asked you a question, old man," the boy said, a sneer painted thick across his lips. "Where d'you think you're going, eh?"

"Inside." With a hawk and a spit first to clear the claggy phlegm from his throat, so the word didn't die a-borning.

"Wrong." And the mouth stretched to a happy smile, without losing any of the sneer. "You just listen to me, now, I'll tell you where you're going. You're turning round right here, and starting to walk; up to that road there, see it, turn left and keep on going. Mind the traffic till you're outside the fence, I don't want any nasty messes on my patch."

And if Ivy hadn't been with him, the Coatman would have surrendered gracelessly and left, with no further encouragement than a shove on his shoulder to get him moving. He'd already taken the first shuffling steps away from the Centre when he heard her voice behind him and stopped again.

"Oh now, now, now. No, no, Mr Security Guard, don't you do that to the Coatman, don't you turn him off. He's with me."

"Aye, and you can just go along with him, can't you? We got no call for your sort round here."

"Oh, and what's that, then, Mr Security Guard, sir? 'Our sort', what is that? Beggars and trash, is that what you mean, is it? Because we're not here to beg, oh no. You won't catch us begging. We've got money, see?" And she held up a handful of cash, just inches under his nose. "Pound coins we've got, do you see them glinting there in all this lovely sun? And we're just going inside to spend some of this money of ours, for a cup of tea and a sit-down. No, we're not beggars."

"You're still filth," the man muttered, keeping his voice low as he glanced around at the curious bystanders.

"Filth, is it?" Ivy echoed shrilly. "Filth, did you call us? You listen to me, Mr Big Security Guard, you see this dress I'm wearing? Washed it with my own hands yesterday, I did, put it on clean this morning. *I'm* not filthy, no, old Ivy's clean as the days are long." Wisely she said nothing about the Coatman, but went stridently on for all to hear. "And all I want is a cup of tea in a comfy place, *and* I've got the money to pay for it. That's not so much to ask, is it? Is it?"

"You can get tea down there, at one of the stalls . . . "

"Oh, and what about the baccy for my old love the Coatman? Can't buy baccy down there, at one of the stalls, now can I? A bit of baccy and a cup of tea, that's all I'm looking for. Just to spend some of this nice money in your nice shops, and what's wrong with that, then?"

The gathering crowd was beginning to murmur now. The guard sensed the critical atmosphere building around him, scratched his neck under the rim of his cap, said, "Christ, it's not worth it. Not for two quid an hour, it's not. All right, you can go in," to Ivy, "but not him, get it? He stays out here."

"And what about his cup of tea, then? His little sit? He's got to rest those tired old legs of his . . . "

"Well, he can bloody rest them out here, can't he? There's benches to sit on, he can have his little sit on one of them. And you can bring him his cup of tea, you can get him a carry-out. Buy him a burger while you're at it, I don't care. But he's not going in. Now shut up and get moving, or I will turn you both off. It's what I should do anyway, it's what my boss'll do if he catches sight of you . . . "

Ivy snorted, took the Coatman's arm and made a great production of conducting him to the nearest empty bench and settling him down.

"Now you just wait here, old love," with a scornful glance at the hapless guard, "and don't you fret yourself. *He* won't touch you, and Ivy won't be long, no. She'll be back soon, with a cup of tea to warm you, poor cold old man, and some nice fresh baccy for your tin. Yes, and some papers for your clever fingers to roll a cigarette in, and matches to light it after . . . "

So the Coatman sat and watched her leave, watched her hobble away through the doors on her bad feet; looked around defensively, and pulled the hood of his parka higher over his face as he saw a young man with a TV camera training the lens right at him.

A minute later there was a touch on his shoulder, just firm enough for him to feel through the insulation of all his coats; and there was the cameraman, smiling down at him, the big camera still riding high on his shoulder.

"Excuse me," in a soft voice the Coatman could barely

hear, "my name's Charlie Campbell, I'm with Two Rivers Television. Me and my friend here with the microphone, we were just wondering if you'd like to talk to us for a bit, tell us about yourself . . . "

But the Coatman only snorted and spat, hunched himself deeper into his coats and waited for them to go away. Which they did, after a little; so he could turn his head back to the bright glass doors and watch, and wait for Ivy.

*   *   *

Andrew's lunch was a sandwich, eaten in haste and in motion, hurrying through the malls. He'd given himself twenty minutes, and even that was pushing it; strictly speaking, he ought to have stayed outside and snatched something with Bill Bruce, keeping himself on call. But he had his own personal reason for getting away, something he'd overheard by chance on a teenager's ghetto-blaster out in the sunshine half an hour ago, something he couldn't ignore.

So he'd broken away and come looking; and the first familiar face he found was the wrong one, was Calum ploughing his chair through the crowds, blithely confident of their getting out of his way.

"Hey, Hook! What are you up to? Thought you'd got yourself glued to the media people."

"Yes, well . . . " Andrew swallowed the mouthful he'd been chewing, said, "I was hungry," waving the remains of the sandwich in evidence, "and it seemed like a good chance to get away for a bit."

"Uh-huh. Can't take the pressure, I suppose. Yuppies getting to you, were they?"

"Something like that."

"Right. You'll be going back now, though?"

"I'd better, yes. Show willing, you know."

"Oh, I know. I also know the quickest way out from here, and you're going in the wrong direction."

"Er – yes, I suppose I am, but . . . "

Calum chuckled, and stretched out a twisted hand to pat Andrew lightly on the arm. "But there's someone else you want to see first, I know. Don't worry, boy, your secret is safe with me. You'll find her down in the next hall, dispensing her favours. There's a queue, mind, or I might have claimed one myself. Cheap at the price, I reckon."

Another chuckle, and the chair rolled slowly away. Andrew scowled; he hadn't realised he was being that obvious. Did *everybody* know? But no, probably not. Of all the people he worked with at the Centre, Calum was closest, and saw most of him on duty and off; if anyone was going to spot it, he'd be the one. And he wouldn't talk, Andrew could trust him that far.

So he shrugged and went on his way, finishing the sandwich quickly and then ducking into a public toilet to rinse his mouth out, to dilute the flavours of ham and mustard a little. That was only polite, after all; and for all he knew she might be a rampant vegetarian who'd find even a hint of meat utterly repellent. Though if she was, she'd have problems with what she was doing today. Hamburgers, hot dogs and bad breath, she could count on all of those . . .

Sure enough, there was a long queue when he finally found her; and she wasn't hurrying through it. Even from his place at the end of the line he could hear her talking to the punters as she took their money, sharing a joke or a double-entendre with each of them, making sure they got their money's-worth. Giving them what they'd expect.

But he moved up slowly, pace by pace, and barely gave a thought to how much time this was costing him, how late back he'd be. At last he was standing at the head of the line, looking down at her, registering her reaction and waiting hopefully for a smile to follow the surprise.

"Hullo, Dee."

She scratched vaguely at her Mohican, pushed her fingers through it as though to check that it was still vertical, it hadn't wilted with the shock; and yes, here came the smile as she said, "That's cheating, Andrew."

"Yes, I know. But . . . " *But all's fair in love and war, and this is both; only for God's sake don't say it, don't push your luck, man . . .*

"Well. All right; we're going for a record here, I can't afford to turn customers away. But it'll cost you a fiver. Friends come extra."

He shrugged, took out his wallet, dropped a note into the bucket she rattled at him.

Then she passed the bucket to the man at her side, stood on tiptoe, put her hands lightly on his shoulders – and he barely had time to put his own right arm around her waist, to

feel her resilient body pressed momentarily against his before she'd touched her lips briefly to his cheek and was
pushing him away already. "Mark him down, Harry. How
many now?"

"Um, hundred and fifty-three, I make it. If you're really
going to count that. She's short-changing you, mate."

"Not really," he said, keeping his voice easy, squeezing
Denise's shoulder in farewell, walking away.

And looking back just the once, with terrible timing:
seeing her with her arms tight around the next boy's neck,
kissing him with concentration, full on the mouth. One
hundred and fifty-four, and counting.

*   *   *

– and that's when it ends, really, or when it begins. When
the kissing has to stop.

Call it the end, or the beginning; or say it really began
hours ago with the first, the secret death, say that this is just
another step along the way. Say what you like, it doesn't
matter. What happens is what counts, after all; and what
happened is this.

A man called Stuart Thompkins had just arrived at the
Centre for a day out with his family. He'd found a place to
park his car, helped the children off with their seat-belts in
the back, had a quick word with his wife Joan about where
they were going first, how they were going to spend the
afternoon.

Then he'd set off for the nearest entrance to the malls,
reckoning that she was right; best to get the shopping over
with, before they took a look around. He'd led the way
through the crowds, cheerful and confident, knowing that
Joan was just behind him and keeping an eye on the kids.

He was almost at the doors when he heard gasps, mutters,
some woman's high laugh behind him; and he'd already
been turning to see what was up when he heard something
else, sullen staccato barks that made no sense, no sense at
all.

And when he looked round, what he saw made no sense
either. He saw some people frozen, some already backing
off with hands pressed to mouths or pulling at others' clothing, a few lying strangely on the ground. He saw one person
turn to run, and then more, dozens more; but above all he

saw his youngest, Nicola, sprawled on the bricks of the plaza with her yellow dress turning dark and wet. He saw his son Thomas standing close beside her, doing nothing, only staring. He saw Joan jerking like a puppet, her mouth working soundlessly. And then he saw something – someone – else.

He saw a soldier, or at least a man in full combat gear: camouflage jacket and trousers, boots, black balaclava pulled down to leave only his eyes and mouth showing. A man running, with a rifle in his hands and his finger on the trigger. He heard that sound again and understood it this time, quick bursts of fire from an automatic; and saw Thomas's head explode, saw his wife crumple silently and fall.

Saw the rifle turn towards him, the man pause in his running; and felt a kick in his stomach that knocked him back, heard screams faint and fading, saw blue sky hung before his eyes and a dreadful, burning sun.

1400:

and Andrew had made his way outside, was heading back towards the broadcasters' pantechnicons when he heard the screaming. He checked, turned – *somewhere around Entrance B, two hundred yards from here; and what the hell's going on?* – and had already started to run when he heard something more, a loud explosion that stilled the screams for a moment.

Answered his own question as he ran, *some fool kid's throwing fireworks. Big ones. Christ, that's all we need . . .*

Thought that he should have asked for a walkie-talkie, just for today; he could have called in some guards and the St John Ambulance. But no, it shouldn't be necessary. There ought to be a guard there anyway, they were stationed at all the doors. If not, the racket would draw one soon enough.

He ran around one wing of the complex but still had one more to go, a long greenhouse extension for the garden centre. Even from here he could see the first signs of panic in the crowds beyond, people running and shoving, shouting unintelligibly. It seemed strange, an overreaction to a firework; but that was punters for you. *En masse* they were stupid as cattle, and as dangerous if they started a stampede.

And maybe they weren't overreacting after all, if someone had been seriously hurt. Or if the cretins who'd started this were still standing there, lighter in one hand and firework in the other, ready to do it again . . .

Again Andrew wished for a walkie-talkie, so that he could at least listen in to the messages being passed; and even as the thought occurred, he saw two men in uniform come out of a fire-door a few yards ahead, one listening intently to his radio.

They were police, rather than the Centre's own security guards; but that was just as good, or better. Andrew drew to a stop beside them. "What's going on?"

The younger man just glanced at him, and turned his attention back to the radio; but his senior looked at the badge on Andrew's lapel and said, "You work here, son?"

"Yes."

"Know your way around?"

"Yes, but . . . "

"Good. Stick with me, then. I can use you."

"Why? What's *happening*?"

"There's been a shooting incident; maybe worse. That last bang sounded like a grenade to me. Simon, you get down to the cars. Call HQ, and tell them it's the big one. I want ambulances, fire engines, the lot; and tell them to get the brass down here, sharp. They'll want to call in the Tactical Squad, too, shouldn't wonder."

The constable nodded and hurried off away from the Centre, towards the road.

"What's your name, son?"

"Andrew Scott."

"Come on, then, Andrew. Let's have a look."

*　　　*　　　*

Charlie Campbell and Guy were working again, taking stock shots of the packed malls between interviews; Bill might find them useful, and if not the library would be glad of them.

Charlie had his lens trained on an overcrowded escalator and was following the line of heads down to the floor below, half expecting to find himself filming an accident any second, when the plate glass window of a sports shop beyond suddenly exploded.

He grunted in surprise, gestured to Guy to stay with it, zoomed in to catch the face of a man bleeding from a dozen superficial cuts – and saw the man jerked violently out of frame. Panned the camera around to find him again, and found him down on the floor, both hands clutching at his neck as blood spurted out between his fingers.

"Jesus . . . "

Now Charlie registered the voices screaming, the running feet, all the sounds of a crowd in panic; and realised there was something more going on down there than a shattered window. He pulled the focus back for a wider view, saw half a dozen people down as scores more fought to escape. He saw – and his camera recorded – people kicked and trampled in the rush; he saw people falling on the escalators, and others clambering over them; he saw one abandoned toddler stumbling between the bodies on the ground, wailing thinly, its hands raised high in anticipation of some adult's arms lifting it out of danger.

Sorry, kid, Charlie thought grimly, holding the camera rock-steady on the shot. *Looks like they're all out of heroes down there; and I've got a job to do. Couldn't get to you anyway*, added as a brief salve to his conscience. *But in sweet Jesus' name, what . . . ?*

The question was answered then, before it could be properly framed. A man came running into view from one of the malls that met at this concourse, and Charlie focused on him automatically, thinking, *here comes your hero, kid . . .*

He couldn't have been more wrong. And he knew it a moment later, as the man checked, lifted a gun halfway to his shoulder and sprayed bullets indiscriminately into the retreating mass of people.

Charlie kept the camera rolling, nothing else he could do from his position a floor above. Except duck, of course; but Christ, this was the chance of a lifetime, this was national news material. And the guy hadn't looked up once – not yet – so there were only ricochets to worry about, and a ricochet could get you anyway, no matter how low you ducked.

So he zoomed in for as much detail as he could catch at this range, and for a second or two the man stood obligingly still, as if trapped and held by the camera's eye. Then he turned and ran again, behind the escalators and away down another mall, gun stuttering to clear a path ahead.

Charlie followed him out of sight, then swept the lens slowly back across the all but emptied concourse: picked out the shards of glass and the blood that streaked and pooled on the tile floor, the bodies stirring and crawling and falling again, the bodies with no life at all. Focused at last on the toddler, sitting now and silent in the midst of a bewildering devastation.

Then he took his eye from the viewfinder, glanced at Guy, said, "Come on, fast! We can follow him from up here, maybe catch him at the next bank of escalators."

"Hell, Charlie . . . Shouldn't we *do* something? Those people . . . "

Guy's hand sketched a movement towards the floor below. Charlie started to speak, started to say, "What, you're a doctor now? We can't help them . . . "

But his eye followed the movement anyway, and he saw the chaos nakedly now, without the shield of his camera's neutrality; saw the toddler and the stillness that was only underlined by the odd movement, the single blood-spattered figure lurching painfully to its feet.

And his head turned again, to plot the course the killer had taken, further into the Centre; and he thought, *Sue.*

Thought, *Sue. And John Mark . . .*

*   *   *

On the far side of the greenhouse was a wide gravel court used to display more hardy plants in the open air. It had been a restful place the last time Andrew had seen it, almost a garden: flowers and herbs growing in wooden boxes, shrubs and saplings in individual tubs. Now it looked more like a bomb-site, the whole area laid waste by the charge of a terrified crowd. There was scarcely a pot left upright, scarcely a plant without its roots stripped bare to the sun.

Andrew followed the hurrying policeman through the mess, lifting his feet high in a futile and stupid attempt not to add to the damage. Looking around – purely to avoid looking ahead, knowing that this wasn't the worst of it, that this was nothing compared to what was waiting for him fifty yards further on – he saw pale faces staring out at him from behind the illusory safety of a glass wall. Looking back he saw people still running, parents carrying their children over the road and lovers dragging each other by the arm, scattering between the parked cars on the far side. Others were gathering in little knots on the road itself, thinking themselves out of danger there, curiosity fighting self-interest and achieving a balance at this little distance; while a few more courageous than the rest – or more prurient – were making their way cautiously back up the slope towards the Centre, to offer their help or simply to get a better view.

But whether he looked around or looked back, wherever he looked, Andrew's feet still took him forward; and soon the crunch of gravel under his shoes gave way to the softness of a grass border, and then unyielding tarmac. And then there were no choices left, nothing to look at but the real truth of the day.

And it was a truth captured by his first wary glance at it, embodied in that moment; because what he saw was bodies, more bodies than he could count or believe to be real, to be true. And when his eyes flicked numbly back to himself, to his feet – when they rejected the truth of those bodies – he saw that he was standing in a thin, meandering stream of blood.

When he could move again – and it took a while, it took a great effort of will to do it, to concentrate his mind on the simple mechanics of movement – he walked slowly and stiffly between the fallen to where his policeman was standing listening to another.

" . . . Yes, sir, just the one man. Got up like the SAS, he was. Came from over there," with a nod of his head towards the separate security complex. "Running, and firing indiscriminately. Went up to the doors here, looked like he was going straight in; only then he stopped, and threw something into the crowd. And then there was this explosion, and . . . " And a helpless gesture of his hand, not enough fingers on it to count the bodies.

"Right. Did you see him go inside?"

"No, sir, I didn't see; but I'm sure he did. He must have done."

"No one tried to follow him?"

"Not that I saw."

"All right, constable. Do what you can for these people, and I'll talk to you again later."

Andrew's eyes followed the man as he walked hesitantly over to a child's sprawled body, crouched, felt for a pulse that clearly wasn't going to be there. There were other policemen arriving now, doing the same, giving what help they could to those who were still alive; but pathetically few of them, and with pathetically little in their gift. Mostly they watched the road, waiting for a miracle, or at least for a fleet of ambulances.

Among them Andrew could see a couple of the Centre's own security guards, as lost as the police or more so. He lifted a hand to beckon one of them over, then aborted the gesture as he heard his name spoken.

"Andrew. Are you with me?"

"Uh, yes. I suppose . . . " He turned his head, met his policeman's sharp gaze.

"Good. I know how you feel, lad, but stay with it. I'm going to need you. First thing is to evacuate the Centre. You must have contingency plans for that?"

"Yes, of course. It, it should be happening now. The men on watch in the control room, they will have seen all this over the cameras, they should be putting it out on the PA right now. They're not stupid, they'll know to act without orders, a situation like this . . . "

"Well, let's just check, shall we? Which way?"

*   *   *

A quarter of an hour after leaving the girls, Rudy had regretfully abandoned his big idea.

He'd found what he was after soon enough, a rack of leather jackets even better than the ones he'd seen in town, in a style that would really suit Liane. They were even more expensive, too, but that wouldn't have mattered if his plan had come off. If they hadn't all had wires threaded through the sleeves, wires that ran to a very visible alarm box on the wall; if they hadn't been tagged as well, to trigger the extra alarm by the store's doorway. If there hadn't been a security guard in shirtsleeves and cap leaning against the wall right by the doorway, his suspicious eyes watching Rudy's every move . . .

Rudy fingered the jackets regretfully, found Liane's size and double-checked the price, daydreamed a little about somehow finding the money and buying the bloody thing straight; and was startled almost out of his skin by a voice at his shoulder, "Do you need any help at all?"

He flushed, turned to face the assistant, knowing that he looked guilty as hell; and had to try twice before he managed to get any words out of his tight throat.

"No – no, thanks. I'm just browsing, really."

"That's fine. Just give us a shout, if you want anything."

She started to walk away, and it was only Rudy's pride, a sudden, desperate need to show himself as a genuine customer that made him call her back.

"Tell you what, there is something. Um, I'm looking for a jacket for my girlfriend, see, for her birthday? And, well, you're about her size and everything, and I dunno whether this'd fit her or not. Could you just put it on for a bit, let us see how it looks? You've got the same hair, too, so . . . "

The assistant grinned. "No one's ever asked me to do that before, but I expect it'll be okay. Hang on, I'll have to get the keys off the supervisor . . . "

So Rudy watched while the girl turned off the alarm, disentangled the jacket from its protective wiring and modelled it for him in a fit of giggles. It wasn't the first time he'd done this, played the legitimate shopper to get past an alarm system and then waited for his chance to slip away with the goods; but he had no thought now of stealing the jacket. Not with that other alarm by the door, and the guard hanging around.

It was still just for show when he took the jacket and went over it minutely, testing the stitching and checking every zip; saying, "It's dead nice, isn't it? How does it feel on?"

"Terrific." More giggles. "Too bad you're not buying it for me."

"Yeah." He gave her a smile, thinking, *No chance. You against Liane? Don't make me laugh* . . . "Well, look, it's a pity, 'cos I wanted to surprise her; but . . . "

But there were suddenly screams in the mall outside, loud enough to drown out the ubiquitous Muzak. Rudy and the little assistant turned to look, to stare as they saw people running, stumbling, charging in panic past the wide windows. Everyone in the store was watching now, some moving closer to the door for a better view. The security guard stepped outside as the crowd thinned, gazed back down the mall for a moment; then Rudy saw him fumble urgently for the walkie-talkie clipped to his belt.

And saw him thrown impossibly back against the door-frame, as all the glass splintered around him; saw him slide slowly to the ground, with blood leaking through his shirt.

Now they were screaming inside the store as well as out, voices pitched higher even than the wailing alarm set off by the broken windows. Rudy tore his eyes away from the fallen guard, fought to control his skidding, twisting mind; barely noticed a man in combat fatigues go sprinting past, as he focused his attention on the shop's staff.

His own assistant was standing frozen, hands pressed to her cheeks and mouth open soundlessly. He forced his shocked and trembling body into one quiet pace backwards, another; then – seeing that no one had so much as a glance to spare for him, that the only other movement in the store was hesitantly forward, towards the guard – he slipped sideways between mirrored pillars and racks of clothing till he came to the fire-exit.

WARNING! said a printed sign on the double doors. *This exit is alarmed! Do not use it, except in emergency!*

Well, this was an emergency, wasn't it? And the alarm was going off already . . .

One last look back, then he worked the long handle on one of the doors, pushed it open and slid out with the leather jacket – Liane's jacket now – still clutched in one sweating hand.

Found himself in a narrow corridor, breeze blocks and concrete and harsh lighting; turned from left to right, *which way now, then? How do I get out of here?* – and saw a security camera hanging from the ceiling just a few yards away, seemingly focused right on his face.

Spat a nervous curse, and started to run . . .

*   *   *

Andrew led his policeman past the barrier at a sprint, into the security complex. There was no one on duty in the gatehouse; Andrew registered that as he passed, frowned, shrugged it off. They had bigger things to worry about right now. Round the corner of the building and a moment's thought, not to take his usual way inside; instead he headed for the entrance nearest to the control room. Jerked it open – and stopped dead, only moving again when the policeman pushed at his back.

There was a cluster of people in the corridor, gathered around the door – the *closed* door – into the control room. A couple of uniforms, outnumbered by suits and skirts: a mixture of security and administrative personnel, all of them known to Andrew, all of them tense and anxious as they banged on the door, called through it, looked round one by one to see who was coming in.

The policeman shoved his way through, to try the door for himself; then he said, "I'm Inspector Holborn. What's going on here?"

"It's locked," a voice answered him, "and the men inside don't answer."

"Spare key?"

The question was general, but his eyes picked Andrew out.

"There's a set of masters in my boss's office. One of those ought to do it."

"Any other way in? Or a window?"

"No. I don't think so . . . "

"Be sure."

Andrew thought for a second, calling up an image of the control room in his mind. He hadn't been in there for months, but . . . "No. Definitely. There isn't another door, and there's certainly no window."

"Right. Fetch those masters. You two," as Andrew turned away, "see if you can break the door down. I've got to get in there, quick. Someone else go for an axe or a crowbar. Hurry!"

Andrew ran for the keys, came back with the big ring heavy in his hand, just in time to see that it was redundant. Some hefty kicking had splintered the wood around the lock; and as he watched a shoulder-charge finished the job, crashing the door back against its hinges.

Peering over the heads of his colleagues, Andrew saw the bank of monitors, all of them grey and dead, no pictures coming through. He saw the men who should have been watching for trouble, one in his chair and one sagged into a corner, both covered with blood, both clearly as dead as the monitors; and he choked with the others on the overpowering smell of petrol.

A moment later Inspector Holborn hurtled into him, sending him sprawling on the floor of the corridor. He heard the inspector's voice screaming, "Down! Get dow – "

And then there was a flash and a roar, and his whole body was lifted and shaken by a punch that struck him everywhere at once, that sent him reeling and tumbling into the black.

*   *   *

The band had set up in the centre of the fake village square, with fake cobbles under their feet and a fake well behind them. The few inches of water in the well gleamed with coins, and there were more in the genuinely wooden bucket that dangled above, under a coy little roof.

"Punters!" Richard had said disgustedly. "Any excuse to chuck their money away. I just hope they're going to fish that lot out and add it to today's total, that's all."

"Expect so," Penny had said non-committally, still angry with him.

"Penny, my love, you have a touching faith in human nature."

"No, I just think this place has good PR. Adam, have you got the posters? May as well let the people know who they're listening to. You never know, someone might want to book us."

"Sure." Adam had produced a roll from his bag, unfurled two posters emblazoned with the band's name, *Hot Ginger*, and pinned them to the roof of the wishing-well. Then he'd taken a green marker-pen out of his pocket, and written an addition in big capitals. "Just for today. Hot *Green* Ginger, how do you like that?"

"Terrific."

So the gig had started with a smile, despite undercurrents of bad feeling – or band feeling, perhaps, because there was nothing new there, it was familiar territory. They were four highly disparate individuals, and hardly a week went past without conflict somewhere between them. The patterns changed, different members found themselves at each other's throats one day and playing peacemaker the next, but the levels of friction were constant and perhaps necessary.

And there was always the music to bring them together at last, water in the desert, port in a storm.

So it was today. Penny might have started the session growling at Richard, but it needed only a few minutes of playing together to make her forget her irritation and find herself falling as ever under the spell of his particular genius, his strong but generous mastery of the guitar.

Song followed tune followed song, their voices and instruments melding in three- and four-part harmonies intercut by long, intricate solos. *Midnight Train*, *Black Eyes*, *Sweet Georgia Brown* – it was a repertoire of classics they played, their regular busking set, and it drew them a large audience with kids fighting for the privilege of carrying the bucket around.

And for Richard – well, there was the music, of course, there was always the music like a shawl, like a cocoon to wrap him around, Adam's guitar to toss the tune to and catch it coming back, Laura's fiddle to follow and Penny's bass to bring him home again; but today – now – there was something more.

There was Julian, who'd shaken Robbie off and come to find them sooner than ever he'd expected, ever he'd dared to hope: Julian spotted suddenly at the back of the crowd, Julian with his head turned towards the imitation half-timbered tavern, seeming to watch the waitresses – sorry, the serving wenches – in their low-cut bodices and long skirts, seeming barely to be aware of the band. Julian fooling everyone else, perhaps, but not fooling Richard for a second.

So let the rest of the band play for themselves, for the public, for Friends of the Earth or the hope of another booking; Richard played and sang for Julian alone. He didn't have any choice. *This is fixation, Rich*, he told himself sardonically, retuning a string between numbers and fighting not to glance up, and failing. *This is obsession,* as his eyes traced the curves of Julian's ear, followed the line of his jaw, cursed the women who stood between them and blocked his view; but he shook his head before the idea had time to settle. He'd been here before, after all, more times than he could count. Forget the world's labels, he had his own word for it. *Nah. This is love.*

But that was the end of it, just then; the end of all songs for

Richard, for Julian, for Hot Ginger. The cheers and whistles and applause were just dying down, Penny and Adam were murmuring about what to do next, Laura was waving her bow excitedly to underline a suggestion, a demand. Richard was lifting his head to catch Julian's eye, to hazard a wink and a grin. None of them was more than distantly aware of the sound of running footsteps somewhere beyond the crowd, footsteps that came abruptly to a halt. Certainly no one looked round, until one of the girls in the tavern started to scream; and by then it was far too late.

The gig that had started with a smile ended with a bang; and after the bang, there was a slow rattle in the sudden stillness. That rattle was a yellow bucket fallen from a dead hand and rolling awkwardly across the cobbles, spreading coins to mark its path. Empty at last, it toppled into the designer's best joke, the drainage channel that had never had a function before; it lay on its side in the open sewer, and began to collect the blood.

*   *   *

" . . . We'll have to send the men in, John. There's no other way now. I want them in teams, with megaphones if you can get them; no one goes in on his own. Try for a security guard with each team, they'll know the lay-out, but for God's sake get the place clear. That's the priority . . . "

Andrew opened his eyes slowly, and found himself lying flat on his back, staring at a thin sapling in a cage of wire mesh. He turned his head in search of the voice that had roused him, ignoring the stab of pain in his neck as he moved, and saw Inspector Holborn a couple of yards away, talking to a police sergeant. Beyond them was the security complex, with thick black smoke billowing out of the open door and the guttering red glow of fire inside.

Andrew rolled onto his side, feeling a soreness in every muscle; put his hand flat on the parched earth beneath him, and tried to push himself up. He made it halfway, then a wave of weakness dropped him down onto one elbow with his head spinning and the blackness threatening once more.

Looking up, he saw the sergeant running off towards the Centre, while Inspector Holborn took two quick paces over and crouched down beside him. Hatless now, with soot marks on his face and his hair scorched, an angry burn showing on the back of one hand.

"How are you feeling?"

"Sore, dizzy – okay, I suppose." *Alive.* "What – what about the others?"

"We got some of them out. They're waiting for the ambulance now. You were lucky, son." *Luckier than them*, unspoken but very much there in his voice; and clearly far luckier than the rest, the ones they didn't get out . . .

Andrew closed his eyes, not to see the burning building and the deaths of his friends, not to see anything of this terrible day; but the inspector only allowed him a second before slipping an arm firmly round his shoulders and saying, "Can you get up? Come on, I'll help . . . "

Andrew groaned, forced himself to his knees and then his feet, clinging shakily to the inspector for support.

"What . . . what was it, in there? Some kind of bomb?"

"Grenade. I saw the lever come flying out from between that guy's legs on the chair, that's how I knew. Simple, really. Tie a bit of string to the pin, pass it round behind a pipe or something, and fix it to the door. We come along, open the door, that pulls the string and jerks the pin out. Three or four seconds on the fuse to get people inside, plenty of petrol splashed around beforehand, and Bob's your uncle. Lots of bang, lots of fire, no control room."

Lots of bodies. But then, who's counting now? Andrew grunted, too dazed even to wonder which of his colleagues had survived, which he had to mourn. "So what happens next?"

"We go down there."

He pointed, and Andrew looked. There was the Centre, clean and bright in the strong sunlight; and there were the people. Policemen and bodies, he'd expected those; but there were others too, ordinary people, issuing out of every door he could see. Some running, some clutching or carrying each other; one he could see crawling, dragging a leg that left a stain on the ground behind him. *Leave them alone,* he thought wearily, *and they'll organise their own evacuation. Or the gunman will. Save you the trouble . . .*

Aloud, he said, "You don't need me."

"Yes, I do. For the moment, you're the only one I've got who knows this place."

"Get someone else, then. For Christ's sake, there's enough of them around. Get my boss, or Mr Pritchard, the security chief, he's the guy you want. Or Johnnie Lee, why don't you get him? He knows it better than anyone."

"We're looking; but we haven't found them yet. They're inside, somewhere."

"Well, put a call out, for . . . " He stopped before the sentence was finished, remembering that with the control room ablaze the Centre's PA system was useless, as were the individual walkie-talkies. Hence the policemen going in with megaphones; there was no other way to spread the news to the malls the killer hadn't reached. No way to work out where he was, either. They were blind, deaf and dumb with the control room dead; the madman couldn't have picked a worse place to start. Or a better, from his point of view . . .

That thought stopped Andrew in his tracks, before he'd moved six faltering steps with the inspector.

"Tell you one thing, about this guy . . . "

"Yes?"

"He knows how this place runs. No, more than that. He's *known*, or he would never have got in here. Get a list off the gate, who's been in and out of the compound. That'll help you narrow it down. Unless he came over the fence, round at the back there; but it's still got to be someone who knows their way around. Someone who works here, or visits a lot."

"Good. You see? I said I needed you."

Yeah, sure. Couldn't have thought that out for yourself, I suppose, a big smart copper like you? Pull the other one, it doesn't hurt as much . . .

*   *   *

The Lees ate sparingly when they were alone, as an antidote to business lunches. Today, with a big dinner to come, they were content with a lobster salad and a bottle of Chablis; and they were almost finished when a young policeman pushed his way in through the door and said, "Can I have your attention? Quickly, please . . . ?"

In the curious silence that followed, Johnnie just had time to notice other police in the mall outside, directing a crowd past the windows. Then,

"Can you clear the restaurant, please, and leave the Centre immediately. The nearest exit is fifty yards that way, uh, to the right, and there'll be someone there to tell you what to do. But go now, this is an emergency . . . "

A buzz of conversation and uncertain movements around the room, people gathering up bags and jackets, watching to see what the others did, no one liking to be the first to stand and leave.

The head waiter made his way quickly between the tables towards the constable, but that young man forestalled him, his voice cracking with tension.

"Yeah, you too. All the waiters, everyone. Come on, move! You've got one minute to get outside, all of you . . . "

Then he headed through the restaurant, making for the kitchens; and as he passed, Johnnie reached out a hand to delay him.

"A moment, officer. What is happening?"

"We're evacuating the Centre, sir. If you'd just follow instructions . . . "

"Tell me why."

"There isn't *time* . . . !"

And the constable pulled his arm free, sweat glistening on his face; but Johnnie thrust himself to his feet, stood four-square in the boy's path and said, "Wait. I am Johnnie Lee, I own these buildings . . . "

"Are you? Good, the Inspector's looking for you. Tell someone when you get outside, they'll show you where to find him. But please, just get out of here? And tell the rest of 'em who you are, maybe they'll listen to you . . . "

Johnnie felt a sudden impulse to shake what he wanted out of the boy, and fought it down with an effort. Reminded himself that this wasn't one of his security guards, not an employee; and that added another finger of anxiety to his demand, because surely it should have been, surely the Centre's own personnel should have taken charge in any crisis? "Just explain to me, please, what this is all about. Quickly!"

"There's a guy gone crazy with a gun, right? He's killed a lot of people already, and he's in here somewhere, and we don't know where . . . "

Deliberately or not, that was said too loud for privacy, loud enough for the other customers to hear. They stopped muttering then about practical jokes and students in fancy-dress, stopped worrying about walking out without paying the bill; they were suddenly up and moving, rocking tables and spilling wine, sending chairs skidding across the tiles as they struggled towards the door.

And still Johnnie only stood there, caught in confusion, his usual decisiveness stripped from him by a few short words. His mind was filled with visions of a killer running wild through his dreams, turning them all to nightmare; and in the end it was Linda who had to take charge, tugging urgently at his sleeve, propelling him out of the restaurant by main force just moments ahead of the kitchen staff and their shepherding policeman.

*   *   *

Denise had called a five-minute toilet-break from her mammoth kiss-in, leaving her tally-keeper Harry to control a queue of impatient males, most of whom were sniggering and offering to come with her.

She ducked into the nearest ladies' with a sigh, and a grimace of distaste for the job she'd taken on. *All in a good cause*, she reminded herself forcefully; but still her mouth was sore, and she was bored already with the seemingly endless procession of young men urgent to thrust their sour tongues halfway to her tonsils and grab a quick feel for good measure.

Well, you brought it on yourself, girl. Never volunteer, that's what Grandad used to say. Should've listened to him, he was dead right . . .

For a wonder there was no queue for the cubicles, no one else in the toilet at all. She had a quick pee, then ran a tap at one of the basins and produced a toothbrush and paste from the pocket of her dungarees. At least she could clean her mouth out, and start in again reasonably fresh . . .

Scrubbing away vigorously, she heard the tinny voice of a loudhailer in the mall outside. Couldn't make out the words, though, above the gushing tap and the sounds of her own brushing; and wasn't much interested anyway. Just a promotion of some kind, most likely. A day like this, with the Centre so full, they weren't going to miss the opportunity to push some new consumer miracle down the throats of the ever-gullible public.

She spat into the basin, rinsed out her mouth, drank a little water straight from the tap and pushed herself upright. *Better get back to it, I guess . . .*

Turned to the door, just in time to see it swinging open; and saw a man coming in, a man with a load of gear in his arms, glancing edgily back over his shoulder.

"Wrong door, old son," she advised him cheerfully. "Little boys' room is on the other side."

He looked at her then, and she bit down hard on the jokes. She'd never seen a guy looking so desperate, not even Matt at his worst.

He dragged in a couple of rough breaths that didn't seem to do him much good, shook his head, said, "You shouldn't be here."

No, that's the wrong way round, mate. It's you that shouldn't be here, I'm entitled . . . But she couldn't be flippant confronted by a face that frantic; instead she just said, "What's the matter, chum?"

He sagged against the tiled wall, and wrapped his arms tighter around what he was carrying; and Denise had time to recognise it as a professional video-camera, time to wonder if maybe he'd pinched it and the hue and cry was on, time to question what she'd do about it and not find an answer, before he spoke again.

"Haven't you heard? You should get out of here. Go on, quick. They're evacuating the whole Centre."

"They're *what*?"

"There's a lunatic running loose somewhere, dressed up like a soldier, with a rifle and grenades and God knows what. He's killing people wholesale, I, I saw them die, some of them. I was filming, and it just started happening, I filmed them dying . . . "

"Jesus . . . " She thought quickly, made a guess at what the loudhailer had been saying, knew that Harry must've been warned and should be safe by now. "Well, come on, then. There's an exit just over the mall, we can walk straight out . . . "

Linked her arm with his for a bit of moral support, the guy seemed to need it; and stared disbelievingly as he shrugged her off, as he said, "No. I'm not going."

"Why the hell not?" And then, glancing at his camera and jumping to an obvious conclusion, "Don't tell me you want to get some more pictures? That's crazy, mister! I mean, it's not worth it, you could *die* out there . . . "

"Not that. Not, not now . . . " And his head jerked towards the door as they heard the loudhailer again and staccato voices shouting, coming closer. He stepped quickly into one of the cubicles, started to push the door closed with a glance of mute appeal. Without really thinking about it, Denise slipped inside with him; and a moment later, they heard someone come banging in, calling, "Anyone in here?"

God, if he looks in the cubicles – what the hell's he going to think? But he didn't look in the cubicles; the silence seemed enough, and he went running out again.

The cameraman slumped suddenly, sinking down onto the toilet seat.

"Okay, that's a reprieve," Denise said. "But you'd better have a bloody good reason why you want to stay, and you'd better tell me quick. I can always call him back, and let the police drag you out."

"My wife," he said simply. "And my kid, they're in here somewhere."

"And by now they're most likely outside with everyone else, looking for you and getting worried," Denise said caustically. "For God's sake, mister . . . !"

"I've got to be sure."

"Sure. Right. So what are you going to do, wander round shouting for her? Have you got any *idea* how big this place is? It'd take an army to search it properly."

"They could've been hurt . . . "

"Well, yes, I suppose they could. But even if they are, they'll get help soon enough; the police are right here, they know what to do. They've had enough experience. So come on, let's just clear out and let them get on with the job, eh? The maths says your wife and kid are going to be safe, anyway. There's a quarter of a million people here today; the odds of this madman hurting your two are infinitesimal. He's got a much better chance of hurting us, if we don't get out of here . . . "

Still talking, she dragged the man to his feet and pulled him over to the door, thinking how familiar all this was. The circumstances were different – could hardly be more different – but close your eyes and she could just as easily be at home and lugging Matt around, bullying him, taking his decisions for him and talking, talking, talking . . .

She pulled the door open and put her head out cautiously. Silence, no movement – the mall had been cleared incredibly fast, and now it looked deserted of police as well. And, thank God, deserted of crazed gunmen . . .

"Okay, come on. Quick now, the way out's just over there . . . "

She hustled him across the tiled floor, between a bench and a litter bin and on towards the exit; and they were just fifteen, maybe twenty feet from their goal when a panelled section of wall suddenly flew open off to their left.

And there, framed in this unexpected doorway, was a man: tall, dark, bulky-looking, silhouetted against a strong light behind him. Wearing combat jacket and boots, looking like a soldier.

Looking like a soldier . . .

*   *   *

After the music and its ending, after the music died he lay wrapped in its death, in a numbing silence. The silence filled him, consumed him, drank mind and body both. It stole the world away, and time; it stole his very name from him, so that he had nothing to do but drift within it, lost even to himself.

But after the silence – and too soon after – came the pain. With that came the knowledge or memory of his body, the borders of himself restored; so that he knew this pain, this clamorous agony was confined inside his skull. It beat and battered at him, shrilled and ricocheted through his brain like all the devils of hell giving voice in a terrible crescendo.

And after the pain was movement, but not of his own making. He could remember his fingers, what and where they were, but he couldn't have moved a single one of them himself. Certainly he couldn't have lifted his head as it was lifted now, couldn't have rested it against something firm but yielding, couldn't have pressed the palm of a hand against his brow . . .

The tormenting racket in his head subsided slowly, became nothing but a strident whine between his ears; and at last he found or generated enough will to force his eyes open, just a crack.

Saw red and white, a blur that resolved itself eventually into a face of sorts: impossibly pale and streaked with blood, but a face nonetheless.

Saw the face mouthing words, and at first heard nothing above the noise that filled his skull; but gradually, reading the patterns more than listening to them, he made sense or a kind of sense from both the face and the words.

" . . . chard? Richard, can you hear me?"

It was Penny's face, the face was Penny and he was, he must be Richard. And with the name he recovered the rest of himself, more than his body. His history, his life came back to him; and after it something of what had happened, to bring him to this.

He moved one cautious arm, and then the other; tucked his elbows underneath him, pushed himself up a little and lifted his head from its pillow on her leg. Shook it, and the whining died to a buzz as he blinked and looked around him.

And saw people and pieces of people thrown in mad savagery across the floor, in a mess of blood.

Let his head drop back to that comforting pillow, her leg; and said nothing, only stared up at her in search of some explanation, some excuse.

"I don't, I don't *know*," she whispered. "But they're . . . Adam and Laura, they're both dead. And, and everyone else, too. Everyone who hasn't gone. And I thought you were too, only you're not bleeding or anything, I couldn't see anything wrong with you, so I just, I just prayed . . . "

Richard's mouth worked, worked hard; finally found a name, and a way to say it.

"Julian?"

"I don't know. Was he here? I haven't, I couldn't bear to look too closely . . . "

And he could understand that; but for himself he had to look, he had to know. So somehow, with a lot of help, he got himself up on his feet; somehow managed to walk, to keep his feet on the wet cobbles; somehow forced himself to look at faces – where there were faces still, where the faces weren't torn and splintered into masks of blood and bone – until he found Julian.

And found himself a miracle, because Julian wasn't dead either.

Not quite.

*   *   *

Denise had never moved so fast in her life. She almost flew those last few paces to the exit, with the cameraman keeping pace at her side, her fingers locked tight in his sleeve. They slammed into the doors and sent them crashing open, came staggering out into bright sunshine; and ran on across the tarmac, neither of them risking so much as a glance behind.

It was a policewoman who stopped them at last, appearing suddenly from around a corner, holding out an arm to check their mad career. Even then they didn't just come to a polite and obedient halt, not with that hectic urgency on them, not with that doorway gaping wide at their backs, offering a direct line of fire. They swerved around the woman, heading for the more solid protection of bricks and mortar, the cover of the corner; and as they passed Denise snatched blindly at the woman's hand to drag her into safety with them.

Then they did stop. Then they did more than stop, they collapsed: the man sagging against the wall, sliding slowly down onto his haunches, his arms still wrapped all but unconsciously around his camera; Denise simply dropping flat onto a border of grass, her lungs heaving and a cold sweat prickling across her shaven scalp.

The WPC took a moment to pull her uniform straight, then said, "What's that about, then?"

"We – we saw him," Denise gasped. "The gunman. He's just back there . . . "

"Are you sure?"

"Well, he came – he came out of the wall, it was dead scary; and what he was wearing, it's what this guy said," indicating the cameraman with a jerk of her head. "Army stuff. Ask him, he saw him earlier. Got him on film, he said . . . "

"Wait a minute."

The policewoman turned aside, switched on her walkie-talkie and spoke into it, taking a cautious glance round the corner as she did so. Then she came back to Denise.

"Got your breath back, have you?"

"Uh, yeah . . . " Or *no, not really, it takes longer than this, it's going to take days before my heart calms down; but I'm ready to pretend.* She scrambled to her knees, to her feet; pushed both hands through her hair, and tried a weak smile. "Why?"

"I'm to take you to the inspector, straight away. Both of you," with a glance down at the oblivious cameraman. "And the camera. The inspector wants that tape."

She got no reaction from the man, so she looked back at Denise. "What's the matter with him, he's not hurt, is he?"

"No. He's worried. His family's here somewhere and he can't find them. I had to drag him out of the Centre, he wanted to stay in there and search . . . "

"Uh. Got a name, has he?"

"Dunno. We haven't been introduced. We, er, we met in a ladies' toilet . . . "

And hard, painful little giggles thrust themselves suddenly, stupidly up her throat and out of her mouth, giggles like bubbles that rose and burst and just went on and on, rising and bursting beyond any hope of control.

*   *   *

Old Ivy's eyes saw more than most people would have credited; and her mind remembered what she'd seen, oh yes. No fool, our Ivy, and no madwoman, let them think what they liked.

Particularly, she'd seen the secrets of the Meldon Centre. She'd seen the hidden doors with their passageways behind, she'd seen people come in and out of them, and made a special effort to remember. Secrets were always useful to know, especially in a place so thick with security, with guards who'd turn her out as soon as look at her. Sometime, she'd thought, sometime she might have cause to hide in here; so she'd hugged the secret to her, kept it close against a future need. And told no one, not even the Coatman. Maybe she'd get the chance to surprise him with it, to lead him suddenly out of trouble; and she liked to surprise people, did Ivy.

So today – fighting to keep her feet in a panicked crowd, to keep her grip on two capped beakers of hot tea, confused and bewildered and cut off from the exit by a frightening crush of bodies – she'd let herself be shoved and elbowed to the side, to the wall. She'd felt her way along, pressing her shoulder against panel after panel, until at last she'd felt one give beneath her weight.

Slipped through, and let it swing shut again behind her; and found herself in a grim grey passage, facing a dead end, a solid wall cutting her off from the way she wanted to go.

So she turned and went the other way, rather than face the madness of the malls again; tried to find another passage to bring her back, or any door out into the open.

But one stairway led her down into basements and storerooms, and no way out from there; and another took her up again into a baffling maze of corridors that soon had her tearfully helpless, hopelessly turned around.

Nothing to do but keep on walking, keep on looking for an exit. But before she could find one, she found something else; and maybe old Ivy's eyes weren't so good after all, because what they told her she was seeing – well, it just couldn't be, that was all.

So she shuffled closer, peering, until she was sure; and when she was, when she was close enough to touch and absolutely certain, that's when horror took her and drove her back, nothing on her mind now but finding a better place to hide . . .

Calum Rafferty hadn't been lucky today. You could say there was nothing new in that; born with bad cess in his bones, he'd had to fight his own disabilities and other people's prejudice every day of his life, and there's not a lot of luck in a scenario like that.

But today the gods had really gone to town on him. He'd been caught like Ivy in a chaotic stampede of terror, without understanding at all what had caused it. Like Ivy he'd been helpless to withstand the rush, trapped as he was in his slow chair; and like Ivy, he'd used his brain and his knowledge of the Centre's secrets to escape into the sudden peace of the service ways.

But once there, things had really turned sour on him.

Unlike Ivy, he knew his way around back here; and as soon as he got his bearings he'd set out confidently for a ramp that would take him and his chair easily down to the nearest exit door.

And he hadn't gone more than fifty yards before he met his ill luck in person, face to face.

Or eye to eye, at any rate. You couldn't call it a face that he found himself confronted with: more of a blank, a face-lessness. There was a mouth, yes, stretched into a tight smile; and above that only eyes, dark and wild, staring through a slit in the black balaclava.

Mouth, eyes and hands, that's what Calum saw: and the hands moving to lift the rifle they carried.

Calum's own hands moved in response, in fear, as his mind finally understood the crowd on the other side of the wall. His weak fingers gripped the joystick of his chair and tugged at it too slow, far slower than the finger of the man who faced him – if he was a man at all, and not simply Calum's bad luck turned real, turned all too solidly real –

on the trigger of his gun.

Bullets smashed into Calum's frail body as the chair began to turn, throwing him sideways, his head hanging over the arm and all his light weight leaning now on the control.

The man left him then; but the ill luck didn't. Because he wasn't dead, not yet. His body clung almost as stubbornly to life as his fingers did to that little joystick; after so many years of struggle against the odds, it wasn't going to give up now without a fight.

So it fought, and failed at last; and Calum died slowly, agonisingly, a victim of his own heart's strength as it pumped the blood around his ruined body and found less to pump with every passing minute, as it finally faltered and stopped for lack of work.

And the blood gathered in a puddle beneath the chair, tried to run away across the concrete; but each fresh channel it found was checked by the wheels of the chair as it turned on the spot, turned and turned and kept on turning, quite unheeding of the dead and stiffening fingers at its controls.

And that was what Ivy had found in the frightening emptiness of these grey corridors: a wheelchair that span in circles, seemingly of its own desire, with a dead man slumped in the seat. Or a dead midget, a dwarf, a twisted and distorted creature that could scarcely have looked human even before all the blood ran out and over the torn body.

And that was what sent her scurrying for cover, for somewhere to hide, some place of darkness where nothing lived or died or was dead already, where nothing moved at all.

THE BOOK OF THE DEAD

III: After the First Death

Oh, this.

This, now, this is better. This is so much better.

His feet may be clay, but his head is glory; which only goes to show that he was right all along. He knew himself, and his worth. And he's proving it today, painting it high and wide and handsome for the world to see.

Those that have the eyes for it.

He steps forward into the blood, smells the panic, sights a target. Raises his weapon and shoots, takes the target out. And yes, this is how it's meant to be. Death can come easy to his hands and to his heart, it can be as quick and as meaningless as this. It doesn't have to hurt.

It doesn't have to hurt him.

A grenade now, lobbed into the middle of a milling crowd; and after, hunting through the stillness, he finds a boy naked, broken but unmarked, blown entire out of his clothes. But even this doesn't touch him, doesn't come close. A naked boy is a long, long way from a naked father, this death an impossible distance from that. There's no connection, only a memory stirred and ignored, abandoned in the heat of action. No time for that now.

And if not for that, then how much less for the other, this morning's unintended, undesired death? Surely now, with his finger on the trigger and his face on tomorrow's news, surely he's got no time to dwell on what she did to him today.

He pauses for a little knifework, a misericorde for the temporarily living and another reminder – as if it were needed, as if – how simple it can be, to let life out.

He cleans his blade and looks up, looks around. Sees nothing moving, nothing more to be done here; and sets off to run again, in search of further work.

Yet even as he runs, his mind beats to an earlier rhythm than his rapid feet; he hears a clear and terrible voice above the distant shouts and the constant muzak; he sees the light of the morning behind the neon glamour of the malls.

Whether he's got time for it or not, he carries the blood and terror of this morning with him, every step he takes. It's a constant, lurking threat, a dimming of the glory, a shadow on the sun. A bullet will chase it briefly back, a grenade will give him cover for a while; that's why he works so hard, why he takes every death that's offered him. For another coating of gilt on the day, a deeper shine before the glory fades.

Because fade it will, fade it must. That's the dreadful, gloating logic that pursues him, running hard at his heels. However far he pushes this, there will have to be an end to it at last. A time will have to come when the malls are empty, when there's only him among the corpses; and though that too won't last forever, it'll last long enough. He'll have time then to be overtaken by his stalking horrors, with no more deaths to offer in propitiation, nothing in the bank.

It's the fear of that which drives him on, as much as the lust for fame. He slaughters for self-protection more than self-advertisement; but even as the body-count rises, he knows it won't be enough, it can't be.

He can never, ever get enough of killing now.

THE BOOK OF HOURS

IV

1500:

and Penny rubbed a hand uselessly across her eyes, still didn't wake up, couldn't make all this into a dream; so she turned her gaze and her attention back to Richard.

He was kneeling over Julian's slack body, working feverishly on the boy's jeans, easing the saturated denim down. His hands were suddenly red to the wrists, as collected blood escaped in a gush; Penny saw him check, heard him make a strange, soft noise in his throat before he rolled the unconscious Julian over onto his stomach.

Looking, Penny felt a moment of gratitude that the boy *was* unconscious, that he wasn't awake to know what had been done to him. There was a great hole torn in the back of his thigh, a crater of ripped flesh with shards of bone showing and blood pumping out to fill it.

Again that sound from Richard, that muted despair; and his eyes met hers across his lover's body, searching for something more than she could give.

When he spoke, though, his voice was crisp and decisive. "Get me a guitar-string, quick. Spares in my case."

She hurried to obey him, came back with a packet of strings in her hand.

"What are you going to do?"

"Tourniquet."

He had already ripped the packet open and was fumbling to uncoil one of the strings when she said, "Should you? I thought, I'd heard that they didn't do that any more, it does too much damage . . . "

"He's bleeding to death here, what the hell else can I do? I'm not a fucking doctor . . . "

And she said nothing more then, only watched while he wrapped the metal string twice and three times around Julian's leg, below the swell of the buttock and just above that terrible wound. Then he snatched a pen from his pocket and thrust it under the string, twisting it round and round, drawing the wire savagely tight. They watched it bite deeper and deeper into Julian's flesh, watched until the pooled blood no longer stirred in its hollow, until they were sure the flow was checked.

Richard breathed out, long and slow, then reached for Julian's wrist. Held it lightly, frowned, shifted his fingers a little – and shivered, said, "I can't find a pulse, Penny. Maybe . . . "

Maybe that's why the blood's not flowing, right? But all right, I won't say it if you won't. "Here," she said, "let me try. You're not a doctor, remember?"

And never mind that she wasn't either, she had to give him something to hang onto, even if it fell disastrously short of hope.

So she took Julian's hand in hers, swallowing a little at the cold, clammy – *okay, say it, the dead* – feel of his skin; laid two fingers across his wrist, and waited. And prayed.

And at last, "It's okay, Richard. I can feel something, I can." *Or I think I can. I could be wrong, it's been known.* "Sort of a flutter. Dead weak, but I think he's still alive. Can we turn him over? Without you losing that tourniquet? We'd know better then, we'll be able to see him breathing." *Or not.*

"Yeah. Go careful, though . . . "

So they eased Julian over, onto his back again; and both thought – or claimed – that they could see a little movement of his lips and chest, that they could feel a stirring of the air above his mouth.

"So what now?" Penny asked.

"Now you go for help. And hurry."

The tone of his voice had her halfway to her feet before she could think. But then she looked around for the first time since they'd found Julian alive; saw all the others, the ones who weren't; and said, "No, wait. I can't leave you here."

"I'm staying."

"Yes, of course. I didn't mean that. Only, what if he comes back? That, that madman who did all this? If he finds you sitting out here . . . "

Richard only shrugged. "He won't come back."

"You don't know that. He might. There sure as hell isn't anyone to stop him. And, and it might take a while to get help here, there must be so many others hurt . . . "

"So what are you saying?"

"I think you ought to move. Into one of the shops, say, get yourselves in a corner where he won't see you. And – yes, look, there's a clothes shop over there. If we get Julian in there, you could make a sort of a bed for him, keep him warm. He really needs that, he's freezing cold . . . "

"I don't think we should move him," Richard said hesitantly; but Penny sensed his uncertainty and seized on it, feeling the initiative swinging over to her at last.

"How the hell would you know? You're not a doctor. Come on, Rich. I'll take his shoulders, you get his legs. And keep a grip on that tourniquet, for God's sake . . . "

So they carried Julian twenty yards into a menswear shop, and built him a nest of coats; and then, driven by Richard's returning urgency, Penny finally left them. She halted by the door for one last look, and could barely see Richard's back, bent over his lover's makeshift bed. Satisfied, she hurried off, nervousness keeping her hugged to the sides of the arcades and her eyes constantly moving, ready to duck into the nearest doorway at the first hint of danger.

*   *   *

Rudy finally found his way out of the service areas and back into the Centre proper – but it was a Centre bewilderingly different from the one he had left. Then it had been loud, exuberant, packed from wall to wall; now he stood in an arcade that was eerily and utterly empty, only the constant muzak serving to dull the echo of his solitary footsteps.

He opened his mouth to call, to try to find at least some evidence of life; and bit the sound back before it was past his lips, remembering the stolen jacket still clutched in his hand. He had to do something about that first, he had to hide it. Whatever was going on here, there was still the chance of a security guard or a policeman walking round the corner any second, challenging him to produce a receipt, charging him with looting . . .

He looked around and spotted a toyshop just ahead. A careful check through the window reassured him, no one there; so he slipped inside, went behind the counter and rummaged until he found a large carrier bag. The jacket went into that with room to spare. He resisted the temptation, the challenge of the locked till; he wasn't here to steal, he just wanted to make himself safe and get the hell out. The world had turned crazy, ever since he'd seen that guard getting himself shot, but this was the craziest thing of all. Like the *Marie Celeste* on land, this was. Dead creepy . . .

Still, on the way out he passed a table piled high with the latest cartoon dolls, that Deena was mad keen on; and it was almost instinct to grab one of those and stuff it in on top of the jacket. That way, even if Liane sneaked a peek inside, she might not see her present under the other.

And that was the moment, thinking of Liane, when he suddenly didn't care any more about the jacket, didn't give a damn about anything but finding her and Deena, being sure they were safe.

Because he remembered the guard falling, the store window shattering, all the blood; and more important, he remembered the crowd stampeding outside, all the screaming and the panic. That's why the place was empty now, for sure, because some guy had run wild with a gun in here. And if one person had got shot, then maybe others had too . . .

And that thought, those pictures were so vividly in his mind that he didn't stop to wonder if maybe the gunman was still around, still uncaught; if maybe he was in danger himself. He just hurried to the end of the arcade, where an electronic map showed him where he was in the Centre and plotted out a route in flashing lights that would take him to Dreamland. He scanned that quickly, and started to run again; and only ran faster, after his feet took him past the first little knot of bodies.

Bodies alone, bodies in groups: some obviously shot, others terribly ripped apart. Twice he ran through showers and streams of water, where the sprinkler-systems had switched themselves on to douse a fire.

And then there were the others, the bodies that moved . . . Some he saw crawling or limping, hauling themselves along the walls; a couple of times arms reached out towards him, voices called, racked voices crying out for help. Even then he didn't stop. He couldn't find space in his mind for them, filled as it was with images of Liane and Deena like this, bleeding and dying, perhaps dead already. He did slow down, though, almost to a walk. At every junction he looked left and right and saw the malls quiet and empty, not a body in sight; but the way he went – the way he had to go – there were always more. Death guided him, as much as the signs to Dreamland; so that it seemed that he followed a path of blood, carrying a burden of terror that grew heavier with every step.

At last he came to the wide, bright entrance into Dreamland. And here, finally, he did stop. His heart was pounding in his chest, his lungs fighting to drag air in through a tight throat; but it wasn't the long run doing that to him. It was his body's rebelling against what lay ahead, desperate not to take another pace forward, not to confront the truth of what he saw in front of him.

What he saw was Little Red Riding Hood lying dead across the Yellow Brick Road, her blood staining the golden tiles that tempted children in. Beyond her was a miniature boating lake with Bugs Bunny floating in it, face down, his fur half torn away to reveal the flayed ribs of the man beneath.

And on the bridge arching high over the lake was the body of a child, a little girl unstitched by bullets. She wasn't Deena, he knew she wasn't Deena, her hair was the wrong colour and the clothes weren't right; but still, she could have been. And it could be that Deena was no different from her now, that she lay somewhere in the wreckage beyond the lake, just as still, just as broken. Maybe this little girl was only there to be a signpost, another of death's neat footsteps to lead him on his way . . .

So he didn't go that way, over the bridge. He followed the Yellow Brick Road instead, around the edge of the lake, looking all the time, searching for what he most dreaded to find.

Mostly what he saw around him was proof of panic, of hurried flight: toys and push-chairs abandoned in the path; shopping crushed and flattened in its wrappings; one young boy, eight or nine by the look of him, stone dead without a mark on his body. Rudy shuddered, picturing him trapped in the surge of bodies, suffocated by the sheer weight of people. Lifted off his feet for a while, perhaps, carried along in the rush before finally being allowed to fall, to die beneath the feet of his playmates and their parents.

And Rudy found himself hoping, praying that Liane and Deena had been right there, among the killers. That Liane had fled in terror with the rest, Deena clutched screaming in her arms, conscious of nothing more than a sudden stumble in her passage as her own feet added their little contribution to the boy's death . . .

But somehow he didn't believe it. Most people must have got out, sure; but still he went on looking, driven by a dreadful certainty that his girls weren't among them. They'd promised to meet him here, in Dreamland; and he was horribly afraid that it was a promise they meant to keep.

So he didn't surrender to hope, and slip away to search for them outside. He went on looking here, in this desolation of dreams; and at last spotted something that was at least another guide for his eye, another of death's jesting clues.

The last time he'd seen it, the track of the roller-coaster had soared and swooped perilously over and under and between all the other attractions, the gaudy cars speeding round it in the shapes of dragons and unicorns, a catch for the eyes and irresistibly tempting. He couldn't count how many times he'd let Deena tease him into a ride, how many times he'd lied about her age to get her on; couldn't forget the way she pressed her warm little body against his, clutching at him for security and screaming with delight as they'd been thrown around the circuit once and then a second time, going faster with every passing second, rising and falling and hurtling through crowds of onlookers with a yell of laughter . . .

But that was then and this was now; and now the track had been torn apart by an explosion, the broken ends of it hanging above the hall, above a tangle of fallen cars and twisted rails. There were bodies there too, inevitably, teenagers and children caught inside the falling cars or tossed out as they fell. He could see one wide trail of blood leading away, where someone perhaps a little luckier than the rest had managed to slither out of the ruin and drag themselves off to live or die somewhere else.

But what caught Rudy's gaze and held it wasn't the piled wreckage, or the death it had created. It was a simple thing, a foolish thing: a yellow balloon tied to the shattered wing of a proud red dragon-car and jerking impatiently at its long string as it was pulled this way and that by the currents of air in the vast hall.

And sure, they must have given away hundreds, maybe thousands of those balloons today, and most of them to kids. He could see a couple more of them now, even, bobbing away up by the ceiling, far out of reach. But still his eye came back to the tethered one – which must have been tied there since the cars fell, and what for, what did it mean if it wasn't a sign? and a sign for him? – and there was a tremble in his legs so strong they could hardly carry him over the floor towards it.

Carry him they did, though, they had to. And when he reached it, when he stood by the dragon's snout he looked up for a second to track the balloon's movement back and forth, half wishing that he could stand forever like this, caught between one world and the next.

Then he looked down.

Liane lay at his feet with most of her body mercifully hidden beneath the crushed wreck of the dragon, nothing to be seen of her below her ribs. Her eyes were closed, but her mouth was open and moving slightly, giving him at least a little hope to mix with the horror. Her brown hair was clotted dark with blood, but he couldn't see any damage, any cuts on her drawn, pale face. Perhaps it was someone else's, the blood, that was something to hope for. Her T-shirt had been ripped open in the crash, and a flap of it had fallen back to expose one small, pale breast; and the first thing he did as he knelt beside her was reach out a shaking hand to give the shirt a tug, to pull it up and cover her again.

She must have felt that, or sensed him there some other way, because her eyes flickered slowly open. He saw the wide, dark pupils shrink against the light, and struggle to focus on his face.

"Rudy . . . " Her voice was a whisper, the most of it hidden like her body, maybe broken like her body; but it was enough for now. Enough to build a dream with. "I knew you'd come, Rudy. I said you would . . . "

"'Course I came." He touched her cheek lightly and snatched his fingers back, hating the chill he felt there and the message of it; then cursed himself silently and took her slack hand instead between both of his. Rubbed it, squeezed it, waited for a response and got none; saw how her eyes moved to follow what he was doing, and thought, *She can't feel it. Christ, she can't feel a thing . . .*

"Can you pull me out, Rudy?" she asked, in that cracked whisper. "Please? I can't do it, but you could. And then you could carry me out of here, I'm not too heavy for you . . . "

He looked again at the twisted steel of the car and how the edge of it was pressing so deeply into her stomach; and shook his head slowly. "I'm scared to try," he lied, "in case moving you brings it all crashing down again. We'll have to wait till the fire brigade gets here, they'll get you out."

"Okay, Rudy. I don't mind . . . " She coughed then, much louder and more harshly than she was speaking; and a little gobbet of mixed blood and phlegm shot out of her mouth and fell into her matted hair.

After that she couldn't talk at all for a while, breathing took all that she had to give. Rudy used the time to pull the jacket out of the bag he was still carrying, wad it up and slip it under her head for a pillow, the most that he could do. Except stay with her, of course, and there was no question about that.

Still one question that he had to ask, though, for all that he was sure now of the answer and terrified of hearing it.

"Liane, pet, where's – where's Deena?"

"I don't know. Gone . . . I'm sorry, Rudy, but I couldn't . . . I couldn't make her stay. I got her to . . . to leave her balloon on the dragon there, so's you'd know where to find me . . . but she was so scared, poor love, she just went running off . . . "

It was more than he could take in, at first. "You mean – you mean she's all right? She's not hurt?"

"No. I, I had my arms round her, see, when we fell . . . and she landed right on top of me. She wasn't trapped, like I am . . . and even her balloon didn't burst. But she, she wanted you, and I couldn't . . . I couldn't help her, I couldn't even hold her. It's silly, but I can't make my arms work." Another fit of coughing, and more blood leaking in a dribble from her mouth. She licked at it fretfully, gave the pain time to die a little. "After a bit she wouldn't wait any more, though I said you'd come, if we just waited . . . She was half out of her mind, with all the shock and everything, and me just lying here . . . So she said she was going to find you, and I couldn't make her stay. Just the balloon, that was all I could think of . . . "

"That was dead smart of you, sweetheart." And never mind the cold of her, or the white skin and the blood on her chin making her look like a vampire more than a girl, he bent over to kiss her anyway, in a flood of relief. "So where did she go, then, out after everybody else?" They'd look after her, sure they would, a little girl alone – and never mind that young boy dead in the stampede, that couldn't have happened to Deena. Not now, when he knew she'd been safe.

"No. I saw . . . I saw her go . . ." And she coughed again, and blood came spitting unheeded from her lips; and this time he could hardly bear the delay till she could talk again. "I said, she was looking for you . . . and she knew which way we'd come, where we left you. She went back."

Back. Back into the echoing, empty malls, with all the dead to scare her witless and no Rudy to find; and for all he knew the killer still haunting the place, still looking for a little more death . . .

He was on his feet again without having to think, and was held back only by Liane's voice, touched suddenly with panic.

"Don't leave me, Rudy . . ."

"I've got to, pet. I can't just let her go wandering out there, I've got to find her."

"No. She's okay, I told you she's okay. Someone'll look after her . . ."

"There isn't anyone there, Liane. It's empty, the whole place." *Except for the dead, and the dying.* "She can't handle that, she'll go crazy. I'm sorry, I've got to . . ."

"No!"

But he was moving already, starting to run once more with his mind reeling between grief and terror, between the knowledge of Liane behind him and the desperate hunt for Deena ahead. And it might be that he was running simply in order to find Deena more quickly, and spare her at least something of her dreadful walkabout. Or it might be that he was running in the hope – the dream – of getting back to Liane in time, before she died.

Or perhaps that was what drove him like a spur, the certainty that she really was dying there. Perhaps he thought he could outrun the certainty, find a little doubt somewhere if he could only move fast enough.

Then again, maybe it was none of those. Maybe it was simpler still.

Because she found her full voice, Liane did, as he moved

away; and she hurled it after him, like a hammer on the hard anvil of his soul.

Screamed his name, screamed, "Rudy! Don't leave me, Rudy! Don't leave me . . . !"

And maybe that's why he ran, only to get away from the girl he loved, only to escape her pain.

*   *   *

Carol Easterman had fallen asleep at last to the lullaby of television, murmuring at the foot of her bed; and it was television that woke her now.

Woke her with the sounds of gunfire, drawing her abruptly out of her dreams. Her eyes startled open, focused in bewilderment on the screen, saw the image of a man in close-up, his face hidden by a balaclava. Then he ran, and she saw the gun he carried, and the khaki back-pack; and as he disappeared out of shot, the camera pulled back to show glass and blood and people lying dead, a solitary child sitting bemusedly in the middle of it all. Carol swore softly, thinking it was just a film. Some story about terrorists or the SAS – if there was a difference – and nothing to touch her, nothing she wanted to see. Certainly nothing to be worth the waking up.

But even as she reached for the remote control, the picture changed. Cut to a man in shirtsleeves standing in a car park, facing the camera with a microphone in his hand and a long brick building behind him. And high on the bricks was an illuminated logo, and the name spelt out in neon beside it: *The Meldon Centre*.

Carol drew her hand slowly back under the covers, as the man spoke.

"What you've just seen was filmed an hour ago by one of our camera teams, who happened to be on the spot when this nightmare began. A little later I hope to be talking to Charlie Campbell, the man who took that footage, about what else he saw in there. Charlie was one of the last people to be evacuated from the Centre, and I gather was extremely lucky to escape with his life.

"Right now, no one quite knows what's going on. It's a scene of utmost confusion here; the police have a terrible job on their hands, trying to establish some kind of control over the situation. There are tens of thousands of people milling around, some in hysterics, many searching desperately for their families or loved ones, praying that they're not among the dead or injured. All the roads to the Centre are blocked, in both directions; the emergency services are having great difficulty getting here through the queues of traffic. The police have put a temporary ban on anyone else driving away from the Centre, in an effort to clear the roads, and they've appealed to the public not to come however worried they are about relatives who may be here. You are asked to be patient, stay at home, and call one of the emergency numbers, which we'll be giving you again in a few minutes.

"Regrettably, it seems that other people are turning up simply out of curiosity, coming to gawp. I spoke to Inspector Holborn about this a few minutes ago, and he said – "

At that point the reporter broke off to glance aside, apparently listening to someone out of shot; then he turned back to the camera.

"I've just heard that the Assistant Chief Constable has arrived by helicopter, and that he's on his way over now; also that Mr Johnnie Lee, the man who owns the Meldon Centre, is with him. We're not quite sure why they're coming in this direction, but I'll try to get a word with them . . . "

There was a minute or two of confusion then, as the reporter consulted again with his unseen colleague, and the camera's lens jerked away from him to scan the length of that windowless brick wing and the car park that fronted it, seeking and finally finding a small group of people walking hurriedly towards a pair of huge lorries emblazoned with the logo of Two Rivers Television.

The reporter intercepted them just as they reached the steps leading up into one of the lorries; and Carol heard fractured chunks of dialogue:

"Excuse me, can I just – "

"No time now, I'm busy – "

"This won't take a – "

"Later, there'll be a statement later – "

"Come on, out of the way, you, you heard him – "

"Mr Lee, could you spare me – "

"No comment. No bloody comment."

Fractured faces, too, the camera showed her those, people who'd reached the limits of their training or expectations and been pushed unexpectedly far beyond. It was a relief to see them vanish into the lorry, to see the narrow door slam shut behind them; Carol knew that look, but hitherto had only seen it on patients or their distressed relatives, confronted with cancer or Aids or one of death's other disguises.

The reporter faced the camera again, not unduly harassed by his failure. "Well, I'm sure we'll get a word with someone later on, as the situation develops; and hopefully, an explanation of why they're interested in Two Rivers' outside broadcast facility. But meanwhile, I think we can go over to Sally Roberts at the King George Infirmary . . . "

And the picture cut away to a view of Carol's workplace, another reporter standing outside Casualty with an ambulance just pulling up at the entrance behind her.

"Thank you, Tom. As you can see, the first victims are just beginning to arrive, with the expectation of many more to come in the hours ahead. No one's hazarding a guess yet about numbers; there's really nothing to go on. It could be that there are hundreds of dead and injured in the Centre still, but we just won't know until the police feel able to move in.

"Meanwhile, off-duty staff are turning up here in droves, as they are at every other hospital in the region. Doctors and nurses are flocking back without being asked, knowing that every ward here is already seriously understaffed, and that each extra worker could mean an extra life saved . . . "

Carol groaned softly, consulted her conscience and her feet. The former said yes, the latter no; and conscience was outvoted, two to one. For the present, she'd just stay in bed and watch television. If there really was a crisis, then she'd turn out for it. Maybe. But it hadn't happened yet, and the hospital could no doubt cope without her, for another hour or two at least . . .

1600:

and the emergency vehicles were coming through at last, as the police cleared every other car off the road to let them by. They came with blue lights flashing and sirens wailing, fire engines and ambulances, police vans by the score; and then – at least as far as Andrew could see – they did nothing.

He watched squads of armed policemen in flak jackets deploy themselves around the entrances to the Centre, finding cover behind low walls or parked cars, training their weapons on the doors; he saw others cautiously climbing the fire-escapes to take up positions on the flat roofs. But this was a purely defensive perimeter, an exercise in containment, and it kept the firemen and ambulance officers standing uselessly by their vehicles, well behind the guns.

The dead and wounded had already been removed from the ground outside the Centre, and one fire engine had dealt quickly with the blaze in the security complex, so that the bodies could be carried out. But that was only the tip of the iceberg. There must be dozens, might possibly be hundreds of victims inside the Centre proper, many of them urgently in need of medical attention if they weren't to join those who were dead already; and it seemed as though nothing was being done to reach them.

Andrew sighed, and walked slowly back up the metal steps of the pantechnicon. The inside was reminiscent of the wrecked control room, with its banks of monitors and the console in front, microphones on stalks and sliding switches; but this was narrower by far, more a corridor than a room. More cramped, and far more crowded. Bill Bruce was there, sitting at the console with a couple of assistants, though none of them was paying any attention to the pictures on the screens. Control had been patched through to Two Rivers' headquarters in the city, leaving them free for the moment to listen to Inspector Holborn, who was leaning over Bill's shoulder talking quickly. The Assistant Chief Constable was there with Commander Jakes, the man in charge of the armed officers, the Tactical Squad they called it. They were watching another rerun of the video showing the gunman inside the Centre, discussing his weaponry quietly between themselves. Johnnie Lee was there with his wife, looking for once utterly overtaken by events, his shoulders slumped and his stocky body seemingly shrunken, abandoned by the magnetic charisma and the self-confidence that had always been so much a part of his personality. No one was paying any attention to him. Even Linda seemed barely aware of his presence; though she stood at his side, her eyes were turned away to watch the video with an intense concentration.

" . . . What we want," Inspector Holborn was saying, "is the use of every camera you've got, that can be plugged into these screens. This place is simply too big for us to cover every exit properly; but if we can establish your cameras at judicious points around the perimeter, it'll be a great help. The one up in the airship, too, that'll be useful. We can control the whole operation from here, watching the monitors for any sign of movement and calling a squad in straight away if he shows himself."

Andrew vaguely heard Bill objecting about the danger to his camera crews, and the inspector offering reassurance; but he'd stopped listening already, started easing himself through the crush towards the far end, where one more figure sat hunched on the floor, hugging her knees, crushing herself as small as possible.

He crouched down beside her, reaching out his right hand to touch her shoulder.

"Dee? You okay?"

She lifted her head, and gazed at him dully. "Not so's you'd notice, no. I can't, I can't hack this . . . "

"You want to get out of here?"

She just shrugged, *nowhere else to go*. Andrew settled his back against the wall, hesitated, then slipped his arm loosely around her, all the comfort he could give.

"Where's your friend with the camera?"

"Charlie? He went off. Looking for his wife and kid. I told him to wait, I said chances were she'd come looking for him here, but he wouldn't stay."

"I'm not surprised. I don't think I could just wait around, if . . . " *If it was you.*

"Maybe, but it's still stupid, going off like that. It'll be a fluke if he finds them, there are so many people here."

"I don't know, love. What I heard, they're getting it well organised out there. They've got volunteers splitting every-one up alphabetically around the car parks, making lists, sorting out who's missing and chasing them down. He'll find his family all right."

"Well. I hope so." She chewed on her lip for a minute, then said, "I just can't take it in, you know? Something like this, it's too big to be real, almost. And, and I need to pee, only I don't know where . . . "

Andrew bit back on an unexpected laugh, said, "There's a portaloo, just outside."

"Is there?"

She still didn't move, though. Andrew thought that per-haps she was daunted by the crush of people between them and the door, or else more simply by the sheer fact of moving, of leaving the inadequate refuge of her corner.

Either way, he could help her in this at least. He pushed himself to his feet and reached down a hand.

"Come on," he said gently. "I'll take you."

As they squeezed past, Inspector Holborn was asking John-nie Lee about maps of the Centre, and getting a vague, listless reply. Andrew could have stopped, could have said that there were full architectural plans in his office, could have volunteered to fetch them at a run; but not with Dee's chilly fingers linked so tightly with his own. Not with her finally turning to him, his finally being able to give her something she needed.

*   *   *

Penny was alone in the cabin of the portaloo, had been there for quite a while now. And she wasn't planning to leave yet, not till she'd got her head together. Not till she'd forced down the panic, forced herself to *think*, to find another argument to throw at the police.

They'd spot her, she knew that, as soon as she went outside. She was well within the cordon here, close to the walls of the Centre itself; and if they found her before she'd had time to come up with something irrefutable, they'd just escort her away, behind the lines. "For your own safety, pet," they'd say; and that would be that. Julian's death, that would be, safe and sure.

She leant heavily on the stainless steel basin, staring at her reflection in the cracked mirror above. She could read the exhaustion on her face, and the shock that was still with her, that still had the power to set her body shaking and her mind skittering away. She could see streaks of blood still on her pale skin, despite the frantic cold-water scrubbing that had left her hair damp and that same skin tingling; and wasn't sure if those streaks were there for others to see, or if it was only her imagination that painted them in, a memory turned physical, coded into the cells of her body.

Above all, she could see her own failure writ large in her eyes, in her mind; could see it and relive it all in a moment. See herself finally finding a way out of the Centre, running over deserted tarmac till at last a policeman intercepted her, brought her to a group of senior officers. Hear herself gabbling out her name and her story, urging them to do something, to get in there and help Julian, help Richard; see them making notes, hear them saying it wasn't possible. Not yet, they said, not till they had a better picture of the situation. Waiting for orders, they said.

She'd begged, she'd pleaded, she'd got nowhere; and then they'd passed her on to a WPC to be taken away, to join the crowds beyond the cordon. So when she'd seen the portaloo, she'd snatched at the chance of a temporary haven the right side of the lines: somewhere to stop and think at least, maybe to find an answer, a way to get the boys out in a hurry.

She'd told the policewoman she had to use the toilet, and not to wait. "There must be other things you've got to do, and I, I could be a while. I can't join everyone else looking like this, I want to get the, the blood out of my hair . . . "

And then she'd run up the steps into the cabin, and locked herself in the single cubicle inside; and five minutes later, when she checked cautiously, the policewoman had gone.

But that was some time back. Penny had grieved for her dead friends and shivered joylessly over her own escape; had ached for Richard and wondered whether Julian still had so much as a fingertip's hold on life. And now she stared at herself in the mirror, met her failure eye to eye – and heard voices outside the cabin, footsteps coming in. She scuttled quickly into the cubicle, shoving the bolt across and realising the futility of it even as she did so, because there was only the one. Unless the newcomer just wanted to use the basin or the mirror she was sure to wait, and Penny couldn't simply sit it out without attracting the attention she was so eager to avoid . . .

So she perched on the toilet seat and waited, prayed to hear water splashing from the taps and those unwelcome footsteps going away again. And instead heard the cubicle door rattle, and a soft voice asking, "Is someone in there?"

Her breath caught in her throat, making a noise halfway between a sob and a snarl; and eventually, reluctantly, she said, "Yes. Just, just a minute . . . "

Stood up, hesitated, flushed the toilet; unlocked the door and walked out, to find herself face to face with a short, slim girl in dungarees, who wore her dark hair in a bizarre but oddly familiar Mohican.

The girl smiled faintly, and slipped past her into the cubicle. Penny let out a long, slow breath, and slumped uncertainly against the cabin wall. At least it wasn't a policewoman caught her lurking in here. Whoever this girl was, maybe she'd just use the toilet and go.

After a couple of minutes the toilet flushed again, and the girl came out. Again her eyes met Penny's, this time with a little controlled curiosity, a hint of surprise at finding her still there; and again a half-memory nudged at Penny's mind, that haircut with that face, something known about this girl, something she'd seen somewhere . . .

The girl went to the basin and washed her hands, shook the water off and reached for a paper towel. She rubbed vigorously, dropped the sodden paper into a wire bin, made for the door – then turned, and looked back.

"Are you all right?" she asked quietly.

Penny gave her a half-smile. "Got the runs," she said. "I'll have to go again, in a minute. No point leaving, really, I'd only have to come back."

"Oh. Right . . . " The smile was returned in full measure; and Penny had the impression that the girl might have added something more, in different circumstances. Just a word, female camaraderie at its lightest, "bad luck" or something like it. If they hadn't both known how untrue that would have been today: if to have been out here and in danger of fouling her jeans wasn't good luck stretched to its limits, a day like this . . .

So the girl smiled and said no more, and her heels clattered on the steps going down, going out. Where a man's voice greeted her, "Okay, love?"

"Yeah, I guess . . . "

Then he said something else, asked a question or made a suggestion: Penny caught the mood of uncertainty, but not the words. And after that she didn't hear any more, because her hands were clenched on the rim of the steel basin and she was back to staring at herself, hunting for a bit of resolution or original thought and finding nothing but guilt, nothing but failure and weakness. When you came right down to it, nothing but death.

*   *   *

Linda Lee stood in front of the monitor, conscious of the policemen's attention fixed on her, of her husband's disturbingly unfocused, straying away; and she shook her head.

"It could be. I don't know . . . Johnnie?"

He turned his head back, gazed at the screen, shrugged. "You know him best, Linda."

"Yes, but . . . " She sighed. "It's not clear enough, the picture. Not with that balaclava, you can't see anything but his eyes. And they're in shadow."

"Forget about the face," Inspector Holborn urged quietly. "Look at his body, the way he moves. The way he runs. You've been out running with him, your husband said."

"Yes." *And I know his body better than most, though I'm not going to tell you that. Or have you guessed? You're sharp enough* . . . She glanced at the inspector briefly, couldn't tell anything from his impassive expression, turned again to the monitor.

Linda was regretting already the question wrung from her after the fifth or sixth showing of this footage, the uncertainty that had driven her to say, "Johnnie, is that – is that Carl . . . ?"

The policemen had overheard, asked who Carl was, taken the possibility seriously. She'd explained that there had been an argument that morning, that Carl had disappeared from his flat when he was supposed to be with her. They'd phoned through to town, ordered a squad car sent out to check up on him; and now they rewound the tape and set it running yet again, trying to win a more positive identification from her, yes or no.

She couldn't give them what they wanted, though. Even suppressing her own strong desire for it not to be Carl, trying to judge clinically and objectively, she couldn't be sure. All she could do was shake her head, say, "I don't know. It might be, that's all. I'm sorry, I can't be any more definite," and turn away, fiercely hoping that they'd settle for that.

Behind her, she heard the Assistant Chief Constable say, "We could get the pictures enhanced, Frank. That might help. Set the technicians loose."

"Yes, sir. We'll do that, of course; but it takes time. We don't have the equipment or the men any closer than Leeds, we'll have to send the tape down to them. And I doubt we could expect anything useful back before tomorrow."

His superior grunted, and Linda felt Inspector Holborn touch her arm lightly. "In the meantime, I think this is worth pursuing, Mrs Lee. Maybe it's a red herring, but it's still the only lead we have. And I'm right, aren't I, that this Carl would know his way around here?"

"Oh, yes. He's spent a lot of time here, with me."

"Could he have bluffed his way into the security complex without you?"

"Probably. They'd know him by sight, I should imagine . . . Why don't you ask them? There's always a man on duty at the barrier."

"He's dead. We found him in his booth a little while ago. He'd been stabbed; most likely the first, as our friend went in. Or your friend."

That stung, as perhaps it was meant to. "It doesn't have to be Carl, you know," she snapped back. "It's only the combat jacket made me wonder, and hundreds of men wear those."

"Thousands," the inspector agreed. "But how many of them have got an insider's knowledge of this place? And how many have vanished from sight this morning?"

Linda shrugged helplessly. "Find out. That's your job. You should, you should check up on everyone who works here, see who else can't be accounted for . . . "

"Oh, we're doing that. It's a slow process, though. And while we're waiting, I'd like to talk to you, if you don't mind. In private," with a quick glance towards Johnnie. "I want to know a lot more about Carl, and especially the way he was acting this morning. That row you had."

"That was personal."

"I'm sure; but I'm afraid I'll still have to ask you about it. It could be important, you see."

Could have been the trigger, you mean, that pushed him over the edge? Linda thought about it, couldn't see it; but then, she couldn't see Carl as a mass murderer, either. Most likely no one ever could in the people they knew, even after it had happened; it would always be impossible to imagine of your brother, or your wife, or your son.

Linda nodded briefly, accepting the inevitable. *I'm going to tell you about it after all, aren't I, Inspector? Not that it'll be news to you.* And then, thinking of news, and newspapers: *Well, let's pray that I'm right, or wrong. Both. Let's pray that it isn't Carl. I can do this once, maybe, in private; but not in court. Not for the world, for the papers, for Johnnie to confront over breakfast. I couldn't, I wouldn't do that. Not for the world . . .*

*   *   *

Down by one of the car parks -- a long, slow trudge from the Centre, from the bench where Ivy had told him to wait -- the Coatman sat on the ground with all his coats drawn about him like a tent to exclude the world. Only his sunken eyes stared out from under his hood, to say that the tent was inhabited.

A long trudge it had been, a slow trudge, yes, with his feet aching already from the walk here and the coppers nagging at him, bullying, shoving him along. He hadn't wanted to move at all, Ivy had said wait and that's what he meant to do. That's what he told the coppers. But they swore at him and pulled him up, pushed him forward, said they'd carry him if he didn't walk.

So he'd done that, he'd walked: muttering and reluctant on his complaining feet while he cursed all coppers and all security men and everyone who'd ever turned him off. They'd brought him here, over the road and into a car park packed with people; and here they'd left him at last.

He'd turned his back on the hysterical crowds; pulled his hood up higher to cut out the sobbing, the occasional screams, the names being desperately shouted; and sat himself down by the roadside where he could watch the blurred and distant outline of the Centre, watch all the coming and going, watch for Ivy.

And now – still watching, as best his weak eyes would allow him – he heard footsteps coming from behind him. A firm, fast clicking of heels: *that* wasn't Ivy. So he didn't look round, not even when they stopped, when a woman's voice addressed him.

"Can I have your name, please?"

He didn't move, didn't speak. After a second the heels clicked again, and a pair of legs appeared right in front of his eyes.

"Um, excuse me, could you give me your name?"

This time he did raise his head, just far enough to see a middle-aged woman, smartly dressed, pen poised over a clipboard and her face frozen. Deliberately, the Coatman leant forward and spat a gob of yellow phlegm between her legs.

She scuttered back a couple of quick paces, half-turned to leave him; then took control of herself with a visible effort, and came back.

"I must have your name, please."

"Coatman."

"What? How do you spell that?"

"I'm the Coatman."

"Is that your name?"

"Coatman. Just you write that, write the Coatman." Names were a weapon and a power in this world, he'd thought that once today already, he thought it often. Long time since he'd given his old one away; certainly wasn't going to give it to some nosy old cow with a clipboard. The Coatman was enough. Enough for him, plenty enough for her.

"Well, all right." She scribbled, then said, "You should go to the blue car park, uh, Mr Coatman. If you wouldn't mind."

"I'm not moving."

"We're asking everyone from A to C to assemble in the blue car park. It's just a short walk, off to the right there; and it'll make it so much easier if everyone cooperates. People know where to look, then, for their families . . . "

"Got no family." *Not any more.* "You got Ivy down on that list?"

"Er, who?"

"Ivy."

"What's her surname?"

"Just Ivy." He didn't know her last name. Probably neither did she. Certainly she wouldn't give it out for the asking.

"Well, no, I haven't. This is G to I here, but I don't think we've come across an Ivy. We're not properly organised yet, though. And if she's looking for you, it'd be much better if you went where you ought to be, to the blue car park. Then when we do find her, we could tell her where you were . . ."

"I'm not moving." And, "You find Ivy. Fetch her here." And that was all. He spat again, *conversation over, nothing more to say*, searched among his pockets for his baccy tin, turned his head towards the Centre again. Watched for Ivy.

*   *   *

Coming down the steps from the portaloo, Denise found Andrew fidgeting uncomfortably, struggling with something inside himself.

"Okay, love?" he asked distractedly.

"Yeah, I guess . . ." She had half a mind to say something about the poor girl trapped inside with diarrhoea, just to lighten him a little, try to lighten herself; but clamped down hard on the temptation. It wasn't funny for the girl, that was certain. She'd looked terrible, under the harsh fluorescent lighting. And it was probably shock or sheer terror that had turned her bowels to water in the first place. Not a tummy bug, surely. Nothing so trivial . . .

So she said nothing, left the talking to him; and what he said startled her out of all sympathetic concern for the stranger, brought her sharply back to her own fears and distress.

"Look, Dee," he said, "will you be all right by yourself for a few minutes? Go on back to the lorry, you'll be safe there."

"Why?"

"Something I've got to do . . ."

She waited, but he didn't explain; so she said, "Well, what?"

"I want to fetch something from the office. Plans of the Centre, the inspector was asking about them. Might as well make myself useful."

"I'll come with you," she said flatly.

And, equally flatly from him, "No."

"Why not?"

"No point both of us taking chances." He gestured up at the high, blank walls above them. "No windows on this side, there's no danger of him taking pot-shots at you. But there's a couple of open entrances between here and the complex, and the garden centre, that's all glass. Stupid, to expose yourself to that . . . "

"You're going."

"Hey, look, I'll be okay." And, greatly daring, his hand slipped forward to rest reassuringly on her waist, where she let it lie, unprotesting. "I mean, the police are swarming all round there, they've got barricades of cars and sharp-shooters and everything, I'll be fine . . . "

"So okay, I'll come too. We'll both be fine." And when he shook his head, she went on urgently, "I just don't want to be kicking around here on my own, that's all. You're not the only one who needs to be doing something. And I've got no good reason to be here, now that I've told them what I saw. They'll send me back with everyone else, beyond the road there; and I can't handle that, it'll drive me crazy . . . "

She watched him hesitate, and cheated: lifted her hand to his wrist, slid it slowly up his forearm, fixed her big eyes on his face and whispered, "*Please*, Andrew . . . ?"

Hated herself for doing it, for taking such an unfair advantage of him; but it got her what she was after, as she'd known it would. As it had to.

"All right," he said, moving his hand again, taking hers lightly, as firmly as he dared. "Come on, then. But keep your head down, out in the open. Promise."

"Sure."

They made their way cautiously around the wings of the Centre; and hadn't gone far before they were stopped by a policeman in a flak jacket, with a rifle in his hands.

He asked who they were, where they were going; and when Andrew said they were on an errand for Inspector Holborn, he said, "All right – but I'd better come with you."

At his insistence they went the long way to the security complex, down to the road and around, keeping some distance between themselves and the Centre.

Once there, it took Andrew only a couple of minutes to unearth a cardboard roll of plans from his office; then they left the complex – with just a glance from Andrew at a smoke-stained door and the pooled water in the passage beyond, just a momentary tightening of his hand on Denise's to remind her that some of his friends had died there, that he'd come close to dying himself – and hurried back.

Their escort left them when they reached the safety of the walls. They headed towards the television vans; but as they passed the portaloo, Denise checked suddenly.

"Hold on a sec. There was a girl in there, she's not well; I just want to see if she's okay. Do you mind?"

"No, sure. Go ahead."

She ran up the steps into the cabin and found the girl there, right enough: caught her with a startled, defensive look on her face, halfway into the cubicle and moving fast.

"Sorry," Denise said. "Bad timing?"

"Uh, no, not really." The girl stood where she was, one hand on the cubicle door. "Did you, uh, were you looking for me?"

"Sort of. I just wanted to see how you were. I was thinking, if it's really bad there are dozens of doctors around, they must have something for an upset stomach . . . "

"Oh." The girl looked blank for a moment, then said, "Yes, but they'll be rushed off their feet, with all, with all that . . . "

"I don't think so. Everyone outside the Centre's been taken away by now, everyone who was hurt, I mean; so they're just hanging around, mostly. They can't get in yet, the police won't let them."

"I know that." And she knew it as more than hearsay, that much was obvious: Denise could see the knowledge stamped on every muscle of the girl's body, and the pain that came with it.

She's left someone in there, Denise guessed. *Someone she loves, someone she's frightened for . . .*

Aloud, though, she only said, "So how's about it, shall we go and find a doctor? I'll come with you, if you want."

"No. I don't need a doctor." That was confession more than denial, but a question followed it hard, before Denise could work out the implications. "Who – who *are* you, anyway?"

"Me? Denise Anderson. I work for Radio Nova. Why?"

"That's it. I knew I'd seen you somewhere. They've got your picture up in the foyer, haven't they, at the studio?"

"Along with everyone else's, yes."

"I remember yours," the girl said. "We were there to record a couple of songs, a few months back. For one of the daytime shows."

It was a strange conversation in the circumstances, in the surroundings; but Denise crushed her swelling curiosity, and simply asked, "Who's 'we'?"

"Me and, me and the band. Hot Ginger, we were called . . . "

And then the girl's face crumpled, and so did her legs. She clutched at the cubicle door, but couldn't find the strength to keep herself up; and by the time Denise reached her she was down on her knees, both hands still tight and white on the door's edge and her face buried in the crook of an elbow.

*   *   *

There are ways and ways, to search for a little girl lost in a vast and intricate chain of buildings. Rudy had done the sensible thing at first, moved quickly but quietly, retracing his own route more or less and checking the shops along the way, looking for places a child could hide in.

But he'd found nothing, no trace of her. He'd passed dozens of exits, and knew that Deena might have blundered out of any one of those by chance or design, might even have been taken out by someone else astray in the deserted Centre. She might easily be safe by now, outside and waiting for him . . .

But though he could hope for that, there was no way he could check up on it, no way he could be certain. Not unless he went outside himself, to look for her; and once out, he doubted if he'd be let back in again.

So he stayed, and went on searching; and passed slowly from a constant expectation, a forced confidence – *she'll be just around the next corner, of course she will, she's bound to be. Or if not, the corner after that. I'll find her, any minute now I'll find her. I'm her big brother, I always find her when she's lost or in trouble* – passed from that to a desperation that took him near to panic again.

Jesus, I've got to find her soon. I've got to. And safe. Not hurt, not . . . Jesus, no, not dead, not that . . .

But still he hadn't found her; and now he'd abandoned all his caution, left it behind somewhere with his confidence, with his hope. Now he was more than half lost himself and just running heedlessly, running without thinking, up one mall and down the next and shouting her name all the way.

"Deena! Deena, it's Rudy. Where are you? *Deena . . . !*"

He shouted until the name itself turned strange in his mouth, lost all its meaning and turned into a noise with no significance, except that he had to keep on shouting; and he ran until he couldn't run any more, until his legs were trembling and his ribs aching with the simple effort to breathe. And even then he couldn't stop, he couldn't stop moving; he dragged himself along the walls and staggered across the open spaces, and forced his ravaged throat to do it one more time, to make the noise that might yet work a miracle.

"Deena . . . ?"

And finally, finally he got a response. Not what he was looking for, not what he'd been straining his eyes so long to see: not his small sister stumbling round the corner with her arms held out and her shrill voice calling his name.

No, what he saw was a door opening where he hadn't even seen there was a door, a section of a long wall swinging back; and a man looking out, looking down the mall right at him.

Rudy stared back in a dazed confusion, startled beyond all reason. Then slowly, so slowly, his mind took in what the stranger was wearing, the combat jacket and khaki trousers, army boots; and never mind that the hands were empty. Alarm still stiffened Rudy's legs, terror still sent him bolting back, away, *get away, get out of sight and for God's sake keep quiet . . .*

So he ran again; not far this time, he couldn't, but seemingly far enough. Round a corner, down an escalator in five strides, almost falling at the bottom but somehow staying on his feet, ducking round another corner and into a shop. Finding a storeroom at the back, burrowing into the darkness of it like any animal at bay. Crouching behind a pile of boxes, trying to listen for footsteps and hearing nothing but his own breath whistling and screaming in his ears like a siren, like an advertisement, *here I am, I'm hiding. Count to ten, then come and get me . . .*

But no one came, though there was time enough to count a hundred, count a thousand or more. Time enough for Rudy to get control again, just a little, over his body and mind both. Time to lose the panic, and start to think.

He didn't have a gun. Maybe he wasn't the same guy, not the one I saw before. What if he's here to help – what if he's a real soldier, even, what if they've sent the army in? I could have told him about Deena, asked him to look for her. Christ, I'm never going to find her myself, not like this. She could be anywhere by now. I've got to get help; and I could've had it already, I bet that's what he's here for. If I hadn't been so shit scared . . .

At last Rudy drove himself out of the safety of his dark hiding-place and back into the malls. Not running now, and certainly not shouting, he scouted cautiously back up to where the man had come from, that unsuspected door.

Felt his way along the wall, and found the panel that moved; pushed his way through into a narrow corridor, looked both ways and saw nothing, tossed a mental coin and turned left.

Came to a flight of stairs and followed them down, found a service lift, an emergency exit and two more corridors. Another job for the coin, and heads again. Left again . . .

Soon he was as disorientated in these back ways as he had been earlier, when he'd stolen the jacket. He felt cold and depressed, cursed almost, surely punished. He was never going to find that guy again, or Deena – or if he did she'd be cruelly dead, just a limp bundle of rags and sticks in his arms, nothing of his sister left in her. And his fault, that would be. Like Liane, deserted in Dreamland – that was his fault, it all came back to him. He shouldn't have left them, before. And he should never have left Liane after, it had all been waste and loss; but if he went back now, if he made his way back to Dreamland he'd only find her dead too . . .

He wasn't even desperate any longer, only despairing; and so blinded, so gutted by it that it took a moment or two to register what he was seeing, longer to react.

There was a man standing poised in the corridor ahead, with his back to Rudy. A man pushing open another of those panel doors, peering out . . .

Rudy licked his lips nervously, and squinted against the harsh light. Made out the green and brown blotches of camouflage on his jacket; and decided that was enough. Right or wrong, he couldn't take any more of this.

"Hey . . . "

The man span round fast; and Rudy just had time to see that he'd got it wrong again, that this time the hands weren't empty. Full of rifle they were, and the rifle spitting loud . . .

1700:

and they'd shifted ground temporarily, from Two Rivers'
pantechnicon to the large police van now parked alongside:
leaving Bill's assistants behind, losing Bill himself as he went
off under escort to organise the moving of his cameras, but
adding Penny to their number. That had been Andrew's
idea, justified to the inspector by the information she could
provide on conditions inside the Centre. That was little
enough, in all truth, but little had to be better than none at
all.

So she was at a table, bent over a chart with Denise at her
side for company and comfort, retracing her route from the
Tudor Village. Reliving it in her mind and on paper, using a
red felt pen to mark in the approximate positions of the
badly wounded and the dead she'd passed on the way,
starting with her own friends in their hiding-place and
putting in too many, far too many small red crosses between
that and her final escape.

What she knew of the killer's path she had added in a
single dotted line in blue: a line that came from nowhere,
simply started in the middle of one mall, ran down to pause
in the open square (with a bracket beneath, the time he'd
got there; she'd been able to tell them that at least, more or
less accurately), and then went off at an angle, up another
mall.

Red crosses, and a blue line. Andrew peered over the
girls' shoulders, and wondered how Penny could bear to do
it: to reduce everything so far, to map the dead so neatly,
place and time . . . And scowled and moved away, reminding himself that she wasn't obliged to react according to his
expectations. Making maps was better than hysterics and
helplessness, more useful to everyone, herself included.
And there'd be time enough later to give the dead their due

memorial. When it was over, when they could be sure there were no more to be added to the list.

"I think it's time to move in, sir." That was Commander Jakes. "From here, as we said." He tapped another chart, picking out one entrance with his finger.

"Soon, yes. Get them ready. But watch your backs, Michael. Go slow."

"Oh, aye. Slow and careful, I'll see that the men understand that. We've got smoke and gas, we'll use those from the start. It'll not be easy, it's a warren in there; but we can seal the malls off one by one, and drive the bastard back. Flush him out, or pin him down in the end. I wish I knew how much ammunition he has left, but it can't be much. He's been . . . generous with it. I doubt there'll be much resistance from him now."

"Don't forget about all the service corridors," Andrew put in quietly. "If you're not careful, he could double back on you."

"Aye, we'll watch that. I'll put teams in there too. It'll be a question of liaison more than anything, making sure they don't get ahead of the men in the malls; but they've all got radios, and they're well trained for this. I think we can do the job."

"I'm sure of it. I – " The Assistant Chief Constable broke off, as a uniform sergeant came in hurriedly, breathing fast.

He looked around, spotted Inspector Holborn and came across.

"Something's going on, sir," in a quick, low voice. "At one of the fire-exits, just round the corner from here. It was open, and we saw someone moving inside. It could just be someone who'd got trapped, making their way out; but they're holding back."

"Any communication?"

"Well, we've got a loudhailer, we told them to come on out, good and slow; but we didn't get a response. They're still there, though, I'm sure of that."

"All right, sergeant. I'll come."

"I think it's a bloke, sir. And, I don't know, it's all shadows in there; but I thought I saw camouflage patches on his clothes . . . "

That report was enough to bring more than the inspector out. His seniors went with him, and so did Johnnie and Linda Lee; and as Andrew walked slowly after them across the tarmac, he found the two girls suddenly at his side.

"I want to see," Denise said. Beyond her, Penny's eyes said, *I don't want to be left alone*; and he nodded, and took Denise's hand because if they both got what they wanted, why shouldn't he? Her fingers hesitated fractionally, then clung tight; and her other arm slipped itself lightly around Penny's waist.

Linked like that, they followed around the wing of the Centre to a loading bay. No lorries here now: only a line of cars parked nose to tail across the access, armed police crouched behind the barricade, their weapons and their eyes trained on the far wall. Steel shutters twenty feet high closed off half a dozen loading-points; but in one corner were a pair of double doors painted drab green, with a sign on the brickwork above. *Fire Exit – Do Not Obstruct*, the sign said; and one of the doors was standing half open, letting a path of sunlight fall inwards across the concrete floor.

Andrew could see nothing moving in or around that track of light; but he and the girls ducked low as the others had ahead of them, and scuttled along crab-like behind the cars. He was half-expecting the three of them to be questioned and sent back, told impatiently to keep out of the professionals' way; but it seemed that no one had time to spare for them, at the moment.

At any rate they were left alone, unchallenged and utterly disregarded. Andrew counted that purely as good fortune, which might not last; and he pulled the girls down into the unoccupied shelter of a car two short of the people they'd been trailing.

"We'll stay here," he murmured. "Safe enough. And close enough to see . . . "

What they saw, a minute later, was Inspector Holborn rising far enough to rest a loudhailer on the roof of the van that gave cover to himself and his superiors.

"This is Inspector Holborn speaking." His voice crackled and boomed in the enclosed space, echoing back at them from blank walls. "There are armed police here. Walk out slowly, with your hands in the air, and you will be in no danger." A pause, during which nothing happened, no one moved. Then, "I repeat, there are armed police covering the doorway. Come out with your hands up."

No response.

"If you are hurt," the inspector's voice crashed out again,

"push the door open wider, so that we can see you. People will come to your aid. We have doctors and a stretcher available, if they are needed."

That was what the police were expecting, then, despite the sergeant's report; what Andrew himself expected, in his heart of hearts. Just another victim, who'd made it this far and then lost their nerve for the final stretch, in the face of guns and the vicious sunlight. Lost nerve, or lost strength. Andrew had a sudden mental vision of a crumpled body in the shadows just beyond the door, leaking its life away without the power to move again, even to show itself; and wished urgently for someone to be stupid enough to walk up to the doorway and take a look. Wished that he had sufficient courage – sufficient stupidity – to go himself.

And then bit the wish back, crushed it to death in his mind, as there was a movement in the darkness behind the door. A movement that resolved itself into a silhouette, a man: who came walking tall and strong out through the doorway, letting them all see his combat jacket – *top marks, sergeant* – and his khaki trousers, his army boots laced up ankle-high.

Letting them all see the child, the young girl in his arms.

He stopped, just two paces from the door, and stood still. One arm held the girl close to his chest, where she was clinging tightly, her face buried in his shoulder. The other hand stroked her pale hair, and Andrew had the impression that his lips were moving, that he was talking to her softly. Impossible to hear, of course, at this distance.

Not impossible to act, though, apparently; because he heard a quiet voice say, "I can get a head-shot, sir. Drop him right there, he'd never know a thing."

"No. Wait."

Inspector Holborn put his lips to the loudhailer again.

"Come further out, into the open, and put the child down. Do it now, and do it carefully. Move slowly at all times, and keep your hands where we can see them."

The man lifted his head, turned it to locate the inspector; and Andrew saw Linda Lee flinch, where she was kneeling on the ground staring over the boot of a car. A moment later he felt Dee nudge him gently, saw her lips move, read the message. *That's the man we saw, Charlie and me . . .*

"No," the man responded, in a shout paled by distance. "One of you comes to get her. Just one of you, alone. And no guns. She's scared of guns."

"That will not be possible. Do as I instructed. Walk into the centre of the bay, and put the child down."

"No."

"Then set her on her feet, and let her come to us. You stay where you are."

"She won't." There was impatience in the man's voice now, impatience clearly to be seen in the jerk of his head. "I said, she's scared. You have to come and get her." And when no one moved, he lifted his hand from her hair and spread the fingers wide, scorn rising high over that impatience. "Look, no guns. I won't hurt you. Just come and get her, will you?"

"I'll go, Inspector." That was the man who'd claimed he had a clear shot; Andrew recognised his voice, saw him flick the safety catch on and lay his rifle down on the ground, already halfway to his feet.

"No!" Commander Jakes. "Stay where you are. And pick up that rifle!"

Reluctantly, the man followed orders, his thumb shifting the safety off as he took careful aim again.

Time crawled by, second by dangerous second. The man stood in the doorway, and waited; the police crouched behind the vehicles, and waited. Andrew waited, and watched; and at last it was Denise at his side who broke the stalemate, broke the silence.

Who exploded suddenly, "For God's sake, she's only a bloody kid!"

Who pulled her hand free of Andrew's, and stood up; who scrambled between the cars, ignoring all the shouts and cries of warning, the orders to come back; who walked slowly forward through the bright day, towards the man and the child.

Andrew rose up on his haunches, his right hand clenched into a fist, a cold sweat prickling all over his body. His mind taunted him for a coward, his every instinct was urging him up and out, to go with her, to protect her; and it was only his common sense that held him back. That said she'd be safer going alone, that there was danger for her if the man saw him bursting out of cover and running forward. A girl on her own was no threat, surely, just precisely what the situation called for. She should be all right, she had to be, if he only stayed where he was, kept down and kept quiet . . .

So he did that, though it gutted him; and he watched, and saw Denise reach the man. Saw her small body park itself firmly in front of his, saw her reaching up to take the little girl, couldn't hear what passed between them as she did so.

Instead, he heard:

"Jackson?"

"Not a chance, sir. She's bang in the line of fire."

"All right. But keep tracking, be ready."

And wanted to scream at them, to tell them to put their guns down, all of them, not to risk an accident now. Couldn't find his voice, though, in the panic of the moment; and mercifully didn't need it, because no guns went off, there wasn't an accident or a deliberate shot from a man with no orders and an itchy trigger-finger. Denise took the girl, and settled her on her hip; turned, and began the long walk back with her head bent down to the child's ear, hugging her close and murmuring to her, not looking at all where she was going.

And behind her, the man ducked quickly back through the doorway and into the darkness, exploiting the shield of her oblivious body for that last crucial second. He was gone before anyone could call out to stop him; and now Andrew did move, heedless of the chance that this was all a trick after all, that bullets might suddenly come blasting from the shadows inside. He edged between the cars and sprinted up to Denise, his urgent fingers desperate to hold her, to shake her, his tongue to swear at her for taking such a risk; but she just blinked up at him, squinting against the sun. And the calmness, the rightness on her face left him bereft again, reminded him that he had no rights where she was concerned; and all he could do was mutter, "Do you want me to take her?"

"No. Of course not."

"She's not too heavy?"

"She's fine."

Denise dropped her head again, kissed the little girl's hair and said, "Come on, sweetheart, tell me what your name is. I'm Denise, and you're safe now, I'll look after you, there's nothing to be scared of any more . . . "

And the girl looked up, wide-eyed, her face pale under a coating of filth; and said, "I'm Deena."

And looked at Andrew, blinking; and looked around, and said, "Where's Carl?"

*   *   *

Julian's watch bleeped softly, on Richard's wrist. He switched the alarm off with fingers that trembled slightly, and checked the time to be sure it wasn't playing up. Hard to believe that another hour had passed already, that he had it all to do again. But he couldn't argue with the figures showing clearly in the bright shop light, the seconds that flicked away in front of his eyes.

So he sighed, slipped his hands under Julian's cold head and lifted it off his lap, moved it carefully onto a pillow of camouflage jackets. Shivered, and rubbed his palms on his trousers, to wipe off the chilly sweat that had dampened the boy's short hair and left it clinging to his scalp; then pushed himself effortfully to his feet.

He stretched, to ease his cramped and complaining muscles. He shook his head sharply, against the muzziness of shock and his own uncertainties. He curled and uncurled his fingers, to work some life back into them; above all, he needed them strong and sure.

And then, still doubtful but determined, he knelt again beside Julian, and lifted back the heaped coats and jackets that blanketed his legs.

It was difficult with the boy lying on his back, he couldn't see what he was doing; but this was the second time, and he reached under his lover's thigh almost without hesitation. Felt for the biro in the wire, and found it; lifted the leg an inch with his other arm, and began to untwist the tourniquet.

It was Penny who had started this, Penny's words reinforcing something he'd read himself about the danger of leaving a tourniquet on too long. Richard had had time to think since she'd left him, time to remember. Too much time: endless minutes ticking away, while he watched and waited for her return, for the help that never came.

He'd taken Julian's watch, for lack of one himself, and kept an eye on it; and after an hour, he'd steeled himself to do this. Done it nervously, clumsily, not knowing if he was saving Julian's leg or killing Julian. But the boy had seemed no worse afterwards, if no better; and now – still alone, still no sign of rescue – he was doing it again. No wiser, only a little more practised.

He turned the biro stolidly until the guitar-string lay loose on Julian's skin, like a snare unsprung. A glance at the watch, and he moved his hand a few inches, to lie cupped beneath the great hole in Julian's flesh. After a minute, blood began to drip onto his fingers. A noise forced its way out of his throat, half grunt of satisfaction, half moan of fear; but he waited, watched the time, forced himself to let the blood flow for five minutes before he tightened the tourniquet and covered the leg again, moved back to lift Julian's head to its place on his lap.

Five minutes in every hour: that's what he'd decided on, and that's what he'd stick to, whatever it cost him. Whatever it cost Julian. He reset the alarm on the watch, to keep him to it; turned his eyes to the shop window and prayed for someone to come before the next hour was up, before he had to play God again.

Leaning his head back against the shop wall, he felt the ventilator blowing cold, conditioned air against his back. He'd already borrowed yet another of the thick padded jackets from stock to keep himself warm against that constant flow, and had set himself deliberately in front of it to shield Julian.

Now, though, the air was bringing something more than chill with it. A freak of the system handed a gift to Richard, his first contact with the world outside: just the briefest of contacts and strictly one-way, but still enough to reassure him that the world hadn't actually gone away.

He heard a noise, a dull clatter that grew louder, that hung for a few seconds on the artificial breeze. A moment's frowning thought placed it, identified it in his mind; and he licked his lips, and explained it softly to his unheeding lover.

"Helicopter, that was," he murmured. "Police, I expect. What you might call a pork chopper. Pigs might fly. But at least we know they're there." And then, as the double edge of the gift bit deeply, as he laid his hand for a second on Julian's brow and tried to will some of his own body's heat into the cold skin, the colder bone beneath: "So if they're there, why the hell don't they come? What's keeping them?"

And his question was answered by another sound, footsteps dimly heard. He lifted his head, and froze; watched through the glass door with fearful eyes as a figure moved among the bodies in the square.

A figure in combat gear, with a pack on his shoulder and a rifle in his hand.

*   *   *

The little girl sat damply on Denise's lap in the pantechnicon, on a chair pulled back from the console, as much out of
the way as they could manage.

The police had tried to take the girl away, in the hectic
minutes after the exchange in the loading bay. They'd said
there was a tent for lost and abandoned children, and a WPC
had come to add Deena to her list of charges; but Deena had
screamed, clung to Denise's neck and refused to go.

In the end it had been Andrew who'd resolved the stand-
off, at least temporarily. He'd pointed out that Deena could
be useful, that even her child's-eye view of the situation
inside the Centre could add to their tally of information.
Inspector Holborn had acquiesced, to the point of asking
Denise to get the child settled enough to answer a few
questions; and had brought her here to the TV van to do it,
saying that he wanted to conduct an experiment, when they
were ready.

The questions had established that Deena's full name was
Nadine Bellamy; that she'd come to the Centre with her big
brother Rudy and his girlfriend; and that she'd been on a
walkabout through hell – "looking for Rudy, 'cos Liane was
hurt, like everybody" – when Carl found her. Carl was nice.
He cuddled her, and said he'd take her away from the scary
place and all the hurt people. Then he'd brought her out,
and promised that Denise would look after her; and please,
she wanted Rudy now. She wanted him *now*.

She'd said all that to Denise in a tight, strained little voice,
worn out from too much crying, too much fear. Inspector
Holborn, eavesdropping from a yard away, had grunted,
and fiddled with the console controls for a minute to produce a freeze-frame close-up of the killer on one of the
monitors.

Then he'd said, "Deena? Look up a minute, pet, and tell
me if this is Carl. If this is what he looked like, the first time
you saw him."

Deena had looked up hesitantly, squinted in confusion at
the screen – and screamed, and buried her face in the bib of
Denise's dungarees.

"Satisfied?" Denise had snapped in a raging fury at his
unsympathy, wrapping both arms round the trembling little

girl and rocking her gently to and fro.

"No," bluntly. "That tells us nothing. A 'yes' would have been useful; but 'no' would still have had a question-mark over it, and she hasn't even given us that much. So okay, she saw a man like this," his finger stabbed at the monitor, "and she's terrified of him. Of course she is; if she saw him, she probably saw him shooting. And then she saw Carl later, and he was *nice*." With a sour emphasis on the simple word. "It doesn't mean they weren't the same man. If he'd left the gun somewhere and taken the balaclava off, she'd never know."

"That doesn't make sense," Denise had protested, speaking over Deena's head, literally and she hoped metaphorically as well. "If he'd killed all those people, why the hell would he take the risk of coming out like that, just to rescue a lost girl? He'd be more likely to strangle her."

"Not necessarily. Maybe he's out of ammo, and he doesn't want to dirty his hands. Or maybe he's cleaned himself out with all the shooting, and he's coming down off the rush. He's had his thrill, and now he's just tidying up in there, making sure he's got the whole place to himself. Him and his dead." The inspector had shrugged, and rubbed at his temple with a wince. "Christ, if I don't know why he started, how should I know why he's stopped? Ask the psychiatrists. It gives me a headache just thinking about it. All she's told us is Carl was nice to her; and I'm sorry, that's not enough."

Denise had snorted, and dropped her cheek onto Deena's fine hair; had crooned to her softly under her breath, had held the small body close, had been only distantly aware of the inspector's heavy footsteps departing.

And now – five minutes later? ten? – she was still sitting there, still holding Deena; and the little girl was just starting to pull herself back from nightmare. Turning her wet face up towards Denise's, rubbing clumsily at her eyes, whispering, "I want Rudy. *Please* I want Rudy . . . "

"I know you do, pet. People are out looking for him, I promise. They'll find him for you." *If he's here to be found, if your nightmare's over yet.* "It'll take a bit of time, though. There's an awful lot of people out there, and he could be anywhere. You'll just have to be patient. Go on being brave, like you have been . . . "

Deena sniffed, and nodded dubiously. Then she wrapped

the fingers of one hand tight round a dungaree strap and said, "Your name's like mine, isn't it?"

"That's right," giving her a big smile, a reward for being brave. "You're Deena, and I'm Denise. It's even more like, when I'm talking to Andrew. He calls me Dee, and that's ever so like Deena."

"Rudy calls me Dee. Sometimes he does." She was obviously pleased with this. "Is Andrew your boyfriend?"

"Er, no, pet. He's just a friend." *Poor bastard.*

And then there was a shout from one of the women still at the console, and a hasty, muttered conference with an overseeing policeman, who went outside at a run shouting for the inspector. Denise stood up curiously, shifted Deena's weight onto her hip and walked the couple of paces over to the woman's shoulder.

There was a live screen in front of her, relaying pictures from a newly-positioned camera. One picture, rather, a wide view of the Centre from the riverside. Showing in the foreground the familiar barricade of vehicles, the crouching police, the pointed rifles and handguns; and beyond them, so small an image it was only the quality of these monitors that allowed her to see it, an emergency exit standing open.

A man standing in the exit, with another figure in his arms . . .

Then Denise was shouldered roughly out of the way, as the inspector came charging back in with others behind him.

One glance at the screen, and then, "Yeah, we've got it," snapped into the radio he was holding. "Stay back, don't do anything. Ask him who he is, what he's up to. And tell that cameraman to give us a close-up, if he can. He's just a matchstick from here."

But the cameraman was doing that already, from instinct or professional pride, or else an understanding of the need: zooming in to give them a reasonable view of the man's actions. It was the same man, that was obvious; they didn't need Deena's interested comment, "That's Carl. He's helping someone else now, isn't he?" to identify him. Didn't need the radio's commentary to tell them that he was laying the figure – a woman, they could see that much, and see also that she was badly injured, too hurt to walk on her own – quickly but carefully down on the ground in front of the exit.

And didn't need the curses that came over the radio then, or the thin voice that underlay the curses, the vain commands for him to stand still and explain himself, to tell them that the man had turned and vanished back into the Centre again.

"Well, is he or isn't he?" That, from the Assistant Chief Constable: a question which Inspector Holborn could do nothing but shrug off, unanswered and unanswerable.

"I don't know, sir. But send the men in. Let's get this over."

*   *   *

Rudy didn't like it, when he opened his eyes. Keeping them shut was better. Not seeing the bent legs, the white trousers with the great dark stain on the hip; nor the glimpses of T-shirt, black-red and sodden. Nor the pool of blood trapped between leg and chest, especially not that. That was best, not to see the pool of blood. Not to see it spreading.

But he'd done that for a long time now, kept his eyes closed against the truths his body was telling him. And he couldn't do it any longer; he couldn't just lie there and drift away.

With his body smashed like this, maybe past repairing, he'd lost all the urgency that had sent him hunting for Deena. She was alive, or she was dead; that was out of his hands, almost out of his thoughts. Big brother couldn't help her this time.

All he wanted now was to get back to Dreamland. Maybe it wouldn't be too late, even yet. Maybe he could still catch Liane before she'd gone too far. Maybe they could go together, the two of them, hand in hand in Dreamland. He'd like that.

So he forced his eyes open, and kept them that way. Looked at himself dispassionately, trying to work out the damage; and couldn't, didn't know enough. Nothing to do but try.

He moved an arm, a hand. Placed it flat on the floor, and pushed.

Lifted his body an inch, two inches up; and suddenly knew a lot more about the damage. Fell back sweating, biting his lip hard, not to scream. Waited, counted his heartbeats from five to ten to twenty; and tried it again.

And again, and again. Getting a little higher each time, and learning a little more.

Eventually he had himself sitting up, sagging against the wall; and stayed that way for a while, just breathing. Breathing was difficult, and it hurt. It hurt a lot more now he was upright. His T-shirt was soaked, it was dripping; so he decided not to look at that any longer, certainly not to look underneath.

Instead, he looked at his legs. Thought about them slowly, all the way down from hips to feet; and finally tried to move one.

This time, he did scream.

Screaming was good, though, he realised that almost straight away. It fooled the hell out of the pain. You moved, you started to scream; and you could move a lot more while you were screaming. The pain didn't notice, it was too busy listening to the scream. Licking its lips, enjoying itself.

Soon he had both legs lying straight out in front of him. He'd had to help one with his hands, it wasn't working too well; but it was there, next to its mate, neat and straight and ready for action. He thought perhaps the hip was shattered on that one, it would explain the blood and the reluctance to do what he wanted. That was okay, though, he didn't need them both. He could hop, if he had to. He won a hopping-race at junior school, one time.

Well, maybe he could hop. It was a theory, anyway.

He bent the other leg, the good one; pulled it right up, knee under his chin and foot flat on the floor. Put his hands back against the rough solidity of the breeze blocks behind him, rested, closed his eyes — *just for a second, honest* — and started to work his way up the wall.

It took a long, long time. It took a lot of sweat and shivering, a lot of crying, a lot of air; and that was almost the hardest thing, getting air enough to make it all the way. He had nothing spare to scream with. Too bad, that was.

But he got there in the end: standing on his one shaking leg, feeling that good cold wall biting at his back. Watching the blood find new paths to follow down his trousers, red snail-tracks across the white.

Then he thought about hopping. He thought about it for a while, taking his time; and felt dead pleased with himself for figuring out what the problem was in advance, before he tried it.

Problem was, he was going to fall over. Not the first hop,

maybe, maybe not the second; but he would, sure thing. It was a tumble just hanging around, waiting to happen. And when it did, he'd have all the getting-up to do over again.

So he didn't hop, no. He inched and wriggled, heel and toe along the corridor, keeping his back and his hands firm against that lovely clinging wall, leaving splodges and streaks of blood to mark his trail. Drips and smears on the floor, too: drips when he managed to keep his bad leg up in the air, smears when he didn't, when the toe dragged.

It was a slow way to travel – *never going to catch her at this rate, Rudy boy. She'll be well gone, cold and gone* – but travel he did, all the way down to the door. Rested again, when he got there; then gentled it open with his fingers, reached around, caught at the wall on the other side and pulled himself through.

Still a long way to go, much further than he'd come. Much, much further. And his head was swimming already, swam a little more as he thought about the open spaces he'd have to cross between the malls. No walls to hold onto there. Maybe he'd have to try the hopping after all. And if he fell – no, let's be sensible, *when* he fell – well, he'd just have to crawl, that's all. Pull himself along on his arms, use his good leg to push a bit. He'd get there if he had to slither on his belly; and it might come to that, even. Slither and scream.

His bad leg, now that was going to be difficult. More difficult, it was difficult enough already. Loose, it felt. Swinging around.

Still, maybe it'd work itself all the way loose, and just fall off. Then he could leave it behind. That'd solve the problem. Wouldn't hurt so much, then. If it wasn't dragging.

He tried to think which way to go, which way was Dreamland. Wasn't sure, so turned right, towards where he could see a concourse, a bank of escalators. There'd be a map there, that'd get him straight.

After a bit he realised that he was backtracking, reversing the way he'd come on the other side of the wall. *Would've been quicker to just walk through it*, he thought; and giggled.

And was still giggling when a hand closed firm on his shoulder.

His head jerked round, hard enough to make his neck snap, almost; and he lost the perilous balance he'd been clutching, and started to fall.

Would have fallen, if the man in the combat jacket hadn't

caught him, and held him upright.

"Easy, mate. Just hang on, I'll get you out."

Dark eyes, and cropped dark hair. No smile, and no particular gentleness; just strong arms, and a solid grip. Just what he needed.

"Which . . . " Rudy stopped, took another of those problematic breaths, and tried again. "Which way is Dreamland?"

"Eh?" The guy frowned, then shrugged a little. "In here, out there. What's the difference?"

"That's . . . that's where I'm going."

"Nah. You're going to hospital, mate. I'll get you outside, then they'll look after you. No sweat."

"*No!*" Breath enough to shout, a little. "I don't want to go out. Got to get to Dreamland. Catch Liane."

"Oh." The frown cleared slowly. "You mean the fairground place, where the kids go?"

"Yes."

"Look, you need help. They got doctors out there . . . "

"No. I need . . . to get to Liane. Catch her, quick."

"She won't be there. There's nobody here now."

"She's there. I've seen her." And when the guy still looked stubborn, shook his head unbelieving, Rudy finally found the right words. "She's trapped, in the wreckage. She's dying. I want to see her."

"You're not in any great shape yourself, kid."

"I know . . . I know that. It's what I want."

"But . . . Okay, what the hell. I'll get you there." With an arm round Rudy's shoulders, the man stooped, put the other behind his knees. Straightened easily, carrying Rudy like a child; and did smile now, just a little, as he started to walk down the mall.

As he said, "It's your funeral, mate. And I'm not kidding, either."

1800:

and awake again – solidly and permanently awake by this time, no hope of dozing off again, of finding succour in dreams – Carol Easterman was still in bed, still resting her feet.

Still watching television.

They'd been filling in for the last couple of hours, showing reruns of old quiz games and travel programmes; but every half-hour or so they'd cut in with newsflashes between the pap, on-the-spot reports from the Meldon Centre and the local hospitals.

And now – as she munched mechanically on a bowl of cereal, with a cup of tea waiting to follow, and a bar of chocolate – now they'd gone back to the Centre one more time, with promises of something more exciting for their eager viewers, action at last.

On the screen, there was an increasingly familiar view of the Centre from a distance, with dark figures milling around one entrance; and over that a sharp, edgy commentary:

" . . . What we've heard, what we believe is that squads of armed police are finally ready to move into the Centre. As we understand it, that's what you're seeing now, the final preparations before the operation begins. I'm sorry that the pictures aren't clearer, but the police won't allow us any closer to the building. Through my binoculars, though, I can see men checking their weapons one more time, others fitting gas-masks over the balaclavas they wear for security reasons. I'm told that they're hoping to use tear-gas to flush the perpetrator out. It'll be a long, slow business, though, we're assured of that. No one knows where in this vast complex the man may be hiding; and the police are desperately anxious to avoid any more deaths, particularly among their own men.

"Further back from the entrance, I can see teams of

doctors and ambulance staff preparing to follow the police in, to bring out the dead and wounded. There are helicopters standing by to ferry the critically injured directly to hospital, as well as a fleet of ambulances for the less serious cases.

"One curious fact that has come to light in the last few minutes is that there seems to be a man operating independently inside the Centre, helping people to escape. He's been seen on at least two occasions, bringing out a little girl and an injured woman. We understand that the police filmed him doing so, using the cameras commandeered from Two Rivers Television; and we're hoping to obtain the tapes to show you later. The man has been provisionally identified, according to Inspector Holborn, though his name has not been released; there's even a suggestion that he may be the gunman himself, though no one has yet explained why, if so, he should be helping people to safety. I –

"Wait. I think there's something happening at last. Yes, I can see men moving up into the Centre now, through this wide entrance-way they've chosen as a starting-point.

"They're walking in quite calmly – slow and watchful, but with no visible air of urgency or danger. They're going in in single file, with perhaps as much as ten yards between one man and the next; and there are two lines of them, one keeping to the left-hand wall and the other to the right. I make it a dozen men in each line, with more assembling behind them.

"There are stretcher-teams moving forward now as well. I don't think the police are going to allow them in just yet, but it surely can't be long before they start to bring out yet more victims of this insanity. At the moment, no one is venturing an official figure on how many may have died in the slaughter; unofficial estimates vary widely, from as low as thirty to a high of over one hundred. The police say it's proved impossible to build up an accurate picture from the accounts of the shocked survivors. It seems that the only limiting factors will have been how much ammunition the killer had with him, and the man's own psychological condition: to put it bluntly, how many deaths it will have needed to satisfy his blood-lust. And that, of course, no one can answer yet. It may be, it may well be that he's still not had enough: that so long as he has bullets or grenades to spare, nothing will stop him short of his own death or disablement.

"So there's no question about it, the police are going to be very careful indeed. I understand that their men have been instructed to respond immediately, if they should come under fire. The Assistant Chief Constable has said that while he would of course prefer to bring the man out alive, he's not prepared to risk the life of any one of his men to achieve that. And to be frank, from what I've gauged of the mood here, I think it's very unlikely that we will see the perpetrator coming out on anything except a stretcher, with a blanket over his face. I wouldn't say that any of these men going in are trigger-happy, they're too well-trained for that; but they're excellent shots, and they've been here all afternoon, they've all seen the bodies being cleared away and the distress on the survivors' faces. They all know what to expect inside, many more bodies and more suffering; and their mood is very, very grim.

"There are two more squads lining up now, following their comrades inside. I wonder what's going through their minds as they pass out of the sunlight and the fresh air, and into deadly danger. They're all so unnervingly quiet, so calm. There's no one shouting, no one running or diving for cover against anticipated bullets. Watching them, I'm reminded of my time in Northern Ireland, the armed patrols I've seen through Bogside and the Falls Road; and I think there's no doubt that the lessons of Ulster have been well learned, and are in operation here. Keep close to the walls, keep a good distance between you and your mate ahead, so that one burst of fire can't catch you both; and keep alert. Keep calm, but keep alert. Be aware that a bullet can come from any direction, at any time . . . "

*   *   *

Desperate though he was, half crazy though he knew himself to be, Charlie Campbell was nevertheless playing things very cool. He'd have to, to get back through the police cordon.

He stood on the verge of the perimeter road, with hundreds – no, with thousands of others, the punters trapped here and the curiosity-seekers come to gawk. They were watching the action, most of them, the ones who weren't turned stupid by grief and hope mixed, who weren't staring blindly at the blank brick walls; but not Charlie. He was watching the guards, the young constables set here to keep the public back behind the lines.

Specifically, he was watching the two nearest to him, the obstacles he had to evade. He'd been biding his time for half an hour or more, his interest camouflaged by the crush of people around him; and at last the long wait had paid its dividends. One of the two had been utterly distracted by what was going on behind him, to the extent of turning his back on the crowds and gawping with the best of them; while the other was temporarily besieged by an urgent crowd of pressmen, struggling to hold them back with one arm while he manipulated his radio with the other, calling for reinforcements.

Now was his chance; and Charlie took it, walking briskly but steadily forwards, over the road and onto the grass beyond. Not looking back, not allowing any doubt to appear in his own mind or anyone else's: simply a man with a mission, who had every right to be where he was and to go where he was going.

And just to confirm that to any questioning observer, he headed straight for the heart of things, the police command unit that they'd set up in and around the Two Rivers' pantechnicon.

He had an excuse, if he were stopped and challenged *en route*. He'd heard that the police had annexed all the cameras, to give the men in control an overview of what was happening; they were using Two Rivers' crews to man them, and Bill Bruce to keep charge at the console; and Charlie was looking for Bill, to volunteer. No one could argue with that. He was a trained cameraman, and he could quite legitimately offer to take over for a while, give another guy a break.

As it turned out, though, he didn't need the excuse. No one asked him his business before he reached the high-sided lorries; and standing outside the police's own big van he found a small group of people he recognised, civilians like himself.

He joined them quietly, nodded to Denise and the guy, what was his name, Andrew, and said, "You're still here, then?"

"Yes." Denise sighed, and pushed a hand through her drooping Mohican. "No one's asked us to go, they're all too busy, or else they think we might still be useful, somehow; and, well, I'd rather be here than back there." She gestured vaguely towards the milling crowds Charlie had escaped from. Then, remembering, "Did you – did you find your family, Charlie?"

"No." And now, having to say the word, he felt the despair rising again inside him; despair and certainty, an overwhelming conviction. "No, they're not there. I've been all around, where they ought to be and everywhere else, and no one's seen them, no one knows . . . " He looked up at the massive weight of the Centre's walls, and shivered. "They're in there, still. They have to be."

"Not, not necessarily. Maybe they got out early enough, and got away . . . "

"No. Sue wouldn't leave without telling me she was safe." He had no doubt in his mind now, and little hope. To make that clear, to make himself clear, he went on in a soft, steady voice, "I'm going back inside. I have to find them."

What surprised him then, insofar as he still retained the capacity for surprise, was that no one reacted particularly to that. Andrew grunted, and Denise said nothing at all; she only looked sideways at the other member of the group, a girl Charlie hadn't seen before.

"Me, too," the girl said. And when Charlie blinked, when he looked the question at her for lack of words, she explained. "I've left friends in there. And one of them, he's badly hurt. He needs help, that's why I came out, to get it for him; and no one would do anything, they just said wait. I know the police are going in now, but I've been looking at the maps and listening to them making plans, and it could be hours before they reach my friends. That's too long."

She stopped for breath, looked around at the others, and seemingly got a silent permission to go on. "It's not so far, from here to where they're hiding. I know the way, I checked it a dozen times on the map. And with four of us it'd be easy, if we can just get hold of a stretcher. We could go in, pick them up and come straight out again; it wouldn't take ten minutes. And it's so big, this place, the odds must be hundreds to one against, against running into anyone in there . . . "

"I'm not coming out again," Charlie said. "Not once I'm in. Not till I find Sue, and the baby. But – aye, I'll come with you, if you want. I can help with the stretcher."

"We've got to get one first," Andrew pointed out. "That's not so easy, we can't just walk up to one of the first-aid stations and take it. They'll have questions to ask."

"Say someone's fainted," Charlie suggested, "and we can't bring them round."

"No good, we thought of that. They'd come themselves. There are too many of them here, with not enough to do. And we can't wait till they're all busy. That'll be a long time yet, and then they'll be needing all their stretchers."

"No. We can't wait." Charlie thought for a moment, said, "Do we have to take a stretcher in with us? Can't we find one inside somewhere, or fake one? All we need is a couple of poles, and something to go across them. Coats would do."

Andrew stiffened suddenly. "Christ, but I'm stupid! Of course there are stretchers in there. There are first-aid rooms with everything you can imagine. And I've got keys for everything now. It'll add something to the time, mind; but I can find one, for sure."

"Right. So how do we get inside?" That was the all but insurmountable problem, as far as Charlie could see; the one he'd been beating his brains against for a long time now. He might have been able to dodge the kid policemen in the cordon, to get this far; but the four of them could hardly saunter past the barricades up here with a word and a casual wave.

"Andrew gets us in," Denise told him. "He says he knows a way that isn't watched."

"Oh, aye?"

"There are advantages to working here. And having keys." Andrew jingled those keys, where he'd hung them from a loop on his belt, and looked around the group. "Are we really going to do this, then?"

"Yes." Positively, from the girl – Charlie still didn't know her name, but this wasn't, this really wasn't the time to ask – and from Charlie himself. Denise hesitated, or waited for those explicit confirmations, and then nodded.

"Okay. Everyone ready? Then let's go, let's do it."

*　　　*　　　*

Carl – Rudy had got that much out of the guy, at least, learnt his name if nothing else – Carl wasn't particularly gentle, carrying Rudy through the malls. Not deliberately rough, either, just ungentle. Uncaring, maybe, simply not bothered that Rudy was hurting.

He was strong, though, he had that much going for him. And he knew his way around. Rudy watched the bright shop-fronts go past as Carl picked his way through the massive complex, slow but certain; and gradually his sluggish mind noticed something else about the guy.

"You're not scared." It came out as a statement, rather than a question.

Carl glanced at him briefly, said, "No."

"Why not?"

A smile, almost a smirk. "What's there to be scared of?"

That, said as they bypassed a huddle of bodies. Rudy shook his head dizzily. "Well, getting hurt. Getting shot."

"No bugger's going to shoot me, kid. You neither, long as you're with me."

He was seemingly so sure of that, he took no precautions at all: walking confidently through the arcades and the open concourses, never so much as glancing around for signs of danger.

And his confidence was infectious, finding a wary handhold in Rudy's mind too, so that he stopped wondering when the bullets would catch up with him again, to finish what they'd started. Stopped questioning whether they'd ever make it as far as Dreamland; and, inevitably, started fretting once more about the time it was taking to get there. This was a faster way to travel, no doubt of that – but fast enough? That was something else, and something to be doubted.

Then Carl stopped abruptly, with a jolt that set Rudy almost to screaming again. Pain lashed him, so that his sight blurred and breathing came harder than before; and through it all, through the pain and the fear and the not being able to see what was going on, he heard Carl's voice, dimly, as though on the far side of a wall of water.

"Wait here, kid."

"What . . . ?"

"Just wait. I'll be back."

And there was another jolt as Carl put him down, almost dropped him onto the flooring with his back against a wall. This time Rudy did scream, in a voice thin as his blood, as his thoughts, thin as his hold on life.

"Take it easy." From the sound of it, Carl was already moving away as he said it. Rudy forced his eyes open, and for a moment could see nothing but a swimming redness. He blinked hard and his vision cleared a little, enough to show him one more mall, two moving figures. Another blink, and one of the figures was Carl, the other a boy ten or twelve years old, staggering a little, one red arm clutched to his chest.

Rudy couldn't see, couldn't tell for sure: but the arm seemed to end just below the elbow, didn't seem to have a hand attached.

Carl picked the boy up in one swift movement and kept on walking, around a corner and out of sight.

Rudy let his eyes close again, and went back to breathing.

He was still doing that, still breathing when he felt something cold against his cheek. Something cold and hard that did more than touch, that turned his head and pressed it back against the wall, that added one more sharp discomfort to Rudy's long burden.

His eyes opened in protest, cleared slowly, focused; and he found himself looking up the length of a rifle, looking into a mask that showed him nothing but eyes and mouth separated and surrounded by black.

And the mouth moved, shaped hard little words, said, "You're not dead."

Not yet, Rudy thought. And, *Soon, though.* And, *Very soon, I think*, surprising himself with the clarity of it, and the calmness. *Too soon, I guess. Sorry, Liane. I did try.*

"You weren't here," the mouth said. "Five minutes ago, you weren't here. That's how I know you're not dead." And then saying it for him, as if recognising that Rudy lacked the strength to speak for himself: "Not yet."

Rudy could see the hands that held the rifle, see them quite clearly now; so he saw when the finger moved on the trigger, and his whole body jerked in anticipation, and even the pain went away, just for a moment.

But nothing happened, except a little click and the mouth stretching into a wide and terrible smile.

"No bullets," the mouth said. "Not in that magazine. I used them all."

The rifle was pulled away from his face; and Rudy watched quietly, almost placidly, while the man unclipped the magazine, thrust it into a pocket of his combat jacket and took a fresh one from another pocket.

"It's all right," he said, "I've got plenty. I knew I'd need plenty of bullets."

And the magazine went into the rifle, locked into place with another, a louder click; and Rudy thought, *Now, then. Do it now, and get it done.*

The rifle turned back towards him, so that he gazed into the barrel's mouth, knowing he'd never see the bullet come; but then it was jerked away and tucked under the man's arm while he reached again into one of his pockets.

And came up with a grenade.

"Mills 36," the mouth said. "Old friends are best." He tossed the grenade into the air and caught it again, one-handed. Rudy watched, and went on breathing.

"A pin," the mouth said, "a lever – and a bang. Seven seconds, on this one."

The man pulled the pin and tossed it away, stood there holding the grenade. Holding the lever in, Rudy saw, with his fingers.

"You can move," the mouth said. "Or you wouldn't be here. You weren't here before. But I don't think you can move far in seven seconds, can you? Not as far as I can. And not far enough."

He opened his fingers and the lever flew out, clattering away across the tiled floor. The man tossed the grenade neatly into Rudy's lap, span round and ran out of the limited circle of Rudy's vision, entirely out of his mind.

Seven seconds . . .

One: and it didn't tick or anything, it just sat there in the cleft between his legs, dirty green and the size of a fist; and Rudy looked at it, and sat there, while somewhere in the back of his mind a quiet voice was counting.

Two: and Rudy thought he should do something, get up and run, scream for help, something; and did nothing. Except count, of course, he did that. He couldn't help it.

Three: and he thought of Liane, remembered how hungry he'd been to reach her before she died.

Four: and he tried. He did try. He told his legs to move, to hurry, to get him away from there. But they couldn't hear, or weren't paying attention; or else they'd grown too used to being carried, being rescued. Maybe they were just waiting for Carl. At any rate, they didn't so much as twitch.

Five: and he used his arm instead. Lifted the great weight of it, moved the hand, watched carefully to see that his numb, sweating fingers closed good and tight on the grenade's metal casing.

Six: and he meant to hurl it high and wide, to do the best he could to go on living; but his arm was too heavy to manage. There was no strength left in him, no trace of the old skills that had sent beer-cans over walls and stones through windows. He saw the grenade fall just a yard or two away, bounce and slide another couple of feet; and thought, *That's it, then.* And thought,

Seven . . .

*   *   *

Andrew had led his little group directly away from the Centre, across the grass to the ring-road, the car parks, the massed crowds. Policemen noted their passage, but made no move to stop them.

Behind him Andrew could hear the muttered curiosity, the surprise of his companions; but he offered no explanations. They'd understand in a minute. For the moment he could find something to enjoy in their bewilderment, in his private knowledge of the Centre's secrets; and was grateful for anything to set against the building tensions in his mind. What lay ahead was a lion's den by any definition, and his imagination was cringing already from the thought of walking into it in cold blood. Laying his life on the line, and Dee's, and the others'. Trusting only to luck, tempting fate with a vengeance, and all to save a stranger's life when so many strangers were dead already, one more would hardly notice . . .

The crowd was starting to thin out at the back. People were getting into their cars, driving at a slow walking-pace through the aisles and towards the exits. There was a lot of shouting and blaring of horns, marshals running to and fro trying to clear the way while others scribbled registration numbers onto their clipboards. The police must finally have given permission for the punters to leave; though they wouldn't all go, of course. The sensation-seekers would stay until they were forcibly evicted, and so would the desperate ones, those who'd lost friends or family in the panic, who could do nothing now but cling to whatever shreds of hope they could find and wait for the news they dreaded most.

But still there were thousands who wanted only to get away; and the resulting confusion was perfect for Andrew and his allies.

He headed at an angle across one car park, to a fenced-off area that lay between that and the next.

And there he stopped; there he locked his fingers tight in the mesh of the eight-foot fence; and there, at last, he turned.

And found them all still with him, looking pale and tense and puzzled as their eyes asked the questions. *What now? Where do we go from here?*

"This is it," he said quietly.

Frowns, quick little shakes of the head; and Dee talking, saying, "I don't understand. How do we get into the Centre?"

"Secret passages, pet. This is the transformer station," with a nod at the squat, square building that stood well back inside the fence. "All our power comes in through here; and there are big conduits underground, to carry the cables. Man-size."

"Is it safe?" Dee asked, looking at the red *Danger!* signs on the fence and on the building, the jagged lightning-bolts warning of high voltage inside.

Andrew felt a rough, painful choke of laughter force its way up and out of his throat. *Safer than a lion's den, sweetheart,* he thought; but said only, "There are walkways, for the maintenance crews. Just follow me close, and for God's sake don't touch anything."

*   *   *

Seven had passed, long passed.

Also *eight*, *nine* and *ten*.

Rudy had stopped counting after that, only watched the deadly little lump with a tension that was strangely increasing, now that it was past its time – that was slowly, steadily turning to terror.

Stupid to be so afraid now, when he'd felt almost nothing

before; but afraid he was, frozen into an immobility that had nothing to do with his injuries. He watched the grenade, and wondered if he would see it explode; if his suddenly-sharp mind would have a moment to understand before sharper steel fragments ripped him into a mess of blood and bone.

He watched, and the first minute ticked away.

And the second minute, and the third . . .

And then there was a shadow, a movement at the end of the mall, a figure against the light; and briefly he thought the man had returned to ask why there had been no explosion. Perhaps to blame, to punish Rudy for the failure.

But he saw no rifle, no black balaclava mask; and that's how he recognised Carl.

Forced his stiff jaw to open, his paralysed throat and tongue to call a warning: "Watch it! There's a, a grenade . . . On the floor there . . . "

Couldn't point, but didn't need to. Carl looked, and nodded. And stayed where he was, quite calm.

"Turned up, did he? How long back?"

"I, I don't know. Seven seconds, he said; but it's been more than that, minutes it's been . . . "

"Must be a dud. We won't chuck it around, though, eh? Just in case."

And Carl came loping down the mall, side-stepping neatly around the grenade. Stooping over Rudy and picking him up again with that casual, careless strength, sending the familiar agony surging through him. His nerves were a long way from dying yet, that was for sure, further maybe than the rest of him; but Rudy clenched his teeth into the tough fabric of Carl's jacket, and thought he'd never been more glad to feel anything.

"Get us out of here," he whispered.

"Sure."

Carl carried him down the mall and out into one of the Centre's theme areas, a mock mediaeval village. Rudy looked back over his shoulder, still seeing the grenade, still fearing it; and remembered that the killer too had come this way. Thought he ought to warn Carl, but changed his mind before he'd found the words to do it. There were half a dozen ways on from here, it'd be terrible bad luck if they came face to face with the guy again; and Carl wasn't worried anyway. He'd made that clear already. And it was strange, but – back in his arms again – Rudy wasn't really worried, either. Carl had a charmed life in here, or believed he did; and so long as they were together, perhaps the charm stretched to include Rudy too. After all, it had only been after Carl left him that the man had come . . .

For a brief, treacherous second, Rudy wondered what Carl had in his pockets. Ammunition clips, perhaps, and a balaclava? A rifle stowed carefully somewhere out of sight . . . ?

But no, that didn't make any kind of sense. And the voice had been different, not even close to Carl's rough London. Whatever was going on, it wasn't that.

After a minute, the pain ebbed a short way out of Rudy's body again, a little way out of his mind; leaving space enough for just a brief curiosity.

"What did you do with the kid, then?"

"Took him out, didn't I? Like I was going to, with you. Still could, if you want."

Rudy thought about that: thought about ambulances, hospitals, doctors. Thought about being free from fear and free from pain, freed maybe from the shadow of death if they got to him quick enough.

And said no to all of it. Said, "No. Take me to Liane."

Rudy's mind came almost loose from his body on this last stretch. Ducking away from the realities of constant pain and a dragging, clutching weakness, he could barely hang on to where he was and where he was going, who he was going to. He'd left all curiosity and all questions a long way behind; he accepted Carl now simply as someone far beyond his pale understanding, someone who happened to be there and had the will and the power to help him, nothing more.

There was no movement along the route they followed, no more signs of life. Only the dead; and Rudy was barely conscious of them, his eyes fixed on Carl's unheeding feet, walking steadily step by step through the carnage.

At last – after a time that was immeasurable, that meant nothing in Rudy's floating world – he saw bright yellow tiles on the ground beneath Carl's boots, and shimmering water contained behind a wall; and knew that he'd made it, he'd hung on long enough. He'd come back to Dreamland.

"Where now, then, mate? Where is she?"

The first time Rudy hardly registered the words, didn't realise that they were a question, and aimed at him.

But then Carl's face was hanging in front of his eyes, asking again, pulling Rudy back from his drifting separation. Slowly he rediscovered his mouth and tongue, remembered their use and found an answer of sorts:

"Balloon. A yellow, a yellow balloon . . . "

That was all he could manage, to share the image in his head, Liane and a balloon inextricably linked. But it seemed to be enough, because Carl grunted and started forward once more.

Back in his body, reattached to his pain, every step was a jolting agony to Rudy; and this time there was nothing he could do but bear it, choke on it, somehow endure. He didn't dare float off again, for fear he'd never make it back a second time.

He didn't look ahead and try to spot Liane, or the balloon that seemed in some odd way to have become Liane, her features moulded in his mind onto elastic yellow. All he did was count the paces, count the pain that told the time; and forty-seven times a foot went forward, forty-seven times a scream cramped his body, found no way out through his throat. And then,

"This her, then?"

A head, a girl's head was lying motionless by Carl's boot. Rudy squinted, squeezing out the picture of a yellow face, a balloon-face, fighting to remember how she ought to look, how she had looked before the balloon; and said, "Yes."

"Looks dead to me, kid."

"Doesn't . . . Doesn't matter."

And it didn't, not any more. Coming back, being here; that was all that counted. Maybe chasing after her and catching up, maybe not.

"Put me down."

And Carl did that, kicking rubble aside to make a space for him. Rudy made one final, tremendous effort: swung the dead weight of his arm through the resisting air, and closed his fingers around Liane's wrist. He wasn't feeling for a pulse, or even for the simple reality of her, the touch of her cold flesh against his. His eyes were all that were left to him now; all he wanted was to see it, his hand on her arm, the two of them linked, locked as tightly as he could achieve.

Didn't think to say thanks, to Carl; didn't even notice the

sound of booted feet moving away.

Just looked, and saw, and didn't fight the drifting when it came again. Didn't want to.

1900:

and Denise watched nervously as Andrew fumbled among the many keys on his ring, trying to find the particular master that would let them into the transformer station. The gate in the fence had been no problem, but this was taking longer; and somewhere inside she was half-hoping that he wouldn't have the right key after all, so that they wouldn't be able to go through with this crazy adventure.

She looked around to see if anyone had spotted them yet, a policeman or some other official coming to interrogate, to forbid; and found her gaze caught instead by something much closer, Penny's anxious and determined face, with Charlie's just behind. Denise regretted her treachery in a moment, almost despised herself for it, seeing again the reasons why they were going in. Finding them again obvious and inarguable.

She groped for Penny's hand and gripped it loosely, looked again for watchers and this time felt nothing but relief when she saw no one. And then there was the solid *clunk!* of a lock turning, loud against their silence, and Andrew pulled the heavy door open.

"Inside, quick . . . "

They hurried through into near-darkness, only a little late sunlight finding its way in through the ventilation slats, lying in bars across heavy grey machinery. Andrew closed and locked the door again behind them, shutting out more light; but Denise saw the shadow of his hand move over a bank of switches, and a moment later bright fluorescent tubes flickered into life above them.

They were standing in a tight cluster on a metal inspection platform, with guard-rails around. Like the others, Denise had her gaze fixed on Andrew; he collected them up with his eyes, and nodded slowly.

"Right, then."

And he led the way off the platform, down an open metal-runged stairway which clattered noisily under their feet.

*   *   *

Johnnie Lee lurked in a corner of the police van, and knew himself to be lurking. Worse, he felt himself growing ever less important, ever more inconspicuous and overlooked, all control snatched from his hands.

The men fighting for that control now were grouped around the table just a yard or two away; and he looked at their backs, at their bent heads, and knew that they were barely aware of his presence. That they'd discounted him utterly some time back, endured him only because of his silence and his keeping well out of their way.

They were working on a map of one section of the Centre, charting their men's slow progress into danger. Beyond them, two men were in constant radio contact with the invading police squads, reporting checks and advances to their superiors at the table.

No one except Johnnie looked up when the door opened, and a uniform sergeant came in with a clipboard.

"Uh, Inspector . . . "

Holborn took no notice, until the sergeant laid a tentative hand on his shoulder; and then he reacted only by shrugging it off, snapping, "Not now. Wait."

No one except Johnnie registered the urgency on the newcomer's face, that drove him to try again.

"Sir, I think you should . . . "

"I said wait, didn't I? So wait!"

And no one except Johnnie, perhaps, would have taken advantage of the moment as Johnnie did then, to re-establish himself a little in his own eyes and those of the men around him. No other civilian would have walked over so determinedly in a vanful of high-ranking police, would have held out his hand for the clipboard and said, "What is that? Let me see."

And for no other civilian, perhaps, would the sergeant have so meekly acquiesced; but he knew Johnnie's face and his position, knew nothing of his current displacement in the hierarchy, didn't even question his authority.

"I've been running a check on the whereabouts of your security personnel, sir," he said, with just a hint of suppressed excitement in his voice. "Routine, mostly; but you'll see, there's a question-mark over one of them."

Johnnie grunted, then stiffened as his eye picked out one name on the list – a name which had a literal question-mark beside it, in red felt pen.

"Peter Kerr?"

"That's right, sir. Do you know him?"

"Of course I know him. I know all my men."

"Well, we've tried ringing him at home, sir, but he doesn't answer. It mightn't mean anything, of course, he could be anywhere; he could even be helping out around here, though no one seems to have noticed him recently, and he's not due until ten tonight. But the thing is, a couple of people thought they caught a glimpse of him earlier, just before all this blew up. And this one guy, he's almost positive it was Kerr; and he says he saw him heading up to the security block. Moving fast, this guy says. And that's not all."

"Well? What more?"

"It's only the one report, sir, so maybe we shouldn't give too much weight to it. But the guy said he was carrying a big canvas hold-all, long enough to have anything you like inside it. A rifle, anything. And he was wearing army gear. Combat jacket, boots, the lot. The guy said he didn't think anything to it at the time, said Kerr was always going around like that off duty; but . . . "

But that was enough to give Johnnie back all the fire, all the inner strength and certainty he'd been lacking. He pushed his way through to the table, slamming the clipboard down on top of the pile of maps. Pulled the startled, reluctant sergeant after him, and snapped, "Listen to this, all of you. Sergeant . . . ?"

*　　　*　　　*

The stairs had brought them down into a pit, sunk below the floor of the transformer station; and now Penny watched as between them, Andrew and Charlie hauled up a trapdoor.

"Okay," Andrew said. "Now, there's not a lot of room down there; but room enough, if we go single file. I've been along it once, out of curiosity, and it's not too bad. There are lights, though they're fairly few and far between. All the cables are in insulated pipes, so don't worry if you brush against them, you won't get electrocuted. Everyone set? – Right, then. I'll go first, then you, Dee; then Penny, and Charlie at the back. Leave the trap up, it'll give us some extra light for the first stretch. Stop, if I say; and if I shout, then for God's sake get down. You've got to remember, we just might run into the gunman down there, he could be looking for a way out by now. Otherwise, keep quiet. We don't want to let him know we're coming . . . "

He gave them a tight grin, then sat down on the edge of the hole and lowered one leg carefully.

"There are rungs set into the wall here, you can feel for them with your feet . . . "

Which he did, climbing slowly down until only his head was showing.

"I'm on the bottom now. Down you come, Dee . . . "

Andrew ducked out of sight, except that Penny could still see his hands, steadying Denise as she followed him down.

"Okay, Penny . . . "

Denise's voice came up slightly muffled, with the hint of an echo behind it. Penny swallowed, flashed a nervous smile at Charlie and crouched by the hole, feeling Denise's hands on her ankle, guiding her foot to the first iron rung.

The climb down was easy, though she still felt grateful for Denise's arm circling her waist in a quick hug when she reached bottom. Then the two girls backed away to leave room for Charlie. He swung himself down on his arms in one lithe movement, disdaining the help of the rungs; and Andrew's voice came out of the dimness ahead.

"Everyone all right? Straight on, then. And try not to tread on the heels of whoever's in front . . . "

The tunnel was no more than five feet high; Penny had to stoop uncomfortably, and she could see that even little Denise was walking with her head low, stray spikes of her disordered hair brushing the concrete ceiling.

The air was damp and stale, with an unpleasant smell to it; and cold too, cold enough to have her wrapping her arms tight around her chest to suppress the shivers. She focused her eyes on Denise's feet and concentrated solely on walking, one slow pace after another. On getting there.

Then she spotted something just below the lowest pipe, something that moved and froze and moved again; and her stifled gasp echoed up and down the tunnel, bringing every-one to stillness.

"What is it?" Andrew's voice, coming back to her in a soft murmur.

"N-nothing. Just a rat, I think. I'm sorry, I just wasn't expecting . . . "

"No. I should have warned you. Plenty of rats, down here. This was marshland before we moved in; and then all the rats moved in on us. Nice and warm, see, and plenty of food. We've got a rat-catcher working here permanently, though he's not called that in the books. Wouldn't want the punters to find out, would we?" With a little chuckle that somehow didn't sound bitter, or even forced; that made Penny sud-denly like Andrew rather a lot. "Don't worry, though, they'll keep out of sight, mostly. On we go, there's a long way yet . . . "

And on they went, single file, keep moving and no talk-ing, no stopping for comfort or encouragement; and more than anything Penny wanted a hug from someone or a hand to hold, just a little impossible contact to help her down this long, long tunnel.

*   *   *

"Peter Kerr . . . " Inspector Holborn seemed to be trying the name out on his tongue, to see how it fitted. He glanced at the Assistant Chief Constable beside him, and got a brief wave of the hand, *you carry on*; then he turned back to Johnnie. "So what do you know about this Peter Kerr?"

Johnnie shrugged awkwardly, more used to being inter-viewer than interviewee. "Little. He keeps himself apart. A hard man, you would call him, perhaps. Reliable, though – an ex-soldier, like most of our security officers. That, or ex-police."

Holborn grunted. "Where does he live?"

When Johnnie shook his head, the sergeant told him. "Out in Allingham, sir. Twenty minutes' drive."

"Married?"

That was aimed at Johnnie again; he hesitated, caught at a faint memory rising in his mind, found time to be surprised that it was there at all before he said, "No. I think, I believe he lives with his mother."

"Get onto her." Fired at the sergeant.

"Like I said, sir, there's no one answers the phone . . . "

"So send a car. Or call up the local bobby, if there is one."

"Yes, sir. Um, if no one answers the door . . . ?"

"Tell him to get in there and have a snoop. Tell him to break the bloody door down, if he needs to. Oh, and sergeant?"

"Yes, sir?"

"Get onto Records, and find out if Peter Kerr has a firearms licence. No, wait." A moment's frowning thought. "Do that first. If he has, tell the local boy to keep well out of it, if he doesn't get an answer at the door. Commander," he glanced across at Jakes, "if there's any chance this guy's our perpetrator, I want one of your teams to check his house out. And I want them to be bloody careful. He's caught us with a booby-trap once already, I'm not risking it again."

"Will do."

"Thanks." And back to Johnnie again, sharp and urgent. "Where do you keep your personnel files?"

"In the security complex. Your men must have seen them already, to obtain that list of names."

"How much more is there?"

"Plenty. We keep detailed records of everyone. And not only their work. Any domestic problems, changes at home, whatever we know will be there."

"Good. Who knows where to find all this?"

"Anyone who understands the system. It's all there."

"Go up yourself, would you? My sergeant'll take you. Get it all dug out, Mr Lee, there's a good chap. I want the lot."

* * *

The tunnel seemed to have been going on forever. Certainly it was far longer than when Andrew had last been down here; someone had come along and stretched it in the meantime, they must have done. Or else he'd led his companions wrong, he should have turned into one of the offshoots of this main low-way and he was currently guiding them to the sewage outfall or the river . . .

But he kept on walking, trying to hide his doubts. He counted the lights, and watched his shadow stretching and contracting as they passed; and at last, at long last he saw ahead what he'd been aiming for. The tunnel widened briefly into a square alcove, before running on again. The wall there had rungs let into it for climbing, and in the ceiling above was another trapdoor.

He stopped, and waited for the others to group up.

"This is it," he said softly, when he could see Charlie's pale face behind the girls. "The trap leads into a basement storeroom. Then we go up some stairs and into the malls. I don't know what we're going to find up there, it could be pretty bad; but if we're going to get Penny's friends out, we can't let it get to us. We've got to be quick, and quiet; and I'm afraid we've got to be ruthless. We can't stop to help anyone else, however hurt they may be. Everyone clear about that?"

He waited for a nod from each of them, and got it. Then he started up the rungs, lifting the trap carefully as he went.

The storeroom was in darkness. As his head came through, he heard a soft scuffle in one corner, and thought, *Rats again*. Paid no more attention to it, but climbed up until he could twist his body round to sit on the edge of the hole. He lowered the heavy trap to lie flat on the floor, as silently as he could manage; pulled his legs up, and got cautiously to his feet.

Dee followed him out of the tunnel, then Penny. Charlie came last, with a glance down at the trapdoor and a murmur, "Should I close this, then?"

"No, leave it."

"We'll never get a stretcher down there." That from Penny, fretful and fidgeting.

"We won't need to, love. As soon as we've collected your friends, we'll go straight out the nearest exit. They're not trigger-happy out there, they'll wait to see who we are; and we could pick up something white to wave at them, that'd help. We'll get bollocked, no question, but we'll get out safe enough."

He led them out of the storeroom and up the stairs into a long service corridor. There he hesitated, torn between two choices. With a little thought and the odd detour, he could find his way from here to a first-aid station and then on to the Tudor Village without their having to set a foot in the public malls; and that could well be the safer option. Certainly it would be a less distressing route, saving them the worst horrors of the slaughter.

But the killer could just as easily be lurking somewhere

back here, hiding in the shadows, avoiding the bright lights
and all the evidence of his handiwork. And if they met him
here – well, these corridors ran straight and true, offering no
shelter, nowhere to hide. At least there was cover in the
malls, and shops with many exits, places to flee to and flee
from . . .

It was Charlie who settled the issue, in the end; or
Charlie's face, rather, just a glimpse of terror tightly suppressed, reminding Andrew of why the other man had come.
He had his reasons, as they all did; and Charlie's couldn't be
satisfied by sneaking around the edges, avoiding the carnage. Privately, Andrew thought his search was hopeless.
Even if Charlie was right that his family hadn't got out – and
it was a big if, things weren't that organised out in the car
parks; it was more a case of stewards and volunteers doing
their best against impossible odds – he was still asking for a
miracle, hoping to find them this way. He couldn't have any
idea how large the Centre actually was, how long it would
take to search it properly.

Still, for his own sake, he had to be allowed to try. So
Andrew pulled open the panel door, and looked cautiously
out into the mall.

He could see no movement, no bodies, not so much as an
abandoned shopping-bag; nothing but the emptiness itself,
early on a Saturday evening, to say that anything out of the
way had happened.

So he went through, and the others followed. Then he
turned left, drawing a mental map of the quickest route to a
first-aid station; and had gone only a couple of paces before
he was frozen to stillness by Penny's hissed, "Wait!"

"What?"

"I know this bit. And that square, where we were playing
– it's that way, isn't it?" Pointing right.

"Yes. But we've got to get the stretcher first."

"How far?"

"I don't know." Checking the map in his mind. "Ten
minutes, maybe. We'll have to go slow."

"And then ten minutes back to here, and the same again
before we get to Richard. It's too long, Andrew. You fetch
the stretcher, I'll go straight there, tell him you're coming."

"Not alone," Andrew said flatly. "No way."

"No." That was Dee, pale but determined. "If you do

that, I'm coming with you."

That was the killer blow, for Andrew. He stared at her blankly, swallowed, shook his head. "I don't, I don't think we should separate. It's too dangerous . . . "

"It's half an hour, Andrew!" Penny again, the words driven at him hard and fast. "And Richard's been waiting hours already, on his own, with Julian maybe dying on him. I can't leave him another half an hour."

Why not, if he's been waiting hours already? But he couldn't say that. He couldn't say anything. Or in the end do anything but watch as the girls turned and left him, went hand in hand away down the silent arcade, looked back only once at the corner for a brief meaningless wave, and were gone.

*   *   *

Peter Kerr did have a firearms licence. The information had come back within minutes, dredged from the massive police computer network on a priority order.

"Two shotguns, a .22 competition rifle and a Lee Enfield .303," Michael Jakes read aloud, peering at the list over Holborn's shoulder. "So what's he doing out there with an AK-47? If it's him, that is."

"It's him." Holborn was convinced suddenly, as if the fact of a sheet of paper in his hands made all other suppositions also fact. "Picked it up under the counter somewhere. He's ex-army, he'll have contacts. Belongs to the local rifle club, too."

"He'd have to. Wouldn't have got the licence, else. Wouldn't have got a licence at all for the automatic, of course, not these days; but he'd know that from his cronies at the club."

"From magazines, more likely. I doubt he has cronies. We'll check out the club, though, someone must know him. I'll get onto that; you send a team out to this village. Use the chopper, it'll save time. And it's not doing anything useful, hovering about up there. Getting on my nerves, that's all."

"I'll go myself," Jakes said. "Hold the men where they are, for now. Let the stretcher-teams in. We'll move on when I'm back."

And at that moment Johnnie Lee, back from the security complex with a sheaf of print-out from the computer, surprised himself and surprised everyone; said, "I want to come too."

They just looked at him.

"He works for me. And you still can't be certain he's the man. You have no proof. If you mean to break into his home, I want to be there."

Jakes raised a thoughtful eyebrow, glanced at Holborn, asked, "How many will the chopper take?"

"Four, plus the pilot."

"Three of us is enough. All right, Mr Lee. But you do exactly what I tell you, understood? And you don't come inside the house until I say."

"Very well."

So five minutes later Johnnie was in the air, squashed between two silent men in black, each with a handgun in a shoulder holster.

Another five minutes found them putting down in a field between an old stone-built village and a modern housing estate, with a uniformed constable waving at them from the gate.

"The house is just over here, sir," the constable panted, leading them at a run towards the estate. "There's a footpath through the hedge, and we'll do better going that way. Less people, to see . . . "

If they were worried about attracting attention, Johnnie thought inconsequentially, they'd have done better to come in a car, despite the extra time. A quick glance back showed him two young boys already climbing over the gate, abandoning their bicycles in the lane behind. The pilot had stayed with the helicopter, presumably to guard it against just such curious children; but let them catch one glimpse of the guns and he'd be utterly redundant.

Through the gap in the hedge, and into the estate. More children playing in the cul-de-sacs, a man washing his car, three grouped around the open bonnet of another: all of them turning to look, to stare as the little group ran by. Johnnie was bringing up the rear, gasping by now, thinking he should have joined Linda on those early-morning sessions in the gym. Too many cigars and business lunches, he wasn't fit for this.

But it wasn't long before the constable stopped. The house was like every other on the street, probably like every other on the estate: a tiny brick semi, already badly marked by the weather. A small lawn at the front, a concrete path leading up to the door; at the back, a fenced garden. The windows screened with lace curtains, no lights showing against the evening sun.

"I've rung the bell, sir, and knocked, but there's no answer. The neighbours say they haven't seen Mrs Kerr all day; and there's enough of them," with a jerk of his head to indicate the close-packed houses all around. "Someone would've seen, if she'd gone out. Her son's been and gone, though. Came back at his regular time from the night-shift, about half six this morning; and went off again in his car sometime after one. Usually he'd still be asleep then, the neighbours say. And Mrs Kerr, she'd be in and out. Always does her washing on a Saturday. There's a line in the garden, she'd be using it for sure on a fine day like this . . . "

"All right. Adams," Jakes turned to one of his men, "you go round the back. Get to the door, and wait. O'Farrell, we'll go in the front; but remember, there could be some surprises inside. Nothing technical, most likely, just nice simple little traps. And don't count on a wall to shield you, not in a house like this. One grenade could bring the lot down."

One man nodded, and vanished around the side of the house; the other moved up to the front windows and peered in.

"You won't see anything," the constable said. "Not through those curtains, you won't. I tried."

Jakes looked up and down the street, and scowled. People were approaching from all directions, moving slowly, the sight of guns both drawing them forward and holding them back.

"What's your name, constable?"

"Higgins, sir."

"Right. Well, Higgins, keep that lot out of the way, will you? I want them fifty yards back, at least. And watch out for the kids, they're the worst."

"Yes, sir."

Jakes glanced at Johnnie, and said, "You, too. Fifty yards. If you want something to do, you can help Higgins with the crowd control. Make like a policeman; they'll believe you, if we're lucky. If not, someone's going to

recognise you and make the connection. Then we'll ge
swamped."

"Reckon they're doing that already, some of them,"
Higgins put in, glancing around gloomily. "They know
where Kerr works, and they know he shoots; a couple o:
them told me that, said they thought he might've gone down
to the club. Doesn't take much, to put two and two together."

"No. Do your best, anyway. Tell them there may be a
bomb. Some of the parents'll hold their kids back, if they
hear that. Just keep them out of my way, right? I don't care
how you do it. And you, Mr Lee – you don't come in till I
say. Remember that."

So Johnnie didn't get to go in with the police, or hard behind
them. Didn't get to go in at all, in fact.

All he got to do was watch while O'Farrell forced the lock
and eased the front door cautiously open, watch from a
distance while he and Jakes slithered inside; and then wait,
minute after tense minute, until Jakes appeared at the door
again.

Johnnie walked confidently forward, and was stopped
dead by a shake of the head.

"Sorry, Mr Lee, you can't go in."

"Why not? It must be safe now."

"Oh, it's safe enough."

"So why must I stay outside?"

"There's a dead woman in there, Mr Lee."

"A dead woman . . . Mrs Kerr?"

"I expect so, she's the right age. But no one goes in now
until the forensics team gets here. Inspector Holborn'll send
them out fast, I expect; but I'm going back to the Centre,
and you'd better come with me. Nothing for you to do
here."

"No. How did she die?"

"Slowly, Mr Lee. Now let's move, can we? I've been away
too long as it is, I don't like being out of touch with my
men."

"Why did you come, then? You weren't needed, those
men could have done the job alone."

Jakes gave him a slow half-smile. "Maybe I also don't like
being left out of the action altogether. Why did you come
yourself, Mr Lee?"

And turned and walked down the path without waiting for an answer, without seeming to need one.

THE BOOK OF THE DEAD

IV: In the Kingdom of the Damned

He patrols ceaselessly in the stillness. Only the air moves here, without his authority.

This is the hiatus he's been expecting, the dead time, the eye of the storm. The ground has been cleared for action. Soon now, he thinks: soon the war proper will begin.

That's what he's been waiting for all this time, what he's been working towards. That's his chance to be a soldier at last, to meet other soldiers in combat. It's what he's always wanted.

But it hasn't happened yet, and the enemy has the initiative now, they can decide the time. They're in control.

He controls his territory, perhaps, but that's all. He can't control himself. He paces the malls quickly, but he can't outpace his memories; and what he remembers is losing control, losing everything, feeling his life run out between his fingers.

What he remembers is her eyes, her mocking, scathing eyes.

Driving home, that's where his memories start. He was driving home through the thin light of dawn, thinking of a meal and bed, thinking a little of the night to come. Asking for trouble, he thought it was, keeping the Centre open all night, loud music and stupid games. Letting teenagers crowd the malls, drinking too much and spoiling for a fight.

That was fine by him, though. A little trouble in the nation's eye, television cameras right there, journalists galore: he couldn't ask for a better chance. Finally he'd be up there where he belonged. His picture on every front page, full colour and full of truth. He'd be a little bloody, a little tired, a little grim – the face of a hero, clear and acclaimed.

Telethon Riot, in giant headlines. *Security Guard Averts Tragedy*.

Hero of the hour, king for the day. That was his due, what was owed to him and all he'd ever asked. They couldn't keep him from it forever, try though they might. Try though they did. The opportunity would come tonight, he was sure of that, he could taste its coming; and he'd be ready. He'd kept himself ready for years now, but this time he wouldn't be disappointed.

So he drove, and dreamed; and came home hungry, thinking only of his supper. His mother would be in bed, of course, but she always left a meal out for him when he was working nights. Cold beef or pork, or perhaps a slab of steak and kidney pie. Man-food, he insisted on that, none of her quiches and salads. And there'd be a can of lager in the fridge to wash it down, and one of his magazines to read while he was eating; the new issue of *Combat & Survival* should be in, she should have picked that up at the news-agent yesterday.

But as he turned into the close, he saw a car parked outside his home, where no car should be; especially not this car, and doubly not at this time, before seven in the morning.

He pulled up short of it, and sat dreaming of nothing now, facing an unbearable reality.

Sat for a long time, a time beyond counting.

At last, his hunger forced him to move, against his horror. He got out of the car, slammed the door, let himself into the house.

Walked into the hallway. A briefcase by the door, a man's coat over the banister. Voices in the kitchen. The smell of bacon.

He rocked on his heels, as his world rocked around him; then slowly, step by reluctant, by appalled step, he made his way down the hall and into the kitchen.

He knew what he was going to find, of course. He knew that briefcase, that macintosh, as he had known the car. Any other time of day, there would have been no surprise in finding them here, him hanging around. The man was a leech, unshiftable. But now, to have him here now . . .

They were sitting at the kitchen table, the remains of their breakfast scattered around them, cups of tea in their hands.

No sign of the supper he had the right to expect after a hard shift, she a duty to provide.

The man was wearing a suit; a small mercy made smaller by the woman's dressing-gown hanging loose, showing no nightgown beneath. Made smaller still by the mildness of her embarrassment, the soft blush rising to cheeks and throat. Scarlet she should have been, and wasn't.

"Mother . . . "

"Peter."

And that was it, that was all; no explanation, no apology. The one wasn't needed, he could see the truth all too clearly; the other he wouldn't have believed, even if it had been offered.

She stood up, and began to stack the dishes.

The man – Laurence Judd, bespectacled clerk, thin and balding hanger-on – cleared his throat into the silence.

"'Morning, Peter." And, getting no response, "Well, better be off, then. I've got work to do; and no doubt you two'll be wanting to talk," with a meaning glance, all its meaning wasted as she didn't even look up from her busy hands.

Judd drained his cup, dabbed at his mouth with his hand-kerchief, pushed his chair back and rose. Walked around to where the woman stood, her hands full of dirty dishes, and claimed a kiss before squeezing past in the doorway, "Excuse me, Peter," and another nervous cough, a nervous smile.

With Judd gone they gazed at each other a moment, mother and son; then she said, "Well. I think I'll have a bath."

Yes, he thought. *You need it. Filthy. His hands on you, and worse. Slimy, disgusting. Run it deep, mother, run it hot,* he thought. *Scrub hard.*

Aloud, he said all that he could think of to say, the only protest he could make. "Where's my supper, then?"

"Oh, Peter, look after yourself, can't you, just for once? God knows, you're old enough." And when he didn't move, when he only stared at her, she grabbed his arm and jerked him forward. "There's the fridge, see it? That's where I keep food, in the fridge. Plates are in the dresser. That's the dresser. Cutlery's in the drawer, by the sink. Anything else you need to know?"

But his eyes weren't following her stabbing gestures. They were focused on her bony hand where it clutched his sleeve, her greasy fingers – and pray God it was only grease, it might have been anything, after what she'd been doing this night – leaving their mark on his jacket.

He wrenched himself free, spoke thickly around the constriction in his throat.

"Don't *touch* me!"

He hacked chunks of meat in a fury, chewed them viciously, washed them down with lager and tasted only sourness. Then he sat brooding, hearing the tick of the pipes and the gush of water into the bath above his head.

You're wasting your time, mother. Wallow all you like, you can't wash yourself clean of this.

His father had been wrong, then. Women were all alike at root, and his mother no different. Bitches and cows. *Rutting bitch*, he thought, seeing it all happen in his mind, in her bed. Judd sweating and grunting, her writhing, gasping beneath him . . .

He closed his eyes, and only saw it better; clenched his fist and felt the bite of sharp metal on his palm, a sudden rush of liquid over his hand. He'd forgotten the can he held. When he looked, he saw it crushed and torn in his grip, frothing lager all across the table and dripping over the edge.

Christ, you, she'd say, when she came down. *You're hopeless, aren't you? Helpless. When are you going to grow up?* And when he didn't respond, as of course he wouldn't: *Well, get out of the way, then,* she'd say, fetching a cloth from the sink. *Let Mummy clean up after you, little boy. What, got it on your trousers, have you? God, looks like you've wet yourself . . .*

And then on her knees, maybe, and her eyes bright with mockery, she'd reach to wipe at him with that foul cloth; and he'd only stand and shudder while she dabbed, stand and wonder if maybe she'd been on her knees before Judd and reaching between his legs too, a little earlier. No mockery in her then, of course; but no doubt she'd remember it, she'd see the comparison and laugh the harder.

And then perhaps he'd murder her, he thought. He'd put his hands round her scrawny neck and squeeze, drive his thumbs in deep, crush her throat like a lager can . . .

So instead he stirred, shifted, pushed himself to his feet against a massive reluctance. He fetched the floor-cloth and swabbed the table angrily, dropped it and used his toe to move it through the puddles on the floor. It wasn't soaking much up, just smearing it around; but at least he'd done something. He hated her for that, for making him do it. *Women's work*, he thought. And a woman's fault, that it needed doing.

Probably he should have changed his wet trousers too, but that was just too much. He kicked the cloth into a corner, washed his hands carefully, slumped back into his seat.

Watched the clock and listened to the noises from upstairs, hands tight-fisted against his impotent rage. He ought to be sleeping now, well-fed and sleeping. He had a long night's work to come, he needed rest and she'd denied it to him. Typical, that was, just another side to the conspiracy. Like his bosses, she'd take any chance to keep him down . . .

At last he heard water running out of the bath, gurgling in the drains. Footsteps on the stairs and here she came again, her dressing-gown belted tighter now, a foolish effort towards decency, towards disguise.

Too late for that. He knew the truth of her now, should have known it long since. Should never have listened to his father.

"I thought you'd be in bed by now," she said, with a weary discontent.

His head jerked in rejection, his voice jerked in complaint. "How could I sleep? After . . . " He moved his hand in a gesture that tried to encompass the unspeakable.

"After what? What's got you so high and mighty?"

"You know."

"Well, all right, I suppose I do. It's me having Laurence here, right? Right?"

"Yes," sullenly.

"Well, you'd better get used to it, son. It's happened before when you've been on nights, and it'll happen again. I used to hurry him out in the mornings, but I won't do that any more. I've got nothing to hide."

No, indeed. She'd rather make a shameful public display of it. And the time chosen so carefully, too. Just when he needed to be calm and settled, ready for anything, she flung this at him. Deliberately, no doubt of that.

"Listen," she said sharply, "I've got a life too. I've wasted too much as it is, running around after you. You do what you like, live in a dream if you want to, but I'm sick of it. Here on in, I'm taking any chance I can find to make things better. And Laurence, he's a good man, he's the best chance I've got."

He shook his head slowly, barely hearing her excuses. It didn't matter what she said, anyway. He knew the taste of conspiracy when he met it. He'd known it all his adult life.

"You've done this on purpose," he said. "Haven't you? You wanted me upset today, so that I wouldn't be fit this evening." He was speaking more for his sake than hers, outlining her plot in order to see it more clearly, the depth of her betrayal. "I need my trigger-edge tonight, you know that. So you planned all of this to be sure I didn't have it. You're like the rest of them, you want to keep me down. Keep me nothing."

"What are you talking about, Peter?"

His hands worked on the table, and he wished it was her throat they were working on. "I could have done, I could have done anything tonight, if I'd been ready for it. If I'd been sharp. Whatever was needed, I could have done. Made myself noticed. When the trouble starts. I could have been in the *papers* . . . "

"Oh, that's right." Her laugh was rich, strident, cutting at him like a knife. "Dream on. Why not? It's what you've always done. Paint yourself a hero in your head, and blame me when it doesn't work out that way. God, you fool. You just don't live in the real world, do you? You can't see what's real, even when it's right under your nose. Like me and Laurence. That's been going on for months now, and you never noticed. You just went on playing with your guns in your private little make-believe world, where Mother looks after her little soldier until he's big enough to be a hero . . . "

"I could've been." He was almost crying now, with the frustration of losing his dream one more time, feeling it fray away between his shaking fingers. The table clattered as he shoved himself violently to his feet. "I could've *done* it tonight, if you, if you hadn't spoiled it for me . . . It's hopeless now, I'll be, I'll be no good with all this going on in my head . . . "

And he dashed the back of his hand across his eyes, blinded as he was by anger and disappointment mixed; but her laughter slashed at him again, so that he could see nothing but her face, and that blurred and dancing.

"There there, little boy, don't cry. Mummy'll make it all better," she said. And there was that mockery flying fast and free, lighting up her eyes; and it shone brighter than ever before, and there was a new delight in her voice as she looked at him standing, as she said, "Oh, dear dear. Have we wet ourselves, have we? Poor little Peter . . . "

And he only wanted to put the light out, that was all. He wasn't thinking of anything else when he grabbed her narrow head in his broad hands, when he put his thumbs over those glowing eyes and began to press. He only wanted to cover that bright scorn, to escape its savage pleasure.

But she screamed and kicked at him with her slippered feet, beat thin hands against his chest; and now he was yelling himself, and he never yelled. Now he was shouting and shaking her, only to keep her quiet, to shut out that voice and silence her mocking for once. And he tightened his grip on her head, dug his thumbs in deeper, just to lift her clear of the ground and shake her better.

He stopped when her screams were only whimpers, and those fading; when she hung limp in his hands, no movement in her except what she took from him. He let her go then, but she dangled a second longer on his thumbs before sliding free, flopping onto the lino.

He looked at his hands, and saw how they were coated with blood and slime; and shuddered, and hurried to the sink to wash.

It was a long time before he could bring himself to look at his mother.

She lay where she had fallen, not quite still yet, little scrabbling motions in her feet and fingers, rare breaths whistling in her throat. She was on her back, with her arms spread wide and her face turned up to the light; but she wouldn't be seeing that light, certainly would never shine it back at him again in jeering derision. Not with those deep-dug sockets where her eyes had been, filling now with blood and other fluids.

Peter stood above her, shaking; reached behind him for a chair, without lifting his eyes from his mother.

Dropped heavily into it, set trembling hands on trembling knees, and watched.

Sat quiet, sat still, and watched his mother die.

It was another betrayal, of course, he knows that now. Her last and greatest.

In dying like that, in putting herself under his thumbs, she took his own life away from him even as she gave hers up. It was the excuse they were waiting for. They'd lock him up and leave him to rot, take the last faint shadow of his dreams away from him. He'd never get another chance to make his mark on the world, they'd see to that. And smile as they did it.

So he left his mother finally, long after she'd left him. He turned to his guns for comfort, cold metal and sharp clean smells; and as he laid them out for oiling he saw a way to change things, to challenge fate.

It wasn't what he'd dreamed of all these years; but it wasn't that far off. True combat for a soldier, a chance to use his skills and go down fighting. And, of course, a chance to make the headlines, make the news . . .

That's what he's been doing, making news; and it isn't over yet. Only the first phase, only the easy part. The real work's still to come, when they send the army in to flush him out; and even now, even now his mother's working against him. Filling his mind with pictures, haunting him when he needs to be clear-sighted and sharply focused.

He shakes his head in denial of her, casts around for something else to fix on, some other picture; and finds it in a moment, in the window of a shop.

Stares in through glass at bank on bank of silent televisions, and sees a view of the Centre. Nothing new in that, nothing surprising; but there's movement too, people going in and out. Men with rifles running in, men with stretchers walking slowly out . . .

He squints to see it better, works out at last which entrance they're invading. It's right over the far side from where he is now, and no easy route to get there. Ten minutes' hard running, at least. And they'll be well established now if they're bringing out the dead already, they must have infiltrated a long time ago. Hours, maybe. While he let his mother distract him, his concentration slip away . . .

He curses aloud – yet one more betrayal, and will they never end? – and starts to run towards the enemy's bridgehead. Too late to drive them back, he hasn't the ordnance; but he can harass them at least, slow them down, intercept their scouts and take them out . . .

THE BOOK OF HOURS

V

2000:

and it wasn't so much the utter stillness in the malls that got to Charlie, nor the bland Muzak that played on so bizarrely into that stillness. It wasn't even the constant numbing fear of a sudden movement ahead, a noise, a blast of bullets to shatter the illusion of being unseen and undetected. What really hit him was the contrast between what he'd seen before, and what he saw now. He'd come expecting to pick his way between bodies, to walk on blood and shattered glass, to smell death on the recycled air; and there was none of that, no sign that this was anything but an ordinary day. Except for the emptiness – and even the Meldon Centre had to empty sometime, and so what if they'd left the lights on? – it looked so ordinary as to make all their precautions seem ridiculous. Why scurry from doorway to doorway, why constantly be looking over your shoulder, why peer so nervously around every corner, when there was clearly no one around?

The world had been made twice unreal, once by the gunman and once again by his absence now, no sign even of his work; and in that double unreality, it was easy almost to forget the danger. Easy almost to laugh at himself, to mock his fears for Sue and the baby . . .

Andrew unlocked a white door with a large red cross on it, and went into the small room beyond; and Charlie hardly bothered to keep watch outside. There was more evidence of the evacuation here, an eating-place with food abandoned and congealing on the tables, drinks spilt and chairs overturned, but still there was nothing moving bar the escalators.

He cast a casual eye around, then turned to see Andrew struggling to lift a rolled-up stretcher from its clips on the wall. Went in to help without another glance behind him, without a second thought; and between them they got the stretcher down, collected a couple of blankets and a pack of dressings, and organised themselves and their burden.

Charlie took the front of the stretcher, tucking the steel-and-canvas roll comfortably under his arm, carrying the dressings in his free hand. The blankets hung handily over the stretcher like washing on a line; and with Andrew at the back, they were ready to go.

Charlie turned automatically back the way they'd come, but was stopped by a quiet word from behind him.

"No, head straight over. I've been working it out, there's a quicker way through to where we're going."

"You're the boss."

So they crossed the concourse, and took another route; and stepped unthinkingly into another world.

For Charlie, heaven to hell could hardly have been a greater change. He simply turned a corner when Andrew told him to, and stumbled over something soft. Held his balance with an effort, and looked down; and found himself looking at a mess of hair and blood and fragments of bone, a woman with her head half blown away, one blue eye staring fixedly up at him.

He might have screamed then, if he hadn't jerked his gaze so violently away: if he hadn't seen all the rest of it leaping into too-sharp focus, a wide panorama of death. There were half a dozen bodies strewn haphazardly across the floor ahead of him, in pools of drying blood; and there was glass everywhere, bags and boxes lying where they'd fallen, a buggy standing incongruously upright and empty in the middle of it all.

"Charlie . . . " Andrew's voice, sounding oddly distant. "Charlie, just ignore it. Just keep going, there's nothing we can do here . . . "

But Charlie couldn't ignore it, and couldn't find the words to say why. He did walk forward a little way, slowly, blindly trusting his feet to keep him upright; but only as far as that buggy. He stopped there, looked at it for a second, two seconds, ten; then drew a deep, sobbing breath, and looked past it.

Dropped his end of the stretcher, with a clatter.

Fell to his knees, still only looking, not thinking at all; and reached out one tentative, trembling hand to touch.

For some reason, John Mark couldn't or wouldn't ever sleep

in the buggy. Sue always carried a sling in her bag when she was out with him, and when he got tired or fractious she'd transfer him to that, strapping him against her body with his head snugly settled between her breasts.

That's why the buggy was empty; and that's why Charlie's fumbling fingers came to padded cotton first, while his eyes were turned still towards her still face.

The cotton felt wet and spongy against his skin; and when he looked, when he couldn't keep from looking, he saw the pink sling dark and sodden with blood. Saw that there was a great tear in the fabric, that within it John Mark lay sprawled across his mother's body like a mutilated doll.

"Charlie . . . "

He just moaned, shook his head, hunched his shoulder away from Andrew's touch; reached to undo the knots holding the simple sling together.

And Sue's eyes opened as he touched her, steadied on his face. Her mouth shaped his name without sound, and her hand stirred and lifted to lie cold on his arm. And that was perhaps the worst, the most dreadful gift of the day, for him or for anyone: the sudden understanding that she'd survived the bullet or the shrapnel or whatever it was that had been aiming so accurately for her heart.

That her life had been bought for her, by the death of their baby son.

*   *   *

Linda Lee had left her husband with the police an hour ago, and had been politely escorted back to the relative safety of the car parks beyond the ring road. She'd been glad to leave – indeed, it had been her idea – even though it meant inevitably running the gauntlet of a frustrated press corps as soon as they heard she was accessible.

Whether Carl was the killer or not, whether he was risking his life in there for some strange motivation of his own, still she knew that ultimately she was responsible. She had to be. It was too much of a coincidence, his mind seemingly blowing all its fuses so soon after their confrontation in his bedroom. She must have cut deeper than she meant to, deeper than she knew; she must have shaken his ego to its very foundations, to send it rocking so dangerously out of true.

And it was that knowledge, the sense of guilt at what she'd set in motion that had finally driven her away from the unspoken tensions and the unbearable waiting. She felt guilty about that, too – guilty for leaving Johnnie, when he was so manifestly in need of any support she could give him – but there was no help for it. She'd simply had to get out, for her own sake; and there are times when selfishness is a virtue, when it offers the only reasonable response to an intolerable situation.

So she'd left him, left them all; and a WPC, looking tiny and ridiculous in an over-large flak jacket, had conducted her to a large marquee well behind the armed cordon. Like the television lorry, this had been annexed by the police, and was being used as a coordination centre. It was busy with stewards and volunteers comparing lists, with distressed members of the public searching for lost or missing relatives, with crying children and harassed constables; and a few minutes later it was busier than ever, as scores of reporters and cameramen descended in search of Linda.

She gave them what little she could, making no attempt to hide her anxiety and exhaustion, knowing and not caring a damn that all the hag-ridden stresses of the last few hours were showing on her face and would show more clearly on the pages of tomorrow's papers. And when they were done, it was still with half an eye on those papers that she did what she did next, helping to distribute cups of hot soup among the crowds. As she'd expected, the photographers came eagerly on her heels.

She played the concerned and charitable wife for the cameras; and even when the cameras were finished with her she went back for more cups of soup, again carried her tray around. It was something to do, at least. Something to keep her busy, to keep her imagination away from the scene she'd left, her husband reduced to a cypher and the police playing games with her lover, tentatively sketching him in as a mass murderer . . .

After almost an hour she was still doing that, still bringing succour to the masses; or more specifically, offering a cup of soup to a sour, silent old tramp sitting by the roadside. Wrinkling her nose at the stink of him but doing it anyway, bending over him with her tray outstretched: "Excuse me, would you like some of this? It's hot . . . "

At first she thought that he was blessedly going to ignore

her altogether; but then, just as she was on the verge of drawing back and leaving him, he lifted his head slightly so that she could see something of his face under his hood, deep-set eyes and a foul, matted beard. He looked at her, at her tray; and said, "Tea? Ivy's bringing me tea. I'm waiting for Ivy."

"Oh. Are you?" That was possible, even likely; there were booths and caravans serving drinks free, with long queues of people waiting. But a momentary curiosity held her there, made her ask, "Who's Ivy?"

"She's in there." And he jerked his head forward, towards the distant Centre. "She told me to wait, said she'd bring some tea out. And some baccy. So I'm waiting, see? Like she said. I'm waiting for Ivy."

"Oh. Yes, I see. But . . . " But chances were, if she'd got herself caught in the Centre and hadn't found her way out yet, chances were that she was dead or seriously injured, this Ivy of his. And despite her disgust at the state of him, despite the fact that yesterday she would have hurried past him without a second glance, Linda still felt an unexpected sympathy. Death was a great leveller, and guilt a greater; and she was learning a lot about guilt today, and the various forms it dressed itself up in. It was because of guilt, because there was no one close to her trapped or lost to the killer – except Carl, perhaps, always excepting Carl – that she stayed then, that she pressed him. "But this isn't tea, you see. It's soup. Wouldn't you like some soup? Um, while you're waiting for Ivy to bring you the tea?"

His eyes gazed at her steadily, saying, *Don't play games with me, woman. I know what's going on in there, as well as you do. And if I choose to pretend I don't, to pretend I'm still peacefully waiting for my friend to bring me tea, that's no reason for you to patronise me. Don't treat me like a child.*

And after a moment or two, after he'd taken his time to be sure the message had got through, a scarred and filthy hand lifted itself to her tray and closed around one of the plastic cups.

*   *   *

In the end, Andrew just left Charlie where he was. Not alone, exactly, you couldn't call it leaving him alone: but leaving him, yes. Walking away.

Saying, "Look, Charlie, I've got to get back to the others. You don't have to come, we can manage; but I brought them here, and I can't just let them get on with it. So what we'll do, we'll shift Penny's friends outside and then we'll come straight back for you, okay? Shouldn't take more than twenty minutes, I reckon. Maybe half an hour, but we will come back, I promise. Then we'll get you and Sue out of here too. And, and the baby . . . "

Charlie didn't react, showed no signs that he'd even heard.

"It'd be good if you could just get off the mall, in case that guy comes through again. When you're up to it, take Sue in there, will you, into that clothes shop? That's where we'll look for you, if you're not here."

Still no response, and nothing for Andrew to do now but get to his feet, lift the rolled stretcher and balance it awkwardly under his arm, give Charlie a final, ineffectual squeeze of the shoulder in farewell.

"Good luck, then. Half an hour, I promise. No longer."

And he walked away.

The long stretcher was heavy and difficult to handle alone, dragging uncomfortably at his shoulder. He swore softly under his breath, hurried as much as he could and forgot to be careful. Thinking that he was nearly there now, thank God, just one last stretch of mall to go, Andrew turned a corner, eased his aching muscles, lifted his head for the first glimpse of his goal – and saw them.

Saw the two girls, standing stiff and silent against a section of panelled wall.

Saw the man who held them at gunpoint from a few yards' distance: the man who was already moving, stepping back, swivelling his rifle round to cover Andrew.

"Here's another," the man said, almost conversationally. "You two don't move, you don't move an inch."

And they didn't; though Andrew wanted to yell at them, to scream that there was a hidden doorway into the service areas just feet away from them, that they could dive through and run for it while the man and his gun were turned Andrew's way. That any chance was better than no chance at all . . .

They didn't move, and he didn't scream, he didn't make a sound. He just stood frozen and fearful, cursing himself for his carelessness, staring down the rock-steady barrel of the rifle.

"Drop it," the man said. "That thing you're carrying, drop it there. What is it?"

Andrew forced the words out against the near paralysis of his mouth, of his whole body. "It's a stretcher, that's all. And blankets. We just came in to help, to take some people out . . ."

"Drop it."

Andrew dropped it; and they all stirred at the noise it made in falling, and were still again.

"Right. Now come here. Stand there, next to those two."

Andrew's legs didn't want to do it; but the rifle jerked to reinforce the command, and swung towards the girls again. The threat was unstated, obvious, very real. So Andrew walked slowly down the mall, towards the gun, towards his present death. Couldn't do anything else, with Dee in such danger.

He stood on her left, and felt her cold hand reaching for his, gripping hard through the slick of sweat. He squeezed back, a silent message of inadequate comfort. *At least we'll die together, hand in hand; and I suppose that's how I'd choose it, even if you wouldn't, love . . .*

Pressing his shoulders back, he felt the hinged panel behind him give, just a fraction; and thought, *I could pull her through with me. Now, while he's not expecting it. Just yank and shove, and run. We might make it. Penny wouldn't, of course, he'd stop to shoot Penny before he came after us. That's what might buy us time enough to get away. And one death has got to be better than three, anything's got to be better than the three of us just standing here, waiting for him to kill us. Penny'd tell us to go, she'd see that, she's bound to . . .*

He thought all that, and didn't do it. Just stood there, watching the man, watching his finger on the trigger, waiting for the end.

And for a long time, the man did the same: stood there and looked at Andrew, looked at Dee, at Penny. Said nothing, and did nothing; echoing their stillness and their silence.

Time enough for Andrew's gaze to jerk away from the deadly promise of that trigger-finger, to be drawn upwards to the man's eyes. They would have been remarkable in any context, brightly and blazingly blue; against the matt black wool of his balaclava, with the white showing clear all around the pupil, they were terrifying. *Mad,* Andrew thought, *he's utterly mad; but then, he'd have to be, wouldn't he?*

Then the man spoke, his voice tight and trembling.

"Three of you," he said. "Three spies, up against the wall. That's where you belong. Where you'll stay. We'll skip the blindfolds, and the cigarettes. No time for that. Summary execution, that's all you get. All you deserve."

And because he was mad, and because he so obviously, so madly meant it; because he was already stepping back and lifting the rifle-butt towards his shoulder, Andrew did the only thing that was left, the only thing he could think of.

Said, "You can't kill us, you know," and took a pace forward away from the wall.

The rifle jerked round to cover him. "Get back, spy. Up against the wall. Now."

"It won't do you any good." Praying that the madness would hold, would keep the finger still on the trigger just a second longer, Andrew walked calmly towards the gunman. "It won't work, you see. You can't kill us. Look, I'll show you."

Fighting to suppress an inward shiver – *don't think about it, for God's sake, just do it, do it now* – he reached out and closed his left hand firmly over the barrel's end, pushing it high towards the ceiling.

"Go on, then," he whispered. "Shoot. You'll see, you can't hurt us."

The gunman stared at him, then at his hand; and Andrew saw the mouth stretch into a thin smile.

He didn't hear the rifle go off, was barely aware of his hand exploding. Because it did hurt, Christ it hurt; his vision blurred and every nerve in his arm was screaming, his body was shaking and prickling with sweat, all he wanted to do was curl up on the floor and hug the pain close until it went away. But he had to cover that, he couldn't let the gunman see. *This job ain't over, boy. Halfway, maybe; see how the guy's staring? But there's more to do, and that'll be worse. Hang in there . . .*

And he straightened, slowly; squared his shoulders, and lifted his left arm. Metal rods and shards of shattered plastic thrust out from the cuff, wires dangled; he swung them idly, casually in front of the gunman's eyes and said, "See? I told you. You can't hurt us. Want to," – *God help me* – "want to try with the other one?"

Lifted his right hand, and spread it in an open invitation.

The gunman's head swivelled sharply back and forth between smashed mechanics and soft flesh. It cost Andrew more even than he'd imagined, to hold his one hand up and keep it there; but he'd be dead if he didn't. And so would Dee, and so would Penny.

He was gambling on the madness, because he had nothing else to gamble with; and at last, he won. The gunman took one step back, two; then turned and ran stumblingly away from them up the mall, round the corner, out of sight.

Andrew stood motionless until even the sound of the man's feet had faded. Then, slowly, he let his hand fall to his side; slowly he drew his other arm in to his chest, and slowly he turned to the girls.

Dee came uncertainly towards him, her eyes fixed on the shattered stump he was cradling against his shirt.

"How – how bad is that?" she asked, lifting a hand towards his elbow and letting it fall again, just a moment short of touching.

"It's bad."

"I remember, you said it always hurts to take it off. And to have it, to let him do that . . . "

"Yeah. Well, it worked, didn't it? We're alive. And we wouldn't have been, otherwise."

"You're bleeding."

He looked down, and saw without surprise that she was right: bright drops of red were staining his sleeve, dripping onto the floor. Just as well the gunman hadn't seen that. Or maybe not, maybe the sight of blood leaking from a plastic hand would only have added to his confusion, thrown him even further into his madness.

Whatever. The thing was done, and the killer gone: their lives saved and the price paid. Only the interest owing now, the days of pain and disability, the weeks of facing the world one-handed before a replacement could be ordered and somehow paid for, manufactured and flown over from Japan.

Andrew glanced across at Penny and saw her still standing tight, staring at him, her hands pressed flat against the wall for support. Saw the open fear on her face and forced himself to smile, to say calmly, "It's all right, love. It was artificial, that hand, just a prosthetic. Didn't you know?"

She shook her head.

"Sorry, didn't mean to scare you too. It was all I could think of, to scare him . . . "

He turned back to Dee, and it was easy to keep the smile there for her. He touched the back of her neck lightly with his fingers, sharing the apology round as he'd shared the smile, *Didn't mean to scare you, either. Just him, and me.*

Then he checked the shops on either side of the mall and said, "Let's get out of the road, shall we? That bookshop'll have a storeroom at the back. We can hide out in there, till this is over. Quicker than looking for a way out. And I, I don't think I can walk very far . . . "

Indeed he was swaying on his feet already, could feel himself ludicrously rocking side to side.

Dimly, he heard Penny's half-hearted protest, "But, Richard and Julian – they're just down there, it's only a couple of minutes away now . . . "

Andrew couldn't have answered her, his mind turning inexorably inward. But with Dee there, he didn't need to. He felt her arm coming firm around his waist, heard her crisp response.

"Don't be stupid, Penny. That's the way that guy went, right? We can't risk running into him again. I'm sorry about your friends, but they'll have to take their chances like the rest of us. Come on, help me with Andrew, will you? I want to get him out of sight, then have that hand off and look at the damage . . . "

No one had ever seen Andrew's arm at close quarters, barring himself and his doctors. He'd never allowed it. Even his boss the former nurse had been fended off, allowed to inspect the hand itself but not to look below the shirt. He thought dazedly about having Dee be the first, about her tentative fingers undoing the straps and buckles, lifting the wreckage away to expose the scarred, distorted flesh beneath. That had been ugly and inhuman enough in its original state, after the amputation; it was far worse now, with wires worming out of the red skin and tiny plugs and sockets bonded to his flesh to accommodate his technological miracle of a hand.

Andrew thought about Dee being the first to see that in all

its gross unglory; and realised that he didn't give a damn.
I'm glad, pet. Crazy, but I am. Glad it's going to be you . . .

*   *   *

"Any chance of more reinforcements, sir?"

That was Commander Jakes, looking up from the radio
handset he'd been murmuring into.

"Michael . . . " The Assistant Chief Constable sighed, and
shrugged helplessly. "We've got three hundred officers de-
ployed here. The whole region's dangerously under-policed
as it is; I've got people back at HQ permanently on the
phone, tracking down everyone who's on leave and calling
them in."

"I know, sir, but I'm having to leave guards at every
intersection to stop this guy doubling back on us, and I'm
running short already. I can't go much further without extra
men. Could you get on to another region and borrow some?
With weapons, we're short on those too. It's either that or
shift to what we were discussing earlier, the hunter-killer
squads; and that's chancy."

"I'll do what I can."

The Assistant Chief Constable reached for a telephone;
Johnnie's eyes moved on to where Inspector Holborn was
standing with a photograph in his hand, talking to a uniform
sergeant.

"Get some copies made of this, and release it with the
statement. That should keep them happy, they love pictures."

"Yes, sir."

Johnnie caught a glimpse of the photo as the sergeant took
it: Peter Kerr, the standard head-and-shoulders shot included in everyone's file.

Lifting himself quickly, hurrying over before Holborn was
once again too busy to spare time for Johnnie:

"You are giving Kerr's name to the press?"

"That's right, Mr Lee. And his photo, as you saw."

"And if you are wrong, if the killer is not Peter Kerr? You
still have no proof . . . "

"With his mother murdered and him vanished, we've
reason enough to be looking for him. The statement doesn't
say categorically that he's the man in the Centre; and the
media's well acquainted with the laws of libel. Their

lawyers'll be watching every word until we give them positive confirmation."

"If you do. It could still be coincidence."

"All right, if. And if we're wrong, if it isn't Kerr, it'll still be as well to have the public on their guard against him. There's little enough doubt that he killed his mother. He's a dangerous man, Mr Lee. But I don't think we need be too concerned about him suing us for libel. I reckon it's him, right enough. I don't believe in coincidence, not to this extent. Do you?"

He turned away without waiting for an answer; and Johnnie went back to his chair, to his own interminable wait. To the ticking of the clock above his head, to his private little hell: and no, he didn't believe in coincidence either. Not to this extent. He believed in Peter Kerr, in his guns and grenades and his terrible power to destroy; and sitting in the middle of that destruction, Johnnie didn't need a photograph to see Peter Kerr. The man's handiwork was all about him and his face danced behind Johnnie's eyes, it smiled at him, clear and direct. *Look what I've done,* it said, *I've broken your favourite toy, I've killed your baby. And I'm not through yet, just you watch. Just you wait . . .*

And Johnnie watched, and waited; and gradually – minute by minute, second by slow second – Johnnie remembered how to hate.

2100:

and Richard was the first of those left in the Centre, the first of those left alive to realise that finally something was happening.

It wasn't what he'd been waiting for so long, Penny coming back as she'd promised. At first he didn't know what it was, couldn't be sure that it wasn't just the gunman playing games, setting off a couple of grenades to amuse himself and his audience of the dead. To bring the house down.

But he heard a distant and muffled thud, and lifted his head to listen; and heard another a few moments later. Thought maybe he'd heard something else too, the crackle of an amplified voice too far off to distinguish words.

Stroked Julian's hair, glanced indecisively from the boy's glistening white face to the closed door of the shop, and back again; and made up his mind in a rush.

"You wait here, sweets," he murmured, sliding Julian's head gently off his lap onto a pillow of jackets. "I'll just go and see. Won't be a minute. And don't you worry, I'll be careful. I'm not going to walk into that bastard now, not after all this . . . "

He pushed himself to his feet and went slowly over to the door, feeling the stiffness and uncertainty in his legs as he eased it open. He stood listening while his eyes darted from one open mall to the next. He saw nothing at first, no movement; but thought he caught it again, that faint suggestion of a voice speaking through a megaphone. Coming from the left, if it was there at all. And he'd seen the killer come running from that direction a while ago, sprinting madly across the square to vanish again on the far side.

Nothing to stop him doubling back, of course, going round another way. But still . . .

Richard hesitated in the doorway, looked back to check on Julian, not exactly expecting to see the boy sitting up and taking notice but looking anyway, just in case; then he turned his head again and heard another of those soft thuds.

Saw a stream of white smoke way down at the far end of a mall, where it joined another open intersection; saw the stream turn to an eddying, obscuring cloud, and felt his heart race as he hurried back to Julian's side.

"They're coming, sweets, they really are. Not long now and they'll be here, they'll look after you. Just, just hang in there, a bit longer. Don't you dare give up on me now, you hear . . . ?"

Best would be simply to sit and wait: to spend these last few hopeful minutes as he had spent the despairing hours up to now, staying quietly with Julian in the safety of their nested corner. But he couldn't do that with rescue so close, with adrenalin surging in his blood, urging him to action. He got to his feet again, went back to the door and saw a bank of smoke billowing down the mall towards him.

He felt his throat sting and his eyes start to water, as harsh chemicals caught at his breath; and then he heard the voice one more time, closer this time, close enough to make out some of the words:

" . . . *with your hands in the air . . . repeat, armed police . . . surrender now, walk slowly towards my voice with your hands up. Leave your weapons on the ground . . .* "

But Richard was coughing now, choking on poisons. Dimly through his weeping eyes, he saw a canister arc out of the smoke to land just twenty yards away, its contents hissing violently out to flood and foul the air.

Tear gas, he thought. *They're using tear gas, to be sure. And Julian – he can't take that, it's too much. He's hardly breathing anyway. It'll kill him, if he gets gassed on top . . .*

No thoughts now of sitting and waiting patiently for rescue. He slipped out of the door and let it close behind him, for what poor protection it might give to his lover; and he ran stumblingly on his aching legs, desperately into the smoke.

He had to find someone fast, tell them to lay off the gas. Tell them they didn't need it, the square was safe; make them bring a mask through for Julian, before it got to him. But he couldn't see for the pain in his eyes, the streaming tears and the smoke; and he couldn't shout with his throat burning and his lungs all but shut down, clamped and wheezing for clean air. All he could do was run, force his legs and his body on and hope to run through it, to find help and sense beyond.

He ran utterly blind, caroming off a shop window with a bruising jolt, gashing his thigh on a concrete bin that almost brought him down. But he stayed up, and stayed running; heard the voice again, louder and closer, and thought, *Nearly there now, I'm nearly through . . .*

And his foot kicked something on the ground, something small but heavy, he felt it go flying away ahead of him like a harbinger of his coming.

And he heard a voice, another voice: muffled but close, barely yards away.

Heard it yell, "Grenade! Get down . . . "

And Richard stopped running a moment later, felt himself flying instead, floating, the floor gone from under him.

Didn't have time enough to wonder, let alone to understand. Didn't have the time even to realise that he was falling, not floating.

And was gone, long gone before his body hit the ground.

*   *   *

Penny sat on a box of books, beside and between unruly stacks of books, beneath shelves of books; and felt a foolish yearning to run her eye selectively over the titles, to pick one out and pass the time in reading.

She didn't do it, of course. She couldn't have focused her mind long enough to read the titles properly, let alone concentrate on pages of print. Its only value would have been as a gesture; and as a gesture it would be meaningless, both to herself and her companions.

So Penny sat and did nothing, only watched Andrew's face recover slowly from grey to pale, about as good as it was going to get.

He was sitting on the floor, slumped against the wall in the only clear space the stockroom afforded. Denise was on her knees beside him, still now as Penny was still, with the remains of his artificial hand cradled ridiculously on her lap.

She'd refused all further help from Penny, Denise had, when once they'd got Andrew in here and sitting down. She'd eased his jacket off and discarded it, unbuttoned his shirt cuff and rolled the bloodied sleeve up to his shoulder while he just sat there, head back and eyes closed tight against the damage. Or else closed against the girls' seeing the damage, or against their seeing the arm at all. Penny couldn't be sure which; but then she was too confused, too shocked and distressed to be sure of anything. She couldn't even work out what the relationship was between Andrew and Denise: whether they were lovers or old friends or simply strangers thrown together by crisis, as she had been thrown together with them.

Andrew's shattered hand had been hanging half off his arm, torn loose by the bullets' blast. Denise had fumbled with unpractised fingers at the straps that held it on – *not lovers, then,* Penny had thought, *or she'd know the trick of it, she'd have surely done this before* – and then spent minutes more disconnecting it from slender wires that snaked sickeningly out through the misshapen and bleeding stump below his elbow.

For lack of bandages, Denise had unrolled Andrew's

shirtsleeve again, folded that around the stump and tied it in place with a length of stockroom twine.

"How does that feel?" she'd asked, her voice hardly louder than a breath. "Better?"

Andrew still hadn't spoken, he'd only moved his head in a faint nod.

Denise had sighed, stretched up to kiss his cheek lightly, then settled back on her heels again with the detached prosthetic held in her hands, on her lap.

Since then, she hadn't moved at all; and looking at her now – seeing her gaze so firmly fixed on his defeated face and the way her human fingers played with his of broken plastic, as if that were the only part of him she dared to touch – Penny thought, *Lovers, after all. She'd have to be. Wouldn't she?*

But maybe not, even now. After all, Penny wasn't moving either; and Penny too was watching Andrew, tracing the slow improvement in his colour and aching for the baffled hopelessness of his spirit, so clearly drawn on the slack skin of his face.

So they all three of them sat silently in that silent room, waiting for the world to change again.

And change it did, at last, as it had to.

It was the silence that left them first. Or rather the silence stayed with them, stayed inside them; but it allowed itself to be penetrated by sounds from outside, sounds from the mall.

Sounds from movies, really: running feet and soft explosions, shouts and a metallic megaphone voice, the sudden rattle of a gun as suddenly silent.

They stayed as they were, unmoving and unspeaking, only their eyes betraying the first stirring, the first expectation of hope. Like any hostages, without the strength to influence events in their favour or against, all they could do was keep breathing; and that was enough for all of them, with the air turned strangely harsh and stinging, faint traces of smoke and chemicals coming to them under the closed door.

They waited, with the endless patience of the utterly lost. A long time they waited, before there were soft noises from the bookshop beyond the door, cautious feet finding their way towards them. And still they didn't or couldn't move more than their heads towards the sounds, didn't do more than wonder whether this was death or salvation. Penny felt herself almost beyond caring. If it was the gunman, then let him come . . .

The door crashed inwards with a violence that couldn't shatter their shared stillness; and gunman it was, a large and shadowy figure, face hidden by a balaclava and rifle sweeping the small room, its dark eye searching from corner to corner.

But not the same man, no. This one wore black, and his finger stayed motionless on the trigger, holding the bullets back.

After a frozen moment his thumb moved on the safety-catch, and he hoisted the rifle up onto his shoulder.

"Okay, folks, come on out of it. You're safe now. Made my day, you have," he added conversationally, one eye closing in an impossible wink. "Nice to find some living faces, in all of this."

They were far beyond responding. After a second or two he came further in, slipped his hand under Penny's arm and lifted her gently but irresistibly to her feet.

"Up you get, pet. There's some people outside, they'll look after you. Cup of tea and a chat, shoulder to cry on. They'll get your names off you, too. Chances are there's someone out there going to be dead pleased to see you . . . "

He held her a moment longer, to be sure she wasn't going to drop again when he let go; then he turned towards the others, ready to mete out the same rough comfort.

And stopped dead, with a muttered "Christ . . . !"

Looking past him, Penny saw what he was seeing: saw Andrew with his arm cut off below the elbow, with the shirt-sleeve tied around it and stained scarlet.

Saw, and found herself talking at last, her voice doing its own thing, high and shrill and unstoppable:

"It's all right, guy, don't you worry about him. He's the original bionic man, he comes to pieces . . . "

And felt herself doing the same, coming utterly to pieces as the words splintered into a hiccuping, sobbing laughter, sharp as glass and falling, falling like shards of broken glass, falling apart . . .

And coming back together again, after a time beyond clocks or counting: slowly and painfully coming back, clutching at the scattered straws of her sanity, weaving them with hesitant fingers into a raft that could at least hold her above the flood, at least for a while.

Coming back to the stockroom, to a sense of bitter shame, an embarrassment that was stupid in the circumstances but nonetheless real; coming back to Denise's arm tight around her shoulders, Denise's voice murmuring calm nothings into her ear.

" . . . Easy now, Penny, it's okay . . . "

"Oh, lord . . . " She lifted a shaking hand to her face and found it wet, found that she was crying. Sniffed, blinked the tears away or tried to, said, "I'm sorry . . . "

"Don't be silly. I'd have gone hysterical myself, most likely, only you got in there first." A friendly shake and an unexpected kiss on the cheek, and Denise's eyes examining her carefully from just a few inches away, giving the lie direct to what she'd just said. That girl was rock-solidly in control, had probably never been further from hysterics in her life.

Penny sniffed again, fumbled for a tissue and blew her nose hard, straightened her back and looked around.

Andrew was up on his feet, standing in the doorway, watching the two of them. His bloody arm was hanging down at his side; his other hand – no, his one, his only hand – was clamped tight around the jamb for a support that was all too obviously needed.

"I'm, I'm okay now," Penny said, giving Denise a weak but determined smile. "Honest."

"Sure?"

"Yeah. You . . . " *You get over to your boyfriend, he needs you more than I do.* She didn't say that aloud, just with a gesture of her head, but Denise got the message. She gave Penny a final squeeze, and walked across to Andrew.

"Come on, then. Hitch yourself onto me, that door's not taking you anywhere . . . "

Through the bookshop, going slow, no hurry now; and on into the mall. There were people hurrying here, men carrying stretchers, some in uniform and some not. Volunteers from the public, Penny guessed those would be. Stretchers going to the right, towards the square, empty; and stretchers coming back loaded with bodies under cotton dust-sheets, improvised shrouds.

There was a group of armed men standing a little way

away, anonymous in their balaclavas, talking urgently.

"It's orders, John. Not enough men to go on the way we are, and no hope of reinforcements, apparently, not for hours yet. Split up into small groups, scour the place and find the bastard, that's what the Commander says."

"Well, I don't like it. It's slow, sure, the way we've been doing it; but it's been safe. We'd be losing that. It's a hell of a risk."

"I know that. But if we haven't got the men . . . "

Penny's attention drifted away, following the empty stretchers; and after a moment her feet started drifting too, down the mall towards Richard and Julian.

Leaving Denise and Andrew, forgetting them entirely, she walked off in search of her friends; and found them both before ever she reached the square, or the shop where she'd left them.

Found Julian first, and could hardly believe it when it happened.

There was a stretcher coming towards her, just one more in the chain, four volunteers struggling with the awkward weight of it but smiling as they struggled; and no makeshift shroud draped over this one, just a body wrapped in jackets, a head of streaked blond hair suddenly and shockingly familiar.

Penny stopped, and stared; and the stretcher-bearers stopped too in response to her outthrust arm, to her question.

"Is he, is he alive?"

"That's what they said, love. What the doctor said. I dunno, me, he's cold as – as anything, but the doc says he's alive, he's got a chance. What, you don't know him, do you?"

"Yes. Yes, I do. But where's Richard?" She got nothing but blank looks and shrugs to that, and went on more urgently, "There should've been a guy with him, he wasn't hurt at all. He only stayed to look after Julian . . . "

"Sorry, love. I didn't see no one. Just this boy, in a shop he was, all wrapped up ready for us. Wasn't no one else there except the doc."

"Maybe he's gone out already," offered from the back end of the stretcher. "I know they used tear gas in here, maybe that drove him out, like . . . "

Penny nodded, but wandered on anyway; and found two

men standing over a body.

"Christ, it wasn't my fault! I'd never have done it deliberate. But it was all smoke, and then there was this grenade, and I didn't know it was a dud, like, how could I? I couldn't see any cover, I thought I was going to get blasted; but there was this guy coming for me, and I saw his jacket, camouflage like we was told to look out for – so I shot him. Of course I did, what the hell else was I going to do?"

And Penny looked at him, looked down at the body; saw a combat jacket like the ones that had cloaked Julian, stained and soaked with blood –

– and saw Richard's face above it, collapsed in death.

2200:

and it was Denise who stopped suddenly, on their slow walk back to sanity; Denise who said, "Where's Penny?"

"Dunno . . . " Andrew shrugged one-shouldered, shook his head, didn't even turn to look. Couldn't, probably, with the weight of his own collapse so heavily upon him.

But she could, and did.

She saw Penny's tall figure stooped, slumped towards a body on the ground, seemingly held up in defiance of all the laws of gravity: certainly by no will, no strength of her own. Saw, and disengaged her arm from Andrew's the same moment.

Said, "Wait here," and hurried back into the old and wounding world again.

Found Penny crying, as she'd guessed: tears leaking unregarded down her cheeks while her hands hung rather than reached towards the man on the floor.

Denise put her arms round the taller girl and just held her for a minute, paying no attention to the men standing by. Then she asked gently, "Is that Julian, is it?"

She expected a nod, was confident of it; and was deeply

shaken and enlightened both, abruptly understanding the intensity of Penny's grief when she got the opposite.

"No. No, it's not Julian. I saw him, they said he's going to be all right, maybe. This, this is Richard . . . "

There was nothing that Denise could say, that would have any validity in the face of such vicious irony; but she said it anyway, her voice murmuring softly on, making gifts of hopelessly inadequate words while she tried to draw Penny away from the body.

"No," Penny said, finally divining her intention. "No, I want to stay. I want to go with him."

"That won't be possible, I'm afraid," one of the men said flatly, making no apology for listening in. "This body can't be moved at present."

"Why the hell not?" Denise demanded, suddenly furious. "You're taking all the others out of here, what's so different about him?"

The man didn't answer that, he simply repeated himself. "This body can't be moved. It would be best if you left with your friend now, please. We need to secure this area."

Denise's anger would have kept her there, kept her fighting; but surprisingly it was Penny who moved to obey him, seeming to have no defences left and no taste for the battle. She turned her gaze slowly away from Richard's face, though it took an effort of her whole head to do it. One arm lifted itself, found its own way to Denise's shoulders and lay across them like a dead weight, nothing living about it.

Nothing living in Penny's eyes either, or in her voice as she pushed the words out like bubbles of pain.

"Let's go, then. Let's get out."

*　　　*　　　*

Just as Rudy's body had clenched itself unforgivingly around his labouring lungs, still working against his will, against his explicit instructions, so his mind too had clenched: had seized hold of the last thread of his consciousness and refused to let go.

Trapped in this linear, this one-track life, he absorbed facts sequentially, one after another, too cramped to find any space for reaction or response:

Fact: that Liane's hand lay stiffly linked with his, cooling from the inside, from the bones out.

Fact: that his head was turned the other way, towards the open spaces of Dreamland and the mall beyond.

Fact: that he could hear gunshots, very close.

Fact: that a man was running into his field of view, running crouched from cover to cover, turning to fire and running again.

Fact: that the man was gone, had vanished into the wall; but

Fact: that the gunfire still continued.

Fact: that Liane's clawed hand had jerked at his, like a summons.

Fact: that he could still move, for her; that his head had turned, rolling over on his neck in an instant and unquestioning response.

Fact: that if she had been dead before, dead and cooling, she was doubly so now; because a ricochet had torn her apart from shoulder to waist, ripped her open to show him the bright messes of her body.

Fact: that he could still move for himself too, could turn his head again the other way.

Fact: that there were three men now following the first, two creeping cautiously towards the wall that had swallowed him, inching their weapons ahead of them, while the third sheltered behind the wreckage of the fallen roller-coaster and spoke into a hissing radio, only yards away from Rudy.

Fact: that the man said, "Team seven, team seven to control . . . Perpetrator gone to ground through a service door in the west wall of the playground place . . . No casualties on our side, no hits observed on him . . . Understood, sir. Will await reinforcements and further instructions . . . Yes, sir. And, Commander? Send a medical team with a stretcher." His eyes now fixed on Rudy. "I think we've got a live one."

*   *   *

Perversely – and why not, on a perverse day in a perverse world? – Carol was out of bed now, getting up at bedtime. Not dressed, she was shuffling around in the kitchen in her dressing-gown and slippers, scrambling some eggs to eat in front of the television.

She could hear it now, the volume turned up loud in the living-room:

" . . . Here at the Meldon Centre there's still no positive news, nothing certain. The police have refused to confirm rumours that their new tactics have borne fruit, that one of their roaming hunter-squads has actually come into contact with the gunman and that they are now moving to isolate him in one particular wing of this vast complex.

"However, what I can tell you is that the recovery teams have brought out a further four seriously injured victims in the last half-hour, together with thirteen more bodies. This brings the total of dead to forty-three so far, with over a hundred people injured. The police say the death-toll will undoubtedly rise higher, though they are refusing to speculate about the final figures.

"And now from the Meldon Centre, from the scene of the worst mass-murder ever recorded in Britain, this is Nigel Felton handing you back to the studio . . . "

"Thank you. I'm sure we'll be joining Nigel again, as soon as there's anything further to report from the Centre.

"Meanwhile, the police have issued the name and photograph of a man employed as a security officer at the Meldon Centre, whom they are very anxious to interview in connection with another incident, the discovery of a woman's body at her home in the village of Allingham.

"Mrs Olive Kerr was found murdered just before eight o'clock this evening. The man the police wish to question is her son Peter Kerr, aged thirty-three. He is described as five foot ten inches tall, with short dark hair, blue eyes and a stocky build. The public are warned that he may be dangerous, and they should on no account approach him.

"When asked about the possibility of Peter Kerr being the gunman at the Meldon Centre, Inspector Holborn would only say that all things are possible . . . "

If she'd heard that, Carol might well have taken issue with

the inspector, might have argued that some things simply weren't conceivable; but she was hearing nothing now.

She was only standing in the living-room doorway, where the names had drawn her; only staring at the picture of Peter on the screen, but hardly seeing it after the first shocked recognition.

Seeing pictures in her mind instead, memories resurrected and made solid, dredged from the dark corners where she'd abandoned them to fester and die.

2300:

and the door opened, swung silently open. The silence of it might have been the end of her, it might have caught her napping, that sneaking silence. But there was light too, bursting in from the bright and treacherous corridor, good as a shout to warn her.

She stayed frozen, huddled in her corner where the light couldn't reach. Narrowed her eyes against that raucous light, squinted at the doorway; saw the figure of a man, a big man outlined by the light.

Heard him chuckle softly, happily.

Watched him coming in, closing the door behind him; and thanked all the gods in her vast pantheon that there was still a little light leaking from the open trapdoor in the floor, enough for him to see by. That he didn't reach for the switch on the wall.

She'd had a look down that trapdoor, oh yes, after the people had come up through it a while back. She'd seen the dim and threatening tunnel below; and when she'd had her look she'd scurried back to her corner, nice and safe. No tunnels for her, thank you very much. You didn't know where a tunnel might take you, or who you might meet on the way. There might not be anywhere to hide, down a tunnel. Better to stay hidden, stay here . . .

But the big man didn't think so. He took one look back at

the door and laughed again, like a farewell, goodbye to all that; and then he swung himself down into the hole, into the tunnel.

And pulled the trapdoor shut after him, holding its weight easily one-handed above his head, lowering it slowly and snugly into the floor while Ivy watched unblinking from her corner.

*   *   *

Andrew gazed in loathing at the neat job a doctor had made of rebandaging his stump: at the clean whiteness of it, the open declaration of his disability. No blood seeping through the precautionary stitches in his flesh, no pain seeping under the barrier of drugs. No hope of pretending even to himself that this was a fresh and honourable wound, that he was only another casualty of the day's grim war.

Not so much as a sling to hide behind; only the vivid bandages and the arm cut short for all to see and take note of. *This man is missing a hand, he's handicapped.* Pun very much not intended, naturally.

He walked out of the big marquee that was almost empty now, little work left for the doctors here and less expected. The dead were being taken somewhere else, not to disturb the living; and there were few of those coming out of the Centre.

He walked out, and his shadow stretched grotesquely ahead of him into the rectangle of light falling from the marquee's entrance. Stretched towards the darkness beyond and joined with it, melted into it as he kept walking, vanished altogether as he stepped across the border.

Night had come at last, though the Centre denied it, light blazing from its every entrance as it tried to extend the day. Andrew stood in the dark and gazed at it from a distance more than physical; and noticed without surprise that he was still fidgeting to find some camouflage, reaching the stump towards an impossible pocket then wrapping his hand around it, pressing it tight against his chest.

Standing in the dark.

And he couldn't even turn to Calum, for some cheerful abuse: *Lost your hook, then, Captain? Or are you just playing for the sympathy vote?*

The Dalek was gone, exterminated; he'd learned that

sometime in the last hour. Someone had told him, he couldn't remember who, hadn't noticed.

A hand tucked itself under his arm suddenly, unannounced. Too weary to startle, he looked around, looked down.

Saw Dee.

She'd taken time out for some restoration work, while he'd been with the doctor. Her face was scrubbed clean, and her Mohican trademark rode high above her shaven scalp, erect as a cockatoo's crest. He pictured the expression of bleak determination that would have been on her face as she did that, as she worked on her hair; pictured her seeing it in the mirror before her, recognising it for what it was and her motives for what they were, and carrying on regardless; and thought, *Jesus, girl, is it any wonder that I love you?*

"How is it?" she asked. "Seriously?"

"Can't feel a thing."

"Liar," she said bluntly. "And don't," she said, "*don't* tell me you're drugged up to the armpits so it can't hurt any more. I know that, I've been watching. But it still can. It still does, doesn't it? Doesn't it?"

"How's Penny?" he said, answering her with evasion.

"Flipped. I mean, really flipped. The police wanted her, for information about Richard. His full name and address, where he was when she left him, what he'd said, what he meant to do. All of that. But she couldn't even talk to them. So they gave her a sedative and took her off in one of the ambulances, I don't know where." And then, fiercely, "That's what I *mean*, it still hurts. Not me, though, not so much. Penny, Charlie. You. And don't pretend, I know what it cost you, what you did in there. You're the ones who've really been hammered, and they can't patch that up with dressings and an anaesthetic . . . "

He said nothing. After a minute they started to move, heading down the slope towards the promise of hot soup from a booth below.

Before they could reach it, though – while they were still picking their way through small knots of people, all that was left of the grieving, the waiting, the spectating crowds – a voice hailed them uncertainly from the shadows.

Or rather, a voice hailed her.

"Den . . . ?" it said, just that. Just her name, or half of it. And half was enough, seemingly, because she tore herself free of Andrew's clutching, denying grasp. Turned and stared, said, "Matt?"

And Matt it was, Matt it had to be, this unknown young man taking a step, two steps towards them, coming to a dead stop.

"Oh, Matt . . . "

And Dee did the rest herself, took all the other steps that were needed; ran at him, hurled herself at him, tangled her arms around his neck and made a mess of that careful Mohican against his chest.

For a moment stolen hard, stolen violently away from time, Andrew only stood and watched, and hated: hated him, hated her, hated himself more.

And then – because he'd never met Matt yet and wouldn't, couldn't do it now, not here, not one-handed and on top of everything – he swivelled on his heel and started up the slope again, quickly into the sheltering dark.

It was nothing but relief when another voice reached him, calling his own name this time, and he was joined in his steady regress by the slim figure of Linda Lee.

"Andrew, have you seen my husband?"

"I think he's still with the police, up at the Centre."

"Good." She fell into step beside him; then, registering his bandages, "Are you hurt? Your hand . . . "

"No, Mrs Lee," lying profoundly, profanely. "I'm not hurt."

And if he heard yet another call from the darkness, if he heard Dee shouting for him, at least he could ignore it as he offered his good arm to Linda, to help her up the hill.

*   *   *

It was darker now, darker than dark with the trap shut; and Ivy didn't like the dark, never had. So maybe it was that, maybe it was the want of light that sent her out of her corner now, scuttling and scrabbling on all fours across the floor. Maybe she only wanted to heave the trap up again and let it lie open, let the light out again.

Or maybe it was the shooting, dimly heard through the door, echoing down the stairwell. Maybe it was the fear of guns that set her moving; maybe she was thinking that the tunnel might be safer after all, if they were back to shooting.

Ivy didn't know what she was thinking. All she knew was

the feel of concrete sharp under the palms of her hands, hard against her knees as she crawled; then smoother wood, her groping fingers finding the edges of the trap.

Cold metal sunk into the wood, a hinged ring to be pulled up and grasped two-handed, heaved against the dead weight of the trap. And she couldn't lift it like this, on her knees. Too heavy it was, for old Ivy's fat arms.

She had to stand, set her feet firmly, bend double and grope for the ring again.

Found it, tensed her shoulders, started to tug –

– and was tugging, feeling the trap lift, feeling her muscles shake under the weight of it, when there were running footsteps outside, the door burst open again, the light she might have been searching for came dazzling in and all safety slid away.

Her head jerked up, and again she saw a man framed in the doorway.

This one had a gun, she could see that too.

She saw him looking down the corridor, saw him lift the gun and spray bullets towards the stairs; then, as if the answering bark of gunfire had kicked him into action, he span lithely into the room, one hand reaching to catch the door and slam it shut behind him.

And he saw her, still standing doubled over with her legs spread and her hands on the ring of the trap. In the last moment of light before the door crashed into its frame again, she saw him seeing her.

And felt a trickle of warmth running down inside her leg as old Ivy wet herself, she did.

*　　　*　　　*

The route back took them past the transformer station; and Linda checked slightly, seeing an armed guard inside the wire.

"Andrew? What do you suppose he's been put there for?"

"Oh. Um, my idea, actually. There's a way out of the Centre, sort of a tunnel . . . I just thought it would be a good idea to keep an eye on it."

Linda nodded, and they walked on; but she kept a curious eye on the building's door and its guard, wondering why Andrew should have been thinking about tunnels, why the police should have listened.

Then she checked again, stopped dead in her tracks as the guard moved, crouching suddenly, his rifle coming up to the aim. A moment later she saw why, saw a crack of light around the door.

"Andrew . . . " A warning soft as a breath, and wholly overridden by the guard's flat barking voice.

"Armed police! Stand exactly where you are, make no movements!"

For a second, the whole world obeyed: the door didn't move any further, neither did the policeman, nor Linda, nor Andrew at her side.

Then, "Throw your weapons out through the door! Do this now!"

And a response, a man's voice coming muffled from inside the building: "No weapons. Ain't got any."

"Identify yourself!"

"My name's Carl, Carl Sindon . . . "

Linda's fingers clenched tight on Andrew's arm.

"Place both hands on the door, where I can see them, and open it slowly. Do this now!"

The door opened obediently, light spilled out across the gravel, bringing with it the shadow of a man; and at last there he was, unmistakably Carl. His hands gripping the edge of the door, and his face in profile, masked by shadows but unmistakably smiling.

"Lie face down on the ground, with your arms and legs outstretched! Now!"

He spread-eagled himself compliantly; and seeing him so unresistant, seemingly so amused, Linda took her first half-step towards the wire and the gate in the wire, towards Carl.

"Wait . . . " Andrew held her back. "That guy's nervous as hell, and he's got good reasons for it. Don't distract him now."

So they did nothing, only stood and watched while the guard used his radio one-handed, keeping his rifle trained on the prone man. Watched and waited, minute after tense minute, until two more policemen came running down over the grass; and then waited a little longer, while the building was searched and locked again, while Carl was handcuffed and pulled to his feet.

Then, as he was frog-marched out of the gate, Linda's

patience and her stillness broke, both together and all at once. She ran towards the three men in a stumble and a flurry of legs, unheeding of Andrew's voice behind her, calling her back; ran until she was abruptly face to face with Carl and never mind the other two, the men with wary suspicion on their faces and guns in their hands.

Stood there, stared at him, found herself with nothing to say.

While he grinned at her, open and easy; while he said, "Hi, Linda. How's things?"

Coming back to the command post with Andrew, following Carl and his escort, Linda found it greatly and unexpectedly changed.

There were men running in and out of the police van, in and out of the television lorry beside it; voices raised and a thrill of excitement, of achievement, of a resolution finally in prospect.

Commander Jakes and the Assistant Chief Constable hurried past with barely a glance, with no interest at all. Johnnie was on their heels, still clutching after his lost importance, too preoccupied even to notice his wife. Inspector Holborn stood on the steps of the van, watching them go; he spared Carl a glance and a second's thought, said, "All right, you'd better bring him in. I'll find time for him in a few minutes, maybe."

"What's happening?" That was Andrew, asking in a voice that obviously expected no answer.

But got one, briefly. "We've run him to ground," Holborn said. "In that storeroom where you got in before."

"Yeah? You'd better send some more men, then, to cover the tunnels. You don't want him slipping away now."

"Done, already. But I don't think he'll be slipping away." A pause, and then the rest of it, the bad news. "He's got a hostage."

0000:

and the reporters had found Denise shortly after Matt did, catching them both in the car park, her extravagant hair like a beacon to guide them. They'd learned from someone that she'd been into the Centre, met the killer and come out alive; and for Denise no less than for Linda earlier, facing the cameras and the questions was a part of her job. Her boss would have slaughtered her if she'd ducked out. It was grand publicity for Radio Nova; and a few minutes of national fame wasn't going to do her own career any harm.

So she'd smiled through her exhaustion, knowing that the lenses would be picking up both; she'd held tight to Matt's hand, for the cameras and the comfort, for both; and for something more than a few minutes, for close on half an hour she'd given the starved newshounds all she could.

She'd played down Charlie's role, in an effort to spare him as much as possible; and she'd made a hero out of Andrew. *That'll teach him to go off like that*, she thought, drowning guilt under a petty anger. And that was what finally freed her from the focus of press attention, as the whole corps departed in search of a one-handed man, more photographs and a fresh angle on the story.

She and Matt got in the car quickly, and drove away; but not far. Just up the slip-road to the motorway, where they pulled over and parked illegally on the hard shoulder.

They had a fine view of the Centre from here, isolated on its triangle of land with the dark bands of the two rivers meeting at its apex. For a minute or two they just sat there and looked at it; then Denise reached across and took Matt's hand again. Not for the cameras this time, solely for herself. She pressed it tightly, palm to palm, felt the responding strength in his fingers and thought, *I couldn't have done this with Andrew. Not from this side, I'd have been holding plastic. Or nothing, tonight . . .*

She shivered, and turned harshly away from her thoughts; turned herself physically towards the chief cause of Andrew's distress, the boy who had claimed her too soon; and said, "Thanks for coming, Matt."

"Did you think I wouldn't?" The words and the voice aggressive, and the aggression totally fake, belied by his grip relaxing slowly, his thumb stroking gently across her knuckles.

"I didn't think," she said. "I couldn't, there just wasn't the space for it."

"Soon as I saw it on the news, I came down. And they said you'd got out, people had seen you; but then I couldn't find you. And I just kept looking, going round and round that bloody place, asking everyone. People were drifting away all the time, there was hardly anyone left by the end there, and still no sign of you; and I thought they were wrong, I thought you hadn't got out after all. I was frantic, by the end. Going crazy, shoving people out of the way, yelling for you. I almost beat up this one guy, this copper who told me to quiet down. Did take a swing at him, I think. I'm not sure. He was pretty close to belting me, and all. But then he said he'd seen you himself, you'd just come out; and I loved him then, I could've kissed him. He said to get a coffee and just wait, so I did that, it was easy then; and then there you were, and . . . "

And he was dry, seemingly, after so many words in a rush, all out of talking. He just looked at the view, looked at her, shrugged, shook his head. No hint of a smile, but she didn't need that.

"Matt, love . . . " She stretched across and kissed him gently on the stubble of his cheek, tasting salt, sweat or tears or both dried sticky on his shining skin.

"Make that appointment for me, yeah?" he said abruptly. "With the doctor. You do it."

"I will. I'll do that. For both of us. I'll do it tomorrow."

"No. Not tomorrow."

"Matt . . . "

But he was laughing at her, incredibly; a wild, rampant laugh shaking his whole body. "Tomorrow's Sunday, stupid."

"Christ, is it? Still?" She felt like an earthquake victim, dug out after days in the dust and terror. She looked at her watch, said, "No, no it isn't, it's Sunday now."

And was crying suddenly, as an earthquake victim might after days in the dust: crying alone, as an earthquake victim would, barely conscious of his arm circling her shoulders and his voice murmuring uncomfortable, comfortless comforts.

Cried for one minute, two minutes, five; cried until there was nothing left to cry for, until her mind was exhausted of matter as her body was of strength.

Blinked at him through sore eyes and was desperately, frantically glad that he wasn't Andrew, that he hadn't been there and didn't know.

Said, "Get us out of here, Matt love. Take us home."

And he nodded, said, "Do your seat-belt up, then," and put the car in gear.

* * *

Johnnie knew this place, of course, as he knew every last square metre of the Centre: knew it from the inside out, as it were, from the original vision to the detailed blueprints, from the first hole in the ground to the final touches.

But he didn't know it well, it was probably a year since he'd last been down this way; and he certainly didn't know it like this. Hardly recognised it as any part of his dream, had never in his worst nightmares imagined it so taken over.

He stood well back on the stairs, out of the way and reasonably out of danger. Stood quiet and unobtrusive, finding himself with no sort of role to play here and fearful as a schoolboy of being sent away altogether.

Stood, and looked: and saw, closest to him, standing on a lower stair, the narrow shoulders and stooped back of the Assistant Chief Constable.

Beyond him a broader back, bent over a video camera on a tripod: the police were recording the progress of the siege for review, for training, for posterity. Fixing it in history.

Beyond the camera, two more backs. Commander Jakes in shirt-sleeves, with a revolver visible in a holster under his left arm; and a man in black overalls, head swathed by a balaclava, rifle-butt grounded at his feet.

Then another man in the anonymous uniform, overalls and balaclava: this one tense and ready, back to the wall and rifle pointing to the ceiling.

Then the door, the closed and secret door.

And beyond the door two more men, the first echoing his

colleague's stance on this side – flat against the wall, ready to spin, to kick the door open, to go in shooting; the only difference his weapon, a revolver gripped two-handed – and the other crouched a little further down the corridor against the opposite wall, rifle trained steadily on the door.

Seven men below him, and none of them speaking now, everything said. *Let him sweat a little*, they'd said, *see what he does*. All of them waiting, expectant; and nothing for Johnnie but to wait with them and see what happened.

And sweat.

*   *   *

"Right, then, sonny. Your turn."

Inspector Holborn had finished his interrogation of the telephone, slammed the receiver down and swivelled his chair around. Carl was sitting on the other side of the hastily-cleared table, managing to look quite comfortable and easy despite his wrists handcuffed behind him, despite the presence of an armed and silent guard on either side.

"This is him, I suppose, Mrs Lee?"

"Oh – yes. Yes, that's Carl." Linda spoke from her own chair set against one wall, without taking her eyes from the prisoner, or the prisoner's smile.

"Right. Carl." Inspector Holborn let the name hang in the air for a few seconds, like an accusation; then went on quietly, "Want to tell us what the hell you were up to in there, Carl?"

Carl shrugged, an awkward gesture in the handcuffs; but there was nothing awkward in his voice as he said, "Helping, that's all. Helping people out. Nothing wrong with that, is there?"

"Helping. Right. Being a hero, is that it, is it? Getting your name in the papers?"

"If you like."

"It's what the papers like. And you'd know that, wouldn't you? But I'll tell you how it is, Carl, son – there are two kinds of people the papers like. They like heroes, and they like villains. They're both good for sales. Papers don't discriminate, you see? But I do. That's my job, sorting the heroes from the villains. And that's what I've got to sort out with you now, which kind you are. Either way you get the headlines, don't worry about that. I'm not going to stand in your light. It's just a question of what they say about you, tomorrow morning. Were you the guy who risked his life time and time again, to help a few injured victims to safety? Or was that cover, was it a smokescreen? Push comes to shove, were you the guy who hurt 'em in the first place, the guy who set off the fireworks?"

Linda made a move then, a gesture towards protest; but Holborn stilled her with a glance and drove on mercilessly.

"You're wearing the right clothes, see, Carl. And anyone can put a gun down for a minute, take off a balaclava. Anyone can play hero for the cameras, when they know they're perfectly safe. You can fool the press, all of the time. That's not difficult. Where it gets hard is fooling us. And coming out of that tunnel, when we'd just chased you in at the other end – now that wasn't smart, Carl. One and one makes two, sometimes – but not if they're both the same one to start with. One man going in at one end, one man coming out the other."

"Not me," Carl said flatly, misplacing his smile at last. "It wasn't me you was chasing. I was ahead of him. That's why I come out, 'cos I knew you was boxing him in. Boxing us both. So I slipped out of the box, didn't I? Anyway, you said, he's got a hostage. I heard you. He must be still in there."

"Not necessarily, Carl. A clever bit of misdirection, that's all. You go in, find someone there, scream out about a hostage. Make her scream, too, so we believe you. Then you kill her, nice and quiet, and slip away down the tunnel while we just sit there outside the door, patient as owls, and twice as stupid. Home free, you thought you were, didn't you? Only there was this man with a gun at the other end, you weren't expecting him. So you fall back on the cover story, being a hero. Quick change of hats, is that it, Carl? White for black, swap 'em over and think no one's going to notice?"

Carl shook his head. "I told you, I only stayed in there to help people."

"I heard you. But I don't believe you, that's my problem. I can't see a smart kid like you taking the chance. You could've been blown to bits in there. Why risk it? I bet you never helped an old lady across the street in your life. And even for the headlines, for being a hero – I can't see it, son. Not you."

"Well, that's where you're wrong, ain't it? That's how it was. Except for the risk bit. It wasn't no risk."

"Why not, Carl? He was shooting everything that moved in there."

"Not me."

"Why not? How could you know that?"

"Because he said so, didn't he? I met him, and he said he wouldn't shoot me."

A moment's silence, more than a moment, a lifetime measured in moments: and then Holborn's voice again, slow and careful. "Where did you meet him?"

Carl jerked his head. "In there, where else?"

"When?"

"Hours ago. When it started."

"Okay. So you met him, just bumped into him casual-like, and he stopped shooting the place up for long enough to tell you that you were immune, not to worry about the bullets and the grenades and such, he wasn't going to hurt you? Is that what you're telling us?"

"More or less, yeah."

"Which?"

"Eh?"

"More, or less? Tell us about it, Carl. Take your time, and tell us every last sweet little detail – only make sure it's the truth, Carl, son. No porky-pies, you hear me? I could turn quite nasty, if you lie to me."

"Sure." Carl shifted his shoulders, said, "You want to take these things off my hands?"

"No. You're either a danger to the public, boy, or else you're a danger to yourself; and either way, the last thing I want to do is take the cuffs off. Just tell us the story."

"Well, when the shooting started it was like chaos in there, right? All of a sudden, like. People running, screaming, this great clag-up at the exit; so I hung back, I know my way around in there, thought I'd slip out through the service ways. So I went through, and – "

"Wait. Just hold up a minute, Carl. What were you doing there in the Centre in the first place, all dressed up? What were you looking for?"

"Keeping an eye on Mrs Lee, wasn't I? That's my job," virtuously.

"But you weren't – " Linda started, and checked herself.

"You weren't with Mrs Lee," Holborn finished for her.

"We know that."

"Well, no. I wasn't any too chuffed with her, see? Didn't want to be hanging round with her, playing the good boy. Didn't feel like a good boy. But still, a job's a job, ain't it? And she might have got into trouble, without me. She needs looking after, she does. So I thought, if I could stick with her without her seeing me, I'd be doing the job, I'd be there if she needed me; and I could have some fun with it, couldn't I? Playing spies. So I did that till they went into the restaurant, her and her old man. I couldn't follow her in there. So I hung around outside; and then all the fuss started, the big evacuation bit. And the crowds got too heavy, like I said, so I got out of it."

"Right. Go on."

"Well, I got into the service ways, and I was heading for an exit when there he was, see? Just came round a corner, right at me. Gun in one hand, grenade in the other, the lot. I thought I was a goner."

He paused for effect, and Holborn allowed it, briefly.

"But?"

"But he didn't do nothing, did he? Just stood there, staring at me. And I stared right back, didn't know what else to do. Didn't want to start running, I thought if I did that he'd shoot me for sure. So we stared at each other for a bit, then he says, 'Peter.' Calls me Peter, see? 'You're too late, Peter,' he says, 'I got here first.'

"Well, I didn't know what the fuck he was on about, see? So I didn't say nothing. And he says, 'Or maybe you're too early,' he says. 'But it's all right,' he says. '*You're* all right,' he says, 'I won't shoot you. I'll shoot the others, I'll shoot them all; but I won't shoot you. You're in the army too,' he says. 'You, me, we always were, weren't we? We was always in the army,' he says.

"Then he just turns and buggers off, back round the corner again. And a minute later I hear shooting, but I still don't move, I'm just standing there shaking. Only after a bit I start thinking maybe he meant it, at that. He's flipped, for sure; but it's a good flip, my point of view, see what I mean? Thinks I'm his brother, or something. Maybe he really isn't going to shoot me.

"So I go back out into the mall, and first thing, I go down to the restaurant to see if Mrs Lee's okay. That's my job, right? Only she ain't there, there's nobody there. And there's this bottle of brandy on the bar, and I'm still shaking, right, so I thought one little drink wouldn't hurt . . .

"So I sat there and had a drink or two; and I dunno, I must have been there a while. A couple of hours. I found this telly, see, back in the kitchen; so I sat there with the bottle and watched it all on telly.

"Then the bottle was empty, and I thought if I fetched another one I'd never get out of there, not on my own two feet, I wouldn't. So I thought, time to go, and walked out; and first thing I see, except for the bodies, there's this little girl wandering round on her own. She was in some state, she'd wet herself and everything; only she wasn't scared of me, I reckon she was past it by then. Came when I called, let me pick her up, no trouble. Said she was looking for some guy, so I said I couldn't help her there, but I'd take her to people who could. And I talked to her, like, the way you do with kids, and carried her out. And your lot nearly shot us, they was all too scared to come and get the kid, a girl came for her in the end . . . "

"Mmm, I was there. But then you went back, Carl. Why did you do that?"

"Thought there might be others like her, didn't I? And I was safe, right, he wasn't going to shoot me. He said so. And your lot was too scared to come in, there was only me. So, yeah, I went back."

"He might have shot you anyway. He was shooting anything that moved, he might not have stopped to check you out."

"Well, I thought of that, yeah. But it's a big place, I thought chances were I wouldn't run into him again. And if I did, like, I was the only one moving around, I figured he'd recognise me. And I was right, wasn't I?"

"You mean you did see him again?"

"Sure. Just bumped into him, like, in one of those big squares they got in there. I reckon he knew what I'd been doing, too, getting people out; but he didn't care, he just laughed and said, 'Carry on, soldier.' So I says, 'Hang on, what's your name?' and he says, 'You'll know, Peter. Take a look in a mirror, some time when you're older.' Dead weird, that was. Then he went off again, and I just hung around in there seeing if anyone was alive. Till it got too hot, when your boys finally turned up. I didn't want to get myself shot by the good guys, did I? So I remembered about the tunnel, and came out."

"Mmm. You had a key, though, didn't you? You needed a key, to get out of the transformer station. Where did that come from?"

"Oh, I found Pritchard in there. Security chief, I knew him. Dead, he was, but he had his keys on him. So I took 'em. Thought they might be useful, like."

Andrew spoke then, from the doorway where he was nursing his arm against his chest. "It took us a good while to get through that tunnel, Inspector. Even running, you can say ten minutes, minimum. I don't think the timing holds up, for him to be the gunman."

"I know that," Holborn snapped. Then, after a long, quiet moment, "All right, son, you're in the clear. Get the cuffs off him."

Released, Carl stood up, rubbing his wrists with no visible sense of aggrievement. "You mean I can go?"

"Why not? Being a hero isn't a crime, not in this country. Go on, get the hell out of here. Go find the press, get yourself on the telly." But as Carl made slowly for the door, "Just one thing, Carl. Tell us why you did it, eh?"

Carl looked back at him, looked down at Linda, smiled broadly.

And left, brushing past Andrew, clattering away down the stairs without another word.

Holborn swore softly, then reached for the phone as it shrilled again.

"Holborn . . . What? Who is she? . . . Yes, of course I bloody want her, you cretin. Get her here. Get her here *now* . . . "

*   *   *

Ivy was back in her corner, not liking guns.

Especially not liking this man's gun, the way it pointed at her from across the room.

She didn't like the man, either. He was crouched in the opposite corner, under some shelves, against the wall with the door in it. He'd turned the light on so she could see him better, see his gun; but he hadn't said anything, not for a long time now. Not since he'd made her stand by the door and scream her name out, to tell the police she was here.

She didn't want to be here. She wanted to be out of here,

through the door or down the tunnel, she didn't care; but he wouldn't let her do that, he wouldn't let her move out of her corner.

Or the gun wouldn't.

So she sat on her pile of rags, and pulled them around her like blankets, and played them between her fingers; and he didn't like even so much movement, his gun twitched, ordering her to stillness.

Her eyes jerked around the room, across the shelves till they found something to focus on, something else she wanted.

And having found it, she wanted it more. Wanted it desperate bad, Ivy did. She licked her dry lips nervously, and measured the distance. It wasn't far, just two steps, two steps and a stretch; and he wouldn't mind that, would he? His gun wouldn't mind if she just took two steps and a stretch, and scuttled back quick to her corner with what she wanted.

With her treasure, that nice bright plastic bottle sitting on a shelf up there, just two steps away, a little stretch . . .

0100:

and Andrew had followed Carl down the steps of the police van, had stood for a long time gazing after him into the darkness; was only now coming back into himself, becoming conscious of a warm wind in his face, of the distant noises of the motorway, of his fingers constantly rubbing at the itching stump of his left arm.

He thrust his hand violently into his pocket, and scowled; and turned, as a shadow occluded the light from the doorway above him.

Recognised Linda Lee, and took his hand out of his pocket again to reach it pointlessly towards her, offering her a help she didn't need or apparently notice as she came down.

"Andrew . . . I thought you'd gone."

"No. No, I haven't."

"I don't suppose you can drive, can you? Not with that arm." Or put it another way, *not without that hand.*

"No," he said, "I don't suppose I can. I guess someone'll run me back eventually. They must have put some kind of shuttle service together, for people who've got themselves stranded."

It didn't matter to him. He had nothing – no one – to go home for, only the prospect of endless hours alone with his imagination, pictures of the day. Pictures of Dee. He would have been quite content to stay all night, see the dawn and hope to find some promise in it, hope to see more than the ashes of the night.

But then Linda said, "I could take you. If you'd like. I'm going soon. Now, more or less. Johnnie will stay, of course, but I – there's no reason, nothing to keep me here. So if you'd like to leave now . . . "

Andrew realised suddenly that to her, it mattered very much indeed. While he was looking ahead and seeing nothing to head for, all her attention was turned back and showing her plenty to run from, plenty of reasons to be gone.

So, for Linda – to give her the excuse, *I've got to run Andrew home, he's stuck here; and once I've left, well, there's no point coming back* – he said yes. Said thank you, he'd appreciate that. Very much.

"Good, then." But she didn't move except to turn her head towards the blank shadows of the Centre, except to shudder slightly against the warmth of the breeze. "How's it all going to come out, Andrew? What's going to happen?"

"I don't know." *No crystal ball here, love, you've come to the wrong guy.* "I expect they'll talk him out, eventually. They usually do, don't they?"

"Yes. It's the woman I feel sorry for, his hostage. What was she doing there, I wonder? Just hiding, I suppose. Thinking she'd be safe, down in the basement. And now this. You know, I don't even know her name . . . "

"Ivy." He'd learned that from Holborn's conversations on the phone; he'd been listening, when Linda was doing nothing but watch Carl.

"Ivy . . . ?" It seemed to mean something to her; he saw her frown, felt her reaching to remember. "Do they know who she is, at all?"

"I don't think so, no." Just one of the day's stray victims, nobody special. Nobody could be special, Andrew thought, on a day like this; or else everybody was. It came to the same thing, in the end.

"Ivy . . . Oh, yes." She'd got it now, fixed her memory on the name, on its importance. "There was a man, an old tramp down on the road. He said he was waiting for a woman called Ivy . . . I'd better tell them, don't you think?"

And she already had her foot on the steps to go back up, not needing Andrew's support, his quiet agreement, "Yes, I suppose you better had."

*   *   *

Duty – or its more noble cousin, responsibility – drives different people in different ways.

Specifically, tonight it was driving Carol Easterman out to the Meldon Centre in this last act of a dramatic day, where it had so signally failed to drive her to work before.,

She sat in the back of a police car for the first time in her life, and tried to enjoy the experience, to savour the speed, the flashing blue light reflected off windows as they passed, the wail of the siren that sent other traffic in to the kerb ahead of them. It should have been a thrill, she knew that, and tried to make it so; but duty or responsibility had her by the throat, by the heart, no room for thrills tonight beyond the big one.

She wore a polite little smile for the driver's sake, taking as much care over that as she had over getting dressed; and the smile meant as little as her clothes, had as little to say about her.

She watched the city racing past, unreal around her – unless it were she who was unreal within it, she who was cut out of it by something sharper than a police car's siren. The city and then the bridge, the river beneath, her first view of the Meldon Centre on the further bank: and surely it was dangerous to be driving this fast, even with the siren and the light and the streets half empty? A preternatural caution enveloped her suddenly in a cloud of misgiving. Surely if she were that important, if Carol Easterman counted for so much, surely they should take more care of her, take their time, take every possible precaution?

She opened her mouth to say so, to ask the driver to slow down; then bit the words back, and let her lips fall again into that ridiculous, encouraging smile. It wasn't her physical safety she was worried about, that was only a decoy thrown up by a deeper concern, too shy to show itself without a mask. But her native honesty dug it out as the car swooped onto the slip-road to the Centre, and she looked on it with loathing, with contempt, with recognition.

I don't want to be here, it said, brazen and afraid. *I don't want to talk about my weaknesses, my failures, my Peter Kerr. I don't want anything to do with any of it, and I wish I'd stayed in bed.*

And duty couldn't touch that, responsibility was just a word; and there was nothing Carol could do but look out of the window, see the Centre looming ahead and console herself with the one inarguable fact, that it was too late to back out now.

*　　　*　　　*

"There you are. I've been looking for you, old man."

The Coatman scowled, muttered, turned his head up to squint; and his failing eyes could make out nothing in the murk except the high rounded shape of a policeman's helmet, which only made him mutter the louder.

"Fucken busies, fuck off and let me be . . . "

"Easy, now." The policeman squatted down on the pavement beside him, and pulled a pack of cigarettes from his pocket. "Take it easy, mate. Here, have a tab and relax. I only want to talk to you."

The Coatman knew all about talking to policemen, in the street or in the station; and he knew where talking led you, too. Nights in the cells and days in court, he knew it all. Done it all, he had.

But a smoke, now – he'd been craving a smoke. He was all out of dumpers, and Ivy hadn't come back with the baccy she'd promised him. Hadn't come back at all, though he was still waiting, still watching for her.

So he fumbled at the open packet with his gnarled and clumsy fingers and couldn't manage to work one out, they were packed too tight; could only fumble and curse until the copper did it for him, eased a fag free and pressed it into his hand.

"There you go, mate. Hang on, I've got a light somewhere . . . "

The copper didn't say anything more until the fag was lit and the Coatman's first response, his coughing fit was over. Then, "My name's George. You remember me, don't you? You saw me this morning, I had a chat with Ivy when you got here."

The Coatman grunted, dragged another deep chestful of smoke and coughed again. Always a good weapon, a cough was.

"It's Ivy I want to talk to you about, actually. Someone told us you were waiting here for Ivy. Is that right, is it?"

He shrugged, a small gesture to start with and lost entirely within his layers of coats. Tell them nothing, that was the rule he lived by.

"You see, what it is, old man, we really need to know whether she's still in there. She could be in trouble, see. We want to help her, we want to get her out; but we need to know if it's her or not. All we've got is the name, and maybe it's another Ivy altogether. Must be, if your Ivy came out with the others, if you've seen her at all . . . You can tell us that much, can't you?" The copper knew the rule too, of course he did. They all did. And they'd use it against him, given half a chance. They'd done that before.

But still, Ivy's name was a focus, a sudden clear space in the Coatman's clouded mind and a password to the heart of his fuddled anxiety; and when the copper pressed him, when he asked it again, "Have you seen her?", the glowing cigarette-end made a track in the darkness, as the Coatman shook his head.

"No." And after a moment, he gave more without the copper asking. "She never came out. I'm waiting, see? I'm waiting, but she doesn't come."

"Aye. Well, she can't come, that's what it is. The gunman's got her hostage. Maybe you'd better come on up with me, old man. There'll be some questions, as much as you can tell us, every little helps; and I can't take you to her, but I can get you closer than this. So you can be there ready, when we do get her out."

*   *   *

The car drove through a checkpoint and right up to the walls of the Centre, to park beside a big white van, 'Police Incident Unit' painted on the sides. Carol was briefly surprised by the driver's casual approach, the absence of the ring of armed men she'd seen on television; then remembered that there was no danger now, if what the inspector at the station had told her was true, if the gunman had been hunted into some kind of basement under the Centre. No danger of being sniped at. She was safe from bullets, at least. Though if their suspicions were accurate, if it really was Peter Kerr they had caged down there, then she'd hardly call herself safe.

The car door was opened for her, and a short, sharp-looking man extended a hand to help her out.

"Miss Easterman? I'm Inspector Holborn. It's very good of you to come all this way, at this time of night . . . "

Oh, sure. Public-spirited, that's what I am. And never mind the voices in her head, the soft one that urged caution, the harsher one that laughed at public spirit and called it treachery. She was here now, she'd given herself and her memories over to the police; however polite they might be, they wouldn't release her until they'd wrung her dry.

She sighed, heaved herself to her feet and followed Holborn to the van. Accepted his assistance up the stairs, sank into the chair he offered inside, watched him settle himself on the other side of the table.

Made one final effort to discount herself and her story; said, "I still don't really see how I can help you, Inspector. Even if it is Peter who's been running wild here. I didn't really know him that well, I can't tell you much about him."

Holborn fiddled with a biro for a moment, then said, "Anything you can tell us will help, Miss Easterman. Anything at all. The point is, he doesn't seem to have had any social contacts, apart from yourself. No friends at work here, none at his gun club. No one knew him at all, except presumably his mother; and she's dead. You're the only person to come forward who's had any kind of close contact with him. That makes you very important in building up a picture of his state of mind; which we need to do, quite desperately."

"Look, I'm not an expert . . . "

"We're not asking you to be. Experts we've got. In fact, I'd like you to talk to a psychologist, if you would, in a few minutes. They can be useful, but they need data. That's all we want from you, Miss Easterman, just facts, and your impressions of the man."

Carol watched him playing with the pen, doodling on a sheet of paper; and thought, *I don't believe you, Inspector Holborn, sir. There's something else you want, isn't there? Something you're not ready to ask me yet . . .*

But she said nothing, determined to make him ask; determined to refuse, if it was too much. Duty only went so far, and responsibility no further. She had duties to herself as well, responsibilities for her own well-being. She wouldn't tear herself apart for anyone: not for Peter, certainly not for the police.

"Well. If we can get started . . . " Holborn put the doodles to one side, took a fresh sheet of paper. "Just a few details about yourself first, if you wouldn't mind. For the record. Your full name is . . . ?"

"Carol Anne Easterman."

"Date of birth?"

Carol gave that, and her address; agreed that she was training as a nurse, explained the jobs she'd had before, the redundancy that had driven her at last into nursing. Agreed that he could call her Carol.

"All right, then, Carol. Want to tell me how you first met Peter Kerr?"

No. She didn't want any part of this. She wanted to go home, she wanted to go to bed.

She said, "It was at a singles bar. That smart place, One To One. Other side of the river."

"Uh-huh." Holborn made a note. "When was this?"

"Oh, two years ago, easily. It was new then, just opened."

"Your first time there, was it?"

"That's right. I don't," with a forced chuckle, "I don't make a habit of hanging around in singles bars. It was my friend Audrey got me there. I'd been out of work a few months, and it was really getting to me. I suppose I'd been moaning to her, and she came out with all the usual stuff, how I needed to get out a bit, meet some new people, give my self-confidence a boost. She suggested giving this place a try, she said she'd go if I did. She was on her own too by then, her marriage had broken up the year before."

"I see. So the two of you went along together, did you?"

"Well, no. That was the thing, we'd arranged to meet

there, but Audrey didn't turn up. I got myself a drink – it was happy hour, I remember that, triple gin for a pound; except the tonic was extra, of course, they really sting you for the tonic – and I hung around at the bar waiting for her, but she never came. After a while I went to the phone and called her flat, and there wasn't any answer, so I thought okay, she's on her way, she'll be here soon. So I bought another triple quick, before the prices went up; but Audrey still didn't come.

"I hate waiting around for people like that, especially in public. Playing the fat white woman who nobody loves. I was really angry with her, I was going to just finish my drink and leave; only then I saw this man sitting in a corner, watching me. I mean, I'd noticed him before, he'd been there as long as I had, but this time I caught his eye. He was on his own and nursing a drink, just like I was; and, well, he was quite attractive. To me. Short hair, and a camouflage jacket. He looked strong. Like a soldier. And it was a singles bar, after all, chances were he was looking for company. And I suppose the gin was getting to me, I don't usually drink much; and as I said, I was childishly angry with Audrey. I remember thinking it'd be one in the eye for her, if I found myself a man. It never occurred to me that that was why she hadn't turned up, so I'd do exactly that . . . "

"So what, you went over and introduced yourself, did you, Carol? Is that what happened?"

"That's right. I did." She shook her head in wonder at the memory. "I don't usually . . . It's not my sort of thing at all, thrusting myself on strangers. But it seemed stupid to have spent so much time there, and not spoken to anyone except the boy behind the bar. So I picked up my drink and walked over, and asked if I could join him."

"Did he look surprised?"

"Not a bit of it. He'd watched me coming, all the way from the bar. He just nodded. So I sat down, and told him my name; and then he told me his."

"Peter Kerr, right?"

"Well, just Peter, then; I'd said Carol, he said Peter. But yes, it was Peter Kerr."

"And what did you talk about? Your missing friend?"

"A bit. I explained about her not showing up, and asked if he was waiting for someone too. He said no."

"He didn't try to charm you at all? He didn't say he'd been

waiting for someone like you, for instance, anything like that?"

This time the chuckle just rolled out of her, natural and easy. "Peter? No. Not then, not ever. It wouldn't have occurred to him; and if it had, he wouldn't have known where to begin. I don't think he'd had any experience at all, with women."

Holborn made another note. "Didn't that strike you as odd, at all? For a man who'd been in the army?"

"I suppose so; but by the time I started thinking about it, I knew a lot more about him, you see, and by then everything was odd. It didn't stand out that much. It even made sense, a bit. In context."

"All right. Let's go back to that first meeting, then. You established that he wasn't waiting for someone. So what then? What did you talk about?"

"Oh, I think – yes, that's right, that's when I asked him if he was a soldier. He said yes."

"He wasn't in the army then," Holborn objected.

"No, he said that. But he said he was still a soldier. Once a soldier, always a soldier, I said; and he nodded. He was just like my father. I told him that. Dad was career. He'd been invalided out after the war, but he was still a soldier to the day he died. Peter asked me where he'd served; and then we talked about the Africa campaign, and Italy."

"You both talked? Or you listened while he talked?"

"Oh, I put in my two pennyworth. I'd picked up a lot from Dad, over the years. But – yes, mostly it was Peter doing the talking. He knew it all: every battle, every battalion. I told him he should write a book about it."

"And what did he say to that?"

"Oh, he shook his head. He read books, he said, for the information; but he wasn't a book man, he was an action man. I remember, I giggled over that, because of those silly Action Man dolls; only I hid it, pretended it was just a cough, I didn't want him thinking I was laughing at him."

"No. That was probably sensible." With a bleak look that sobered Carol abruptly, reminded her that maybe fifty people had died here today. Maybe more. "What then?"

"I asked him if he'd actually seen any action, when he was in the army; and he said no. He said he'd been in Northern Ireland, he volunteered, but he never came near any fighting."

"Was he relieved about that, or disappointed?"

"Not relieved." She closed her eyes, trying to fix the memory more firmly in her mind, pick off the emotions that had touched his face and body. "But not disappointed either, not really. Sort of angry. He said they'd kept him away from it, his officers, if there was any chance of trouble. They only sent him on the safe patrols. That's what he said."

"Paranoid?"

"Something like that." She thought about it, and nodded more firmly. "I suppose so, yes. I mean, they wouldn't do that, would they?"

"It doesn't seem likely," Holborn said in a neutral voice.

"They wouldn't have known, to start with, which patrols would be safe. They couldn't possibly be sure. But he really believed it. So, yes. Paranoid. And resentful."

"It was a long time ago."

"Yes, but still. He still resented it. You can understand that, though. I thought I could, anyway. I mean, you join the army, you go through all that training, you stay in there nine years or whatever, and when you leave you've still never fired a shot off the rifle-range – well, it makes it all a bit pointless, doesn't it?"

"Some people think that's the point of an army," Holborn remarked drily. "To keep the peace, not to start a war."

Carol snorted. "Try asking the soldiers. Or Peter, any-way. They trained him to fight and then never gave him the chance to show how good he was, even when the oppor-tunity was there. That was what rankled with him."

"Right." Another careful note. "So what else did you talk about? His job?"

"Not really. He mentioned it, but that was all. I was unemployed, remember. The last thing I wanted to do was talk about other people's jobs."

"The gun club?"

"No. Not then. That came up later, another time."

"You?"

"No. I mean, I wouldn't have minded, I wasn't keeping any secrets; but he never asked me anything about myself. It wasn't his way."

"No. Shoot first and ask questions afterwards, that's his way, right?"

Carol just looked at him.

"I'm sorry. He was a friend of yours. I'll try to keep it in mind. Now go on, please. You were telling me what you talked about."

"Not much more, that first time. He had to go to work, he was on nights."

"Had he been drinking much?"

"No, not Peter. He had a drink, a beer; but he'd been nursing it. I think he liked to keep control."

"All right. So he said he had to go. Did you arrange to meet again?"

"Well, sort of."

"What does that mean?"

"I asked." And it was like a confession, to say so; but hell, that was what she was here for, wasn't it? To confess. "I gave him my number, and said I'd like to see him again. To talk to."

"Uh-huh. And what did he say?"

"He said he'd ask his mother."

A pause; then, "Are you serious?"

Carol laughed, painfully. "That's what I said. And he said yes."

"How did you feel about that?"

"Well, it made sense, in a way. I knew he was living with her, he'd told me that much; and I'd met them before, men of his age still under their mother's thumb."

"Right. But you were approved, were you? He did meet you again?"

"Oh, yes. Several times . . . "

Slowly Holborn took her through each of those several meetings; and slowly Carol stripped her soul bare, told him everything she could remember.

Told him of her increasing physical attraction towards Peter, and how easy it seemed, to want him; and of what came coupled with that attraction, the constant edge of discomfort, the sense of never getting near to the heart of him. How uncertain she was of his own feelings, how strong his barriers were. How he'd never say a word or make a gesture of affection, how he'd back off hard if she did: pull himself free from her arm, or shake her voice out of his head. How he'd meet questions with a long, dragging silence that she could neither brook nor breach.

Told him of her excitement and despair, stirred together into a cocktail that thrilled and poisoned, both at once; and told him at last of the final chapter in this strange and inadequate romance, this story of her life: the day Peter invited her out to meet his mother.

Well, it hadn't been like that, quite. The way he'd said it, not trying to hide his deep reluctance: it was obviously the mother's invitation, the mother's insistence. *Really under her thumb, aren't you, Peter?*, Carol had thought.

But she'd said yes, of course she had. She'd gone along. She was curious, and hopeful. Maybe his mother's approval would be a way in to Peter's mind or heart, the key she needed . . .

On a clear day, they say, you can see forever; but it was murky that day, grey and drizzling. They'd driven over the bridge and out into the country, not speaking, Carol venturing nothing against Peter's silence. *Wait and see.*

So she'd waited; and she'd seen, oh yes. Seen the village through her window, the estate, at last the house. She'd hauled herself out of the car, no help from him; had followed him up the path to the front door and in.

Had met Mrs Kerr in the living-room: a thin, short woman, straggly brown hair with hints of grey. Deep lines on her face, and the skull very evident beneath her skin. No family resemblance that Carol could see.

None in the voice either, or the manner of her, direct and brutal.

"So this is your girlfriend, Peter. No beauty, is she? No dream-girl, that's for sure."

Carol flinched back from the heavy sarcasm, then made an effort to recover, thinking, *No, it's not aimed at me, it's all for Peter, poor guy. Is this what he lives with, day in, day out? No wonder he's repressed* . . .

But, "No offence meant," Mrs Kerr said to her, with a twisted smile. "I'm glad of it. At least you're real. I'd had my doubts, till now."

"Oh, I'm real enough." *Too too solid. And wishing I was solidly somewhere else.*

"Well. Sit down, then. I'll make coffee. No doubt Peter can entertain you for a few minutes more."

"I'm sure he can." If Peter wasn't going to stand up to this verbal laceration – and he showed no signs of it, only staring out of the window as if he were utterly uninvolved – then she'd have to do it for him. Try at least. Make an effort on his behalf, and her own.

Left alone with him, she'd settled herself at one end of the sofa and said, "Peter? Is she always like this?"

She'd been ready to offer sympathy if he'd only invite it, but ready too to be put off with a shrug, his common response to anything personal. What she hadn't been prepared for was his complete divorce, his broad back turned to her, his head entirely still. It might have been monumental indifference, or a pain beyond bearing; she'd had no way of telling, and was left helpless by her ignorance, his secretiveness.

So they'd only waited, trapped in that silence again, until Mrs Kerr came back with mugs of coffee on a tray.

"What," she said, "not grabbing a quick cuddle while my back's turned? Peter dear, you're letting me down. You could at least sit with your girl, even if holding her hand's too much to ask."

Again nothing from Peter, not a movement; again it was left to Carol.

"My name's Carol," she said. "And I think we're a little old for holding hands."

"Well, I wouldn't care to speak for you," a sharp glance, perhaps an appreciative glance, someone who fought back at last, "and you wouldn't care to have me do it; but my Peter, now, I can speak for him. As he won't speak for himself, seemingly. And I thought, when he told me he was seeing a woman I thought he was hitting his adolescence at last, you see. Heaven knows, I've been hoping for it long enough. So a little hand-holding wouldn't come amiss, would it? But no, you're right," with a soft sigh, wholly artificial, in shocking contrast to her gleaming eyes and her cynical smile, "this is Peter we're talking about, after all. And Peter doesn't like to be touched, do you, sweetheart? He doesn't like the purity of his body corrupted by someone else's skin. He's saving himself. That's it, isn't it, Peter? He's not scared, I wouldn't want you thinking that. He just doesn't want to be sullied. Other people are dirty, you see. Especially women. He's made an effort, you have to give him that, he's got this far; and it's me you have to thank for that, by the way. I've been leaning on him. But you shouldn't get your hopes up. He's not going to kiss you in the dark, or sneak you up to his room for a quick grope. That's not Peter's style. He's a hero, not a lover. Isn't that right, Peter? And now," putting the tray down and sitting comfortably next to Carol, "now we've got all that straight, come and drink your coffee, Peter. While it's hot."

Peter had turned then, finally: his face working, tears on his cheeks. He'd mouthed something inaudible, unreadable, and charged suddenly out of the room, slamming the door behind him.

Carol had sat motionless within this perfect, this devastating humiliation, while Mrs Kerr made polite enquiries about milk and sugar, while strange noises came down to her from the floor above. The rattling of chains, she'd heard, and a metallic crash; then heavy footsteps on the stairs, the front door flying open.

She'd seen Peter through the window, running to his car with a long case under his arm. Had seen him drive away; and still moved nothing but her eyes, just enough to catch the bitterness of his mother's smile, to be uncertain if that signified victory or defeat.

"Where's he . . . ?"

"The gun club, I expect. He has to practise."

Hunching herself against a shiver, Carol had forced out one more question. "Why – why did you do that to him?"

"I didn't. He does it to himself. I just wanted you to see what you were getting into. Now, you'll be wondering about the buses . . . "

Carol told the story once, straight through, stopping for nothing and not taking questions; then she told it again, in painful and self-immolating detail.

"And I never saw him again, never heard from him."

"Did you try?"

"After that? No, I didn't. It was up to him, not me."

Holborn grunted, stacked his notes into a neat sheaf and set them aside.

"All right, Carol. Thank you. I'm afraid I'll have to ask you to go through it all again with that psychologist I warned you about. But there's something else I want you to do after that, if you're willing."

I knew it, she thought. *I knew you were working up to something more. Something bigger.*

"I'd like you to talk to him," Holborn said, playing with his biro again, as he hadn't throughout the interrogation. "I'd like you to come down and talk to Peter."

0200:

and Ivy had got her bottle, finally.

Desperation – you couldn't call it thirst: not that sere feeling that was in her head more than her throat, the fire scorching her mind, the cracks opening up in her skull like cracks in the earth – desperation had driven her at last to ask. A favour to old Ivy, she'd said. Ivy needs it, she does.

And he'd paid no attention at first, the man in the woolly mask, it was like he couldn't hear her. But when she'd begged, when she'd said please, when she'd started to whine and cry for it: then his eyes had moved, behind their little slit in the black hood. Moved from her to the shelf, they had, back to her again; and his mouth had smiled, slightly, behind its separate slit. His head had nodded.

And his gun had followed her all the way, the trembling, crawling, scuttling way from her corner to the shelf. Had kept its eye on her while she stretched, while she clutched the precious bottle to her chest; and had tracked her back to her rags again.

But she had it now, she had the top wrenched off and the flimsy bottle gripped tight in both hands, with her knees brought up for cover. She had the taste of it in her mouth, the sour purple heat of it withering her tongue and twisting her lips out of true; and best of all she had the first touch of it reaching her mind already. Soft, strong fingers cupped to receive her, to soothe her pains and terrors and draw her down deep to a place of safety.

She'd drunk meths before, often. Drunk worse, too, when she had to. When she couldn't get meths. So she knew the way of it, she drank in little sips at first, all she could bear; and suppressed the shudders in her body and her stomach's churning, knowing they wouldn't last. Soon her mouth and throat were numb, far past tasting what they took; and she drank deeper then, urgent swallows in search of stronger magic.

The voice came at her soon after that. Too soon to fool old Ivy, though it made her jump, almost made her drop the bottle, the way it boomed and echoed through the room. Her thumbs dug into the giving plastic, the meths sloshed in the neck, she saw the man jerk beyond the barrier of her knees, stare around wildly, swivel his gun towards the door. She cackled once, and cut it off as the gun came back at her again.

"Can't fool old Ivy," she muttered. "She's not drunk enough for that, not yet. Not drunk enough to hear voices. Go away, voice."

But the voice wasn't listening, it came back a little quieter, still too loud.

Peter, the voice said. *Peter Kerr. Can you hear me, Peter?*

The man stood up slowly, set his back against the wall, turned his gun to the door and kept his eyes on Ivy.

Peter, my name's Simon. Shout if you can hear me.

The man didn't shout, no. He just stood there, still as anything, still as Ivy in her corner.

Peter. And it was louder again, blasting its way in, shaking the floor Ivy sat on, shaking everything. *Can you hear this?*

"Yes, all right!" the man screamed suddenly. "I can hear you! Turn it down!"

Is this better? Softer now.

"Yes!"

Good. Peter, there are armed police out here. You can't get out. It's over, Peter. Why don't you give yourself up? Let your hostage go, and come out. There's no point going on now. It's finished.

The man said nothing. Ivy took another little drink, and thought, that's me. The hostage. I'm his hostage. He should let me go, that's what the voice said. Nice voice. We're friends, we are, me and the voice. That voice, it's on Ivy's side, that voice is . . .

But not the man, no. He wasn't on Ivy's side, he didn't say go on, Ivy, do what the voice says, get out of here. He didn't say anything.

Peter? Why get yourself killed, Peter, what's the point? The police won't wait forever, you know that. And you're out- numbered, you must be low on ammunition. Give up, Peter.

Be sensible. There's nothing left for you in there now . . .

"I've got a hostage! You do anything stupid and she dies, right now!"

We're not going to do anything stupid, Peter. And neither are you, am I right? You're not going to kill Ivy. That really would be stupid. Where's the point in it? There are so many dead already, why add another? Ivy's got a right to her life.

To her life, and to her bottle – if you could distinguish between the two. Ivy couldn't. She took another sip.

What do you want, Peter? What are you holding out for?

No response. Ivy knew what she wanted, right enough, she wanted to go home, bold and triumphant on the Coatman's arm; but if Peter did, if he knew, he wasn't saying. And Ivy kept her tongue still, her mouth closed gently round the bottle's neck.

The voice went away after a while, after Peter stopped talking to it.

And then there was the silence again, in the room and outside: back from its holiday, refreshed and vigorous. It was too much for Ivy. She hadn't minded it so much before, when the bottle had been singing to her from its shelf, when terror had blanked out everything but the bottle; but she had the bottle now, she had the song of it held tight in her hands and in her head. It made her braver. And the voice, nice voice, that had made her braver too. *You're not going to kill Ivy*, the voice had said; and of course he wasn't, was he? The voice was authority, you could tell that, it was uniforms and orders. He'd do what the voice told him to, in the end.

It was only the silence that made her doubt, that kept her fearful in her newfound bravery. She knew all about meeting orders with silence. It wasn't her way, no, she talked, Ivy did, she could talk her way out of anything; it was the Coatman's little trick to say nothing, to scowl and spit and stand there and wait for the order to go away with the man who gave it. Sometimes it worked, more often it didn't.

But it could be working now, for Peter. The silence said so. There was the silence inside the room, and that was him not doing what he was told; and there was the silence outside, and that might be the voice giving up and going away, leaving him to do what he wanted, orders or no orders. Leaving him to kill Ivy, if he wanted to.

She didn't trust the silence, and she wasn't even sure

about the voice any more, not certain sure, not to bet her life on it. But she had a voice of her own, her own sweet voice she had; and she could talk her way out of anything, given half a chance and a little courage.

So she took another gulp of liquid bravery, and took the chance.

"What," she said, and saw his head spasm towards her, felt his wandering attention clench around her body, "what are you going to do with Ivy, then, old son?" Nothing if not direct, our Ivy. "You and that nasty old gun of yours, what are you going to do? Going to shoot her, are you, shoot her dead and drop her down the hole there? Feed her to the rats? 'Course you're not," answering her own question quickly before he could, before his gun could do it for him. "You wouldn't do that to poor old Ivy, now would you? Not you. Ivy's no threat. No good to you dead, Ivy isn't. No good at all, not to you or the lovely old Coatman or anyone."

"Shut up," he said; but she had him now, already she had the measure of him. Ivy could measure a man up just by a single word, she'd had years of it, more than she could count. Silence defeated her, all her experience couldn't span a silence; but get them talking, get them doing what the good gods had given them mouths and tongues to do it with, and she knew where she stood, straight off. She knew which coppers would let her stay, and which would turn her off; which marks would give her money and which would not.

Which crazy killers would shoot her dead, and which would not.

This one – no. This one wouldn't.

So she lifted the bottle to her lips again, took a defiant, celebratory swig, *Here's to you, Ivy old girl. You're a queen, girl, you're a downright queen*, and said, "What's your name, then, son?"

"I said shut up."

"'Course you did. You don't want Ivy rabbiting on at you, silly old woman she is, lets her tongue run away with her and doesn't know when to stop. But she's curious, see? Killed the cat, curiosity did, and maybe it'll kill Ivy too, sooner or later." *But not today, old love. Doesn't matter how much you wave that horrid old gun around, you're not killing Ivy with it. Not today.* "She doesn't mean any harm by it, though. And there's no harm telling a silly old woman what your

name is, is there? No harm in the world. So what is it, then?
Is it Peter, is it, is that your name?"

"Yes." His eyes stared at her, sharply blue and edgy.
"Peter Kerr. That's my name. Now shut up."

And it rolled through her like a chime, like a charm, *Got
you now, son. Power in names, there is, and I know it. I've
got it, Ivy's got the power.* And she could have danced in her
exultation, could have dropped a deep and joyful curtsey to
him, to a mirror, to herself, Queen Ivy as ever was; but she'd
had half a bottle by now, and that'd put the wobblies in her
good and proper if she started prancing about on her silly old
legs. So she settled for the warmth and wonder of her own
strong magic coursing through her blood, she knew it was
there, no need to show it to him, no need to scare the
daylights out of that silly old gun of his; and settled for a
cackle quickly drowned in another gulp at the bottle of
spells.

"Peter?"

Nothing, no answer above a glare; but it was too late for
that now, too late for him to hide behind his fractured
silence. No cover there, not from Ivy's glorious, shining
magic, her silver tongue.

"Peter . . . "

"Well, what?"

"Why don't you take the hat off, Peter? Take the silly old
hat off, and let Ivy see your face?"

And if he'd said no, flat and blank and solid – well, maybe
he'd have got away with it even then, for a little at least.
Held the magic off a while longer. But he didn't. He was a
fool, he was a victim; he didn't know what he was, but Ivy
did, oh yes. He was a mark, she'd marked him; and marks
didn't say no, not ever. Not once she'd got to work.

He said, "Why?"

"Want to see it, Peter. Ivy's curious again, she wants a
face to go with the name. And it must be hot under there,
you must be sweating and itching in that scratchy old wool.
Take it off." And, sharper even than she knew, Queen Ivy
rising above herself, lifted on the wings of angels, no less:
"The fighting's over, Peter. Take it off."

And – after a pause, after another of those silences come
far, far too late – he held the gun one-handed and bent his
head towards the other, pulled the balaclava off. And

maybe, if she'd been young and spritely and fast on her feet, maybe Ivy could have got out then. Run for the door while he was blind and his gun was taking a rest, no finger anywhere near its clever little trigger. And maybe even the police wouldn't have shot her either, as she burst out under the muzzles of their guns . . .

But she was old and slow and halfway to heaven on the meths express and the thrill of her own power, watching him do what Ivy told him. And her magic would keep her safe, of course it would, no need for desperate, drunken, hopeless staggers towards a dream of safety she'd never reach. No need to insult the magic. Ivy wasn't going to run out of this, no, she was going to talk her way out, head high and cackling. That's what she knew best, what she could do. And it was working already, wasn't it? He was pulling his hat off like she'd said, showing her short dark tousled hair and a pale face, showing her a man lost without his mask, no role to play.

Which made him no kind of man at all, just another mark to dance to Ivy's tune, if she tuned it careful . . .

Peter . . . ?

Voice again, but not the same voice. A new one: a voice with a sigh in it, a reluctant voice, a woman's voice. Ivy scowled. Last thing she wanted was another woman butting in now, coming between her and her mark.

Peter, this is Carol Easterman.

A sad name, in a sad voice: but Peter wasn't sad, no, he was electric. Up on his feet looking wild, gun forgotten on the floor beside him, he pushed his hands through his hair, he sweated, he paced the room; and this was their chance outside to come charging in, to take him, to win the day if they'd only known it. Ivy's second chance to make her own bid for freedom. And again she let it pass without moving an inch from her corner.

Peter, I'm not going to ask why you've been doing this. It's too late for that, it's done now, it's over. And I think I know anyway, I think I can understand what's been going on in your head. All I want to say is, why drag it out any longer, what's the point? There are so many people dead, so many hurt . . . Why go on, Peter? Give it up now, let that lady out and come out yourself. Please, Peter. You won't be treated badly, I promise. There are people out here who can help

*you, it's their job, it's what they want to do. They can help
you get things sorted out in your head, help you see things
straight again . . .*

When she mentioned the dead, he remembered his gun.
Picked it up again, stroked his hand along the barrel,
snapped the magazine off and checked it, slotted it back.

And when she'd stopped, at least for the moment, he
spoke; but not to her, no. He spoke to Ivy.

And his voice was tight and thrumming like a wire as he
said, "You don't surrender. Not in a good defensive position, so long as there's a single bullet left in your clip. You
hold your position, keep your head down and buy time.
Time is a soldier's friend, every minute is valuable. When
you're out of ammo, that's when you surrender. Not before.
Not ever before then. One well-placed soldier well supplied
can hold off a superior force for hours, buy time for his
comrades, wait for reinforcements . . . "

No reinforcements for you, old son, Ivy thought, and was
just too sensible to say, despite the drink that was in her. *No
comrades. You're on your own, boy. Even with me, even
with poor old Ivy under the barrel of your gun, you're still on
your own, and you know it.*

And then, from outside, the woman again, stupidly saying
it all:

*What are you waiting for, Peter? There's nowhere to go
from here. You can't get out, you must realise that; and
there's no one going to come bursting in to rescue you. It's
just you, Peter, it's all up to you when this finishes. You've
got to come out sometime, why not do it now and get it over
with? Please, Peter. I'll help, as much as I can. We'll all help.
It won't be so terrible, nobody's going to beat you up or
anything, we're all trying to understand . . .*

And his face contorted, his hands snatched the gun to his
shoulder and pointed it at the door, his finger trembled on
the trigger; and it was a long, long minute before he lowered
the gun again. Before he rubbed a hand across his sweating
face and looked at Ivy, and she wondered what he was
seeing as he said, "No. You don't waste ammunition, when
your supplies are limited. You conserve it against a future
need. You don't let the enemy taunt you into shooting it off
without a target."

And now . . .

No more military lectures now, nothing from him, no words, no movement except the trickle of sweat down his shiny face. Even his eyes were still at last, his head back and gazing fixedly at the ceiling as if he was the one who'd been drinking, not her.

And nothing from outside, either. No voices except her own, running on slurred and unstoppable, gushing out of her like drink from a broken bottle and nothing for either of them to do but listen to it, lick a little maybe from their fingers, watch the rest of it soak away into the absorbent silence.

" . . . He's my love, see, the Coatman. You wouldn't have thought it, would you? Wouldn't have thought a fat old woman like me could find herself a sweet love out on the road. But Ivy did it, she found her man. And she loves him, she does. There's no one like the Coatman, not for Ivy.

"He was a teacher once, you know. He was a clever old man, when he was young. And he was married, too, he had another love before Ivy. Wife and kiddies, the Coatman had. And a job and a car, and a house that was his, his very own house. Home to the same door every night, dinner on the table and the same bed to sleep in, and his woman to cuddle while he slept.

"But she took it all away from him, she did. Took his house and his car and his kiddies, took all his love away from him; and now all he's got is Ivy, and he doesn't know how to love her properly, he can't remember, poor old Coatman.

"You got yourself a love, then, Peter, son? Have you? Or you're a soldier, you love your guns, is that it? Your nasty old guns take all your love away from you, do they, drink it all up? You shouldn't have been a soldier, Peter, you should've come out on the road with us, me and the Coatman. You do that, leave the silly guns behind and come with us. We'll find a sweet love for you, handsome boy like you are. Someone to keep you warm at night, the way the Coatman won't keep me, he can't remember how. There's them as do, them as'll do it for you, Peter, if you only don't point nasty guns at them . . . "

And on and on, her voice reeling, staggering, hurrying on after her swirling mind; and nothing clever in it, nothing tricksy, nothing planned. Only the words tumbling out of her, and if they made sense, if they found a path to follow it was the magic that put it there, or else it was the drink.

But the drink was gone now, the bottle empty and so light it fell out of her silly fingers and rolled halfway across the floor towards Peter; and the noise of it made him jump, silly old bottle that it was, it scared the boy so that he snatched up his gun again and pointed it at her, and breathed so hard she could hear it all the way from the other side of the room.

And why she could hear it so clear was that there wasn't any other sound to drown it, because she wasn't talking now, for a bit there she wasn't even breathing.

But she did that when she remembered, when the bottle had stopped rolling, when he'd stopped panting at her so hard. She breathed deep, and gave him a big smile.

"Nothing left in it," she said. "All gone. But there's more, there's another bottle up there on that lovely old shelf. All right if I get that, is it, Peter, if I just go over and help myself?"

And she pulled herself upright, clinging to the wall; stood swaying for a moment, scowled down at the wobble in her knees; and took one carefully solid step and then another, keeping both hands tight on the bottom shelf and watching her feet to check that nothing sneaked up to trip her over.

Came within arm's-reach of the bottle, lifted her arm and reached; and Peter stopped her.

Stopped her dead.

"No," he said, and that's what stopped her. His voice was enough, she didn't need the picture in her suddenly steady head, his gun pointing at her broad back.

"Leave the bottle," he said.

"It's only a bottle," she muttered sullenly, crying bright tears at him that he couldn't see from behind her. "Only a bottle, only a drink for Ivy, a little drink. She's thirsty. And you don't want it, Ivy offered you a drink before, you said you didn't want it . . . "

"Leave it," he said, "and just keep walking."

"Keep walking, he says, when it's all she can do to stay on her feet, poor old girl. And where's she supposed to walk to, without a drink to keep her going? Over the hills and far away, is it, nice long hike through the country? Ivy's good at that, but she needs her drink, she does."

"Go to the door," he said, "and get out." And then fiercely, when she still didn't move, except that her hand still clutched and clawed towards the bottle: "Go on, you stupid bitch, get the hell out of here."

0300:

and Johnnie Lee saw the handle turn, the door begin to open.

He didn't need to shout a warning, didn't need even to think about it. Every pair of eyes, the muzzle of every gun was focused on that crack, that bare inch of gap between the door and its jamb.

For the space of a breath – a slow, difficult breath, the air seeming to gel around Johnnie as the corridor had gelled before him, each man caught and held by the moment – nothing more happened. The door opened no wider, forced no response beyond that heavy stillness.

But then there was a hand worming its way through the narrow gap, with something clutched precariously between its fingers; and that might have brought a response, might have splintered the door with eager bullets if Jakes hadn't found his voice in the suffocating silence.

"Hold your fire!" he shouted, once and then again; and in the aftermath of his shout, Johnnie saw what Jakes must have seen that second quicker, perhaps just in time.

It was an old, arthritic hand, a woman's trembling hand that hung in front of them, that consumed their gaze; and dangling from it was nothing more deadly than a dirty length of rag, that might once have been white.

"Ivy?" Jakes called. "Is that you?"

"Yes, yes, it's me! It's Ivy, only old Ivy, and I want to come out! Don't you go shooting at me, now, there's only me coming. Peter's staying here, but he says I can come out, he's letting Ivy go and she doesn't want you shooting at her, so just you be careful with those guns of yours . . . "

And the hand waved the cloth violently up and down, to underline her fear.

"All right, Ivy. We won't shoot you. Just listen very carefully, and do exactly what I say. Do you understand?"

"Yes, yes. We're listening."

"Good. Now don't do it now, wait till I say. Don't do anything yet. But when I tell you, then open the door just enough, and walk out very slowly. *Very* slowly, Ivy. And tell Peter to keep well back out of the way, out of sight. If my men see him behind you, it'll make them very nervous; and we don't want to risk an accident now. So you tell him to keep right out of the way, out of sight."

They heard Ivy's shrill tones gabbling inside the room; and meanwhile Jakes waved a hand at one of his men, a silent order to clear away the listening device and the loud-speaker that obstructed the doorway, together with their trailing cables.

Then Ivy's voice came back at them, "Hullo? Hullo?"

"Hullo, Ivy."

"Done that, Peter's in his corner, you won't see him. And he says he won't shoot anyone, he just wants me gone, he says."

"That's good, Ivy. That's very good. Okay, now open the door a bit wider, so that we can see you. Do it very slowly."

The door crept back on its hinges, and Johnnie could see a short, bulky figure framed in the gap.

"That's right, Ivy, you're doing very well. Just right. A little bit wider, now . . . Okay. That's enough. You can get out now, can't you, a little slip of a girl like you?"

There was a cackle of laughter, then, "You tell those men to put their nasty guns down. I can see them, pointing at me. I don't want none of them going off."

"They won't go off, Ivy. I promise. You're perfectly safe. Just come out now, nice and slow."

And nice and slow she came: an old woman in ridiculous clothes sidling through the doorway, taking her time, inching her feet across the concrete floor. At the last she stumbled, tripped and would have fallen if Jakes hadn't stepped quickly forward to catch her.

He hoisted her up onto her feet again, and grinned down into the wrinkled, filthy face; and behind them the door slammed shut again, pushed by an unseen hand.

It was the psychologist, Simon Breen, who thrust his way unceremoniously past Johnnie to take charge of the old tramp. A plump, sweating little man, his voice was as moist and giving as his hands as he said, "Well done, Ivy. You did really well in there, we're all terribly proud of you . . . "

The old woman blinked at him blearily. "Where's the Coatman, then? You haven't gone and lost the Coatman, have you? I want him . . . "

"And you shall have him, my pet. Anything Ivy wants, Ivy can have tonight. The Coatman, too. We found him for you, in the crowds outside. He's fine, we've got him waiting. There's a few questions we'll have to ask you first; but you be a good girl, tell us what we want to know and you can have the Coatman straight after, and anything else you fancy. A room in a hotel, perhaps, would you like that? A nice comfortable bed, and a hot bath before? And a meal? That's for both of you, you understand, you and the Coatman. A reward for being wonderful. A *double* room, perhaps, a double bed? Would you like that?"

He was steering her as he spoke, supporting her, bringing her up the stairs towards Johnnie.

"Nah," she said. "The Coatman wouldn't like that, he wouldn't. Doesn't matter what Ivy likes. You just get us home. Give us a bite to eat, and get us home."

"Of course, if that's what you want. Just a few questions first, then some hot food and a ride home in a car . . . "

"Bloody police," she said amiably. "Always bloody questions, isn't it?"

Johnnie flattened himself against the wall, to let them pass; and turned his head aside from the woman's owlish stare, the reek of meths on her breath.

"Mr Breen?" That was Jakes, calling up softly from the corridor. "Any advice?"

"Leave him," positively. "Don't do anything until I get back. Just wait, and let him sweat a little longer."

Whether Peter Kerr sweated behind that door, Johnnie didn't know; but Johnnie sweated. Johnnie was shedding pounds in this cold stairwell, his body giving itself away too late to save his dream.

Breen came back at last, and held a muttered conversation with Jakes. They were only a yard or two away from where Johnnie stood, just a little below him at the foot of the stairs; if he'd tried, if he'd wanted to, he could have listened to every word. Even without his trying, a few phrases worked their way in through his defences, enough to give him the substance of the conversation. Should they maintain the siege and try to talk Kerr out, or was now the time to go in with force?

It was Kerr's fate they were debating, and a Johnnie Lee just twenty-four hours younger might have had his own contribution to make to that debate, might have had a lot to say. But he was too far detached now from that dogmatic and determined man, could barely remember the part, let alone play it with any conviction. The morning's headlines were written and printed already; the Centre's future and his own were decided, and needing only the passage of a few weeks or months to become known. In the light of that, it was immaterial whether the police brought Peter Kerr out alive or dead. Johnnie was simply past caring.

So he paid no attention to the discussion below him, or the inaction in the corridor beyond. He had become a disinterested observer of his own life, as uninvolved as the camera that was taping everything for future reruns. Standing where he was, above and behind the camera, he knew that the tape would hold no record of his ever having been there at all; and that seemed right to him.

But then there was a soft warning cry from one of the men stationed by the door.

"Smoke, sir . . . "

Jakes spun round, Breen fell silent, even Johnnie moved his head to see; and yes, there was smoke, trickling out from under the door.

No one spoke, everyone waited for Jakes to respond, to react; and in that last moment of his indecision, everyone heard the muffled *crack!* inside the room, the single shot.

"Positions," Jakes snapped. "We're in."

Even now they were careful, they were wise. A small explosive charge was taped to the door and fired, blasting a neat little hole in the fibreboard. Two stun grenades were tossed through, and Johnnie felt the concussion of them even from his distance.

It was Jakes himself who kicked the door open and went in first, went in running with a pistol in his hands and his men a moment behind; and still Johnnie only stood and watched, stood and waited while smoke billowed out into the corridor.

THE BOOK OF THE DEAD

V: Finis

He's free at last, rid of the mistake he'd made, the unsoldierly temptation of a hostage. Back in his proper place – the hero alone with his weapons, taking a stand, laying his life on the line – he breathes easy, closes his eyes and composes an ending to suit the day.

Closes his eyes, and sees the soldier making his own choices to the last. Sees him start a fire with the meths and those old rags, sees him put an honourable finish to it all with a single bullet between the eyes; sees him go out in a blaze of glory, his spirit rising in the flames.

Closes his eyes, and sees the soldier who never gives up, however hopeless the odds. Sees him sow confusion with a small fire and a single cartridge left to explode, to fool the listening enemy; sees him slip quietly away down the trapdoor, and take his chances in the tunnels. If there are men waiting for him down there, he's a little ammunition still, one grenade; and the concussion'll kill if the shrapnel doesn't. He can find an exit, take his chances, fight his way to freedom or die trying.

Closes his eyes, and sees the soldier . . .

Author's Note

I like shopping. I spend a lot of time in malls and shopping centres in and around my home city; and it probably needs to be said that the Meldon Centre is not intended to represent any of them. Instead it's an amalgam of them all, curiously mixed with matter from my own imagination.

Similarly no character in this novel should be taken to represent any real person, living or dead. They are all of them products of my invention and nothing more.

On the other hand, no one could have invented Carol Smith. She is *sui generis*, and owed more than I have room to say. Many thanks also to Nick, Amanda and Bill; to Mike and Philippa, to Ian and Mary, to Nick and Manda and to Simon and Jill. And to PSJ, Marten and Patricia; and of course Sara, Pat and Jon, and many others. You know who you are . . .